BOOKS BY J.D. KIRK

A Litter of Bones

Thicker Than Water

The Killing Code

Blood & Treachery

The Last Bloody Straw

A Whisper of Sorrows

The Big Man Upstairs

A Death Most Monumental

A Snowball's Chance in Hell

Ahead of the Game

An Isolated Incident

Colder Than the Grave

Come Hell or High Water

Northwind: A Robert Hoon Thriller

CHAPTER ONE

IT HAD BEEN a good night up until that point. Drinks had been consumed, laughs had been shared, and sexual advances had been laughed off, while at the same time tacitly encouraged.

Not seriously, though. Not properly. It was flirting, that was all. Neither woman had any intention of so much as snogging either of these lads, much less anything else.

They *were* fit, mind you. Dark hair, dark eyes, complexions so smooth that their skin might well have been burnished with ultra-fine-grit sandpaper. And well-built, too. Tall, long limbs, but not gangly. They were in good proportion.

"In proportion in all the right places," the men had said, which had earned more laughter and an excited *whoop-whoop*.

And they'd been fun, the guys. They had the gift of the gab, the two of them. Always smiling, always cracking jokes, always saying the right thing while pressing another drink into a hand that had just moments ago been waving a 'no thanks.'

By the time last orders came, both women were struggling a bit to get to their feet, but strong arms had supported them, holding them up, guiding them to the door.

They'd wanted to detour via the bathrooms—take a minute or two to get themselves together, to discuss their game plan on how they were going to ditch these two charmers and get a taxi home. They both had work in the morning. Two different classrooms at two different schools, each crammed to bursting with overly-excited five and six-year-olds.

They had to get home, knock back a couple of preventative paracetamol, go to bed, and hope that the morning didn't come too quickly. That was why the trip to the bathroom was necessary. From there, they could plot their escape. Call an *Uber*. Make a break for it.

"It's fine, our place is just around the corner," a smooth voice had whispered.

"Toilets are closed now, anyway. Just hold it for a minute," another had soothed.

The cold air had hit them like a one-two punch, sharpening their senses with one strike, while making their heads spin with the other.

How much had they drunk? There had been wine to start with—there was always wine to start with—but they recalled pints, and shots, and big gulps of things that burned all the way down.

Things that had seemed like a laugh at the time but that now, with firm hands on their arms and on their arses, tasted sickly and sour.

"We should get a taxi," one of the women said, her eyes darting to the blurred shape that was her friend. "We'd better get home."

The response had surprised her.

"Yeah, course. No problem."

The man at her arm smiled. Even through her drunken haze, it really was a very nice smile.

The hand on her back withdrew and became an offered arm for her to hang onto.

"Let us walk you to the rank, though, yeah? Least we can do."

The women relaxed. Agreed. That *was* the least they could do, actually, after getting them this drunk.

And besides, you never knew who was roaming around these back streets of London at this time of night. Having a couple of big lads on escort duty was safer than walking themselves.

The streets around the pub seemed to have been set out with the express goal of causing confusion. Neither woman had been to that bar before, but the club had been too loud, and the dance floor too crowded, and the men had mentioned they knew a place nearby where they could talk. Have a laugh. Get to know each other better.

The pub had been quieter. Much quieter. Dead, in fact. But they'd got a round in, fed the jukebox, and made the most of it. And it had been fun. For a while.

But the fun was over now.

There was a van. Old. Battered. The paintwork scarred by scratches and scrapes, the wheel arches pitted with dots of brown rust. It didn't move, and yet it seemed to come at them out of nowhere, its back doors appearing in the mouth of an alleyway as they staggered past.

No, not *past*, the women realised. Not exactly.

Towards.

"What are we doing?" one of them asked, as she was led closer to the vehicle. She turned to look in the direction they'd been headed—the direction where she assumed the taxi rank lay —then turned back and met the warm, soft lips of the man whose arm she was holding.

He smelled nice. Better than the street around them, certainly. She sunk into the kiss for a moment, then a yelp and a metallic thud made her pull away.

Her friend was pinned, her back jammed up against the

van. She was trying to wedge her handbag between herself and the much larger man pressing himself against her, but it wasn't proving much of a deterrent.

"Get off," she was saying, the words slurring as they tumbled from her mouth. "I want... I don't... Just, get off."

"Hey! Leave her alone!" the woman protested, then she gasped as the hand on her arm tightened. Locked.

The smiles on the men's faces were still there, but they were different now. No longer cheerful or friendly, but something else. Something cruel. Something *wrong*.

Keys were pulled from a pocket. The lock of the vehicle's rear doors *clunked* at the press of a button.

"Just get in," one of the men instructed. "Come on, relax. We're having fun, aren't we? Then just come on and get in."

"No, don't. Don't. I don't want to, I just want to—"

The back of a hand cracked across her jaw. Fingers tangled in her hair, grabbing, pulling, sending shocks of pain through her scalp.

They tried to scream then, the women. Tried to call out for help, but hands clamped over mouths and tightened around throats, and they were suddenly off-balance, feet tripping them, the whole world twirling in big birling loops as the van door was wrenched open and they were shoved towards the darkness that waited inside.

And then...

The light from the alley reflected off a pair of eyes set back deep in the shadows. There were gasps and grunts of surprise, not from the women, but from the men shoving them.

"What the hell?" hissed one.

"Who the fuck are you?" demanded the other.

There was a creak as the man in the back of the van rose to his feet, rocking the vehicle on its rear axle.

"Me? I'm nobody. Just consider me a concerned citizen. Don't you fucking worry about me." The accent was Scottish, the voice as rough as a badger's arse. "It's you two limp-dicked arse tumours you should be worrying about."

A foot swung suddenly from the shadows. The toe of a well-worn boot connected with the tip of a chin. A head snapped back. A gargled cry of pain was followed by the hollow *thunk* of a skull hitting pavement.

"Taxi rank's that way, ladies," the guy in the back of the van helpfully informed them.

Except, he was no longer in the back of the van. He was standing between them now. The other man was bent double, his eyes wide, his hands grabbing at his crotch as he sunk to the ground with a gargle and a whimper.

"I suggest you go fuck off home now," the Scotsman said.

He was smiling, and his smile was somehow even more disturbing than those of their assailants had been.

He cracked his knuckles, cricked his neck, then he bent and caught one of the fallen men by the foot, like he was going to drag him away and eat him for dinner.

"Me and these two gropey wee cocksmears are going to have ourselves a cosy wee chat."

———

Bob Hoon enjoyed these little moments. It was the theatre of them that appealed to him. The building of tension in that calm before the storm.

He appreciated the looks on their faces as they came around to find themselves gagged and bound. He enjoyed the muffled howls of panic before they realised that no amount of struggling was going to help them. The way their red-ringed eyes followed his hand as it reached into his tool bag and came out with something blunt and heavy, or pointy and sharp, depending on how the mood happened to take him at the time.

Sometimes, he liked to come up with other ways to scare the

shit out of them, as much for his own amusement as anything else. Spontaneous, out of character singing was a preferred choice of late. It really put them on the back foot.

On one recent occasion, he'd sung the entirety of *Hey Diddle Diddle* into the face of a would-be rapist, then had left him hogtied in his own filth for a few hours trying to figure out what the fuck all that had been about.

By the time Hoon came back, the bastard's imagination had gone into overdrive, and he would've given up his own mother if Hoon had asked him to.

It was a pity that he hadn't known anything. Nothing Hoon needed, anyway. Nothing that could help him.

He had high hopes for these two, though. They didn't strike him as the usual seedy *lads out for a good time* types he'd been rounding up of late. These two seemed organised. They hadn't just seen an opportunity and gone for it, they'd planned things in advance, right down to the positioning of the van.

You could easily believe that they'd done this sort of thing before. Hell, you might even call them *professionals*.

A professional was exactly what he had been hunting for these past few months, so to end up with two at the same time...?

"Must be my lucky fucking night. Eh, lads?" Hoon announced.

There was very little echo in the back of the van. The walls and rear doors had been lined with thick foam padding, most of it ridged like the inside of an egg box to help muffle the sounds within.

Professionals. No doubt about it.

"No' so much yours, though, I should probably warn you both now that it isn't your lucky night at all," he continued.

He hummed below his breath as he reached into his tool bag again, and this time he pulled out a pair of child's safety scissors. Frowning, he gave them an experimental *snip*.

"Fuck knows where these came from," he said. He smiled at the men. "Funny the things you pick up, eh? They're blunt as a dolphin's bellend, so no idea what I'm going to use them for." Hoon placed the scissors down on the thick, dirty rug that covered the van's floor. "Still, I'm sure between us we'll come up with something."

He was kneeling, and sat back so that his arse was resting on his heels. The two men lay on their sides, tied together, locked face to face in an embrace, their hands bound behind each other's backs. Hoon had gone to the trouble of stripping them both naked. He found that this generally helped focus every-one's attention.

"You didn't have ID on you, so we're going to need to come up with names for you," he said, considering them both. He ran his tongue across the front of his teeth, his eyes narrowing until, finally, he pointed at each man in turn. "Humpty Dumpty and Laser Tits. That's who you'll be." Hoon sucked in his bottom lip, then gave a nod, satisfied. "Aye. Those suit you down to the fucking ground."

He returned his attention to the bag, took out a yellow snooker ball, and then produced a sock into which the ball was carefully inserted.

"Actually, speaking of which, I mind a few years back, there was a bit of controversy over the whole Humpty Dumpty thing," he said, giving the sock an experimental *swish* as he tested the weight. "Some BBC kids' show changed it. Made it so that all the king's horses and all the king's men did actually manage to put him back together again. Gave it a nice happy ending for the weans watching at home."

He gave a shrug, indicating his indifference to the whole thing.

"And you think, aye, fair enough. Go on yourself. There's enough fucking doom and gloom doing the rounds, might as well mix it up a bit. Except, some arsehole of an MP—can't mind who—he lost his shit. Said we were mollycoddling three-year-olds. That they needed to learn to live in the real world." Hoon looked across to his hostages and raised both eyebrows. "The fucking real world! I mean, for one thing, it's a story about a gang of horses trying to rebuild a sentient egg. I don't think anyone's mistaking it for a fucking documentary, I don't care what age they are."

Hoon set down the sock, pulled out a small leather pouch, and unzipped it to reveal a selection of dentistry tools.

"And secondly—and I remember thinking this at the time—how few fucking concerns must you have in your life that you've got time to worry about shite like that? What kind of Tweedledee fantasy dreamscape must you inhabit where you can waste even one fraction of a second fretting about the fate of Humpty fucking Dumpty? I don't know about you two, but I want to think my MP has got better things to do with their time than shite the bed about nursery rhymes. Know what I mean? I want the bastards to have real problems to concern themselves with. Urgent problems. *Pressing* problems."

Hoon breathed on the dental mirror and wiped it on the front of his combat trousers. He nodded his approval, then glanced back at his captives.

"You know, like you two have?"

One of the men—Laser Tits—tried to eject some protest through his gag, but Hoon raised a finger and sharpened his features until silence returned.

"Don't you worry, lads, you'll have plenty of opportunity to talk. I'll make fucking sure of that. That's the whole reason we're here, after all. You'll get your chance," he promised. "Just not now. Not yet. It's just more fun if we do it the hard way. More fun for me, anyway."

He fished in the bag again and this time took out a square of folded cardboard. Opening it, he slipped a photograph out and turned it to his captives without looking at it himself.

"This is who you're going to talk about," he told them. "This young woman here. Take a look. Take your time. You're going to tell me where she is. You're going to tell me who took her, and where I can find them. And then, assuming there's enough of you left by that point, I'm going to—"

There was a knock on the back doors of the van. A side-of-the-fist *thumping* that could be felt as much as heard.

Down on the floor, both captives raised their heads, eyes bulging, like they might be able to stare straight through the metal, or summon whoever was outside using willpower alone.

Hoon placed a finger to his lips and slowly, quietly, reached for the sharpest implement he could find.

There was a rattling of a handle being tried, then another round of knocking. The foam padding made it difficult to hear much of what was happening out there, but Hoon got the impression of murmured voices. Of footsteps scuffing up the side of the vehicle towards the front.

Humpty Dumpty grunted. Squirmed. The business end of a scalpel was pressed against his throat, ending his attempts to draw the attention of the people outside.

Hoon heard the rattle as someone tried the handle of the driver's door but found it locked. He listened, breath held, as the voices outside muttered, then faded away into silence.

He waited. He counted. Five seconds. Ten. No more movement. No more sound.

"Alone again," he whispered, giving Humpty Dumpty a friendly slap on the cheek. "Now, as I was saying..."

The rest of the sentence was swallowed by the screeching of metal on metal. Hoon shuffled right up to the wall that divided the storage area from the cabin, shielding his face with a hand as sparks filled the back of the van like the trailing tail of a firework.

"The fuck?" he spat, switching the scalpel to his left hand and snatching up the sock with the snooker ball inside.

The noise was excruciating. The sparks buzzed him like angry fireflies, smouldering where they landed on the foam, and making his naked captives twist and roll in a futile attempt to escape the brief burning pinpricks of pain.

And then, as suddenly as it had started, the racket stopped, and a ringing silence rushed in to fill the void. The last few sparks died in the air. For a moment, all was still.

Until, with a screech and a groan, both back doors of the van toppled outwards, and landed on the uneven tarmac of the alleyway.

There were guns. That was the first thing Hoon noticed. Three, all pointed at him. Heckler & Koch MP5 submachine guns. Even if the wielders hadn't been wearing the black helmets with 'Police' emblazoned across them, he'd have recognised the weapons right away. He'd used them himself often enough.

A fourth man was lurking behind the firearms officers. Hoon took an immediate disliking to the smug-faced prick with his hair slicked back, and his hands tucked into the pockets of an expensive-looking wool coat. Unlike every other bastard making up the scene, he had a smile on his face, as if there was some sort of joke playing out here that only he was bright enough to get.

"First up, I'd just like to say, I'm a great admirer of yours, Mr Hoon," he announced, and there was a self-assured, rich boy twang to the delivery that made him even more unpalatable. He smiled, maybe even winked, though the spots dancing in front of Hoon's eyes made it hard to tell. "Now, how about you put down the torture instruments, and we can avoid any of these gentlemen having to shoot you in the face?"

CHAPTER TWO

HOON HAD COME QUIETLY. Or as quietly as he was capable of, anyway. The Armed Response Unit hadn't exactly left him with many options on that front. He'd promised Humpty Dumpty and Laser Tits that he'd see them again soon, and then had allowed himself to be handcuffed and led to the back seat of a blacked-out BMW.

The smug-looking bastard with the wool coat had slid into the driver's seat a few moments later, while two of the armed officers squeezed in beside Hoon, flanking and squashing him with their bulky armour.

"What about those two fuckholes in the van?" Hoon asked.

Up front, the driver had flashed a smile in the rearview mirror. "The men you were about to torture, you mean?"

"Torture, my arse," Hoon scoffed. "Since when did a few paperclips beneath the fingernails ever hurt anyone?"

"Since always. And, in answer to your other question, we're letting them go. Assuming we haven't already done so."

"You let them fucking go?" Hoon had stared at the back of the driver's head for a dangerously long time, his jaw clenching until his teeth groaned in their sockets. "You saw their fucking van, right? You know what they've been doing."

"Oh, don't you worry, Robert," was the other man's reply as he looked ahead and fired up the engine with the press of a button. "We know everything."

That had been over an hour ago. Now, Hoon sat shackled to a table in a pokey wee interview room in a police station somewhere in east London. They'd crossed the river at one point, headed south, but Hoon hadn't recognised his surroundings, and they'd bundled him in through the station's back door so he hadn't had a chance to clock the sign out front.

There was no mirror in the interview room. No fixed recording equipment, either. It was old school, which he appreciated. There must have been a dozen or more stations between here and where they'd lifted him. They'd brought him to this nick for a reason.

Either someone didn't want a record of this meeting, or they intended to give him a thoroughly good kicking and wanted some privacy in which to do so. Whichever it was, it was going to make for a very interesting evening.

He'd gleaned very little on the car ride over. The ARU lads had kept their mouths shut the whole way, and the prick in the driver's seat had mostly responded to Hoon's questions with smirks and winks.

They hadn't checked him in properly. No paperwork. No handover into custody. His request for a phone call had been met with a chuckle, and a, "We'll see what we can do," before he was brought in here to this room and cuffed to the metal loop that was fastened securely to the table.

He'd been in here alone for twenty minutes now. With no window and no cameras, it was pointless making a fuss, so he'd put his head down on the table and tried to catch up with some sleep.

As was usual of late, sleep had failed to come for him.

He'd been so close. Those two lads. He'd been so close to a breakthrough, he was sure of it They knew something. They knew something about *her*.

And now, they were out there somewhere, and he was locked away in here.

And the girl—Caroline—was lost to him once more.

The door of the interview room opened. The face that appeared was not the snidey wee fuck he'd been expecting. She was dressed in a big waterproof jacket and a pair of saggy tracky bottoms instead of the pristine uniform she'd worn on the other occasions they'd met, and so it took Hoon a moment to recognise her.

"Deirdrie?" he said, once he'd concluded the necessary mental gymnastics. "The fuck are you doing here?"

"Please don't call me that. You can address me as Chief Superintendent Bagshaw," the new arrival instructed, her tone making it clear that she was in no mood for his shit. She wiped her eyes with a thumb, clearing away the last remnants of sleep. "And believe me, Mr Hoon, I'm not here through choice."

Hoon looked her up and down as she took a seat across from him. She was one of the highest-ranking officers in the Met, and from what little he knew of her, not the sort of person to be easily bossed around. If she wasn't here willingly, then someone powerful had to be pulling some strings.

He'd crossed paths with her a couple of times soon after arriving in London, and while she hadn't helped him with his mission, she'd mostly stayed out of his way and left him to get on with it.

Until now.

"I thought I told you to keep your head down and stay out of trouble?" she said.

Hoon shrugged. "I did."

"You call this staying out of trouble?"

"I've been doing the tourist thing," Hoon said, glossing over his current situation. "Did some sightseeing. Ate jellied eels. Waved at the fucking Queen. All that bollocks. I even went to see *Wicked* last week."

Bagshaw blinked in surprise. "*Wicked?*"

"Aye."

"As in... the musical?"

Hoon tutted. "Naw, as in the actual witch of the west. Aye, of course the fucking musical."

"Right. I see," Bagshaw said, the furrows in her brow revealing how hard a time she was having processing this. "I have to say, you surprise me, Robert. That doesn't exactly strike me as your scene."

"Aye, well, I'll try and no' take offence at that. I'm a complex individual, Deirdrie. I'm a veritable fucking soufflé of hidden layers, me."

"So it would seem." The chief superintendent didn't want to ask the question, but curiosity got the better of her. "And what did you think? Of *Wicked*, I mean."

"Absolute fucking horseshit."

Had it not been so late, and had she not still been resentful over being dragged here, Bagshaw might actually have smiled at that.

"Right. Well, maybe you don't surprise me *that* much. The reason I'm here is that they wanted me to talk to you before they came in to speak to you," she explained. "They thought you might trust me."

"Well, they're wrong. And anyway, who the fuck's 'they?'" Hoon demanded, but Bagshaw chose to ignore the question.

"They want..." She sighed. It turned into a yawn that she struggled to stifle. "They want to offer you some sort of deal. I don't know what or why. I don't care, and I didn't ask."

"Again with the 'they.' Who's this fucking 'they' you keep talking about?'"

Bagshaw tutted and shook her head. Clearly, it wasn't just

Hoon's shit she couldn't be bothered with. This whole pantomime was getting on her nerves. "The Security Service," she said, then she sat back and shrugged. "Like I say, I don't know why, so don't bother asking."

"The Security Service?" Hoon looked to the door, frowning. "As in...?"

"As in MI5. Yes."

Hoon sucked in his bottom lip, then spat it out again. "Aye, didn't think that horse's arse-crevice looked like polis, right enough," he said. "Too smug looking. Which is fucking saying something, when you think about it. What does MI5 want to talk to me for?"

"Didn't you hear what I just said? I have no idea."

"Rhetorical question, sweetheart," Hoon snapped back at her. "Don't go getting your knickers in a fucking twist."

Bagshaw slid a hand across the tabletop, slapped the scuffed wood, then stood up. "Right, well, that's me done my bit. You're on your own from here."

"Your bit?" Hoon gave her another look up and down. "What, that's it? They brought you in just to say that?"

"Oh, no. No, they wanted me to say a lot more. Gave me a big list," the chief superintendent replied. "I was supposed to soften you up. Throw my weight around a bit. Warn against the consequences of vigilante justice. Threaten you with prosecution. All that. They wanted me to, and I quote, 'make you nervous.'"

"But?"

"But it's been a long day, Mr Hoon, and it's late. It's late, and frankly, to use the sort of parlance you're most familiar with, I cannot be fucked with any of it." She put a foot up on the chair she'd just vacated, tied the lace of a battered old white trainer, then returned it to the floor. "And we both know you're too far gone to be concerned by anything I have to tell you, don't we?"

Hoon ejected a throaty laugh that lasted all of two seconds. "Flattery will get you everywhere, Chief Superintendent," he said, then he gave Bagshaw a nod. "Cheers for no' wasting either of our time trying."

"I assure you, that was entirely for my benefit, not yours." She crossed to the door, knocked twice, and gave a nod to the guard on the other side when the hatch slid aside. "Good luck, Mr Hoon," she told him as she waited to be let out. "With... whatever this is."

"Always a fucking pleasure to see you, Deirdrie," Hoon replied. "I'll keep you posted."

"God, no. Please don't," Bagshaw said, then the door opened and she vanished out into the hall without so much as a backward glance.

Hoon strained to hear the whispered conversation that took place out in the corridor, but other than the odd word and a general sense of annoyance from both parties, he didn't pick up very much.

The discussion didn't last long, and almost as soon as the whispering stopped, footsteps squeaked along the corridor in the direction of the interview room.

The same self-satisfied scrote from earlier knocked a couple of times on the open door, then practically skipped on in. He'd ditched the wool coat now, revealing a crisply-pressed light blue shirt buttoned all the way to the neck, and sleeves rolled up with such precision that they could be mistaken for mirror images of each other.

He'd wrestled his tie into a full Windsor with the same degree of skill and accuracy, and then tucked it out of the way over his shoulder like he was about to eat soup and wasn't willing to risk the stains.

Without the coat, he looked smaller. He wasn't short—a touch below average height, maybe—but he had a physical frame that didn't seem to have heard of testosterone, much less ever produced any. Cover his face, and you'd be forgiven for thinking he was yet to enter puberty.

Include everything above the neck, though, and his age became more apparent, although it was still difficult to pin down. He could've been mid-thirties with a hard life behind him, or late forties with a charmed one. His gelled hair looked almost plastic, like it had been moulded onto the top of his head back at whatever Chinese sweatshop of a toy factory had shat him out.

His footwear was a little unexpected. While the rest of his outfit looked like it could've come as part of a Mormon fancy dress costume, he wore an ageing pair of black and white trainers on his feet. Comfier than dress shoes, no doubt, but they didn't exactly fit with the rest of his getup.

He carried a box file, jamming it between his forearm and his ribs so as to keep his hands free for carrying a steaming hot takeaway coffee cup in one, and a shiny silver pen in the other.

"You good, Bob?" he asked, lowering himself onto the recently vacated chair on the other side of the table. He sat the cup down, and placed the pen and box file on the table beside it. The smell of the coffee was so strong that Hoon could almost inhale the caffeine hit.

"I'd say I'm quite some fucking distance from 'good,' now that you're asking."

This made the other man laugh. "No, I'd imagine it's not how you planned your evening going. Apologies for spoiling your fun out there. We wanted to talk to you."

"And it couldn't have waited twenty minutes?" Hoon asked.

"What, until you'd finished your little chat with your two new friends, you mean? No. Sorry. We couldn't just stand by and let you do... well. Whatever it was you were going to do."

"I was just going to pursue one or two lines of inquiry, that's all," Hoon said. He shrugged. "And then, depending on how things went from there, maybe set them both on fire. I hadn't planned that far ahead."

"Yes, well," the other man said, his smile dropping, if only for a moment.

It returned with gusto when he opened his box file. Rather than produce the stack of paperwork that Hoon had been expecting, he instead removed something square-ish wrapped in tinfoil, then peeled it open to reveal a white bread sandwich with the crusts cut off.

"Sorry, missed dinner. And lunch, actually," he said. The sandwich had been cut diagonally into quarters. He picked one up, and Hoon caught a glimpse of a thick slice of cheddar before the whole triangle was shoved into the waiting mouth.

Hoon drummed his fingers impatiently while watching the other man struggling to chew and swallow the dry sandwich.

"Just you take your fucking time, son," he said. "Don't you mind me."

There was some mumbling through the mouthful of partially masticated bread. "Sorry. Want a bit?"

"My maw always told me no' to accept food from strangers," Hoon replied. "Also, that's about the most boring fucking cheese piece I've ever clapped eyes on in my life."

"Piece? Do you mean sandwich?"

"I mean just what I said, pal. Now stop playing with it and fucking swallow, will you?" Hoon gave a grunt of amusement. "And I'm betting I'm not the first person to say that to you tonight, either."

"Ha. Funny. They said you were funny, but... That's good." Hands were brushed together to dust off crumbs, then one was extended across the table. "Miles Crabtree. Sorry, should've said that earlier, but I was a bit, you know, starstruck."

The cuffs weren't restrictive enough to prevent Hoon from shaking the hand, he just chose not to. Miles kept the offer open for a few moments, then shrugged and began cleaning the back of his teeth with a pinkie finger, dislodging lumps of bread and cheese.

"How much did Chief Superintendent Bagshaw tell you?" he asked.

"Not a lot."

"Right. Would you care to elaborate on that?" Miles asked.

"Would I fuck."

"Ha. Right. Yes. It's funny, she did tell me about your use of language. She said, and I quote, 'It's like he's sponsored by the word *fuck*.' But actually hearing it, and the... the *venom* you put into it, it's really quite something."

"Aye, very fucking good, son," Hoon snapped back. "Do you want to remove your lips from around my bawbag for a minute, and crack on with whatever the fuck this is?"

"Fine. OK. Well... Here's the thing, Bob." Miles interlocked his fingers and sat forward, narrowing the gap between them. "I've been admiring your work for a couple of months now. Since all that stuff with the warehouse fire, and those women you rescued—good job on that, by the way—I am becoming... and please, don't let this go to your head... but I am becoming quite the fan of yours."

"Aye, well, I assure you that the feeling's very much no' fucking mutual," Hoon retorted, which only seemed to please the other man further.

"That's it. There it is, right there. It's that attitude I love. You don't care what you say, who you offend, nothing. Just call it as you see it. You just say whatever's on your mind, and to hell with the consequences."

It was Hoon's turn to sit forward. His chair groaned under the shifting weight.

"Believe me, if I told you what's on my mind right now, you'd be tearing up your fan club membership card, asking for your money back, then curling up in the foetal position and sobbing yourself into a fucking coma. You don't want to know what's on my mind, you cheesy-breaded wee fuck. You can't *handle* what's on my mind."

For a moment, Miles sat there in a stunned sort of silence, then he clapped his approval, his face lighting up in a big, beaming smile.

"Brilliant! I loved that!" he said. "I mean, 'cheesy-breaded wee fuck.' It's not even that offensive, but you manage to make it feel genuinely hurtful. It really is quite a gift you have."

Hoon scowled. "Jesus Christ. What is it you want?"

Miles prised the lid off his coffee cup, reached back into the box file, and produced a small bundle of sugar packets. As he spoke, he tore a strip off the top of each packet and tipped the contents into his drink.

"What I want is to help you, Bob," he said.

Hoon snorted, amused by the very notion. "You? A jumped-up wee prick with a face like a haunted Boglin? Help me? Aye, that I'd like to see, pal. What could a spudfingered wee spunk-sack like you help me with?"

"With staying out of prison, for starters," Miles said. He ripped open another sugar pack—the seventh, by Hoon's count—and poured it into the coffee. The scattered brown granules sat nestled there in the foam for a few seconds, before slowly sinking below the surface. "How's your mate, by the way? Book-ish, you called him, wasn't it? I heard he'd... disappeared."

"Aye. I'd heard something along those lines myself," Hoon said, not breaking eye contact.

"You don't know where he is, then?"

Hoon shook his head. "I do not," he said.

This was not, in fact, true. He did know where Bookish was. Roughly, at least, and depending on the recent tides.

"Nice of him to let you live on his boat while he's away."

"Aye, well, he and I go way back," Hoon said.

"Mm," Miles replied, giving the open box file a tap in a way that suggested it held more than the world's most disappointing packed lunch. "I've been reading about that. A brotherhood forged on the battlefield. You must be very worried about him."

"He's a big boy," Hoon said. "He can handle himself."

Miles tipped another pack of sugar into his cup, then produced a thin plastic stirrer and began swirling the liquid around. "I suppose that depends, doesn't it?"

Hoon raised an eyebrow. "Depends?"

"On who he gets on the wrong side of. None of us are invincible, Mr Hoon. Regardless of what we might tell ourselves."

Hoon had a hard time believing that someone with Crabtree's build would even consider themselves to be 'invincible.' Even 'sturdy' would be a push. The bastard looked like a careless sneeze might burst him wide open.

"Is that why we're here? To talk about Bookish?" Hoon asked, but before the other man could answer, he pointed to the mound of empty sugar packets. "And what the fuck's the story there, by the way?"

"Hm?" Crabtree looked down at his cup. "Oh. I don't like the bitter taste."

"Well, don't drink coffee then. That's the whole fucking point."

Miles stopped stirring, ran the plastic stick across his tongue to get the foam off, then set it down on the desk. "Yeah. My wife used to say the same, but sometimes you need the caffeine."

"Then away and get a fucking *Creme Egg* latte macchiato, or whatever shite they're doing at *Starbucks* these days," Hoon suggested. "They were doing some Day-Glo pink atrocity recently. I'm sure you'd be all over that."

"No," Miles said. He took a sip of his coffee and smacked his lips together, like he was trying to get on Hoon's nerves.

"No? What the fuck do you mean, *no*? No what?"

"No, you're not here to talk about your missing friend," Miles clarified. "I'm sure that wherever he is, whatever he's doing, there's a very good reason for it. He is, like you say, a big boy." He locked his fingers around his cup. "No, I'm here to talk about you, Bob. And specifically, like I say, how I can help you." His smile returned. "Or, OK, cards on the table, how we can help each other."

He took another sip of coffee and tried very hard not to grimace.

Across the table, Hoon picked up one of the three remaining sandwich quarters and shoved the whole thing in his mouth. "Fuck it," he said, spraying crumbs over the table. "I'm listening."

CHAPTER THREE

THERE WAS PAIN, and there was screaming, and there was blood.

They blinded him. Deafened him. Narrowed his throat and his airways, and sent his pulse rate spiking in panic.

It had all come out of nowhere. A flurry of blows that had put him on the back foot had been followed by an impact like a horse-kick to the centre of his face. Like the wallop of a sledge-hammer. Like nothing he had ever felt before.

Nobody normal could hit like that. Nobody human.

His opponent had stared at him as he'd fallen. Those chalk-white features. Those burning red eyes. That blank, lifeless expression.

The floor had come up to meet him then. He remembered that much. There was no bounce to it when he hit, not like with the mat or the canvas. It was rough. Hard. Unforgiving. The sound of his skull striking it was like the crack of a gunshot in his ears.

He gagged, coughed. A spray of dark blood and snot patterned the concrete, and sweet, precious oxygen came flooding in.

The floor may have offered an uncomfortable landing, but the cold was welcome against his cheek. All those bodies jammed in together, all whooping and jeering and laughing, had made the room stiflingly warm. Turned the air thick and sour. He'd felt it when they'd announced his name. Smelled it when they'd brought him in. Tasted it as he'd been led through the crowd like a lamb to the slaughter.

But this, now... Block out the pain, ignore the screeching, and this was nice. This was good.

He'd just lie here. Just for a moment. Just until the world stopped spinning and he'd caught his breath. Just until he could see again. Hear again. Feel again.

Wait.

Panic stirred, cutting through the fog that filled his head.

Feel.

He couldn't feel.

His head, yes. He could feel that. His bare shoulder wedged against the floor. Maybe the arm twisted between his upper torso and the concrete.

But beyond that? Below there?

Oh no.

Oh, God.

He saw faces, twisted by the tears and the half-darkness into leering masks of horror, flecks of foam forming around their mouths as they brayed and howled and screeched.

He tried to call to them, to cry out, to beg for their help, but the stamping of their feet drowned out his feeble pleading.

They were animals. Monsters. Things from nightmares.

And yet, so very, very real.

A shadow passed over him. Large. Impossibly so.

Nothing normal cast a shadow like that.

Nothing human.

He heard a hundred intakes of a hundred breaths.

A hundred monsters fell silent.

And the quiet was nice.

The quiet was good.

A foot came down. Fast. Hard.

Red eyes blazed in a chalk-white face.

And a cheer rose up through the warm, fetid air.

"First thing's first. I'm not actually with the police," Miles said.

"You're a spook," Hoon said, still chomping his way through the sandwich.

On the other side of the interview table, the other man failed to hide his disappointment. "Bagshaw told you."

"No. I mean, aye, but she didn't have to. Could smell it off you a fucking mile away," Hoon said. "No way you'd last five minutes in the polis, son. No' unless it's an undercover gig in a fucking primary school."

"Ha!" Miles ejected, and it seemed like he was genuinely amused by the remark.

"Add in the fact that you didn't read me my rights, took me to the arse-end of nowhere, and didn't bother to get me checked in, and it's pretty fucking obvious that this is some shady secretive shite you don't want anyone else finding out about." He returned the other man's smile, but without all the nice elements. "Am I getting close to the mark there, Miles?"

"Not bad. Not bad at all," Crabtree conceded. "Yes, you're right. I work for the Security Service. MI5. Call us what you will."

"And what's your job there? World's smallest secret agent? Do they put you in one of them wee gadget watches and fire you out like a fucking dart?" Hoon asked. He regarded the smaller man more closely, then shook his head. "No. No, that's no' you. You're a fucking pen pusher, if ever I saw one. You're no' out in the field."

Miles almost looked impressed. "Once again, good solid reasoning there, Bob. You're right, I'm generally desk-based. And we're called officers not agents. Although, I don't mind either, and if I'm completely honest, I prefer agents. It just sounds cooler."

He reached into the box file and produced a chunky cardboard folder filled with paper.

"Besides, *Officer Crabtree* was the French policeman in the sitcom, '*Allo '*Allo*, and I'm a little tired of the jokes. If you want to get them out of the way, please do so now."

"Never watched it," Hoon said. "And, anyway, jokes aren't really my strong point. So, how about we cut the shite here, and get down to brass tacks. What do you want?"

Miles picked up one of the two remaining pieces of sandwich, considered it, then set it back down. He idly swept up some spilled sugar with the side of his hand, before pushing it off the edge of the table and onto the floor.

"Have you heard of the Loop, Bob?" he asked. "In fact, no. I know you have, so let me rephrase the question. How much have you heard about the Loop?"

"Not much," Hoon said. He had intended to leave it there, but Miles gave a nod and a wave of encouragement. "It's some big fucking... I don't know. British Mafia. Big scary bad bastards, we're all meant to be shiteing ourselves about."

Miles tapped the tips of his fingers against each other, like five pairs of hands all clapping at once. "Right. So, yeah. Not much, then." He took another drink of his coffee, recoiled at the taste, and produced yet another packet of sugar from the box file. "They're not British. I mean, they operate here, true, but then they operate everywhere. They're a.... What's the best way to describe them? Terrorist organisation? Criminal network? I suppose your Mafia comparison isn't a million miles away, but scale it up. Way up. This isn't a few dozen gangsters, the Loop has tens of thousands of operatives. Maybe hundreds of thousands, all across the globe."

"Bollocks it's that big. I'd have heard of it before."

The look of amusement on Crabtree's face made something stir in the pit of Hoon's stomach.

"Yes, well, I'm sure you had plenty of other things to worry about up there in the Highlands. Stray sheep, or lost climbers, or whatever it was that took up your time. It's understandable that certain things might have passed you by. Besides, secrecy is sort of their whole thing. Well, that and power."

"Power?"

"Oh, yes. The Loop's membership is made up of people from all walks of life. You've got your foot soldiers, yes. Lower league nobodies, like the two idiots you tangled with tonight. And then, up and up we go from there. Police officers. Military. Judges. Politicians. Hollywood actors. Heads of state. It's a worldwide old boy network that can do what it wants, when it wants. Hence the problems you've been having."

Hoon took the bait. "Problems?"

"Finding your friend's daughter. Caroline, wasn't it?" Miles asked, and it was clear from his tone that he already knew the answer. "Caroline Gascoine? You've been looking for her, but you're no closer to finding her now than you were two months ago."

"You know where she is?" Hoon demanded, his cuffs rattling against the desk. "You know where to find her?"

"No. No, sorry," Miles said. "But I might know a man who does. Or who might be able to find out, given the right..." He twirled a finger, as if trying to find the right word to put it on. "...motivation."

"Who?"

Miles let his hand drop down again, then shrugged. "That's valuable information, Bob. I can't go giving that out willy-nilly. Not even to you. Not for nothing."

"What do you want?" Hoon demanded.

Miles leaned back in his chair, stretching and yawning. He glanced at his coffee cup like he was considering another swig, but then chickened out at the last second.

"You know how many people I trust, Bob?"

"I don't give a flying fuck," Hoon said, matter-of-factly.

"Five. Right now? Right at this moment? Five. Five people. In the whole world." He pointed across the table. "Of which you are one."

"Me? Fuck off. Why would you trust me? You don't even fucking know me, pal."

Miles brought a leg up and crossed it over the opposite knee. He leaned an elbow on it, like he was settling in to tell a story.

"Trust is a funny word," he said. "Most people? They look at it wrong. They don't get it. What it means. Not really. In truth, it's about perspective. See, do I trust you to do what I tell you? No. God, no. That would be madness. I hardly know you, and you? Well, you owe me nothing. Not yet, anyway." He shuffled his chair a little closer, and lowered his voice like he was imparting some big secret. "But, do I trust you to be you? Do I trust you to stick to your principles? To do those things you're driven to do? To do what you believe is right? Yes. Yes, I do. Absolutely. No question.

"And, on the Venn diagram of our respective goals at the moment, there's a lot of crossover, Bob. A *lot* of crossover. My needs and your desires are very much in sync right now. I want what you want, and vice versa."

"And what is it you think I want, exactly?"

"You want to find Caroline Gascoine and bring her home," Miles stated. "You want to find the people who took her, anyone who hurt her, and you want to make them suffer. Like you suspect she is suffering." He shrugged. "Well, on the occasions when you manage to convince yourself she's not dead, anyway.

And honestly? You sometimes find yourself hoping that she is. You think that maybe that's for the best."

Hoon said nothing. No confirmation. No denial. Not a word.

"More than that, though, you want to fulfil your promise. You said you'd bring her home. That's what you told them, isn't it? That you'd find her?"

"Who the fuck are you?" Hoon asked.

Miles' smile returned. "I told you. Officer—or Agent, if you'd prefer—Miles Crabtree. I'm with—"

"I don't care about that shite. That's not what I'm asking," Hoon said. "Who the fuck are you really?"

The question was considered a little more carefully this time, before the answer came.

"I'm the man who's going to help you find your friend's daughter, Bob," Miles declared. "And in return, you're going to help me bring their whole organisation to the ground. Tell me, in your *interactions* with all those young lads recently, have you come across the name Godfrey West?"

Hoon leaned back in his chair, lips thin, eyes narrowed. He glanced to the wall, with its lack of mirror, and at the corner of the room where a camera should have been, but wasn't.

"No," he said.

"Right, I thought not. Well, he's—"

"I mean, no, I'm not interested."

Miles, who had been investigating the possibility of trying his coffee again, looked up and frowned. "Sorry?"

"I'm not doing it. The wee fucking partnership you're proposing? I'm not doing it. It's not happening," Hoon told him.

Crabtree let out an incredulous-sounding chuckle. "You... what? I'm offering you the chance to find her. To find Caroline Gascoine. That's what you want, isn't it?"

"I'll find her myself. You've given me a name. Godfrey West. Shouldn't be too many of them around."

Something like panic flashed across the MI5 man's face. "Don't. Jesus. You won't get near him without us. You've got no idea."

"I'll take my chances," Hoon said. "See, you might trust me, son, but something about you... this..." He gestured around the room. "Let's just say the old alarm bells are going ring-a-ding-fucking-ding right now."

"If you go after him, you could blow everything. All my work. Everything we've done."

"I don't care," Hoon told him. "That's your problem. All I care about is getting that lassie home."

"Bob, listen," Miles began, but Hoon was having none of it.

"No, you listen, you goblin-limbed streak of pish. I don't work for you. I don't work for anyone. If you've got information you want to share, I'm all fucking ears. But I'm no' going to balance a fucking ball on my nose and clap my hands to get it."

Miles blinked. "Yeah, that wasn't... I wasn't planning on getting you to do that."

"Obviously no' literally, son. Metaphorically, for fuck's sake," Hoon spat. "What are they teaching you pricks in spy school these days?"

Miles drew in a breath and opened his mouth like he was about to argue further, then shook his head and closed it again when he realised that butting heads with this man was going to get him nowhere.

Perhaps a different approach, then.

"They know about you. The Loop. After what happened. What you did. They know who you are."

"Good. Then maybe they'll come find me," Hoon retorted. "Save me a job."

"You still don't get it. You don't appreciate what they're capable of. Why do you think you were brought in here like this? Arrested? Why do you think we took statements from those lads you'd picked up, and then let them go?"

"Because you're a shower of arseholes?" Hoon guessed.

"For show. To make it look convincing. You're on their radar now. Not high. Not fully. You're a niggle at the moment. A thorn in their side, nothing more. But they're aware of you." He leaned closer, holding eye contact to hammer home his next point. "And that means they're aware of your friends, too."

"Well, good fucking job for me I don't have any," Hoon retorted. He gave his cuffs a rattle. "So, if you'd take off these bracelets, I'll be on my way."

"What about Welshy, Bob? Your old army pal. His wife, Gabriella? Bamber, Caroline's father. Her mum, too, although I don't believe you two are really on speaking terms. They won't differentiate, though. The Loop. They won't make that distinction. They'll all be targets."

He had Hoon's attention now, and pressed the advantage.

"Then there's your old colleagues up north. DCI Logan. DI Forde. DC Neish."

The last name made Hoon's brow furrow. "Who?"

"Anyone you've known. Anyone you've worked with. Anyone you're close to—you have a sister, right? A niece. She has a son. They'll all be in danger. They all *are* in danger. But we can help you protect them. We can bring this network down. You and me. Together. You just have to say the word."

Hoon's muscles had been tensing and tightening during the other man's speech, like he was preparing to tear the metal handcuff loop right out of the tabletop and beat Crabtree to death with it.

"How about I say two words?" he suggested. "The second of which is 'off.'"

Across the table, Miles was unable to hide his disappointment.

"And the first of which is 'fuck,'" Hoon added for clarity. Then, in case the message still hadn't got through: "Fuck off, is what I'm saying."

"Yes. Yes, I picked up on that, thanks," Miles said.

"Well done. Chocolate watch for the big fucking brainbox here." Hoon rattled his cuffs. "Now, are you going to get me out of these things, or do I have to make a lock picking kit out of your shin bones and take them off myself?"

CHAPTER FOUR

THE BOAT GROANED as Hoon descended the narrow stairs to the lower deck, like it was disappointed to see him returning. The feeling, to be fair, was mutual. He didn't particularly like boats at the best of times, and he had plenty of reasons to dislike this arsehole of a thing more than most.

Still, it had a roof, walls, and a bed—or whatever the fucking nautical equivalents of those things were—and if it meant not paying for a place to stay, then he was prepared to put up with it. Just.

He was particularly unimpressed by the ridiculously small toilet that he was becoming increasingly convinced required a degree in astrophysics to operate properly. The kitchen facilities weren't exactly stellar, either, but there was a decent pub just five minutes' walk from where he'd moored the boat, and a kebab shop just a short stagger beyond that.

Bookish's yacht was compact, but distinctive, and Hoon hadn't dared bring it back to its regular mooring after...

Well, after everything that had happened.

It had required a bit of internet research, a few phone calls, and a steep bloody learning curve, but eventually, he'd managed to relocate to a new mooring not far from the Thames Estuary. It was no Canary Wharf, but then given the volume of smarmy, designer suit-wearing, coke-snorting fuckbags making their presence felt in that area—not to mention the bearded hipster twats —he didn't consider that to be a bad thing.

He wasn't sure what the time was when he arrived back, but it felt late. Too late for him to bother eating, anyway.

Drinking, of course, was a different matter.

He navigated the complex toilet protocols, then took a bottle of cheap Eastern European lager from the mini-fridge that was tucked under the L-shaped padded bench. He'd have preferred something stronger, but he'd been trying to keep a clear head of late. Just for now. Just for a while. Just until he found her.

After that—after this was all over—he was going to sit down in a darkened room, and quietly drink his way out of existence. He'd promised himself that much.

The lager tasted thin and watery to his oak-infused palette, and far too fizzy. Still, he polished off the first, ejected an impressively loud burp, then took a second and third bottle with him as he headed through to the small bedroom.

This was the bedroom—or sleeping quarters, or cabin, or whatever the fuck the correct terminology was—where Bookish had holed up for the past few years. Given what Hoon now knew of the bastard, he shuddered to think about what might have happened in this room. It wasn't giving up its secrets, though, and Bookish himself was long past being able to.

He'd taken a cab from the police station to some arbitrary location half a mile from the mooring. From there, he'd wandered the streets, making up the route as he went along, keeping his eyes peeled for anyone following him.

It was almost certainly overkill, just like it had been every other night he'd done it over the past couple of months, but he was fucked if he was letting some people-trafficking jebend get the jump on him. Better safe than sorry, and given the warnings from the MI5 man, tonight he'd taken even more care than usual.

There was nothing he could do about the boat, of course. It was tucked away in a remote... what? Side stream? River offshoot? *Water road?* Fuck knew what the jargon was, though probably not that last one. It was moored on a stretch of water lined with trees, well away from the main river, with only three buildings overlooking it. All three were blocks of flats, and Hoon had spent a few days walking the corridors, checking the lines of sight from the publicly accessible areas, and adjusting the position of the boat accordingly.

If they were going to come after him, then he wasn't going to make it easy.

Taking a seat on the bed, Hoon battered the top of the second lager bottle against the edge of the built-in bedside table. The metal cap carved gouges in the wood before popping off and rolling into the corner, out of reach.

"Aye, just you fuck off, then," he told it, with more venom than it probably deserved. He took another swig, concluded that this bottle was even more disappointing than the last one, then lay back on the bed, the bottle held upright at his hip.

He had a rummage in his pockets until he found the card that the MI5 man had given him. It didn't have much to say for itself, just the name—Miles Crabtree—and a mobile number. That was it. No job title and no address, physical or email.

With a grunt of effort, he rolled over so he could reach the drawer of the bedside table. Inside, hidden beneath a copy of the *Metro* newspaper, he found a bright pink notebook covered in shiny sequins, into the pages of which he slipped the card.

Closing the drawer again, he searched the wall above the bedside table until he found the set of switches that controlled the lights. With a couple of flicks, the inside of the yacht was plunged into cool, soothing darkness.

Hoon inhaled until his lungs were at full capacity, blew it out gradually, then shut his eyes, going through the motions of trying to sleep, all the while knowing that it wouldn't happen. Not now, anyway. Not yet. Not until he was a few more bottles in. Not until the events of the last few months had writhed like snakes through his brain. Burned inside his head.

Not until he'd pictured Bamber's daughter, and all the million-and-one things he feared had happened to her. *Were* happening to her somewhere right now. And would keep happening, until he did something about it.

"I'm trying, Bam," he whispered into the darkness. "I swear, big man, I'm trying."

And he was. He had been. He'd promised he'd find her, and he would not stop until he did.

And now, finally, he had a lead. A name. Godfrey West.

He'd look up the name in the morning. If he started now, he'd never sleep, and he'd already lost count of the number of hours he'd been awake. Every hour unconscious was another hour for Caroline to suffer, but he needed to stay sharp, stay alert, or he might miss something. A clue. An opportunity.

Or worse—hope.

It was harder to stay positive when the exhaustion crept in. Those were the times when his imagination tormented him most. When it fired up the mental cine projector and made him watch her screaming as faceless figures took it in turns to hurt her. To break her. Again, and again, and again.

"No. No, fuck that."

He opened his eyes and sat up. Sleep wasn't coming, and he didn't want it to, either.

Not when there was work to do.

Taking out his phone, he punched in the name 'Godfrey West' and hit the button to search. Down here, below deck, the connection was slow. He finished off the second bottle of lager while he waited for the results to come back.

When they did finally crawl across the screen, they were nothing to write home about. The first result was for a lower league Nigerian footballer who was born in 1996. He was a midfielder, right-footed, and almost certainly not a high ranking member of a worldwide criminal network.

The next Godfrey West on the list had died peacefully at home in 2018, surrounded by his loving family.

There were no more Godfrey Wests after those. Plenty of search results where those two words appeared, but only a handful where they were together in that order, and those were all about the footballer or the dead man.

"Bollocks," Hoon declared.

He returned to the search box, typed in, 'The Loop' and waited for the results to come in. This time, he was able to anticipate them all before they appeared—a board game, a science-fiction TV show, and some sort of drugs charity that he'd looked into for a while, before concluding they weren't connected to the bastards he was hunting.

When the page loaded he quickly scrolled through in case anything new had come up, but everything was pretty much as expected.

He tried combining both search terms, and spent a few minutes reading about the Godfrey Hotel on Chicago's West Loop.

"So much for that," he muttered, then he threw the phone down on the bed beside him, ran a hand down his face, and reached for the third bottle of lager.

Above him, directly overhead, the deck creaked.

It wasn't the usual slow moan of the wood settling in the cool night air, but the sharp, sudden squeak of weight being applied.

A footstep.

Someone was up there. Someone else was on the boat.

Hoon reached behind his head, slipped his hand beneath

the pillow and wriggled his fingers into the set of brass knuckles he had stashed there.

He swung his legs off the bed, got to his feet, then had a thoroughly enjoyable scratch of his arse.

Maybe tonight wasn't going to be a total write off, after all.

CHAPTER FIVE

HOON HAD A COUPLE OF OPTIONS. The first was the most sensible—stay down here, lie in wait, let the bastards come to him, then catch them off guard and leather seven shades of shite out of them before asking them who they were and what the fuck they thought they were playing at. That was the safest approach.

The second option was riskier. Storm up the stairs—which would briefly put his head at the perfect kicking level, and the rest of him at a massive height disadvantage—then go wind-milling in with fists flying in the general direction of anything that might be considered human-shaped. That would be reck-less, though. That would be stupid.

"Fuck it," he muttered, and he took the stairs two at a time.

There were no sudden blows to his skull as it popped up above the deck. No machetes swung down at him. No baseball bats went *crack*.

That was a bonus.

The whispers of the water lapping against the side of the boat were masking all other sound. The only light spilled from the surrounding tower blocks. It wasn't enough to push back the darkness, but enough to give it flavour and texture.

He squinted through the gloom, the hand wearing the brass knuckles drawing back, held ready to swing. He focused, a hunter's gaze, trying to recognise the shapes of the yacht so that he might identify anything unfamiliar. Anything that shouldn't be there. Anything that might feasibly be a threat.

"Bob?"

A hand tapped him on the shoulder, and he turned with a yelp and a, "Jesus fuck!"

Even as his fist began to swing, that part of his brain that had recognised the voice was screaming at him to, 'Abort! Abort!'

He pulled the punch at the last moment, and the woman standing there with him in the darkness narrowly avoided having her face permanently relocated to the other side of her head.

Just as well, too. It was a very nice face. He'd have hated to see it mangled.

"Gabriella?" he wheezed, his eyes still searching for her edges in the darkness. He was aware of her presence, but it was still impossible to make out where the night ended and she began. "The fuck are you doing here? You shouldn't be here."

He realised now that he should've known it was her from the moment he stepped up onto the deck. Even over the smell of the river, her scent was unmistakable. Freshly cut spring flowers and *Dettol*. An elegant woman who had found herself with a dirty job to do.

"You haven't been answering my calls," Gabriella replied. There was reproach in her voice, but a tremble, too, and Hoon realised that the air up here felt cold and raw. "I didn't... I just wanted to see you. To talk. I just..." He heard her draw in a breath, like she was steadying herself. "I shouldn't have come. I know. I just..."

"Were you followed?" he asked.

"What? No. Of course I wasn't followed. Why would I be followed?"

"Go downstairs," Hoon instructed, brushing her questions aside. "Take a seat. I'll be right down."

Gabriella felt his hand on her arm, guiding her to the stairs with a sense of urgency. She didn't resist, and once he released his grip she made her way down the steps and fumbled around for a light switch.

"Leave them off," he told her, anticipating this. "Just for a minute."

Turning, he scanned the darkness around the boat. His eyes were very slowly adjusting, and he could make out vague shapes lining the edges of the towpath. Trees, he thought. And closer, a couple of those big sticky up things you tied the rope to. Nothing out of the ordinary.

His eyes flicked to the buildings standing tall nearby. He didn't let his gaze linger on the illuminated windows for long, so as not to set his night vision back to square one again. Anyway, it wasn't the windows with lights on that were the worry. It was the darkened rooms.

Middle building, fourth floor, two from the right. That one caught his eye. The reflections on the glass were different, suggesting that, despite the cold, the window was partway open, angled towards the sky. The room beyond was in deep, black shadow, and yet...

And yet...

He felt the fine hairs on the back of his neck stirring. He couldn't see anyone in the window, but then he wouldn't. That would be the point. He wouldn't see them, not from this distance. Not in the dark.

But that didn't mean they wouldn't be able to see him. And, with the best will in the world, a set of brass knuckles and a mean right hook were going to be fuck all use against a sniper's bullet.

He cursed himself for not picking his phone up off the bed. He could've lit up the screen, held it in front of him, waved it around. Better to make himself a target now when he was alone on the deck. Better that he get shot than her.

He waited, glowering at the window, but no shot came. No flash. No *bang*. No zipping of bullets through the air as they rushed him into the welcoming arms of oblivion.

Not a fucking cheep.

Turning, Hoon descended the stairs, then felt around in the darkness until he found the switch for the small desk lamp Bookish had used to read by. It was one of those flexible necked numbers, bent down low so the bulb was almost touching the table it sat on. It gave off just the amount of light Hoon needed to see by, and not a single lumen more.

Only then, when the light was on, did he turn to Gabriella. She perched at one end of the padded bench couch in a way that suggested most of her weight was still on her feet. He had always considered her beautiful, from the moment he'd first set eyes on her all those years ago. Here and now, with the lights down low and a slight sheen of sweat glossing her smooth olive skin, she looked like a Renaissance painting.

That was the phrase that came to mind, at least. In truth, he didn't have the first fucking clue about Renaissance paintings. For all he knew, it was all horsey-teethed lassies with crooked noses and bubonic plague. He wasn't an expert on the artworks of the period. Or any other period, for that matter.

Although, he'd always had a soft spot for that one of dogs playing poker.

The point was, Gabriella always looked good, but tonight, even dressed as she was in a thick parka over baggy jeans and walking boots, she looked *radiant*. This only served to annoy him even more.

"What the fuck were you thinking?" he asked her, somehow managing to both shout and whisper in the same breath. "I told you not to come here unless it was an emergency." He took a step closer. "Shite. Is it an emergency? What's happened? Is Welshy alright? Are you alright? What's happened?"

"Nothing's happened. He's fine. We're both... We're fine, Boggle," Gabriella replied. His old army nickname. Something about the sound of it on her lips made the moment feel more intimate, somehow, like she knew him—really knew him—in a way that few others did. "He's sleeping," she continued. "He doesn't know I'm here."

Hoon scowled. The furrowing of his brow turned his eyes into two black holes of shadow. "You left him? On his own? In his fucking condition? Are you wise?"

Gabriella's response was like a cold front moving across the room. "I'm well aware of 'his fucking condition,' thank you. He's my husband. I was caring for him long before you turned up, and I'll still be doing it long after you've moved on again. Like I said, he's sleeping. He doesn't know I'm gone."

"What if he wakes up and you're no' there?"

"Then he'll wait. I do have to leave the house sometimes. He knows I'm never far away," Gabriella said. "He knows I'd never leave him for long." She sighed and sat back, either letting herself relax or too exhausted to remain so tightly wound. "Anyway, he's on new medication. It knocks him out. He won't wake up until six or seven."

Hoon grunted, but otherwise didn't respond. He took another stubby beer bottle from the mini-fridge and offered it to her, but she declined with a shake of the head, then a nod in the direction of the kettle.

"I'd kill for a cuppa, though. Freezing out there."

Hoon blinked slowly, like he didn't quite understand the words she was saying, then turned towards the kettle.

He had been aware, of course, that there was a kettle on the boat. He'd seen it several times. He'd even used it once or twice —the first time for a *Pot Noodle*, and the second to try to remove some stubborn blood stains from a shirt. Neither event could really be considered a success.

"You do have tea, yes?" Gabriella asked.

Hoon had never been much of a tea drinker. When there was no alcohol available, or circumstances temporarily prevented its consumption, then he'd accept coffee, albeit grudgingly. Tea, though? No. He'd have to be particularly consumed by self-loathing before he'd entertain that notion. Tea was the preserve of women, homosexuals, and the Chinese, and while he bore no grudges towards any of those groups, he had no intentions of joining their ranks.

"I'm not sure," he admitted. "I could do you coffee."

"It's, like, one in the morning," Gabriella countered. "I don't want coffee or I'll be awake all night."

She got up. Came closer. Hoon swallowed and bit down on his bottom lip as she stopped right in front of him, close enough to touch. Close enough to hold. To kiss.

This close, she was everything. Every smell. Every sight. All his senses were filled with her and her alone, like there was nothing else in—

A cupboard door *clonked* him on the back of the head, snapping him out of it.

"Ow. Jesus!"

Gabriella winced and failed to suppress a giggle. "Sorry. Your head's bigger than it looks."

Hoon frowned, considering this. "What the fuck is that supposed mean?"

"Nothing," Gabriella assured him. "Just that, you know, you look like you've got quite a small head."

"What do you mean, I look like I've got a small head?"

"I just mean, you know, scale-wise."

This did not appear to answer Hoon's question. "The fuck

do you mean, *scale-wise*? My head's perfectly in scale with the rest of me. I've had fucking compliments about the size of my head, I'll have you know."

Gabriella smirked. "Have you?"

"Aye, well, no' in so many words, maybe," Hoon admitted. "I mean, who the fuck comes out and says that to someone? But you could tell by the way folk look at it that they were bursting with admiration."

"You're funny," she told him, then she produced a cylinder of silver foil from the cupboard and waved it in front of his face. "Tea bags."

Hoon tutted and took the packet from her. "Oh. Aye. I mind seeing them, right enough," he admitted. "There were some other ones, too. Lemon and ginger and... Christ. Lady Grey, or some shite."

Gabriella's eyes darted back to the cupboard on the wall. "Really? Where?"

"I threw them in the sea," Hoon said. "Or the river, or whatever the hell it is."

"It's a river. It's definitely a river," Gabriella told him. "And why did you do that?"

Hoon appeared genuinely perplexed by the question. "What the fuck else was I meant to do with them?" he asked. "I had to get rid of the bastarding things somehow, and you can't exactly start a fire on a boat."

He picked up the kettle and gave it an experimental shake. There wasn't much water in it, but there was enough for a single cup of tea. That would be enough. One cup of tea, one quick chat, and he'd pack her off home. No drama, no long conversations, and certainly no funny business.

No matter how good she looked, or smelled, or *felt* standing there in the half-darkness behind him.

"Right, take a seat, I'll bring it over," he said, clicking the switch that set the kettle to boil. He heard her hesitate, felt her warmth lingering at his back for a moment longer than was necessary.

"OK, cool," she said, her voice artificially light.

Hoon waited until she was back sitting down before saying any more. Even when he did, it was nothing of any consequence.

"Don't know how you can drink tea down here. Water's manky. You know London water is literally recycled pish, aye? That's why it's got that scum on top."

"I'll take my chances," Gabriella replied. She waited in silence for the kettle to boil, and only spoke again once it had clicked off. "Have you had any luck? Finding Caroline, I mean."

Hoon shook his head. "No' yet."

"Yeah. Well. You will. You'll find her," she told him. He said nothing in reply, and when Gabriella spoke again her voice was a little less solemn, like she was trying to lighten the mood. "He misses you, you know? Welshy. He doesn't say as much, of course. I mean, he wouldn't say it, even if he could. He's like you in that regard—he'd never admit to having actual human emotions. But he does. He misses you."

"Aye. Well," was the only response Hoon could offer. Then he made tea in the only clean drinking vessel he could find, and deposited it on the table in front of her.

She considered the dimpled glass pint tankard with an eyebrow raised, then wrapped her hands around it, not yet taking a drink. "Cheers."

"No bother."

"Nick this glass from a pub, did you?"

"I *borrowed* it from a pub," Hoon corrected. "Indefinitely."

Gabriella watched the steam rising from the surface of the liquid for a while, and was still transfixed by it when she finally said what she'd really come here to say. "I miss you, too. Having you around, I mean."

"Aye, well," Hoon said again. "It's safer this way."

"Doesn't feel it," she replied, though she nodded her understanding.

He hadn't stayed with them for long. Not really. Not in the grand scheme of things. A week at most, broken up by a few nights away in between. He'd slept on the couch for some of it. On other nights, he'd half-dozed on the chair in Welshy's room, surrounded by medical apparatus and bags bulging with bodily fluids.

Sitting there on those nights, he'd recounted stories of old friends and days gone by. Made jokes, mostly at his own expense. Held Welshy's hand in silence when the pain in the other man's eyes became too sharp and severe to be blunted by nostalgia.

It couldn't last, of course. Not given Hoon's mission. Not with everything he was planning to do.

Long before tonight—before he'd spoken with Miles Crabtree—he'd known that he was painting a big red target on his perfectly proportioned head. Bookish hadn't told him much about the Loop, but he'd said enough to let Hoon know that the organisation was made up of serious people doing terrible things.

The more he looked for Caroline, the more attention he'd be drawing to himself. That was fine in his book—let the bastards come, it would save him the effort of hunting them—but he wasn't going to bring any of that to Welshy's door. Not in a million years.

Not for a second time.

"Long way to come to tell me that," Hoon said. The words sounded harsher than he'd intended, but she replied before he had a chance to take them back.

"Well, maybe if you'd answer your phone..."

Hoon sighed. "Aye. I know. I just..."

She shimmied along the bench, making room for him to sit. He did, then dropped his arms onto the table and rested his head on one hand. Beside her, in that moment, he felt for the first time in weeks that sleep could come, if only he let it. Like he could close his eyes and drift off into a slumber that wasn't haunted by the nightmares of his own failures.

But he couldn't allow himself to rest. He hadn't earned that right. Not yet.

"The things I'm doing... The things I have to do... I shouldn't be around you. I mean, Christ, I shouldn't be around anyone." He let out a derisory snort of laughter, aimed squarely at himself. "I'm a fucking health hazard, Gabriella. I told Bamber I'd get his girl back, and there is nothing I won't do to fulfil that promise. Nothing. And I don't mean like I'm a fucking superhero, or whatever. I'm no' some square-jawed noble bastard with shiny teeth and a cape."

"I'd love to see you in a cape," Gabriella whispered, but Hoon ignored the comment.

"When I say I'll do anything, I don't mean I'll go out and die a hero's death trying to find her. Fuck all use that'll do anyone," he said, and he sounded slightly bitter about that. "What I mean is there's no low to which I won't sink," he continued. "I was an irredeemable bastard before I came here, and I've had a lot more blood on my hands since then. If it comes to it, I'm going to peel the fucking skin off anyone who knows where Caroline is, strip by strip. I will shatter their bones and feed them their own fucking tongues, if that's what it takes."

He stared ahead for a while, like there was something written on the opposite wall that only he could see. Gabriella rested a hand lightly on the back of one of his. He flinched like he'd been electrocuted, and rose quickly to his feet.

"Having me around doesn't make you safer, Gabriella. Just the fucking opposite. I'm no' one of the good guys. I'm the scabby-eyed monster who lives under the bed. I'm the fucking Bogeyman, and the safest thing for you and Welshy is if I stay far away from the pair of you."

Gabriella stood too, reaching out for him as if trying to calm a startled beast. "Bob, don't say that. That's not you. You're not—"

He clamped a hand over her mouth, silencing her. "Shh. Shut up," he urged, his voice dropping into a whisper. Cocking his head, he listened, then he hurriedly guided her down to the floor when a set of car headlights blazed in through the porthole windows.

They crouched there. Tense. Silent. Hoon's eyes followed the light as it crept slowly across the wall, the engine of a vehicle rumbling along the towpath alongside the boat.

Gesturing for Gabriella to stay where she was, he slid along the floor to a window, pushed himself up with his back against the wall, and risked a glance outside.

He couldn't make out the vehicle in any detail, thanks to its full-beam headlights casting it into silhouette. From the direction the lights were shining, he could tell the car was edging its way up the towpath. Judging by its speed, either the driver was looking for something, or they were lost.

Had he been here on his own, he'd have hoped for the former. He'd have hoped for a car full of hardmen made overly confident by their numbers.

But with Gabriella here?

"Keep driving, you prick. Keep driving," he muttered.

Red brake lights flared. The car stopped, its tyres crunching on the loose grit.

Shite.

"Bathroom. Now. Lock the door," Hoon whispered, tearing his eyes from the window just long enough to shoot a warning look in Gabriella's direction.

She started to stand, but he motioned to the floor, ordering her to stay low and out of sight. Then, as she started to crawl towards what she guessed was the bathroom door, Hoon gestured for her to stop.

"Wait, hold on," he said, a little louder now. Outside, the car pulled a cautious three-point-turn on the towpath, giving Hoon a glimpse of the kebab shop livery on the side. He ducked his head as the lights swept across his window again, then watched the vehicle head back the way it had come, presumably in search of a delivery address.

"Jesus Christ," he wheezed, exhaling two lungfuls of tension. "I didn't know they did deliveries. Bonus."

"What?" Gabriella whispered from the floor. "What's happening? Are they gone?"

"Aye," Hoon said. "Aye, they're gone. It was just a takeaway driver."

Gabriella tutted, then pulled herself back to her feet using the bench for support.

Hoon didn't turn away from the porthole yet. He stole a glance in both directions along the path. Between the unexpected appearance of the car and the open window on that darkened flat, he felt uneasy. Something felt off.

"And you're sure you weren't followed?"

"Yes. I'm sure. I took a taxi and faced backwards. I was watching the whole way," she said. "There was a van parked across the road that I wasn't sure of, but it didn't follow me."

Hoon turned to her. "A van?"

"Yeah. Sort of transit van sized. Been there for a couple of days. Workmen, or something. Probably for one of the neighbours. They're always having something done."

"And you saw them? The workmen? You've set eyes on them?"

"Uh... yeah," she replied, but she sounded less than certain. "Yeah, I mean, I must have. I'm sure I did."

Hoon closed the gap between them in two big steps, his hands clamping onto her upper arms and holding her in place. "I need you to think very fucking carefully, Gabriella," he said, his voice low and urgent. "Did you see workmen?"

"What? Ow, you're... I don't... I don't remember. I'm not sure. Why?"

Hoon released his grip and ejected a, "Fuck!" that made Gabriella shy back in fright.

"What? What's the matter?"

"The van. That fucking van. What would workmen be doing there in the middle of the bloody night?"

Gabriella's face paled. "No, but... it's fine. It didn't follow me!" she reminded him.

"Exactly! Which means it's still fucking there," Hoon spat back, hurrying through to the bedroom.

Gabriella's hand went to her mouth. She staggered, eyes filling with tears like a tap had been turned on. "Oh. Oh, God."

"They didn't follow because they're not after you," Hoon said, returning with his phone, a jacket, and something that looked like a cut-down version of a machete knife. "They're after Welshy."

CHAPTER SIX

HOON no longer cared about keeping the location of the boat a secret. If Crabtree was right, and he'd already come to the attention of the Loop, then chances were they knew damn well where it was moored. No need, then, to do his usual twisting walk through the streets of London before hailing a cab.

They flagged one down almost as soon as they reached the road. Gabriella rattled off the address, then Hoon instructed the driver to get his fucking finger out.

Gabriella had started to dial the police before Hoon had stopped her. He knew from first-hand experience that the Loop had infiltrated the Met. Calling in some random Bobby might make the situation worse.

"Worse how?" she demanded.

"I just... We don't know who we can trust."

"You think someone's gone there to kill him!" Gabriella cried, which drew a concerned look from the driver. He chose not to comment, though, having done this job far too long to get involved in the lives of those he ferried around. "How much worse can it get?"

Hoon stared back at her for a few moments, then begrudgingly admitted that she had a point. She punched three nines into her phone, while he turned and rapped his knuckles against the glass that divided the back of the car from the front.

"What's the problem up there, pal? We joined a fucking funeral procession, or something?" he demanded.

"There's a speed limit," the driver told him. "I can only go so fast, you know?"

"Are you sure you're a fucking taxi driver? I thought you lot were above the Highway Code? I thought that didn't apply to you bastards?"

"I'm not getting points on my licence."

"Well, pull over then and let me fucking drive," Hoon spat.

"I'll pull over, alright, mate. I'll pull over and turf you out of my cab!"

The words hissed between Hoon's teeth. "I'd like to see you fucking try."

"Bob! Jesus, shut up and let him drive," Gabriella cried. She leaned across the gap and slapped him on the leg, drawing his attention away from the driver. The phone was still to her ear, a female voice on the other end talking calmly through the earpiece. "The police are on their way. It's going to be fine."

"Aye, well," Hoon grunted, with a final beady glare at the driver. "I'll believe that when I see it."

———

When the taxi pulled onto the street where Welshy and Gabriella's house stood, the first thing Hoon noticed was the lack of blue lights. If the police were on their way, then they were taking their time about it.

"The van. Where's that van?" Hoon demanded, scouring the street as the taxi slowed to a stop.

"It's... It was there," Gabriella insisted, pointing to what was probably the only empty on-street parking space in the whole of North London. "It was right there."

"Fuck!" Hoon ejected. He tried the taxi's door handle. Locked. He rattled it, then bellowed at the driver to, "Open the fucking door!"

"It don't open until I've stopped," the driver called back. "Health and safety, innit?"

"Then stop the bastard car before I—"

The driver slammed on the brakes, and Hoon's head *clonked* against the dividing glass.

"You did that on purpose, you sack of horse tits," Hoon ejected, then he threw open the door, ordered Gabriella to wait where she was, and went charging up the path that led to the house's front entrance.

This door, too, was locked, though a couple of solid kicks soon put paid to that. Wood splintered. Glass shattered. Hoon was halfway up the hall before the sounds stopped echoing.

"Welshy? Welshy, you alright?" he called, despite knowing full well that the other man couldn't answer.

The door to Welshy's room was closed. Hoon didn't waste time listening for any signs of movement inside. This was no time to get the lay of the land. Instead, he burst in, one hand clenched into a fist, the other clutching the handle of the knife hidden in a pocket of his combat trousers.

He was met by a chorus of beeps and wheezes that told him his old mate was alive, if not well. But then, he hadn't been well in a long, long time.

Welshy's eyes were closed, but the slow rising and falling of his chest in time with the soft clicks of a pump confirmed he was still in the land of the living.

"Oh, thank fuck," Hoon whispered. The knot of fear that had been tightening in his stomach suddenly unravelled, almost bringing him to his knees. He reached for Welshy's hand, and lightly gave it a squeeze. "You're alright. He's alright."

A floorboard squeaked behind him—a low, ominous groan, like something from a horror movie. Not Gabriella. Someone big. Heavy. A throat was cleared. Male. Younger than him. He couldn't say how he knew that, he just knew it. Instinctively.

Large man, thirties, standing right behind him.

He turned swinging, not giving the bastard the chance to strike first. His arm was a piston, his fist a hammer-blow to the middle of the intruder's face.

The impact had the desired effect. Bone cracked. Skin split. Blood and snot fountained over a white shirt collar and down the front of a stab-proof vest, and Hoon managed to mutter a resigned, "Bollocks," before the constable fell to the floor, blinded by tears and choking on big mouthfuls of crimson.

Hoon looked out into the hallway beyond the bedroom door to find Gabriella standing there, eyes wide with shock. "What did you do?" she cried.

"I might as well be honest, I smacked him square in the coupon," Hoon said, indicating the downed policeman. The poor bastard was grasping for the radio on his shoulder, but not having much luck at finding it.

"I saw that! I meant why? He's a policeman!"

"Aye, well, I can see that now, obviously," Hoon retorted. "But I didn't know when I threw the punch, did I? He came sneaking up behind me like a big fucking Creeping Jesus. What was I meant to do?"

"How about maybe *not* punch him in the face?" Gabriella suggested. "Maybe start there? In fact, maybe start with not kicking in my front door? I have a key!"

Hoon scowled. "Well, hindsight's a wonderful fucking thing, sweetheart. But sure. Aye. Go ahead. Blame me for it all, why don't you?"

"Well, it was you who kicked in the door and smacked him in the face, so..."

"I barely touched him!" Hoon protested. "Is it my fault he's got the physical strength of a Cabbage Patch Doll on a hunger strike? No. Is it fuck. That's on him."

Down on the floor, the officer sobbed and choked on his blood. Hoon shook his head and rolled his eyes in contempt.

"Oh, and by the way, for the record?" he said. "He is totally fucking milking this for all it's worth."

———

Fifteen minutes later, and for the second time that evening, Hoon sat in handcuffs in the back of a police car, muttering to himself about the injustice of the whole situation.

They'd helped the downed officer up, tried their best to explain the misunderstanding, and had even made him a cup of tea while they'd waited for backup to arrive.

He'd seemed quite reasonable prior to the other officers barging in. He'd accepted Hoon's apology—begrudgingly given as it had been—and had agreed that he should've done more to announce his presence.

Yes, these things happened in high-stress situations, he'd admitted. Yes, mistakes were made in the heat of the moment. No, he wasn't going to hold a grudge.

As soon as the other three Bobbies had rocked up with their batons out, though, his attitude had quickly shifted. Out went the whimpering wee scrote, and in came someone labouring under the illusion that he was Judge Dredd.

He'd supervised from a distance while the other officers had moved to restrain his assailant. Hoon had started to resist, but a few sharp words from Gabriella had made him see sense, and he'd allowed his hands to be wrenched around behind his back, and the cuffs locked in place.

They'd searched him, of course, patted him down and gone rifling through his pockets. The knife hadn't gone down well with them. Nor, it had to be said, had they been impressed by the brass knuckles, or the second, smaller knife that Hoon had tucked away in his sock.

What they had enjoyed was the notebook they'd found in the big square pocket just above his right knee. He'd stuffed it in there back before he and Gabriella had left the boat, and had sat stony-faced and silent as the constables had made fun of its pink sequins and Japanese Anime-inspired artwork.

He couldn't really blame them. He'd tried quite hard to get rid of the bloody thing for those very reasons back when he'd first acquired it. It had grown on him over time, though. What's more, most of the information he'd gathered about Caroline's disappearance was stored in there in the indecipherable scrawl of his handwriting. Losing it was not an option.

"Be careful with that," he'd warned, watching one of them go rifling through the pages.

"Got sentimental value, has it?" the officer snorted.

"Something like that, aye. I want it back in one piece."

The constable snapped the book shut with a *bang*. "Or what?"

"Or you fucking won't be, princess."

He'd been bundled into the car soon after that. The officer whose face he'd partially caved in was taken to hospital. Hoon spent a few enjoyable moments thinking about the procedure for resetting a broken nose, before the constable who'd gone through the notebook slid into the front passenger seat of the car.

"Comfortable back there?" the policeman asked.

"No' particularly."

The officer grinned back at him. "Glad to hear it. And remember, we can always make you even less comfortable. Just say the word."

"Aye, very good," Hoon sneered. "But I wouldn't waste my time trying to pull the intimidation act on me, son. I've seen balloons that are more convincingly menacing than you are."

He indicated the notebook with a sharp nod of his head. "Now, make yourself useful for once in your life, flick through them pages again until you come across the most boring business card you've ever clapped eyes on, then get me my fucking phone call."

CHAPTER SEVEN

"I WANT THEM MOVED. Somewhere else. Somewhere safe. Both of them. Tonight. Can you do that? Because, if you can't, then you can fucking forget the rest of this conversation."

Hoon was sitting at a different table in a different interview room, wearing yet another set of handcuffs. Only the man sitting across from him was the same as last time, although he wore a much more knackered expression than he had a couple of hours previously, and while he was wearing the same shirt, he'd ditched the tie and unfastened the uppermost button.

"We can do that," Miles Crabtree confirmed.

"The van. Was it yours?" Hoon asked.

"What van?"

"The one parked across the road from Welshy's."

Miles shrugged. "What did it look like?"

"Fuck knows. I didn't see it."

The MI5 man rubbed his eyes, like he wasn't convinced he was fully awake. "I thought it was parked across the road?"

"Earlier. It had fucked off by the time I got there."

Miles' lips moved like he was trying to do some difficult

arithmetic in his head. "So... you're asking if a van that wasn't there belonged to us?"

Hoon stabbed an index finger against the tabletop. "Drop the pained expression, son. You look like a Womble having a difficult shite. You know exactly what I'm fucking asking. The van. Was it one of yours? Have you been watching the house?" He stopped prodding the table and pointed the finger at Miles instead. "And, just so we're fucking clear about this, I will know if you're lying to me, and I will not be best fucking pleased if you are. Keep that at the forefront of your mind while you consider the next few words to come out of your mouth."

"No," Miles told him. "No, it wasn't one of ours. We're a little more sophisticated than that. Not a *lot* more sophisticated, but a little. Most of the time." He produced a pen from his shirt pocket, clicked the end, and held it poised over a small flip notebook he had placed on the desk when he'd first entered the room. "Do you have a registration?"

"I told you I didn't see it," Hoon retorted. "What am I going to do, siphon the fucking number plate out of thin air?"

"I thought maybe your lady friend might have mentioned it."

Hoon became deathly still. His gaze locked onto the man across the table like a predator selecting its prey. "She's no' my lady friend. She's my mate's wife."

"No. No, I know that," Crabtree said. "I'm not suggesting anything's going on between you."

"Aye, well, you'd better fucking not be," Hoon warned. "Or when I get out of these handcuffs, I'll hit you so hard you'll enter the fucking Astral Plane. She's a friend. That's all."

"Exactly. A friend who is a lady. Hence, 'lady friend,'" Miles countered. "I meant nothing by it, Bob. Honest."

"You don't get to call me Bob," Hoon said. "My friends call me Bob."

"Yes, well, I'm very much hoping we can be friends," Miles countered.

"Aye? Well, I'd say the chances of that happening are about two miles north of Not Fucking Likely, pal," Hoon told him. He pointed to the door. "Now, away you fuck."

Across the table, the MI5 man frowned. "Sorry?"

"Welshy and Gabriella. Get them sorted. Get them safe. Then we'll talk."

"Oh. That. Already in hand," Miles assured him. "Got a team working with medics to relocate Gwynn and his equipment. He and Gabriella will be taken to a safe house. He'll get the very best of care. It'll be outside London, up in—"

Hoon raised a hand as high as he could before the cuffs went tight. "Don't. I don't want to know," he said. "But, I swear to fuck, son, you'd better be telling me the truth. They'd better be treated like bloody royalty. Because if they aren't—if you're lying to me—then I will turn you inside out. Literally. Everything that's inside now will be outside, and vice-fucking-versa. And I will take my time doing it. I will fucking *linger* over it. Is that understood?"

Miles smiled, but it was a solemn and sincere thing. "Yes. I think you've succeeded in making your feelings pretty clear there. They're safe. I can't promise much, but I can promise you that."

Hoon stared deep into the other man's eyes, his gaze like a drill boring for the truth until, finally, he nodded. "Fine. OK," he said, relaxing as best he could against the back of his hard plastic chair. "Now, are you going to tell me what the fuck you want from me, or what?"

"Yes. Yes, absolutely," Miles said. He checked his watch, did a double-take, then rubbed his chin with the back of his hand. "It's later than I'd ideally like. But... maybe if we hurry. It might still be possible."

"What might be possible?" Hoon demanded.

Miles leaned forward, steepling his fingers in front of him. "Couple of quick questions before I explain it all." He glanced meaningfully at the mirror on the wall beside them. "Firstly, I assume you have no objection to us taking this conversation somewhere more private?"

Hoon shook his head. "No bother. Atmosphere in this place is shite. What's the second question?"

Miles' smile broadened until it showed a considerable number of his shiny white teeth.

"Actually," he said, and he took his life in his hands by winking again. "I think maybe I'll save that one for later."

———

Miles' car was not what Hoon had expected. Given the man's earlier pristine appearance and what Hoon could only describe as his 'tedious fucking personality,' he'd expected the MI5 man to drive a *Ford Focus.* Maybe a *Skoda* of some sort. A boring company car of some kind, anyway, probably with a filing cabinet in the back and a spare shirt hanging from a hook somewhere.

He had not expected a fifteen-year-old green *Rover* with its door pockets stuffed with half-crushed *Red Bull* cans and chocolate bar wrappers. Nor had he been anticipating the *Peppa Pig* booster seat that he'd had to chuck into the back before he could sit down.

"Sorry, should've cleaned up a bit," Miles said. "Wasn't expecting you to call me back this soon."

"Is this your own car?" Hoon asked. He moved his feet around in the footwell, kicking aside a half-empty crisp packet and a soft toy shaped like a stunted giraffe. "Surely the fucking Secret Service can give you something better than this?"

Miles took several seconds to formulate a reply. In the end, it wasn't really worth the wait.

"That's confidential."

Hoon shrugged, sniffed, and looked out through the side window as the streets of London crawled by. "Suit yourself." He turned back. "What's with the trainers, by the way?" he asked, indicating the black and white running shoes that were currently working the pedals of the car. "No' exactly business attire."

"They were a present from my wife," Miles told him.

"And what, did they come with instructions never to take them off again?"

Miles clicked his tongue against the back of his teeth, but kept his eyes on the road. "Something like that."

Hoon didn't care enough to pursue the conversation any further, so he went back to looking out of the side window.

He wasn't sure where in the city they were. Still somewhere north of the river, he thought, but he didn't recognise it. They'd passed a *Costa Coffee* a few hundred yards back, but given that it seemed like you were never more than that distance from a *Costa Coffee* anywhere in London, this wasn't particularly helpful.

It was after three in the morning now, and the streets were mostly deserted, aside from occasional clusters of die-hard revellers hunting for a club that would still let them in at this late hour.

He shifted his focus from the world outside to his reflection in the glass. His face was superimposed against the city like a ghost, all sallow skin and eye bags. He ran a hand across the lower half of his face, idly wondering how many days it had been since he'd last shaved.

"Where are we going?" he asked, and his breath painted a circle of fog on the cold glass.

"Right now? Nowhere. Just driving," Miles said. "Away from prying eyes and ears. The car is safe. Nobody's listening in. I sweep it for bugs every couple of days."

Hoon turned away from his reflection. "Fucking hell. You sound like a right paranoid bastard."

"Cautious. Not paranoid," Miles replied. "The people we're dealing with... the Loop..." He flexed his fingers, then tightened his grip on the wheel. "Well, you can't be too careful."

"Aye. So you keep telling me," Hoon said. "So far, I haven't seen much to confirm that."

Miles shot him a sideways glance. "What, besides the people trafficking ring you helped break up, you mean? Besides all those people who were trying to kill you?"

Hoon shifted his weight from one arse cheek to the other, struggling to get comfortable in the car's sagging seat. "You'd be surprised how many people try to kill me."

"Ha!" the MI5 man ejected. "Oh, I don't know. Having spent some time in your company, I don't think I'd be all *that* surprised. That's why you're here, if I'm being completely honest."

"So you can kill me?" Hoon asked. He briefly sized the other man up, then concluded he had nothing to worry about.

"Well, no. I can't say I fancy my chances on that front. I just mean that you have a tendency to get under people's skin. You're driven, you can take care of yourself and, well, you're not afraid of doing what needs to be done. In short, Bob, you're exactly the sort of man we're after."

"Mr Hoon."

"Sorry?"

"Like I told you, you don't get to call me Bob," Hoon reminded him. "It's Mr fucking Hoon to you."

Miles nodded. "OK, fine. Sorry. In short, *Mr fucking Hoon*, you're exactly the sort of man we're after. Better?"

"Much," Hoon confirmed. "The sort of man you're after for what?"

Miles glanced in all three of the car's mirrors, then checked his blind spot over his right shoulder, as if making extra sure that nobody was following.

"You have experience of undercover work," he said. "Back in your early days on the police force. Right?"

"Jesus Christ, is there nothing you nosy bastards don't know?" Hoon muttered. "Aye. Long fucking time ago, but aye. So, what are you saying? You want me to go undercover? With these Loop clowns?"

"What would you say if I said yes?" Miles asked, stealing another sideways look.

"I'd say you were out of your fucking mind," Hoon told him. "You said yourself, they're keeping an eye on me. They know who I am. Hard to go undercover if every bastard knows your real name."

"I think you're the one being paranoid now," Miles told him. "Or—and please don't take this the wrong way—a little arrogant, maybe."

"Arrogant? Me?" Hoon spat. "Show's how much you know, son. I'm the polar opposite of arrogant. I'm like *the Beatles* of fucking modesty, me."

Miles side-eyed him to check if Hoon was on the wind-up. Judging by the expression on his face, he wasn't. "Right. Yes. Well. Apologies for my misjudgement."

He indicated left, slowed, checked his mirrors to see if any of the cars trailing behind started to switch lanes, then cancelled the manoeuvre and carried straight on when they didn't.

"We being followed?" Hoon asked, leaning towards the middle of the car so he could get a clear backwards view in the mirror on his side.

Miles shook his head. "Don't think so. Just that paranoia again," he said. "And what I was trying to say is, yes, you're on their radar, but right now you're just a tiny blip lost among countless others. You're a mild itch that doesn't yet need scratching. The Loop is a huge organisation with hundreds of thousands of moving parts, all doing their own thing, all working largely independently of one another, with a few exceptions. They derive profit from a wide range of criminal activities, of which people trafficking and prostitution are just two. Our plan is to insert you into a different sector, where nobody is aware of you."

"Then how's that meant to help me find Caroline?" Hoon asked.

"Because the area we'd be inserting you into—if you go high enough in it, anyway—is headed up by Godfrey West. The guy I mentioned earlier who can help lead us to Caroline. He calls himself the Eel."

"The Eel? What sort of fucking nickname is that?" Hoon scoffed.

"I assume it's because he's slippery."

"Aye, no shit, Sherlock. But, I mean, that's the sort of nickname a fucking five-year-old gives himself," Hoon ranted. He crossed his arms and seemed genuinely quite annoyed. "If you're going to name yourself after a fish, don't go for one of the shite ones. Go fucking piranha, or barracuda, or shark, or something. What's that ugly bastard thing with the wee light on the head and all the teeth? Lives down at the bottom? Go with that. I mean, fuck me, even *the Dolphin* would be better than the Eel."

"Dolphin's not a fish," Miles pointed out. "It's a mammal."

Hoon scowled. "Let's no' fucking kid ourselves here, son. It's a fish. We all pretend it's not, but we all know it is. It's got fins and a big flappy tail, and it swims in the sea, therefore it's a fucking fish. I don't care what propaganda it might be trying to spin to make itself seem more interesting. A fish with a blow-hole's still just a fish, and 'the Eel,' is still a shite nickname for anyone."

Miles smiled vaguely. There was a suggestion of concern to it, like he was worried the conversation was slipping away from him, or that he might have made a terrible error of judgement. Whatever the reason, he worked quickly to get things back on track.

"Well, whatever you want to call him, he's well-connected within the organisation. He's tipped for big things in the Loop. Five years from now, he'll be one of their top players. West knows what's what. He keeps an eye on things, always looking for a way to consolidate his position. He's your best bet for finding her."

"Fine. Great. Then here's the plan. You and me go over there now, tear him out of his fucking bed, I set about the prick with a pair of pliers and a blowtorch, and Bob's your uncle."

Miles slowed the car at a junction, checked furtively in every direction, and didn't speak again until the lights had changed to green and they were back on the move.

"Yeah, it isn't that simple, unfortunately. Getting at him is difficult for one thing. He's usually well protected. And even if we were somehow able to get our hands on him, he's not the type of man who'll just cave in under pressure."

Hoon grunted. "You'd be surprised what a pair of blazing testicles can do to loosen the tongue," he said. "Give me an hour with the bastard, and I'll have him dictating his fucking memoirs."

"I'm telling you, that won't work," Miles said, the words clipped, the tone one of irritation. "We've tried going after him directly, but it was... costly."

Hoon matched the other man's intonation, then raised it. "You're the fucking Secret Service. Go in there with all guns blazing and drag the prick out by his ball hairs, if that's what it takes. Don't let your fucking dreams be dreams, Miles."

Miles almost looked amused at the thought of it. "I think you might be getting us mixed up with *The A-Team*. We gather data, we don't zipline into secure compounds or go battering through walls in tanks."

Hoon adjusted himself in his seat. The chair was quite far forward, and he fumbled around beneath it until he found the lever that let him slide it all the way back. "Well, it sounds to me like you should fucking start. Sounds like it'd be a lot more effective than whatever shite it is you're currently doing."

"Maybe," Miles conceded. He stole a sideways look at the man sitting beside him. "But maybe not."

Hoon went back to looking out the window for a while. They passed another *Costa*. Possibly the same one, but then again, it was difficult to tell.

"If I said yes, when would we start?" he asked.

"Ideally? Tonight."

"Tonight?" Hoon turned back to the man beside him. "Jesus. You don't beat around the fucking bush, do you?"

"Not if I can help it. Which brings me to that second question I mentioned earlier," Miles said. He took his eyes off the road long enough to look Hoon directly in the eye. "How do you fancy spending the rest of the night in jail?"

CHAPTER EIGHT

IT WAS ALMOST four by the time everything had been arranged. The station had been on standby, the officers in charge of the cells carefully vetted to make sure their loyalties didn't lie elsewhere. Even so, Hoon was led in through the back door, and brought to a small private room that was distinctly lacking in people, furniture, or anything else for that matter.

He stood flicking through a bundle of paperwork that Miles had produced from the boot of his car. It had been wrapped in polythene and tucked under the false floor on top of the spare wheel. Hoon had spent a full minute ripping the piss out of this low-tech approach to espionage, before accepting the bundle and starting to read.

"Dale Martelle," Hoon read. His eyes crept down the page to the mugshot of a stocky, balding man who looked like he should've long-since outgrown the list of recent offences on his rap sheet. "Looks like a right arsehole."

"Yeah. He's that, alright," Miles confirmed. "He's small potatoes, though. A thief and a thug, but nothing worse than that. Never been particularly violent, never done more than a couple of months in the nick."

"Just one of them annoying wee bastards that keeps coming back to get on your tits," Hoon remarked. "Aye, I've come across a few of them in my time."

He skimmed over a couple of other pages, taking in a few key details—no close family, a history of drugs, some low-grade gambling addiction—then he handed the wedge of paper back to the MI5 man.

"I mean, I can't be sure without meeting him, but I'm guessing he's got a brain like a fucking scrambled egg. I thought these Loop bastards were all criminal geniuses, or whatever?"

"Well, no. No, they're not that, exactly. The big boys, maybe. Yes. Definitely. But those at the bottom are your average no-marks. It's just that now they're being given direction, rather than being left to their own devices," Miles explained. "And as for Dale, I wouldn't even say he's at the stage of being bossed around. He's on the fringes, hoping someone welcomes him in. They won't, though. He's a liability."

Hoon shook his head. "So why the fuck did you pick him?"

"Because he hears things. He knows where things are going down. And the people you want to get in with, they know him. They don't like him—nobody likes Dale—but they know him enough that he should be able to open a few doors. Where you go from there will be down to you."

Hoon chewed his bottom lip. "And you're sure they're not going to know who I am?"

Miles shrugged. "It's possible they'll have heard the name. 'Hoon.' It's not exactly common. But that's where the undercover part comes in. We're working on your new identity. It'll all be ready for you getting turfed out tomorrow, but this is you."

He passed over a single sheet of A4 paper. Hoon peered down his nose at it like he was judging it and finding it sorely lacking.

"Stephen White?" He looked from the page to the MI5 man and back again. "That's not my name, is it?"

"It is, yeah."

"Well, you can forget that idea, for a start."

Miles frowned. "What? Why? What's wrong with it?"

"It's the most obvious fucking fake name I've ever heard, that's what's wrong with it," Hoon said. "Why not go the whole hog and just call me Sly Incognito? Or fucking..." He clicked his fingers a few times, trying to think of a worse fake name than the one he'd been given. "Actually, no. There's literally nothing more shite than this one. I'd rather be called the fucking Eel, in fact, and we both know how I feel about that."

"It's just a name. It's fine. It's not meant to stand out," Miles explained.

"Aye. Exactly. That's literally the first thing you think when you hear it. It's so obviously meant to blend in that it does just the opposite. If I met someone called Stephen White I'd think, 'Aye, he's fucking polis. That's no' a real name.'"

Miles shrugged and held his hands up, as if indicating his surrender. "Well, it's too late to do anything about it now, I'm afraid, so you'll just have to grin and bear it. You're Stephen White, you've recently moved down from Scotland—"

"Where in Scotland?" Hoon asked.

"Can't remember. It's on the sheet."

Hoon looked down and scanned the page again, then recoiled like he'd been struck. "Dundee? Not a fucking chance am I being from Dundee." He held a hand out and made a beckoning motion. "Pen."

"What?"

"Give me a pen. I'm changing it."

"What's wrong with Dundee?" Miles asked.

"Just the very fucking fact that you're asking that question tells me you've clearly never been there," Hoon said. "Come on. Pen. Chop chop."

The MI5 officer decided that this was not the hill he wanted to die on, produced a pen from his shirt pocket, then handed it over. Hoon drew two sharp lines through the word, 'Dundee,' and scribbled in, 'Kilmarnock,' instead.

"I mean, it's still no' great, but at least it's no' Dundee," he said, and he held onto the pen in case any further changes were required.

"I'm going to give you a few minutes to get acquainted with your new identity," Miles told him. "Then we'll have you taken in. The place is busy tonight, and we picked this station for a reason."

"I'm guessing shared cells?"

"Well done. Yes. Shared cells in the custody suite. So you'll be put in with Dale. He's being held downstairs. Like I say, it's a busy place, so there'll be someone else in there, too. You'll know Dale when you see him from the photo, though. His cellmate doesn't bear many similarities to him."

"What's he in for?" Hoon asked, eyes flitting left and right down the page.

"He got himself into a bit of drunken bother earlier in the evening. Bit of aggro with a bouncer, then he conveniently had a wrap of speed on him when he was turned over that he insists he knew nothing about. He's going to be released in the morning without charge, though he doesn't know that yet. We're letting him stew until then."

"And, what? I'm meant to just waltz in there and become bosom fucking buddies with the guy?"

"Something like that," Miles confirmed. "He's not the brightest, so he shouldn't be too hard to fool. All things considered, we think he's the best chance of you getting inside."

"Inside what, exactly? I still don't know what I'm actually meant to be doing."

Miles winced. "Yes. Sorry. This is all a bit sudden. Ideally, we'd have more time, but when the opportunity came up like this... Well, I wanted to seize it. Once you've made contact and started earning his trust tonight, we'll pull you out and brief you fully. For now, though, just try to make a good impression on the guy, and hopefully, he can get you in."

Hoon tutted. "You're going to make me fucking ask you again, aren't you? Into what?"

"Yes. Yes, sorry. Still being a bit vague. Not intentional, honest, I just—"

"Fucking spit it out!" Hoon barked.

"Right! Yes. OK. So, among its many other activities, the Loop runs an underground fighting ring here in London. Really brutal bare-knuckle, occasionally to the death type stuff. Apparently, a lot of people go in for watching that sort of thing, though I don't see the appeal myself. Those who do are big spenders, too. Lots of gambling, lots of money changing hands. Most of the fighters are here illegally, brought in from overseas. Former Soviet countries, mostly. Kazakhstan. Lithuania. Those sorts of places."

"Lithuania?" Hoon frowned. He held a hand down around knee height, at a right angle to his body. "Are they no' all tiny wee folk in Lithuania?"

"Um, no. No, they're sort of... average height, I think."

"Who the fuck am I thinking of, then?" Hoon wondered.

Miles regarded the hand that was still held just above Hoon's knee, puffed out his cheeks and shrugged. "Munchkins? I don't know. What we do know—though we can't prove it yet— is that they bring the fighters in using a lot of the same routes and mechanisms as they use for the women they've been trafficking in and out. Sadly, we just haven't been able to crack their logistics infrastructure."

"Jesus. *Logistics infrastructure.* It's not fucking DHL. These are people you're talking about."

Miles put his hand to his mouth, stifling a yawn. "Yes. Yes, I'm well aware of that," he said. "That's why we need you to get inside, dig around, and help us put a stop to it."

"What, by throwing myself into a fucking bare-knuckle boxing tournament?"

Miles' eyes widened in surprise. "What? No! God, no. You'll be watching, not taking part! Jesus. No. I mean, I know you can take care of yourself, but from what we hear... Some of these guys..." He shook his head firmly. "No. You're a spectator. You're there to watch the fights, place a few bets, and to keep your eyes and ears open for anything that'll lead us to the Eel."

"This all sounds like a big fucking stretch to me, Miles," Hoon replied. "It's a cock in search of an up, if ever I fucking saw one. No way this is going to end well. Not a hope."

"I admit, it's all a bit hurried. Still, we're confident it's a good plan," Miles insisted.

"A good plan? It doesn't even qualify as a fucking mediocre plan. It's no' even a plan at all. It's barely an idea. It's a vague notion, is what it is. It's a fucking *inkling*."

"It's also your best chance of finding Caroline Gascoine," Miles said. He hesitated, like he was trying to stop the rest of the sentence playing out. "Or at least to find out what happened to her."

Hoon muttered something below his breath, then sighed. He stole another look at the sheet of paper he'd been given, his lips moving silently as he committed the text to memory. Or as much of it as he could be arsed holding onto, anyway.

"And you're sure all my ID and stuff's going to be ready for the morning?" he asked. "I'm not going to be left looking like a knob, am I?"

Miles nodded. "The desk sergeant will give both you and Dale your belongings back at the same time. Everything you need will be in there. Wallet, driver's licence, phone, car keys."

"I'm getting a car?" Hoon asked, perking up at the thought.

"No. It's London. You don't need a car. But car keys help sell the story," Miles said. "We're setting you up with a hotel room booked under the fake ID. Details of that will be in the wallet."

"I'll need cash, too," Hoon said. He wrinkled his nose. "Couple of grand, at least."

"A couple of grand?!" Miles practically shrieked. "Why would you be carrying that around?"

"Because Stevie White's a fucking high-flier, son, that's why," Hoon told him. He tucked his thumbs into a pair of imaginary braces and puffed out his chest. "Big Whitey's always got a bundle of readies on hand, just you ask anyone. And, because if you want to impress a wee scrote like the one you've got down in that cell, you need to be willing to flash the cash."

Miles ran his hand down his face, groaned, then nodded his agreement. "Fine. Two grand in cash," he said. "It'll be there."

"And nothing too new," Hoon said. "Try and no' make it too fucking obvious, eh?"

"Obviously. You might not believe it, but we do actually know what we're doing," Miles said.

"Aye, you're right." Hoon scrunched up the sheet of paper with the details of his alias on it. "I don't believe it," he said, then he tossed the ball of paper over his shoulder, where it landed with a *paff* on the floor.

"Lilliput," he announced.

Miles blinked. "Sorry?"

"That's where the wee people are. Lilliput. That's where I was thinking of. No' Lithuania." He watched the light of understanding fail to come on in the other man's eyes, then shook his head. "*Gulliver's Travels*. Read a book, for fuck's sake."

He clapped his hands, rubbed them together, and grinned with barely contained excitement. "Now then," he said. "I reckon it's high time I was introduced to my new best pal."

CHAPTER NINE

AS HE'D BEEN BRIEFED, there were two men in the cell when Hoon was brought to it. He made a show of resisting the efforts of the 'arresting officer'—a gormless-looking young lad who was too young and stupid to have been corrupted yet, but experienced enough to keep his mouth shut and not to ask too many questions—then hurled a handful of obscenities after him once the cell door was slammed closed.

"I swear these pricks get younger every year," he announced in a big, booming voice that did nothing to endear him to either of the two men in the cell.

Even if he hadn't been shown the photograph of Dale Martelle, he'd have figured out which one he was. He was the exhausted-looking thirty-something with the receding hairline and shaking hands. He was very much *not* the semi-naked skin-headed white supremacist currently slouching on one of the cell's four thinly padded benches.

Identifying the other man as a white supremacist wasn't difficult. The guy's ample chest, arms, back, neck, and face had all served as a canvas for some of the least professional tattoos

Hoon had ever seen, most of which clearly stated where his cultural and racial loyalties lay.

Hoon knew he should ignore the bastard. He wasn't the reason he was there. The reason he was there was currently covering his eyes with a trembling hand, either pretending to be asleep or trying very hard to actually be. That was his priority. That was the entire point of the exercise.

And yet, for a man who prided himself on being almost entirely motivated by hatred, Hoon had never had time for racists. Sure, he understood the urge to detest a group based solely on one defining characteristic. It was just that, in his case, that defining characteristic was *being in his presence.*

Narrowing the focus to one colour, creed, gender, or sexual preference struck him as a massive waste of time. *All* people were arseholes until proven otherwise, and if you chose to ignore that fact and direct your hatred towards one particular subsection, then you were no longer speaking Hoon's language.

Besides, in all his years of navigating a world full of arseholes, the few who had turned out to not fit that description had come in a veritable rainbow of colours.

Despite his instant dislike for him, Hoon might not have bothered with the skinhead, had it not been for the fact that he saw something else in the guy. Something beyond the tattoos and the gelatinous torso.

An opportunity.

"Jesus Christ, pal. I've got some bad news. Do you know you've got a load of racist shite scribbled all over you?" he asked the skinhead, feigning shock. "What the fuck happened? Did a big boy do it and run away?"

The other man's eyes slowly closed, then opened again, like he needed to momentarily divert all his brainpower towards figuring out what Hoon had said.

"You what?" he grunted, which hardly seemed worth the

effort. The voice was low and slow, and East London through and through.

"Fuck me, have you no' noticed? I mean, I could see you were thick as mince the moment I clapped eyes on you, but how the fuck can you have missed all that?" Hoon pointed to the tattoos. "You've got horrible racist Nazi shite scribbled on your... well, your everywhere, if I'm honest. And I hate to break it to you, but it's pretty nasty stuff, too. I'd imagine you're going to be fucking furious when you see it."

"Don't," warned Dale from the other bench. He sounded hoarse. His eyes, when he peeled his hand away, were bloodshot and ringed with loops of dark shadow. Hoon had been on the business end of a hangover often enough to recognise the signs. "He doesn't like you talking to him. Trust me. I'd just... I'd keep my mouth shut."

Hoon turned to the booze-soaked smaller man, then jabbed a thumb back over his shoulder at the skinhead. "Who? Swastika Tits? I'm just trying to help the poor guy out. If I'd been graffitied like that, I'd be fucking raging."

Hoon heard the grunt of the racist heaving his heavy frame up off the bench. He smelled the sour tang of his sweat, and breath that reeked of cigarettes and old lager.

"Aw, shit. Aw, shit," Dale fretted, clutching his ribcage as he struggled to sit up. Pain took his breath away, and he hissed out a warning through gritted teeth. "Watch out!"

The warning wasn't necessary. Even if the skinhead's shadow wasn't clearly visible on the wall, he was a lumbering bastard whose breathless grunting telegraphed his every move.

"Relax, pal," Hoon told Dale. "This big baldy bastard behind me might look scary, but he's just a mini-dicked skinsack full of custard. And no' even nice custard. School dinner custard. *Racist* school dinner custard. If you can imagine such a fucking thing." He shrugged. "He's no' going to give us any bother. He doesn't have the balls."

With a surprising turn of speed for a man of his size, the skinhead's hand clamped down on Hoon's head, its gargantuan fingers splayed wide like the legs of some giant venomous spider.

"Shite. Spoke too soon," Hoon muttered, then he was sent stumbling forward, forcing Dale to slide quickly along the bench out of his path.

Hoon grimaced as he slammed into the wall, found his balance, then shot a reproachful look at the man sitting a few feet along the bench.

"Thanks for the fucking catch there, pal. Much appreciated. Saved me smashing straight into the wall like an arsehole." He clicked his fingers. "Wait, no. It didn't, did it?"

He saw Dale's eyes darting to the cell's other occupant, clocked the shadow, heard the wheeze.

He was reminded again that it was the theatre of it he enjoyed. It always had been. It never hurt to put on a show. He could've dodged that last grab with his eyes shut, but where would be the drama in that?

Spinning, his forearm caught the oncoming skinhead across the throat. It gave a satisfying *thunk*, and panic flashed across the tattooed face.

"Your ribs," Hoon said, turning back to Dale. "Was that this fucker?"

Dale placed a hand on his injured side and nodded once. Hoon turned sharply, brought up a knee, and drove it hard against the racist's ribcage. Swastika Tits staggered, a whisper of pain escaping his swelling throat as he tried to find purchase on the grey brick wall, failed, then slid down it, the rough masonry scraping at his exposed skin.

Hoon was on him the moment he hit the floor, his knees pinning the behemoth's arms to the ground, his thumbs pressing down on the bigger man's eyes.

"I want you to apologise to my friend here," Hoon instructed. "I want you to say sorry for hurting him."

Beneath him, Swastika Tits tried to struggle, but the pressure on his eyes increased and he immediately went rigid.

"I can't hear you," Hoon told him. "I'd hurry the fuck up, because—between you and me—I don't really know my own strength, and I'm liable to pop your eyeballs right to the back of your fucking skull in a minute." He leaned in closer, until the reek of the other man's breath became too much. "And, I have to admit, I'm sort of curious to see what that's going to feel like. Is that weird?"

The skinhead's attempt at an apology was a string of incomprehensible sobs and whispers. Hoon looked back over his shoulder to where Dale was now sitting bolt upright, his face slack with amazement and wonder.

"Did you catch what he said there?"

Dale shook his head. "No."

"No, me neither." Hoon pressed harder, making the skinhead howl in pain, fear, or some combination of the two. "Try again, you clatty bumblefuck. From the fucking heart this time."

"S-sorry! I'm sorry, please! Please, don't!"

"Say you'll stop being a big fucking racist," Hoon urged.

"Wh-what?"

Hoon ratcheted up the pressure again. "Say it."

"I'll... I'll stop being racist."

"No. A *big fucking racist*," Hoon insisted, ratcheting up the pressure.

"I'll stop being a big fucking racist!"

"Say Hitler's a fanny," Hoon urged.

"Hitler's a fanny!"

"Say he's only got one ball."

"He's... Ow, fuck, fuck! He's only got one! He's only got one ball!"

"Good, now sing the opening number from *Starlight Express*," Hoon instructed.

There was a pause, but only a brief one. A pair of thumbs on the eyeballs tended to imbue most conversations with quite a pressing sense of urgency.

"Wh-what?"

"The musical! The one with the fucking roller skates! Sing the first song!"

"I don't know it! I don't know what that is!" the other man sobbed.

Hoon held his thumbs in place for a little while longer, then released them and sat back. "Aye, well," he said. "Maybe there's hope for you yet."

He gave the skinhead a playful slap on the face, then got to his feet and pointed to the corner of the room. "Go stand over there and don't say a fucking word," he instructed.

With some difficulty, Swastika Tits heaved himself to his feet. Whimpering, and temporarily blinded, he limped over to the corner and leaned back, each shoulder touching a different wall.

"Well, face the other way, for fuck's sake!" Hoon told him, like a frustrated nanny dealing with an unruly child. "Jesus Christ, have a bit of common sense, man. You've got a face like a hangman's conscience. Why the fuck would we want you looking this way with a coupon like that?"

He made a pirouette motion with a finger, waited until the skinhead shuffled around so he was facing directly into the corner, then he nodded his approval and turned back to Dale.

"Fucking white supremacist. Can you believe that? Check out the nick of the bastard. How does that think it's superior to anything? I mean, just look at him. He's like a smashed arsehole with legs."

"Eh, yeah. Yeah, totally," Dale said. He still wasn't quite

sure what had just happened, but the look on his face suggested he'd quite enjoyed it. "Thanks for that, um...?"

"Stephen White. Most folks call me Whitey. But, you know, not in a racist way like that purse full of jelly in the corner there." He thrust out a hand for the other man to shake. "And believe me, it was an absolute fucking pleasure to be of service."

———

A handful of hours later, Hoon stood outside the police station, stretching and blinking in the morning sun. Having spent so many years in the grey, overcast Highlands, sunshine still came as something of a surprise to him, and it always took his eyes a few moments to adjust.

It wasn't that there was *never* sunshine up north. Nor was it the case that London was a particularly sunny city. But the differences were enough to be noticeable, and considering that Hoon had always been more of a night owl than an early morning man, it was little wonder that he was finding the glare uncomfortable.

The noise of the city had taken a bit of getting used to, too. It was barely the arse end of eight o'clock, but the streets were clogged by traffic, and the racket was already giving him a headache. The choking haze of diesel fumes wasn't doing him any favours, either.

Buses thundered along in their own lanes past stationary vans and cars. Black cabs took their chances where they could find them, blasting their horns and shooting dirty looks at anyone with the fucking audacity to either try to cut in front, or object to being cut in front of.

Bicycles whizzed through the chaos of it all, weaving through gaps and speeding along the narrow lanes between lines of crawling traffic. A sense of superiority trailed along in their wake, like this was their road and everyone else was only using it with their permission.

Rush hour in London. Was there anything more aggravating?

There was a scuffle behind him, followed by the bump of someone walking into his back. He turned and Dale Martelle flinched at the sight of him, before offering up a shaky smile of apology.

"Sorry, mate. Wasn't watching where I was going." He placed a hand above his eyes, almost as if in salute. It cast a shadow over most of his face. "Too bright out here. Always feel it after a night in the cells."

Hoon grimaced up at the surrounding buildings, the sunlight reflecting off their dirty glass. "Aye, you can say that again," he agreed. He opened the plastic bag containing his belongings—or Stephen White's belongings, anyway—and reached inside for his wallet. "What's your plan now?" he asked.

Dale's eyes had followed the hand into the bag, and locked onto the wallet even before Hoon's fingers had brushed against the leather. The topmost edge of a wedge of bank notes could just be seen protruding from the top. Dale followed them like a fish being drawn to a lure.

"Sorry, what?" he asked, absent-mindedly.

Hoon took the wallet from the bag and tucked it away in one of the side pockets of his combat trousers. Dale's eyebrows dipped briefly like he was trying to work out where all that lovely money had gone, then he raised his gaze to meet Hoon's.

"Sorry, what?" he asked again.

"I asked what your plan was," Hoon said.

The frown deepened further. "My... plan?"

"Fuck's sake, man. Wakey wakey. It's no' a difficult question. You're not on fucking *Mastermind.* Aye, your plan. What are you doing now?"

Dale shook his head. "I don't... I'm not sure. Probably heading home and getting cleaned up." He touched his injured ribcage with the flat of a hand and winced. "Might need to get my side looked at."

"I'm looking at it from here, and there's fuck all wrong with it," Hoon told him. He sniffed. "And I don't know about you, but I'm fucking starving. You know anywhere round here to get breakfast? I'm thinking a big fry-up. My shout."

Dale's gaze crept back down to the pocket containing the wallet, but only for a moment. "Uh, yeah, mate," he said, brightening considerably. His arm fell back to his side, his ribs forgotten. "As a matter of fact, I know just the place."

CHAPTER TEN

FROM THE OUTSIDE, there was nothing remarkable about the cafe, *E. Pellici*. It was on Bethnal Green Road, nine or ten bus stops away from the police station where they'd been held, and Hoon had pointed out at least half a dozen other breakfast places along the way.

Dale, though, had insisted that this place was worth the wait. Standing outside it, Hoon had been sceptical. One greasy spoon was much like any other, in his experience, and while some fry-ups were better than others, he was yet to meet a truly bad one.

He took a bearded guy in braces sipping coffee at one of the outside tables as a red flag, and put a hand on Dale's shoulder before he could lead the way inside.

"This isn't a fucking hipster place, is it? I'm no' going to be offered a soy latte and a bite of a vegan sausage, am I? Because I will fucking kick-off."

Dale grinned. Either his hangover was wearing off, or the thought of all the money in Hoon's pocket was perking him right up. Either way, he was a very different man to the one who'd cowered on the bench in the cell the night before.

"Nah, mate, nothing like that. It's proper good stuff," he promised. "None of that shit."

Hoon shot a dangerous look at the man with the beard, then removed his hand from Dale's shoulder and nodded his consent.

The inside of the cafe was certainly more promising. It was clean, but hadn't been updated in a long time. Hoon didn't like dining in those sleek anonymous modern places that felt more like a science lab than a place to eat food. He despised minimalism. A bit of clutter never hurt anyone, and he appreciated the sauce bottles and salt cellars standing tall in the middle of each table like tiny fantasy citadels.

They were directed to a table in the back corner, handed a couple of menus, and offered tea or coffee. Both men went for coffee, black, and plenty of it, and the waiter—or the owner, maybe—smiled knowingly as he scribbled in his pad.

"One of those nights, was it?"

"You have no fucking idea," Hoon replied, then he turned his attention to the menu.

"What do you think?" asked Dale. He was ignoring his own menu with the self-assured air of someone who had eaten here before and knew exactly what he was after.

Hoon glanced around the place, his gaze lingering momentarily on the carved wooden panels that lined the walls. "Aye, seems alright," he replied, then he went back to reading the menu.

"It's Grade Two Listed," Dale said.

Hoon sighed almost imperceptibly, then raised his eyes from the laminated sheet again. "What?"

"The building. It's got Grade Two Listed status. Because of the carvings, I think."

"Right, aye. Very good." Hoon turned his attention back to the menu, only to be distracted again.

"And because of the Krays."

"The Krays?"

"Yeah. The Kray twins. The gangsters?"

Hoon tutted. "I know who the fucking Krays are. I meant what's the connection with this place?"

Dale rocked his chair onto its back legs and smirked. He looked incredibly pleased with himself, as if just knowing this fact about the well-known London gangsters somehow imbued him with a share of their status. "They used to come here for breakfast every day," he revealed.

Out of habit, Hoon had taken the seat facing the door, so Dale was forced to turn and look back over his shoulder to reveal his next nugget of local history. This resulted in his chair spinning onto one leg, and he had to grab for the table to stop himself falling backwards onto an Asian man sitting at the next table over.

"Shit!" he gasped, hurriedly righting himself. He immediately pointed over his shoulder, like he could distract from what had just happened. "They reckon they had the first run-in with the Old Bill right out front there. They were, like, sixteen, seventeen, whatever. Some fucking copper comes along and tells them to move along."

Hoon raised an eyebrow, waiting for something more to follow. When all he got back was a gormless smile, he returned his attention to the menu.

"High octane stuff. I can see why that drove them into a life of crime, right enough," he remarked, then he flipped the menu over, checked the back, and sighed. "No square sausage."

"You what?" Dale asked.

"This fucking city. No bastard does a square sausage."

Dale stared blankly back at him. "What's a square sausage?"

Hoon scowled. "Have a fucking guess," he urged. "The clue's in the name."

Still confused, Dale positioned his hands so that the space

between them formed a three-dimensional shape. "You mean... like a cube?" he asked. "Like a cube of sausage?"

"What the fuck are you talking about? No, no' a... Why would it be a cube? Who'd want to eat a whole fucking cube of sausage meat?"

"Well, what is it then?"

Hoon stabbed a finger against the tabletop, then drew an outline. "It's a square. It's a fucking... It's a flat square. Like a beer mat."

Dale stared at the finger that was still drawing the same shape on the tabletop, over and over again. His brow furrowed, like his brain was working overtime to crack some difficult code.

"But... a beer mat of *sausage*?" he asked. "Why would you want that? How's that even a sausage? Doesn't the word 'sausage' describe the shape? Like, if something's sausage-shaped, it's shaped like a sausage." He formed the shape of a sausage by pressing the thumb and forefinger of each hand together. "Like that."

"You don't have to mime a fucking sausage for my benefit," Hoon told him. "I know what shape they are. But a *square sausage* is like a normal fucking sausage that's square. Alright? Only, a bit different. And better."

Dale stared down at the table for a while, silently trying to process the last few moments of conversation. Eventually, he asked the question that was bothering him most.

"What's wrong with normal sausages?"

Hoon puffed out his cheeks, set down the menu, and shook his head. "Nothing. Fuck all. I just... It's been a while since I've had one. I've been keeping my eyes open. Forget it. I'm parched here. Where's the fucking—"

Two black coffees were placed in front of them by the same guy who had taken the order. He flashed an encouraging smile as he fished his notepad and pencil from the pocket of his apron. "You ready to eat?"

"Uh, yeah," Dale said, jumping in first. "Don't suppose you do square sausage, do you?"

The waiter blinked. "Square sausage?" he asked. "You mean... what? Like a cube?"

"Doesn't matter," Hoon said, thrusting the menu back at him. "I'll have the full thing. Just give me the works."

"Make it two," Dale said.

"No problem! How do you want your egg?"

Dale got in first. "Poached, ta."

"Fried," said Hoon. "Because I'm no' a selfish bastard."

"How do you mean?" asked Dale.

"Nobody wants to make a fucking poached egg," Hoon informed him. "They're fiddly bastards."

Beside the table, the waiter chuckled. "It's fine. It's not a problem."

"Aye, of course you have to say that, pal. I get it," Hoon said. "But they'll be fucking cursing him in the kitchen. We all know it."

"I just... I don't like the crispy bits," Dale explained.

Hoon held up a hand. "You don't have to justify yourself to me. I'm no' the one you should be apologising to."

There was a long, awkward moment in which neither Dale nor the waiter quite knew what to do. Eventually, Dale turned to the server, offered an apologetic shrug, and mumbled a, "Sorry, mate. I'll have fried, if it's easier."

"It's fine. Honest," the waiter said, tucking his pencil behind his ear. He tore the top page off his pad, shot a friendly—if slightly wary—smile at both men in turn, then hurried off in the direction of the counter.

"What the fuck did you do that for?" Hoon demanded.

"Do what?" Dale asked.

"Try and change your order."

"Well, because you said—"

"The fuck does it matter what I said? You don't even know

me, you shouldn't be letting me dictate what you eat for your fucking breakfast. Man up, for Christ's sake," Hoon told him. "Nobody likes a pushover."

Dale cocked his head to the side a little, studying the man across the table. "What are you, like my guardian angel, or something?"

Hoon laughed. "Hardly."

"No, but..." Dale was regarding him with real curiosity now, like Hoon was a puzzle to be solved. "Kicking shit out of that guy last night, buying me breakfast, giving me all this life advice. What's your game here?"

Hoon took a slurp of his coffee, then shrugged. "No game, pal."

"Everyone's got a game," Dale insisted.

"Not me. I'm just a stranger in a strange land looking to get to know a few folk. You play the hand you're given, and I was given you." He set down the mug. "Speaking of which, you a gambling man, by the way?"

"Sometimes," Dale said, but he wasn't being steered away from the current conversation that easily. "And what, that's it? We share a cell for three hours, and suddenly we're best buds?"

Hoon ejected a harsh, scraping laugh. "Fuck me, no. I can barely stand the sight of you. But the only other choice of breakfast companion was that dough-fingered Nazi fantasist, and he and I aren't exactly on speaking terms."

Dale reached for his mug, brought it up to his mouth, then inhaled the aroma. "What is it you do, exactly?" he asked, studying Hoon through the steam.

"Bit of this, bit of that," Hoon said. There had been much more of a backstory on the notes the MI5 officer had given him —some bollocks about property trading and Bitcoin he'd elected to ignore.

"What, and that's it?" Dale asked. He didn't seem satisfied

by his answer, but neither Hoon nor Stephen White, Hoon had decided, felt the need to prove himself to this arsehole.

"Aye," he confirmed. "Pretty much."

"What were you in for?" Dale asked, still scrutinising him.

Hoon shrugged. "Nothing much. A misunderstanding, that's all. I had a wee disagreement with a doorman at a club."

"Oh? What club?"

Hoon didn't hesitate. "How the fuck should I know?" he asked. "They had lassies and drink. I didn't bother checking the name. The bouncer decided I wasn't welcome. I begged to differ."

"You chin him?" Dale asked.

"Let's just say, there was a butting of heads," Hoon replied. He grimaced. "Can't fucking stand those pricks. Power-hungry bastards, the lot of them."

This, just as Hoon had planned, went over well with Dale, who raised his mug as if in salute. "Amen to that," he said, then both men leaned back as two plates were placed down on the table in front of them.

Hoon nodded his approval of the meal before him. It was a sizeable plate, but there wasn't a millimetre of it untouched by the generous assortment of breakfast goodies heaped onto it. Even the toast—white bread, lightly crisped, with a good helping of butter melting into it—was exactly to his liking.

But for the sake of a well-charred slice of square sausage, it would've been perfect.

"Enjoy, gents," the waiter said.

"Oh, we will," Dale replied, already unwrapping his cutlery from its paper napkin. He cut open his egg—poached, not fried —and made an almost orgasmic sound when the bright yellow yolk oozed out onto his bacon. "Look at that," he urged, trying to draw Hoon's attention. "Isn't that the most beautiful thing you've ever seen?"

Hoon flicked his gaze to the other man's plate. "I mean, it's hardly the fucking Northern Lights. But aye, looks pretty good."

Dale pronged a mushroom with his fork, then pointed it in Hoon's direction. "So, you're new in town, then?"

"Aye," Hoon confirmed, folding up a slice of toast and dipping it into his beans.

"And you're looking for a good time?"

"Always."

Dale popped the mushroom in his mouth and grinned as he chewed it. "Then it's your lucky day, mate," he said. "Because, once again, I know just the place. Only thing is, it's not cheap, though."

Hoon patted the pocket at his thigh, and the wallet tucked away inside it. "Don't you worry, pal," he replied. "Money's not going to be a problem."

CHAPTER ELEVEN

A NOTE TUCKED into the wallet eventually led Hoon to a hotel just off Tottenham Court Road. It was a stone's throw from the British Museum, a place he had never before been to, and which he had no intentions whatsoever of visiting in the future.

It wasn't so much the museum itself that put him off, but the calibre of the arseholes he expected would be milling around inside it. A bit of culture was one thing, but not if it meant being surrounded by tourists and students.

The hotel was a mid-range number, not too fancy, but not too shabby, either. He'd been braced for his new MI5 overlords to have stuck him in an absolute shithole, and had been pleasantly surprised to find out that it wasn't.

A bellhop had moved to intercept when he'd entered through the front doors, only to change direction mid-approach when he'd clocked the fact that Hoon wasn't carrying any bags. Well, unless you counted the bright orange *Sainsbury's* plastic bag filled with cans of lager and *Monster Munch*, which he was clearly capable of carrying himself.

There was a short queue at the front desk, and Hoon stood

in line behind a young couple as they fiddled with credit cards and struggled to understand the accent of the striking Italian woman doing her best to check them in.

She reminded Hoon of Gabriella. Similar hair colour and skin tone. Same warm, patient smile. Unlike Gabriella, she'd had time to apply some makeup and have her hair styled. She was dressed sharply, too, in stark contrast to Gabriella's usual jeans and jumper combo.

Still, despite all that, this woman wasn't a patch on the other.

Hoon tapped a foot and scanned the hotel foyer while he waited, identifying where the lifts were, and mapping out the quickest route to the bar.

Over in the corner, there was a waiting area with a couple of red leather couches, a coffee table, and a TV tuned to *Sky News* with the sound muted. Some politician or other was talking enthusiastically about God knew what, all thumbs-ups and open hands, and Hoon was thankful that there wasn't audio.

Two men sat at either end of one of the couches. They didn't seem to know each other, which made their placement odd. It wasn't a particularly large piece of furniture, and it struck Hoon as much more likely that two strangers would have chosen to sit on different couches, rather than get that close. Especially in London, where briefly making eye contact on a crowded street was considered a gross invasion of privacy.

The men were both around the same age—mid-thirties—but the similarities stopped there. One wore a three-piece suit and had his nose buried in a copy of *The Daily Telegraph,* a big broadsheet newspaper that was obscuring almost all of his face. All it needed was a couple of eyeholes, and the guy would look exactly like a spy in an old cartoon.

Hoon dismissed him as a threat for that very reason.

Nobody trying to go incognito would look so conspicuous, surely?

Then again, he himself was going under the name 'Stephen White,' so clearly MI5 didn't know the first fucking thing about fading into the background.

The other man wore jeans, a brown leather jacket, and a shirt that was buttoned *just* high enough to stop him looking like a sexual predator. He had one leg crossed, and was idly fiddling with the strap of a pointy leather boot while scrolling through his phone. His fingernails were all painted black—either that, or he'd recently trapped all ten of them in a door, which would've been quite the stroke of misfortune—and his hair had that shaggy, just-out-of-bed look that probably took him an hour to get right every morning.

Hoon wasn't subtle about watching them. He glowered at them both, but only the man with the newspaper caught his eye when he was going through the laborious process of turning one of its oversized pages, and there was nothing in the look that made Hoon suspicious.

"Just a couple of pricks having a sit-down," he muttered, then he turned to discover that he had shuffled his way to the front of the line, and was now face to face with the receptionist.

"I'm sorry?" she asked, all smiles and raised eyebrows. The air around her was dotted with intriguingly sweet scents, and up close, her skin was as flawless as porcelain. He realised that she wasn't his cup of tea at all.

Give him some wrinkles and creases. Give him a few pounds of extra weight. Give him scars that burned bright for all the world to see. Hers was a face with no story to tell, and how could you be drawn to something like that?

"Sorry, sweetheart, just thinking out loud," he told her. "I think you've got a room booked for me."

Her smile widened as if she was genuinely thrilled at the thought of him staying there. It was a well-rehearsed move, done for no other reason than to make the person on the other side of the desk feel good about themselves.

Clearly, she had no concept of who she was dealing with.

"Oh, that's wonderful," she said, and she almost managed to sound like she meant it. "It is a little early for check-in, but I'll see if your room is available. Your name is?"

He almost tripped up and gave his real name—it had been a long and sleepless few days, and the belly full of food was working hard to dull his reactions—but he pulled the fake one out of thin air just before his lips could betray him, and then shut his mouth while he waited for her to check the system.

The receptionist hummed quietly as she tapped away at her computer, then gave a nod and turned her attention to a box of keycards beside her.

"OK, here we are. Yes, good! We expected you yesterday, so your room is ready."

"You expected me yesterday?" Hoon asked.

"Yes. That is correct."

Hoon blinked several times, considering this. "So... when was it booked, like?"

"I'm afraid I don't see that information on my system," the receptionist told him. "But I can see that you're pre-paid, everything's taken care of, and you're going to be with us for four nights. Four more nights, I mean, from tonight. Does that sound correct?" she asked, as she walked her fingers across the top of the cards from the front to the back.

"Yeah. Aye. If you say so, aye," Hoon said, still thinking.

Her smile took on a slightly more puzzled air for a moment, but then she decided that it wasn't worth the effort of a follow-up question, and the confusion evaporated before his eyes.

Hoon watched her as she rifled through the contents of the box like she was flipping through the pages of a book. She selected a card which, as far as he could tell, was no different to any of the others. She nodded, though, to indicate that the rectangle of plastic met her approval, swiped it across a pad beside the computer, and then presented it to him in a small cardboard envelope with his room number written on the front.

"You are up on the eighth floor," she told him. She leaned forward and started to point around the corner. "The elevators are—"

"Aye, I clocked them on the way in," Hoon said. He waved his card at her. "Is breakfast included?"

The receptionist checked her screen. "It looks like the company has paid for continental breakfast, yes."

A line appeared on Hoon's forehead. It was just one, but it was a line that anyone who knew him would know to be wary of.

"Continental breakfast?" he said, spitting the words out like he hated the taste. "As in... what, exactly?"

"It's a buffet through in our restaurant," the receptionist replied, still beaming broadly, blissfully unaware of the monster stirring just a few feet away. "Six-thirty until ten. You can have anything from the continental selection on offer."

"So... wait. What do you mean? Cereal?"

"Yes! Cereal, pastries, pancakes, fruit."

Hoon almost choked on the word—"Fruit?!"—and the line on his forehead was joined by a second.

That puzzled look infiltrated the receptionist's smile again. "Um, yes. Like, you know, oranges, bananas..."

"No, I know what fruit is," Hoon said, cutting her off. "But who the fuck's eating it for breakfast?"

"Well... a lot of our guests do. The continental option is very popular," the receptionist trilled. "A lot of our guests favour fruit, granola, and yoghurts over a cooked breakfast option."

"Aye, well, in that case, I've got some bad news for you, sweetheart," Hoon said. "A lot of your guests are arseholes." He slid the key back across the counter to her. "Now, let's be grown-ups about this, will we? And let's get me switched over onto the proper food."

————

Hoon checked out the lifts, saw nothing suspicious, but opted to take the stairs. They were always easier to find from the bottom, and if he needed to get to them in a hurry at any point, he wanted to know where they came out.

By the fourth floor, he was wishing he hadn't bothered his arse. He stopped there to get his breath back for a moment, briefly considered taking the lift the rest of the way, then decided to press on.

By the sixth floor, he was swearing below his breath. This actually helped quite a bit, and a crescendo of *fuckity-fucks* meant he was just getting his second wind when he arrived at floor number eight.

The owners of the hotel had clearly decided that no bugger was likely to take the steps when three perfectly good elevators were available, and the staircase was a spartan thing, with no carpets, and an industrial-style metal handrail running along both sides.

This helped lend a certain sense of opulence to the corridor he emerged onto, which would otherwise have looked pretty much like any other hotel he'd ever set foot in.

Well, maybe not all of them. This one lacked the worrying stains on the walls and carpets that he'd seen in a few. What it lacked in junkies lying slouched on the floor, it made up for in having doors for all the rooms.

Now that he thought about it, in fact, this hotel was definitely one of the better ones he'd stayed in over the years. And, now that he'd got all that breakfast unpleasantness out of the way, a part of him was almost looking forward to his stay.

His room took a bit of finding, but there were regular signposts to guide him through the maze of corridors and intersections. He heard a few TVs playing in the rooms he passed, the rushing of a shower, the repeated creaking of a bed.

He knocked on that last one, voiced an encouraging, "G'wan yersel'!" then continued on until he found the door that matched the handwritten number on his card.

It was the last room on this floor, tucked well away from most of the other rooms, through a set of swing doors and beyond a couple of cleaning cupboards. The placement made it feel like an afterthought, like whoever had designed the layout had spotted a bit of leftover space at the last minute, and shoved a bed in it.

It suited Hoon fine. Nobody except the hotel staff would have any reason to come this far, so anyone milling around outside could be considered a Bastard of Suspicious Intent, and treated accordingly.

The light on the door handle blinked red when Hoon tapped the keycard against it. He tried turning it, anyway, then muttered darkly when the door failed to open. He tapped the card to the sensor plate again. Another flash of red. Another failed attempt.

"Jesus fuck," Hoon ejected. He checked the number on the card—867—and matched it to the one on the door. "It's the right fucking one," he insisted, though it wasn't clear who or what he was addressing the statement to.

He tried again, this time tapping the card against the plate several times in quick succession. Each one earned him a single red blink, and each blink brought him closer to full breakdown.

Hoon was one more flash of red away from kicking the door in when one of the cleaning cupboards opened just along the corridor, and an older woman with hair like a *Mr Whippy* ice cream backed out pulling a trolley.

She jumped in fright when she saw him, said something in one of the Eastern European languages, then adjusted her features into the sort of smile that only existed in training manuals.

"So sorry," she said, practically bowing. "So sorry."

"Nothing to apologise for," Hoon told her. "I'm glad you're here. You know what the fuck's up with this?"

The woman, who he estimated was in her early sixties, fought valiantly to keep her smile in place. Her face was having none of it, though, and it all relaxed into a confused sort of scowl that, to his mind, suited her far better.

"Problem?" she asked.

"Aye, you can fucking say that again."

The cleaner searched around for a response, and seemed utterly relieved when she recalled what was clearly a key phrase she'd been given to recite.

"Uh, uh... *front desk*! Problem? Front desk."

"I'm no' traipsing all the way back down there," Hoon countered. He tapped the keycard against the door handle, then pointed to the red light that flashed up. "See that? Fucking thing. It won't open." He added a second, "Won't open," in a louder voice, in the hope that this might somehow help it punch through the language barrier.

She abandoned her trolley and came shuffling over to him, hand held out for the keycard. He passed it over, folded his arms, and had just assured her that it wouldn't work when the light on the handle flashed green, and she nudged the door open.

"How the f...?" he muttered, accepting the key back.

"Uh, slow. Slow. No go fast," the cleaner explained.

"I did it slow!" Hoon objected. "I fucking... I did it slow, fast, I did it..." He shook his head and jammed his foot against the bottom of the door, taking its weight. "Fine. Doesn't matter. Cheers. Thank you."

He shoved a hand into his pocket, pulled out his wallet, and fished out a fiver he'd been given in his change from the cafe.

"Here. Thanks," he said. "Away and get yourself a Flake for your hair."

The cleaner eyed the offered money with something like suspicion, then took it from him and nodded her thanks. He waited for her to return to her cart before nudging the door open with his hip and stepping inside.

He knew immediately that something wasn't right. The door on his left as he entered—the bathroom—was closed. One of the switches on the wall beside the door was flicked in a different direction to the others, and a faint *whirring* told him that the extractor fan was turned on.

Ducking, he checked the lock and saw through the narrow gap between the door and the frame that the bathroom was most definitely currently engaged.

Fuck that for a game of soldiers.

He threw himself sideways, not giving whoever was in there a chance to react. Wood splintered, and the door gave way, flying inwards under his weight.

The man standing in front of the toilet having a slash shrieked in fright, and sent a spray of piss across the wall and rattling against the glass screen of the shower.

"Jesus fucking Christ!" he cried, desperately diverting the stream back towards the toilet pan while shooting daggers back over his shoulder. "What the hell are you doing, you lunatic?!"

"Miles?" Hoon said, regarding the other man with equal parts surprise and contempt. "Never mind me. What the fuck are you doing?"

"What does it look like I'm doing?" Miles answered, his voice shrill and indignant. "I'm having a pee."

"Jesus Christ. Talk about taking fucking liberties," Hoon muttered. He started to back out of the room, then returned just long enough to indicate the urine dribbling down the walls. "And you can fucking mop that up before you come out, too."

CHAPTER TWELVE

HOON HAD MADE a sizeable dent in the minibar by the time Miles emerged. The MI5 man came out with his hands cupped in front of him, and a somewhat sheepish expression on his face. If he hoped these two things would prevent Hoon from stating the obvious, then he hadn't done his homework as well as he'd claimed.

"You've got pish down the front of your breeks," Hoon told him.

"Yes. Thanks to you." Miles sighed. Despite the slowly expanding dark stain on the front of his trousers, he looked better than he had during the night, with a freshly-pressed shirt and carefully arranged tie. He still wore the same black and white trainers, though, which somewhat ruined the overall effect.

"You'd better not have been using my fucking shower while you were here," Hoon warned him.

"No, I used the shower in my room," Miles told him. "I just... I got caught short. I was expecting you back earlier, and couldn't hold on any longer."

Hoon sat on the bed and peeled the foil top off a miniature

tube of *Pringles*. He'd removed his shoes, taken both bottles of beer from the mini-bar, and was already halfway through the second.

"Help yourself to anything from the Fridge of Delights there," he said, pointing with the neck of the bottle. "My shout."

"That's very generous of you," Miles said. He took out a can of *Coke*. "Considering I'm footing the bill."

Hoon paused with a *Pringle* halfway to his mouth. "You?"

"Well, I mean, not me personally, obviously," Miles said. "The... company."

Hoon nodded, crunched on the crisp, then pointed to the mini-bar. "In that case, chuck us out them *Maltesers*, will you? No point letting them delicious wee bastards go to waste."

Miles looked for a moment like he might offer a counterpoint to this argument, then wisely chose not to bother. He removed the bright red bag of sweets from the fridge, tossed it onto the bed beside Hoon, then took a seat in the swivel chair that sat by the room's small writing desk.

"So?" he asked, sitting stiff and upright on the chair. "How did it go?"

"How did what go?" Hoon asked.

Miles tutted. "You know what I mean."

Hoon tore open the *Maltesers* bag and tossed one into his mouth. "You seem a bit fucking tetchy, Miles," he remarked. "You were all smiles and happy-clappy last night. Who's taken a shite on your cornflakes?"

Miles pinched the flesh above his nose and massaged it. "Nobody. It's just..." His face lit up in a smile. It looked so natural that Hoon would've completely bought it, had he not seen the man's expression a moment before. "There. That better?"

Hoon shrugged. "Whatever. Your emotional welfare is no fucking concern of mine, I was just being polite. Lesson fucking learned on that front. And it went fine."

Miles sat waiting for more. The smile, which he had so forcibly etched across his face, didn't hang around for long. "'It went *fine*.' That's it?" he asked. "That's all you're giving me?"

"What more do you need?" Hoon asked.

Frustration propelled Miles back onto his feet. "Everything! You've told me nothing!" he cried. The volume of his voice caught him by surprise, and he quickly lowered it, though the tone didn't change. "This is a major bloody investigation. I've spent a lot of time, effort, and resources getting to this stage. I've risked everything going after these bastards, and now I've put my neck on the line getting you involved because I think there's a chance—a *chance*—that I can help you find your friend's daughter! So please, don't give me, 'Fine.' You owe me a damn sight more than, 'Fine!'"

Hoon, who had sat alternating between *Maltesers* and *Pringles* during Miles' outburst, tried very hard not to look amused.

"Marvellous fucking speech there, Miles," he said. He thumped himself in the centre of the chest. "Got me right there, so it did."

He replaced the lid on the *Pringles* tube, folded over the bag of *Maltesers*, then set them both on the bedside table. That done, he stood, brushed crumbs off his front, and sat down again.

"First of all, I'm assuming the other guy was a fucking plant of some sort?" Hoon said.

Miles' eyes narrowed as he lowered himself back onto the swivel chair. "Other guy? What other guy?"

"The white supremacist in the cell," Hoon said. "Big beefy fella, face like a baby in mourning. All Nazi tattoos and racist shite scribbled over him. Did you no' put him there on purpose?"

"Aah, yes. Him," Miles said, and a smile tugged at one corner of his mouth. A real one, this time. "No, not on purpose, but it did amuse me when I found out he was in there. I thought you might enjoy him."

"You're no' wrong," Hoon said. "We had a fucking lovely time. I thought you must've arranged for him to give Dale a kicking as a way for me to get on our man's good side."

Miles shook his head. "No. Happy coincidence."

"Right, well, coincidence or not, it worked a fucking charm," Hoon told him. "Once we got kicked out, I took Dale for breakfast."

"Pellici's?"

Hoon hesitated before replying. "You were following us?"

"No. He's a regular there," Miles said. "He tell you the Krays used to eat there?"

"Aye, he was practically beating himself off at the thought of it. Nice place, though. Good breakfast. No square sausage, mind."

"*Square* sausage? What, you mean like a—"

Hoon waved a hand. "Don't even fucking go there," he warned. "Anyway, I cosied up to the runty wee fudd, and long story short, we've got a date the night."

Miles sat forward in the chair. "Tonight? Where?"

Hoon shrugged. "Don't know."

"What? What do you mean you don't know? Why don't you know?"

"Because he was being very fucking tight-lipped about the whole thing, that's why," Hoon retorted. "And I thought if I pushed him on it, I might put the wind up him. So, I'm meeting him at some pub, and he's promised me—and I fucking quote— 'a night I'll never forget.'" He reached for the *Pringles* again. "Which I'm hoping doesn't mean he's going to try and shag me. Because that's going to get very fucking awkward very quickly."

"Where? What pub?" Miles pressed.

"Christ," Hoon said, gazing blankly past the MI5 man. "What was it called?"

"You don't remember?!"

Hoon snorted. "Don't shite your kecks, Miles. Of course, I fucking remember. I'm winding you up. It's the Red Lion."

Miles' chair gave a faint *squeak* as he moved his weight forward a fraction. "The Red Lion?"

"Aye."

"Which one?"

Hoon didn't answer. Not right away. Not for a few seconds. "What do you mean?"

"There's about twenty Red Lion pubs in Central London alone," Miles told him.

"What, is it a chain?" Hoon asked.

"No, they just have the same name."

Hoon tutted. "Well, that seems like a fucking oversight, if you ask me. Did no one bother to check the Yellow Pages before getting a sign made?"

"They date back centuries," Miles said, visibly agitated. "It doesn't matter. What street was it on?"

Hoon stared back at him for a while. "Street?" he said, with the intonation of someone who had never come across the word before. "I don't know."

Miles was on his feet again, practically tearing at his plastic-looking hair. "What? You don't...? Jesus Christ. He must've said!"

"Well, aye, I'm sure he did, but I wasn't really listening by that point."

"Why weren't you listening?!"

Hoon raised his voice so he matched the other man's volume. "Because, as far as I fucking knew, I had all the information I needed! Red Lion pub. Eight o'clock. Boom. Job done," he said. "How was I to know there were dozens of the bastarding things? What sort of fucking system is that?"

Miles collapsed back onto the chair and buried his face in his hands. "Oh, Christ!" he hissed. "They said this was a mistake. They told me. But I insisted. 'He'll be fine,' I told them. 'We can trust him.' And now look. Jesus!"

Hoon regarded the other man with something not unlike disgust. "Pull yourself together, you facecloth. Get me a list up on your phone, and it'll jog my memory. I'll figure it out."

He swigged from his bottle of beer, downed what was left of it, then burped loudly.

"But first, make yourself useful, will you?" he said, and he pointed to a dark blue rectangle he could see through the glass front of the fridge. "And pass me out that fucking *Yorkie*."

———

It didn't take Hoon long to identify which of the city's many Red Lions was the correct one. He prodded the screen of Miles' phone, placing a marker on the map. "That's the boy. It's on somewhere called Crown Passage. I remember making a joke about it being up the Queen's arse, which he didn't seem particularly impressed by." He gave a shake of his head and shot Miles a withering look. "You and your fucking royals. Can't take a joke. Toadying bastards, the lot of you."

"I don't actually believe in the monarchy," Miles said, taking back his phone.

"Fucking hell, keep your voice down," Hoon warned, eyes darting around the room. "Is that no' considered treason in your line of work? They've whipped heads off for less."

Miles gave half a laugh, but said nothing as he was too preoccupied tapping out a message on his phone, his thumbs pecking away at the on-screen keyboard.

Hoon got up, stretched, and crossed to the window. The room was clean enough—if you ignored the broken bathroom door and the lingering smell of piss, at least—but some guests would no doubt describe it as 'in need of modernisation.'

Not as far as Hoon was concerned, though. The dark wood

furniture and wall panels, coupled with the heavy red drapes, lent the place a certain gloomy air, which suited him down to the ground.

Out beyond the drapes, and the ever-so-slightly yellowed mesh of net curtains behind them, the window slid aside to give access to a tiny balcony that looked out over the city. Or part of it, at least.

Stepping out, Hoon was immediately assaulted by the wind. It wasn't the crisp, cold winds he was used to in the Highlands, but a muggy, dirty sort of breeze that trailed diesel fumes in its wake and made his face scrunch up in distaste.

The view was hardly worth it, either. Yes, you got a decent eyeful of the BT Tower, but angle your head just a fraction downward and you also got a bird's eye view of the bins, the contents of which were currently being investigated by a couple of homeless men.

"Jesus," Hoon muttered. "Poor bastards."

Miles, who had finished typing, shoved his phone in his pocket and looked up. "What?"

Hoon watched as the two homeless men were sent packing by a member of the hotel's staff. "Nothing. Doesn't matter," he said, stepping back inside. "Just London."

"Right, fair enough," Miles said, brushing the remark aside. "So, here's the situation."

"Hold on," Hoon said. "Before you start, how come I was booked in here from yesterday?"

"What?"

"The front desk. They said I was booked in from yesterday. We hadn't even fucking met yesterday."

"Oh. Right. Yes, I can see how that might seem a bit..." Miles began, then he shrugged. "I'm a forward thinker. That's what I do. If you agreed, then you'd need a room from this morning. If anyone was to look into you, it's a backstory for where you were staying the night you were arrested."

Hoon's eyes narrowed. He stared at the other man for a long time, then sniffed. "Aye, fair enough, makes sense," he admitted.

"Good. Right," Miles said. "Well, we've got a few hours for you to get rested. We've got clothes in the wardrobe for you, so you can take your pick."

"Aye?" Hoon said, crossing to the wardrobe. He slid aside the doors to reveal at least a dozen different items on hangers—shirts, suits, and even a couple of t-shirts. "Who the fuck puts t-shirts on hangers?" he wondered.

"What? I do. Why?"

Hoon raised his eyebrows, shut the door, and nodded. "Aye, should've guessed."

"What else are you meant to do with them?" Miles asked.

"Forget it. You were telling me the plan," Hoon said.

"Right. Yes. You get rested, then I'll get you wired up, and you can get dressed."

"Wired up? I'm no' getting wired up," Hoon objected.

"Uh... what? Yes. I mean, you have to. We need to know what's going on."

Hoon sat on the bed and looked up at the MI5 officer. Despite Miles now having the higher ground, they both knew damn well who was in charge of the situation.

"I'll tell you what went on afterwards," Hoon countered. He tapped the side of his head. "Memory like an elephant, me. Aye, a proper sharp one, too. No' one of them fucking div elephants that you sometimes see."

Despite his best efforts, Miles allowed himself to get side-tracked by that. "What's a div elephant?"

"Can we maybe try and no' get hung up on the fucking elephants, Miles?" Hoon said, scowling. "The elephants are irrelevant, and no' really the point I was trying to fucking make here. The point I was trying to make is that you can take your wire, roll it up into a wee wiry ball, and then insert it up your arsehole. If these bastards are as switched on as you say they are, they'll clock a wire a fucking mile off. And then where are we?"

"I—" Miles began, but Hoon didn't give him time to finish.

"Well, you'll be right as rain, but I'll tell you where I am in that fucking scenario, will I? I'm dead in a fucking ditch with my balls in my mouth, that's where."

Miles blinked. He had an air about him of someone trying very hard to keep up, but not succeeding particularly well. "Why are your balls in your mouth?"

"Well, don't ask me. I'm no' fucking responsible, am I? I'm no' the decision-maker in that scenario," Hoon spat back. "The point is, I'm no' wearing a wire. Alright?"

Miles held up both hands in surrender. "Fine. Fine, OK. I take your point," he conceded. "But the rest of the plan stands. You rest up, we get you dressed, and we get you to the meeting point for eight."

"Fuck off, *eight!*" Hoon snorted.

"I thought... You said you were meeting him then."

"Aye, but I'm no' going to rock up at eight on the dot, am I? It's no' a fucking first date. I can't exactly arrive bang-on time, or even that fuddbrained wee cockweasel'll start suspecting something."

Miles groaned, buried his face in his hands, then flopped down onto the swivel chair. "OK. OK, fine. Fine. You'll rest up, we'll get you dressed, and then we get you to the meeting point *fashionably late*. Happy? That work for you?"

"No' quite," Hoon said. He picked up his *Maltesers*, unfurled the bag, and took out a small handful of the chocolate-coated balls. "Before all that, I want to hear everything there is to know about this Godfrey West guy."

"I'm afraid that information's classified," Miles replied.

Hoon shook his head. "Aye, well, you're going to fucking declassify it, pronto." He tossed the *Maltesers* in his mouth and chewed noisily. "So cut your shite, and start talking."

CHAPTER THIRTEEN

"SORRY, Uncle Godfrey. Sorry. We're really sorry."

The man on the other side of the curved glass desk said nothing. He hadn't spoken a word since the two young men had been escorted into his penthouse office overlooking the Thames.

The office was starkly minimalist, and yet managed to convey a real sense of opulence, as if each item removed from the room had only added to the overall value. If less was more, then this place, with its single desk and three chairs—two of which had been wheeled in from an adjoining room—in a space that could've accommodated a small cinema, was positively bursting at the seams.

"We're really sorry, Mr West. We didn't... We thought we were doing good."

Godfrey West, who had until that moment been fixated exclusively on the young man he had the displeasure of calling his nephew, now turned his attention to the other man sitting beside him. This involved just a small head movement, and a tiny twitch of the eyes, but it felt like some seismic shift had taken place.

"I'm sorry?" asked the Eel. His accent was South African. Rich, white South African, embroidered at every seam with arrogance and self-righteousness.

Godfrey tapped his ear and smiled, showing a set of pearly teeth. The canines were slightly elongated—just enough to draw the eye and briefly make you wonder if he was wearing a set of vampire fangs.

"Could you repeat that?"

His non-blood relative shot a sideways look at his accomplice, cleared his throat, and tried again.

"We were... We thought we were doing good. We thought it would help, you know, like, the cause?"

Behind the glass desk, a neatly plucked eyebrow rose, forming a single faint crease on a tanned and Botoxed forehead.

"The cause? I see. And what cause would that be?" His gaze shifted back to his nephew, and the carefully controlled temperature in the room seemed to drop by several degrees. "What have you been saying, Charles? You haven't been speaking out of turn, have you?"

Charles West, bastard son of Godfrey's cretinous sister, tried to become one with his chair. Or maybe to phase through it and out the back, so he could make a run for it. Either way, it didn't work. No surprise there—anything this useless fucker put his hand to inevitably ended in disaster.

"No, not... Not like that, Uncle Godfrey," Charles babbled. "Nothing like that, no details, nothing. And Shane's alright, Uncle Godfrey. He's alright."

"Is it your ninth birthday party, Charles?" the older man asked. "Is it Christmas fucking morning where you are?"

Charles blinked. "Eh... what?"

"Is it?" Godfrey bellowed, and his voice echoed like the crack of a gunshot in the sparsely furnished room.

"N-no. No, it's not."

"No. Right. Well, since neither of those things apply, I'm not your uncle. Not in this room." He pointed at the other man without looking at him. "And not in front of loudmouth little shits like that."

Charles's eyes widened in terror when Shane cleared his throat again and began to speak. "Mr West, I think maybe we've got off on the wrong foot here, I didn't mean to offend you, I just..."

The coldness of the look on Godfrey West's face froze the rest of the sentence in Shane's throat. It became a mumble, then a croak, then faded away into nothing at all.

Godfrey unfastened the clasp of his *Omega* watch, checked the time, then set it down on the glass desktop with a *clink*.

"Here's what we're going to do," Godfrey announced. He spun in his low-backed leather chair and sprang to his feet with a faint rustling sound.

Both of the younger men's eyes were drawn to the crotch of Godfrey's tailored pinstripe trousers. The whole area, front and back, bulged, like he was wearing several dozen garments of underwear all at the same time.

Neither man mentioned anything. Neither one questioned. Neither one dared.

"We're going to switch places. I'm going to talk you through what you told me happened—I'm going to be you two, in this scenario," Godfrey explained, walking around the desk to stand behind the two men. "And you're going to be me. You're going to decide what I should do about it."

He placed a hand on both their shoulders, preventing them from turning their chairs to face him, and forcing them to crane their necks.

"Does that sound OK?"

Charles and Shane both nodded.

"Wonderful!" Godfrey said, and his voice was a whisper of

excitement. "So—and please, do jump in if I've got anything wrong—but from what you told me, you sought out two women last night, got them drunk in a public bar, then attempted to—and I think I'm quoting you correctly—'sling them in a van.' A van, which let's be clear, was registered to a company of which one of my other companies is the majority stakeholder."

He squeezed their shoulders, like he was giving them each half a massage. Neither man appeared to be taking any pleasure from their half.

"Does that sound right so far?" he prompted.

It was Shane who piped up, Charles knowing better.

"We were just... They were fit. Well fit. Both of them. We thought they could make some money for—"

"Does that sound right so far?" Godfrey asked again, pressing down more firmly on Shane's shoulder so his chair gave a squeak beneath him.

"Yes, Uncle Godfrey," Charles said, then he flinched like he'd been struck. "I mean, yes. Sir. Mr West, sir."

"Good. Good, I'm glad we're on the same page. I'd hate to be off track," Godfrey said. He released his grip on the two men, but didn't move from behind them. "So, while in the process of *slinging* those women into my van, you discovered that someone else was already in there. Waiting. For you two."

"We don't know who he was," Shane said, then he went rigid in his chair when a hand was clamped on top of his head.

"Charles, can you convey to your friend here that if he doesn't start behaving himself I will cut out his fucking tongue?" Godfrey asked. The question was matter-of-fact. Polite, even. "Can you do that for me? Can you pass that message on? Because there seems to be a breakdown in communications going on between him and I. He seems to have forgotten who he is in the presence of."

Charles met his partner's eye. No words were spoken, but the look that passed between them said all that needed saying.

"He'll shut up," Charles said. "He won't interrupt again."

"Boop!" Godfrey said, rapping his knuckles off the top of Shane's head. "Wonderful! I'm glad we got that little misunderstanding taken care of."

He ran a hand through his hair. It started quite high up on his forehead, and was a shade of black that didn't exist in nature. For all his money and power, a convincing dye job had always somehow evaded him.

"Where were we?" he wondered aloud, then he clicked his fingers. "The man in the van. This... avenging angel with a set of handcuffs and a toolkit. What can you tell me about him?"

"He was crazy," Charles said, jumping in quickly in case Shane was stupid enough to utter a single word. "And big. Really big. Strong. And fast, too. He just caught us off guard. We fought him, but he had, you know, like the element of surprise."

"God. That must've been terrifying for you both," Godfrey said. He bit his bottom lip, inhaled deeply through his nose, then held it there for a moment like he was fighting back tears. His hands returned to their shoulders. "I can't imagine how scared you must've been. Tied up like that. Naked. Exposed. Pressed together in the dark."

Out of the corners of their eyes, the younger men watched Godfrey's hips rotating, and heard the crinkling of the unknown material beneath his trousers. His hands squeezed their shoulders harder, his eyes still shut tight. His lips parted enough to let out just the faintest of moans, then he withdrew a pace and clasped his hands behind his back.

"Yeah, it was... It was pretty scary," Charles confirmed. He looked over to Shane, and saw his own terror mirrored on the other man's face.

"So, it must've been quite a relief when the police turned up," Godfrey said. There was a lightness to his tone that didn't belong there. Didn't feel right. "The police! The Met! Of all people. The Metropolitan Police, finding my nephew like that. In one of my vans. I can only imagine the questions they must've had."

"No, no, not really, Unc—Mr West. Not really," Charles insisted. "They just, they thought he was a lunatic. It was him they were after, not us. They just took statements and let us go, that's all. They gave us a number to call them. They said we might need counselling. Because of the trauma, and that. They were alright. They were nice."

"They were *nice!*" the Eel cried. He raised his hands above his head and clasped them as if in prayer. "They were nice. Oh, that's wonderful! That's wonderful to hear. I'm glad you both were well taken care of. I mean, you'd both suffered enough, right? You'd both had a rough enough night as it was without the police being dicks to you, too."

He looked down at his feet and saw twin reflections of himself in his shiny leather shoes. A slight scuff to the left shoe troubled him, and he polished it against the calf of his right leg until he was happy it was gone.

"Who was he? This 'lunatic' you describe. Who was he?"

"We don't know. We honestly don't know," Charles insisted. "He was just some guy."

"He doesn't sound like just some guy," Godfrey retorted. "He sounds like far more than *just some guy*. I wouldn't be getting this upset if he was *just some guy*." He bent, bringing his mouth close between their ears. "Because I am," he whispered. "I might not look it, but I am, you know? Getting upset."

He gave them a moment to dwell on that, then straightened so suddenly they both jumped in their chairs.

"You want to know the funny thing?" he asked. "About all this? I called in some favours. I asked a few contacts to get me the details of *this guy* you told me about. And guess what? Nothing. Nobody knows a thing about it. Nobody's gotten wind of any of this. Funny that, right? I mean... that is strange, don't you think?"

Charles swallowed. It sounded almost deafening in the oppressive silence of the office.

"I don't know what to say," he muttered. "It was the police. They took us in. They arrested him."

"And yet, there's no record of that," Godfrey said. "Nothing. Anywhere. How do you explain that?"

"I, eh... I mean, we... We can't. We don't know," Charles replied. "We can only tell you what happened."

"What, that you fucked up, you mean?" Godfrey asked. "That in your stupidity you endangered me, and my businesses. And worse than that, you endangered *them*." He pointed upwards, as if indicating some vengeful god perched on a cloud above. "You expose me, you risk exposing them, and how do you think they feel about that? How do you think they feel if that covenant of trust between them and I is put in jeopardy, Charles? How do you think they react to that sort of thing?"

Charles met Shane's eye again. Held it for as long as he dared. When his reply came, it was a thin, croaky thing. "Not well?"

"Not well. That is both understated and accurate," Godfrey told him. "They do not react well. They do not react well *at all*. Which is why I have had to work quickly to make amends. Why I have had to make a show of reaffirming my loyalty. Because, if I didn't—if I didn't make clear where those loyalties lay— then..." He inhaled sharply and shook his head. "Well, let's not dwell on that unpleasantness, shall we? That's the sort of thing that can keep you up at night."

A sound that someone twenty years Godfrey's junior might describe as 'music' blared out from the pocket of Shane's jeans. Both of the seated men flinched, then froze, only their eyes moving to meet across the gap.

Godfrey said nothing for a while, then tutted. "Well, are you going to answer it, then?" he prompted. "It's rude just to leave it ringing."

"Sorry. I'm really sorry," Shane said. He moved to stand, but the hand returned to his shoulder, holding him in place. Instead, he angled his hips to give himself access to the pocket, then produced the ringing phone and checked the screen.

"It's no one," he said, his thumb moving to tap the big red disconnect button.

"No, it isn't. It's your mum. It says so," Godfrey said. "You can't hang up on your mum."

The music continued to play. Shane's gaze crept up until it met that of the man standing above him.

"Go on," Godfrey said, giving a nod of encouragement. "Answer it."

"It won't be... She'll just be wanting to..."

"Answer. It."

Shane took a breath. Shaking, his thumb tapped the green circle that answered the call, and the tinny-sounding music was replaced by the sound of screaming. Of crashing. Of tearing. Of pain.

"M-mum? Mum?"

He tried to kick back, to stand, but the hand was on his shoulder, on his neck, in his hair.

He heard his mum, her voice muffled and distant, crying out his name. He heard her begging, pleading, for whatever was happening to her to stop. *Please, God, just make it stop.*

"Mum?!"

The hand in his hair tightened, twisting it into knots. The edge of the table came up suddenly, the impact detonating like a bomb between his eyes. He saw a flash of white. A sea of red. The ringing in his ears wasn't quite enough to drown out the sound of his mum's desperate screams, and it was almost a relief when the second impact came, and there was nothing in the world but his own pain, and his own suffering.

The tempered glass of the table held up better than the bones of Shane's face. Every blow, every impact—each more frenzied and furious than the one before—shattered skull and ravaged flesh. His nose collapsed. An eyeball ruptured. Blood flooded backwards into his mouth, and into his throat, and into his lungs, and his body spasmed as it was at last allowed to flop forwards onto the glass, arms hanging limply down, the phone slipping from blood-sodden fingers.

Only then, as Shane lay there convulsing on the vinyl floor tiles, did Godfrey show his approval. He clapped his hands, just two or three times, and with very little in the way of enthusiasm.

"Good lad," he told his nephew, who stood over the quivering wreckage that had, until a moment ago, been his friend.

A wash of red stained Charles's hands and painted flecks across his face. His breath heaved in and out, like he'd done a sprint finish at a marathon, and tears and snot ran in rivers down his cheeks and from his chin.

"Like I said, so important to demonstrate where our loyalties lie," Godfrey told him. He indicated the now motionless figure on the floor like it was some sort of inconvenience. "Now clean that mess up. I have a lunch meeting. I'll be back by two. I expect it spotless. Understood?"

Charles nodded. Given how much he was shaking, though, this wasn't immediately obvious. "Y-yes. Yes, Mr West, sir. Understood."

"Oh, please." A leathery hand with carefully manicured nails traced the contours of Charles's face, smearing the blood and tears together. "Call me Uncle Godfrey," the older man whispered, then he leaned in and planted a long, lingering kiss on his nephew's forehead.

He finally leaned back and admired the younger man's face

like it was something to be cherished. "How's your mum, by the way? She well?"

"She's, uh, she's good, yeah."

"Wonderful," Godfrey exhaled. He wiped his bloodied hand down Charles's front until it brushed, just lightly, over his crotch. "Next time you see her, you be sure to give her my love."

CHAPTER FOURTEEN

"SO, HE'S AN ARSEHOLE, THEN?" Hoon remarked. He looked up from his pink sequined notebook, where he'd been making notes. The MI5 man had been reluctant to begin with, but had eventually been worn down enough to provide detailed information about the man Hoon was being tasked with tracking down. "That's what you're telling me?"

Miles Crabtree nodded. "Yes. Basically. Although, a very well-connected, very powerful one. Getting to him will open many doors, and I'm confident—no, I'm *positive*—that one of those doors will lead you to Caroline Gascoine."

Hoon took a moment to read over everything he'd scrawled onto the book's pages, wasted a couple more seconds scribbling out the winking Japanese cartoon character at the bottom, then snapped the notebook closed and slipped it into the bedside cabinet.

"Right, then. In that case, time I got into character and cracked on."

Miles checked his watch, his brow furrowing. "What? But it's barely lunchtime. You've got hours yet. And you said you were going to arrive late."

Hoon got to his feet and headed for the wardrobe, forcing the MI5 man to step aside. "No, I didn't."

"Yes, you did!" Miles insisted. "You said you weren't going to arrive at eight on the dot."

Hoon shot a look of contempt back over his shoulder as he pulled the wardrobe doors open. "Jesus Christ. Clearly, you're no' the one putting the 'intelligence' into the fucking intelligence service, are you, son?" he scoffed. "Saying I won't be there at eight on the dot doesn't mean I'm going to rock up late. I'm no' a fucking savage, Miles. I'm going to be early."

Reaching into the wardrobe, he produced a pinstripe blue shirt. From the way his face contorted as he looked at it, the garment would have been no less appealing if it was liberally smeared with dog shit.

"But first, I'm hitting the shops," he announced. "Because, if I know Stephen White—and I am him, so I fucking well should do—then he wouldn't be seen dead wearing this gear."

Miles' gaze went from Hoon to the full wardrobe, and back again. "But... we already bought all this. I don't know if we have the budget for more."

Hoon returned the shirt hanger to the rail, then gave Miles a couple of gentle slaps to the cheek that might, if you were feeling particularly generous, be described as 'friendly.'

"Well, then. Looks like someone's breaking out the fucking credit card," he said. "And it sure as shite isn't me."

———

Hoon had seen the inside of many's a pub in his time, although the memories of a significant number of them were foggy at best. He knew what he liked in a drinking establishment, though, and the Red Lion on Crown Passage had all of it in spades, from its cluttered walls and dated stained glass windows to the threadbare red upholstery that did absolutely nothing to enhance either the cosmetic appearance or the comfort level of the seating.

There were a good range of beers on tap, a broad selection of spirits mounted on optics on the back wall, and—for this part of the world—an impressive array of malt whiskies sitting on slightly dusty shelves.

The beermats were cardboard, the snacks were predominantly nut-based, and while it had been several years since the smoking ban was introduced, the smell of nicotine still lingered in the ageing woodwork. It wasn't a pub, it was a *boozer*, and Hoon could think of no higher honour to bestow.

He had earned himself a few funny looks from the punters inside when he'd thrown open the front door and announced his presence with a booming, "Alright, ya wanks?"

To be fair, the shirt had probably drawn as much attention as the greeting. It was a black long-sleeved number with bright yellow pineapples scattered across it like polka dots. It wasn't the sort of thing he'd usually be caught dead in, but as soon as he'd seen it he'd instinctively known how much it would wind up Miles Crabtree, and he knew he had to have it.

Besides, Hoon wasn't the one wearing it. Stephen White was, and this was just the sort of thing old Whitey would go for, the brash, loudmouth prick that he was.

There had been no instructions from MI5 to make him a brash, loudmouth prick, of course, but that was the direction Hoon had decided to take the character, although when questioned about it by Crabtree, he could offer absolutely no explanation whatsoever as to why.

Sometimes, you just had to go with your instinct, and his instincts were telling him that Stephen White was an arsehole.

He sauntered up to the bar, admiring the boozer's traditional stylings while simultaneously scoping out the punters inside. There were eight of them in total, one group of four, and two pairs. Or maybe couples. They were all men, but who did what with who these days was anyone's guess. None of the conversations looked particularly romantic, though, and Hoon imagined that this wasn't really the sort of place you went for a date, particularly not at half-past five on a weekday.

The group of four were all young lads in their twenties. Loud. Worked in banking, given the volume and content of their patter. Their current conversation seemed to be some sort of pissing contest about whose investment portfolio management strategy was best. Or something along those lines, anyway, Hoon tuned out at the first mention of 'unrealised returns,' and turned his attention to the two groups of two.

He'd put one of them down as father and son. Builders, he thought. Some sort of manual labourers, anyway. No doubt much better craic than the four chortling muddlefucks in the expensive clobber, though they were currently too busy consuming their pints and the opinions of the printed gutter press to be demonstrating this.

The remaining two seemed a little out of place. They were Chinese or Japanese—he'd never taken time to learn how to tell the difference—and were busily photographing the small basket of condiments that had been placed on their table, presumably in anticipation of food arriving.

They were taking it in turns to hold up sachets of tomato sauce and salad cream, dangling them from the sides of their heads like glitzy earrings, while their opposite number across the table laughed and snapped off yet another set of pictures.

Fair play to them. Whatever kept them happy.

He was met at the bar by exactly the sort of barmaid he'd been hoping for. She had a wrestler's arms and Popeye's chin, and a look on her face that told him she was one wrong word away from putting him on his arse. She was the very definition of surly, and when she spoke it was with an overtone of utter contempt.

"What can I get you?"

"A wee smile wouldn't go amiss," Hoon told her.

"You'll be lucky," she replied, and her expression became even more resentful, as if to prove her point.

Hoon's eyes narrowed. "That a wee east coast twang in there? Newcastle neck of the woods, maybe?"

"Maybe, aye," she conceded, but was no more forthcoming than that. "What you wanting?"

"Pint of Guinness, thanks," Hoon said. "And whatever you're having yourself."

The barmaid reached under the counter and fetched a pint glass, then placed it under the *Guinness* tap and flicked the pump handle down without an ounce of interest or panache.

"Nice shirt," she remarked.

Hoon held out his arms and admired the printed pineapples on the sleeves. "You think?"

The barmaid stopped the tap with the glass three-quarters full to give the stout time to settle, then shook her head. "No," she said. "Where are you headed after this? The Copacabana?"

Hoon grinned. Olde World pub charm, and withering sarcasm. This place was fucking great!

"Don't know yet. It's early days," he said, as she rang two drinks through the till. "I'm meant to be meeting a mate of mine here later. Well, no' a mate, exactly, just some guy I met who offered to show me the sights. Dale Martelle. You know him?"

From the way the barmaid's face contorted, it was clear that she did, in fact, know Dale Martelle.

"Shite. He's not coming in, is he?"

"Aye. Why?" Hoon asked. He took twenty quid from his Stephen White wallet, and slid it across the bar. "He an arsehole or something?"

"With a drink in him, yeah. Bit of a creepy letch."

"What, to *you*?" Hoon asked. It sounded far more shocked than he'd intended it to sound, and he considered himself lucky that he wasn't immediately on the receiving end of a thick ear.

"Aye, well, we're not exactly stowed out with women round here, in case you hadn't noticed," she replied, then she finished pouring his pint and set it down in front of him with a *clunk*.

"You didn't draw a shamrock on the top," he noted.

She responded by dipping her index finger into the smooth white foam and tracing the outline of something shaped less like a four-leaf clover and more like a penis. "There. Enjoy," she said.

Hoon chuckled to himself as he raised the pint to his lips. "Aye," he said. "I could get fucking used to this place."

———

By the time Dale Martelle rocked up to the Red Lion, Hoon was several pints deep, somewhat worse for wear, and best friends with the two Asian gentlemen who didn't speak a word of English. He had, miraculously, resisted the urge to start a fight with the bankers, despite the ever-increasing volume of their voices, and their regular braying cheers.

He was also substantially better informed about the man he was due to meet, despite the barmaid's initial reluctance to engage him in any sort of meaningful conversation. He'd broken her down eventually, and now knew the names of several of Dale's friends, who he worked for, and a pretty solid idea of where he lived.

Not bad for a few hours' work and a few quid in tips.

The pub had slowly filled up in the hours since Hoon's arrival. There were now just shy of twenty punters in there, of which a whole five percent—or, to put it another way, one individual—was of the female persuasion. She sat in the corner looking thoroughly uncomfortable, laughing along just a second or so behind who Hoon presumed were her male work colleagues.

Poor cow. Just doing her best to fit in, but standing out like a sore thumb.

"Wahey! There's the man himself!" Hoon cried, when Dale came striding in.

"What? God. Wait. What time is it?" Dale asked. "What time were we meant to meet?"

"Fucked if I know," Hoon announced, putting an arm around the other man's shoulder. "Couldn't remember when you said to meet you so I thought, fuck it, get in early."

"What's with the shirt?" Dale asked.

Hoon looked down at his arms again and blinked in surprise, like he was only just seeing the shirt for the first time. "What about the shirt? It's a good shirt."

"It's got pineapples on it."

"And?" Hoon asked. He was squinting, like the amount of alcohol in his system was throwing his eyes off balance. "The fuck's wrong with pineapples?"

Dale shook his head. "Nothing. Nothing's wrong with pineapples. I just..."

Hoon slapped a hand on the other man's chest to indicate that he should shut up.

"Shh. Forget the fucking pineapples," he said, and there was a slur to the words that seemed to make Dale nervous. Hoon glanced deliberately around the bar and lowered his voice to a whisper. "This place is shite. No offence, like, but it is. It's fucking shite. This isn't the good time you promised me, is it? Surely to fuck?"

He fished in his pocket and produced the wallet stuffed with cash in a way that managed to be both covert and ostentatious at the same time.

"I've got cash. You said we needed cash. I've got cash."

Dale's gaze lingered on the wallet for a few moments, then he placed a hand on top of it and pushed it down out of sight of the rest of the pub's punters.

"Alright, OK. I know where we can go," he said. "But these are serious people. You can't draw too much attention to yourself. You have to play it cool."

Hoon's grin was a wobbly, drunken thing. "I've got pineapples all over my tits," he boomed, indicating the chest of his shirt with a jerk of both thumbs. "They don't come much fucking cooler than that!"

CHAPTER FIFTEEN

HOON SAT IN A SMALL, smoke-filled room at the back of a low-rent hotel, scowling at the two cards he held in his hand and wondering how the fuck this had happened.

Across the table, Dale gave him a nod and then glanced smugly around at the four other men. Hoon could almost hear the implied, 'Ta-daa!'

Dale, on the other hand, did not successfully decipher the look Hoon shot back at him, which translated roughly as, "You have got to be fucking kidding me," with a long line of obscenities tacked onto the end.

"You in?" asked the geezer on Hoon's right. He was a grey-haired black man in his eighties, wearing a suit that was probably older still. He sat low in his chair, a thin cigar jammed between two fingers of one hand, while the other hand cupped his cards at a downward angle. Dale had identified him as 'Granny Porter,' and Hoon had been too surprised to ask why.

This was not an underground fighting ring. This was a gaggle of sad old farts playing cards for pennies.

"What's the matter, boy?" Granny asked. His voice was low and rich, and while there was a hint of the West Indies to his accent, the rest of it was firmly rooted in the East End of London. "You need to borrow my hearing aid? I asked if you was in."

Hoon discarded his cards, shook his head, and glowered across the table to where Dale was studying his hand. It was obvious from the expression of borderline glee on the fucker's face that he had something decent. A king, at least, judging by the three cards that had been dealt so far in the middle of the table. No way he was getting this excited by the two or the seven.

The player on Hoon's left matched the big blind, then raised it by—Hoon leaned in to check—a whole quid.

"Fuck me," Hoon muttered, sitting back in his chair. "Last of the big spenders, eh?"

The guy on his left—an old boy who was almost identical to the one on his right, albeit a different colour—peered at him over the top of his reading glasses.

"Pardon me?" he drawled.

He had been introduced to Hoon as 'Frenchie,' although there was nothing about him to suggest he'd ever so much as set foot in France. He spoke with a slow Brummie brogue that made him sound a bit simple.

"I'm just saying, it's hardly fucking high stakes, is it?" Hoon said, gesturing at the small pile of cash in the middle of the table.

They'd been playing now for the best part of forty minutes, and the highest the pot had climbed had been just shy of a tenner. At which point, three of the men at the table had been forced to take their heart medication.

"It's not the money. It's the fun," said the guy on Dale's left. He was a little younger than the others, though that still put him in his sixties. The final man at the table had so far said nothing, but his eyes were flitting around everyone else, suggesting he was following proceedings with interest.

"Fun, you say? And when's that due to start?" Hoon asked, checking his watch. "Because maybe I'll fuck off out for a while and come back then."

"What's the matter, Whitey?" Dale asked.

Hoon didn't answer. Not right away. Not until the silence in the room told him he'd missed his cue.

"What? Oh. What do you mean *what's the matter*? This is the fucking matter," he said, indicating the table, and the pensioners huddled around it. "I mean, no offence, gents, but this isn't exactly the big night I had in mind."

"And what did you have in mind, exactly?" asked Frenchie.

"OK, well, see this here? Us, now? Imagine the opposite of this," Hoon said. "That's what I had in mind. Hot women. High stakes. A bit of danger, maybe. No' fucking Bingo night at the Golden Pines."

"It's not Bingo," Dale pointed out, which earned him a tut and an eye roll. And not just from Hoon.

"He knows it's not Bingo," Granny Porter said. "It was a figure of speech."

"Aye. Exactly. Thank you!" Hoon said.

Granny threw down his cards. "And he's right."

"You what?" Dale said. He glanced down at his hand again, then locked eyes with the king on the table, clearly concerned that his anticipated victory was slipping away from him. "Granny, what are you on about?"

"I have wanted to say this for a long time, but never had the damn nerve," Granny said. "I am too old to sit here gazing at you assholes and waiting to die. I've been coming here three nights a week for ten goddamn years. I've sat in this same seat, at this same table, smoking these same cigars, and I don't want to speak for any of you gentlemen, but I am sick and tired of it."

"Fucking preach, brother!" Hoon said, slapping the older man on the shoulder. "This is fucking London. There's got to be something better than this happening somewhere, surely to fuck?"

He and Granny Porter both looked across the table at Dale, who squirmed in his chair.

"Right. Fine. Fine. I might know somewhere," he declared. He looked down at his cards. "But can we at least finish this hand first?"

"Pair of kings?" Hoon said.

Dale's eyes widened. "What?" He swallowed, trying to regain his composure, then forced a laugh. "No!"

Around the table, the remaining men all folded their cards into the middle.

Hoon grinned over at Dale. "Good work. Well played," he said, then he got to his feet and pointed to the prize pot. "Now, gather up your one-pound-seventy-five-pee, and let's hit the fucking road."

———

This was a step up from a smoky backroom poker game, but not by much. It was still nothing like Hoon had been expecting.

It had taken a bit of time to find the place—by necessity, it moved around—and Hoon got the impression that a lot of Dale's contacts didn't actually care for him very much. He could understand why, given that the man was a near black hole of charm or personality.

They'd finally been directed to the back of a pub in the East End, where a gentleman with a clearly problematic steroid addiction had eyeballed Dale and Hoon like he was trying to make them burst open using just the power of his mind.

He had been unsuccessful.

Hoon had been relying on Dale to get them in, but Dale, it transpired, was a useless bastard, and none of his low, mumbled pleading had opened the door.

It was then that the bouncer spotted the older man lurking behind them. His eyes widened until the irises were surrounded on all sides by a sea of white, and he straightened like he was standing to attention.

"Are you... Are you Danny Porter?"

Granny smiled and offered a hand for the doorman to shake. "Once upon a time, maybe."

Hoon watched both men and said nothing while he waited to see how this was going to play out.

"My old man had his photo taken with you after one of your fights."

"Did he now?" Granny asked, still shaking hands.

"He loved it. It was his favourite thing in the world," the bouncer gushed. "He kept it on his bedside table. Used to look at it every night as he was falling asleep."

The smile on Granny's face faltered for a moment, then returned, broader than ever. "Is that a fact? I am truly honoured."

"You coming in?"

"My friends here and I would love to, yes," Granny said. "If it's not too much trouble?"

"No trouble at all, Danny. No trouble at all! It's an honour. It really... Wow. My dad would be dancing on the ceiling if he knew I was talking to you!"

"You want to give him a call?" Granny asked.

"Oh. No. He's dead," the bouncer said.

"Ah. I'm sorry."

"Cancer."

Granny sucked in his bottom lip and gave a solemn nod of his head. "Ah. Damn."

"Yeah. They had to remove part of his face, but it didn't stop it."

"Damn," Granny said again.

Hoon looked between both men as they stood there in

reverend silence, then clapped his hands, snapping them both out of it.

"Well, this has been a fucking rollercoaster," he said. "But if it's all the same with you pair of maudlin bastards, we'll head on inside."

The guard agreed. Another handshake took place, some cash was palmed over, and the three men found themselves being lowered into the pub's cellar on a chain-driven barrel lift that rattled and shoogled as they descended.

"Nicely done, Granny," Hoon said, patting the older man on the shoulder.

Granny shrugged nonchalantly, but looked pleased with the compliment.

"But what the fuck was all that about?" Hoon continued.

Dale jumped in with the explanation, like this might make up for his earlier failings. "Granny used to be a boxer back in the day. Bit of a local hero. He funds a club for young lads now, don't you, Granny? Helps train them."

"Keeps them off the streets," Granny said.

"Aye? You're a fucking dark horse," Hoon told him, then he turned his attention to the cellar they were being lowered into.

It was the heat that he noticed first—the damp warmth of dozens of bodies all crammed into a poorly ventilated space.

The noise followed next. As they'd first begun their descent, the crowd had been almost silent, holding its collective breath, like guests at a surprise party just waiting for the birthday boy to arrive.

Now, over the sound of the lift, Hoon heard the *smack* of flesh on flesh—a few jabs, a couple of solid strikes. The *crack* of a bone followed. And then, the din erupted—cheering and booing in almost equal measure, and the solitary howling of a man in more pain than he could swallow.

"Oh, Jesus," Dale grimaced, putting a hand to his mouth and looking away from where a man with a serious haircut and a bloodied face stood screaming at the sight of the bone sticking out through his forearm.

"Oh, my days. That does look nasty!" Granny Porter exclaimed, but he rubbed his hands together and grinned from ear to ear, like it was the highlight of his week.

The third thing Hoon noticed about the place was the smell. Cigarettes and alcohol. Perfume and cologne. Sweat and blood. The resultant combined aroma was potent and primal. Mixed with the cheering, the jeers, and the screams it lent the place a tribalistic feel, like war might break out at any given moment.

Although, given the state of that poor fucker's arm, it was entirely possible that it already had.

As the lift descended the final few feet, Hoon cast his gaze across the rest of the cellar. It was a relatively large space, big enough to allow a hundred or more punters to crowd around a circle that was about the size, if not the shape, of a standard boxing ring.

There were a few tables and chairs set out closer to the edges of the room, where a smattering of people—women, mostly—sat drinking and looking largely uninterested in the main event.

For the most part, the spectators were all surprisingly well-dressed. Almost all of the men wore shirts and suit jackets, with a few going the whole hog in tuxedoes and bow ties. The women were better dressed still, all of them decked out like they were just stopping off here on the way to some big grand event. The Oscars, maybe. Something with a red carpet, anyway.

And yet, it all felt cheap and seedy. Rightly or wrongly, Hoon had expected something a little... Not classier, exactly, but better than this. Plastic pint glasses lay trampled and broken on the floor, and everyone looked half-pissed, their smart attire all untucked and skew-whiff.

Between the state of them all and the atmosphere, the

whole thing reminded him of a traveller community wedding he'd been called out to while in the polis, which had descended into a riot somewhere during the Best Man's speech.

This place—despite the bloodshed—didn't have quite the same air of unchecked violence about it as that wedding had, but otherwise, both events felt very similar.

"Is this it?" Hoon asked.

"Jesus, you're never fucking happy, are you?" said Dale.

"No' often, no," Hoon agreed. "I thought it'd be... swankier."

"Swankier? It's an underground fight club, not the opera," Dale pointed out, then he sucked air in through his teeth. "Shit, look at his arm."

"No, I know," Hoon continued. "I'd just... I heard it was a big deal. Like all the fucking bigwigs came."

"Who did you hear that from?" Dale asked, and Hoon shrugged the question off before anyone's suspicions could be aroused.

A man was waiting for them at the bottom, and Hoon found himself glancing up at the shuttered hatch above them, half-convinced this was the same guy they'd just left up there. He had the same build—no neck, chest like a whisky barrel, and legs as thick as telegraph poles—and regarded the three newcomers with the same degree of suspicion as his above-ground colleague had. He didn't like the look of them. That much was obvious.

"Who are you?" he asked. The tone wasn't particularly demanding. When you were that size, you didn't have to make an effort to be intimidating, it just sort of happened on its own.

"I was about to ask you the same fucking thing," Hoon retorted, jumping in before Dale or Granny Porter could open their mouths. He gestured around at the cellar. "What's the fucking score here, then?"

The doorman, or lift greeter, or whatever the hell his job title was, gazed blankly back at Hoon, saying nothing.

"What's the matter? You take a blow to the fucking head recently?" Hoon asked him. He motioned again at the chaos and carnage. "We want to get stuck into this. Get a few drinks, have a wee flutter."

The doorman appeared wholly unimpressed by any of this. "You got an invitation?"

"An invitation?" He pointed to the old man in their midst. "Do you know who that is?"

"I don't know who that is, no."

"That's Danny fucking Porter, I'll have you know. *The* Danny fucking Porter."

The doorman continued to look unimpressed. "I still don't know who that is," he said. "Where's your invitation?"

Hoon muttered below his breath, then took out his wallet and produced a crisp banknote. "I've got twenty invitations right here, pal." When there was no reaction from the other man, he slipped out a second note. "Forty invitations?"

Still no response.

"Fucking hell," Hoon muttered, taking out a third twenty. "If I give you sixty invitations, can you give me ten invitations back? Because I feel like my generous nature's being taken advantage of here, if I'm being completely fucking honest."

"I like your shirt."

At the sound of the voice, the doorman stepped aside, and Hoon found himself face to face with what he could best describe as a sack of bones in a nice dress. She was in her thirties, he guessed, and would no doubt be considered beautiful by large swathes of the male population. Far too skinny for his liking, though. It would, he thought, be like shagging a xylophone.

Still, she was elegantly dressed, had gone to the trouble of having her hair done, and the makeup on her face probably cost a month's worth of his old polis wages. More importantly, the muscle-bound goon who had been blocking their entrance clasped his hands and bowed his head as if in deference to this new arrival.

This was a woman worth knowing, painfully protruding ribcage or no painfully protruding ribcage.

"Ta very much," Hoon told her. "I was going to come dressed like a right pretentious bastard, but I was worried someone else might be wearing the same outfit." He flicked his gaze around the room, then settled back on her. "Dodged a fucking bullet there, eh?"

She laughed at that, and it almost sounded convincing. "You're Scottish," she declared, like this should be news to him.

"Well fucking observed, sweetheart," he replied, which drew a snarl from the doorman, and a clenching of his oversized fists.

"It's fine, Hugo," the woman said. Her tone was sharp, and the bouncer immediately backed off again.

"Aye, down boy," Hoon told him, fixing his smile into something particularly antagonistic. The doorman glowered back at him, but said nothing.

"Are you here with the new guy?" the woman asked. She took a sip from a champagne flute—hers was actual glass, and not the flimsy plastic being clutched by the drunken punters—then flitted the tip of her tongue across her plump red lips. "Greig, isn't it?"

"That's right," Hoon said, despite having absolutely no idea what she was talking about. "Greig. The new guy. That's who we're here with."

"What, all three of you?"

Hoon noted her raised eyebrow and the surprise in her voice, and adapted accordingly. "No, obviously not all three of us. Just me. These two are just here for..."

"A good time," said Granny. He smoothed down a suit that had lived through at least two world wars, then brushed a hand through his wiry grey hair. "Hot women. High stakes. A bit of danger, maybe."

The woman laughed again at that, and this time it really did sound genuine.

"Then you've come to the right place. Hugo will show you what's what." She tipped her glass in Hoon's direction, singling him out. "And I'll take you through to Greig." She leaned in a little closer, and the smell of her perfume bloomed to fill the gap between them. "Between you and I, I think you got here just in the nick of time."

CHAPTER SIXTEEN

THE SACK of bones swept through the crowd with a level of confidence that impressed even Hoon.

She glided along, her champagne glass held up at shoulder height, her heels *clacking* on the stone floor. Despite its unevenness, she didn't falter once, and whenever it looked like the sea of punters ahead of her was too dense to pass through, another of the muscle-bound bouncers would emerge from somewhere to shove them aside and form a path.

"I'm Amanda, by the way," she said, glancing back over an exposed, angular shoulder. "But I expect you knew that."

"Aye," Hoon lied. "Naturally."

She seemed pleased at this, and led him towards an area at the back of the cellar where some curtains had been hung from lengths of rope, forming what looked a lot like a row of clothes-shop changing rooms.

Approaching the fourth cubicle along, she mimed rapping her knuckles on the thick black fabric, said, "Knock, knock!" and then smirked like this was some brilliant joke that nobody had ever done before.

There was a pause before the response came. "Um... who's

there?" There was a definite north-of-the-border lilt to the voice, but Hoon couldn't place it yet.

Amanda peered at Hoon over the rim of her glass, then tilted her head in the direction of the curtain.

"It's... Stephen," Hoon said.

Another pause.

"Stephen who?" asked the voice from beyond the curtain.

Hoon rolled his eyes. "Jesus Christ, son, we're no' telling an elaborate fucking knock-knock joke here," he barked. "You decent?"

"Uh... aye. Yeah. Yeah, I am."

Hoon swept aside the curtain to find an infant with a beard staring back at him, wide-eyed and semi-naked. He had been in the process of binding his hands with lengths of grubby bandage —and making an absolute arse of the whole process—but now stood frozen like a rabbit in headlights.

He was black, but light-skinned. Mixed race, Hoon guessed. His beard was a thin, scraggy joke of a thing, neither use nor ornament, and sat uncomfortably on what Hoon could only describe as his 'baby face.'

He had a boxer's build—middleweight, maybe creeping up into heavy—and wore a pair of blue and white shorts styled after the saltire, which was unlikely to win him much support down here in front of an away crowd.

There was recognition in his eyes when he clocked the woman in the dress—that and a flicker of fear, Hoon thought— but when he turned his attention to the man in the pineapple shirt, his look was utterly blank.

"Eh, is there a problem?" he asked. Despite the lad adopting what Hoon assumed was his 'big boy voice,' Hoon was able to more accurately hone in on the accent. Ayrshire. Kilwinning sort of area, most likely.

"You tell me, Greiggy boy," Hoon spat back. He stepped past the open curtain, took hold of the lad's hands, then turned them over while checking out the wrapping. "Look at the state of this. Did you wrap these with your fucking feet, or something?"

"Eh... No, I just..." Greig frowned and blinked, like he was coming out of a trance, then pulled his hands away. "Who are you?"

Out of the corner of his eye, Hoon saw the bag of bones stiffen slightly.

"Who the fuck do you think I am?" he demanded, squinting Popeye-style at the younger man.

The lad, to his credit, stood his ground. Physically, at least.

"Um... Are you...? Did Frankie send you?"

Hoon prodded a finger into the centre of Greig's bare chest. "Bingo," he said, then he caught the edge of the curtain and flashed the woman in the dress a look that managed to be both impatient and apologetic at the same time. "Sorry, hen, you mind if we have a wee bit of privacy here? Lots to discuss."

Amanda ran a finger around the edge of her glass and regarded him silently for a few moments. Then, her ruby-red lips curved into a smile, and she granted the request with a single nod.

"But don't take long," she instructed, taking a step back. "He's up next, and the audience really doesn't like to be kept waiting."

"We'll be on it like a fucking car bonnet, sweetheart," Hoon said, which earned him a bewildered look. He swished the curtain closed before she could seek any sort of clarification, and he gestured for Greig to keep his mouth shut until they heard her heels *clopping* away across the stone floor.

"Look, I'm sorry. I'm really sorry," the lad whispered. "I didn't... I'm going to send Frankie his money. I am. That's what this is for. I didn't mean to... I wasn't going to hide anything from him."

"Aye, well, I should fucking hope not," Hoon said. "You don't mess with Frankie."

"No, no, I know. I know."

"In fact, I don't even want you calling him Frankie anymore," Hoon spat. "I want you to refer to him like he's your fucking primary school headmaster. Which shouldn't be too hard for you to imagine at your age. From now on, you can call him Mr..."

He left it hanging, expecting Greig to fill the space he'd left. He didn't.

"Fuck's sake, son. Keep up." He sighed. "What are you going to call him? Mr...?"

"Cowan," Greig said, bowing his head a little. "I'm going to call him Mr Cowan."

"Frankie Cowan?!" Hoon said before he could stop himself. "That wee fuck?"

A frown troubled the younger man's brow. "Eh... what do you mean?"

"Nothing. Aye. That's him," Hoon confirmed, reining his surprise back in.

He had encountered Frankie Cowan just a few months back, when he'd almost shoved him off a block of flats in Glasgow. Frankie's uncle, Shuggie Cowan, had taken custody of the bastard soon after. Given everything Frankie had done to upset his uncle, and given Shuggie's history of gangland violence, getting thrown off a roof would likely have been the younger Cowan's preferred option. At least that way would've been quick.

"I, eh, I just... I hadn't heard from him in a few weeks," Greig said. "And I just... I thought..." He buried his face in his hands, and Hoon saw his shoulders start to shake. "Oh, God, I'm sorry. I'm sorry. I was going to get him his money. I was. I really was."

"Alright, cool your tits, for Christ's sake," Hoon told him. "If

I wanted to see a grown man bawling his eyes out I'd have bought a fucking mirror and rented *Toy Story* 3." He parted the curtain just enough to allow him a glimpse out at the crowd. There was a flurry of activity going on, with cash being exchanged and betting slips being passed back and forth. "So, what's the story? You meant to be fighting, or what?"

"Uh, aye. Aye. That's my plan. It's how I'm going to pay Frankie back."

A figure in the crowd caught Hoon's eye. He was bouncing up and down on the spot and throwing fast jabs at the air, warming up for what was coming next. He was listening to an older man who was giving him a talking to while punctuating whatever he was saying by karate chopping his open palm.

"Fuck, you're no' up against that bastard, are you?" he asked. He pulled the curtain a little further aside, but Greig didn't move to look.

"What does he look like?"

Hoon answered truthfully. "Like a man who will rip your fucking eyes out through your arse."

Greig did look then. He followed Hoon's gaze, then nodded when he caught sight of his opponent. "He doesn't look that bad. He's not that big."

"He doesn't have to be big. Look at his fucking eyes," Hoon instructed.

Greig squinted. "I don't see anything."

"Exactly. There's fuck all there. He's no' right in the head," Hoon told him.

He'd seen that look many times before. He'd seen it on the battlefield. He'd seen it in back alleys behind pubs, carved into the faces of men standing in circles, kicking and punching a long-motionless mound on the pavement.

Though he didn't care to admit it, he'd sometimes even seen it on the face of the man looking back from the mirror.

It was the look of a man with all the humanity removed. Of a man for whom violence was not only second nature, but *first* nature. A man without an off switch, who didn't know how to stop.

"If I was you, son, I'd find a fucking back door out of here and leg it, pronto."

Greig stood up straight, his arms pinned at his sides, his head raised high. "I can't. I need to get Frankie his money."

"Aye, well, I wouldn't worry too much about Frankie right now. I'm sure the two of you can work out a payment plan or something, in the unlikely event he ever gets back in touch," Hoon told him.

"What?" Greig's face was a mess of confusion. "I thought you... Aren't you working for Frankie?"

"Am I fuck!" Hoon spat, refusing to let a wee scrote like Frankie Cowan be his boss, even in this completely fabricated scenario. "We're more like partners. He fucking works for me, if anything. And I'm telling you no' to worry too much about the money right now. That bastard out there's a much more pressing issue. We'll get fuck all out of you if you're dead."

"I'm not going to die."

"I just saw some lad get his arm broken in that last fight, and —no offence—but he was a big sturdy fucker who looked like he could actually handle himself."

"I can handle myself!" Greig protested, though he didn't sound entirely confident. "I've fought before. Loads of times. I nearly went pro back home."

"Went pro?" Hoon looked him up and down. "What, like became a rent boy, you mean?"

"What? No! Not that!" Greig spluttered. "I mean, I nearly went pro at boxing."

"Aye?" Hoon raised both eyebrows in surprise. "Like... proper boxing?"

"Yeah."

"Actual boxing? No' on the fucking *PlayStation* or something?"

"Proper actual boxing," Greig insisted.

Hoon sniffed, shrugged, then went back to watching events through the gap in the curtains. "Aye, well, sorry to be the bearer of bad news, but that guy's still going to be the fucking end of you, son. Unless..."

"Unless what?"

"Nothing." Hoon shook his head, and let the curtain fall closed. "Doesn't matter."

"No, what? What was it you were going to say?"

Hoon shook his head again, more firmly this time. "I can't. I don't have time." He jabbed a finger upwards into Greig's face. "And you owe us fucking money, I'm hardly going to help you, am I?"

"But... this'll help me get the money," Greig insisted, gesturing towards the curtain. The crowd was starting to get rowdy now. They were growing impatient. "This'll help me pay you back. What were you going to say? Unless what? He's going to be the end of me unless *what*?"

Hoon let out a long sigh of exasperation. "I mean... Fine. I was going to say, unless I'm in your corner."

Greig blinked. "What, like a coach?"

"Like a coach. Exactly. Because, fuck me, you look like you're badly in need of one."

The younger man took a few moments to consider this, then shook his head. "No. No, I don't need anyone. I'm fine on my own."

Hoon shrugged. "Suit yourself, son," he said. He took out his wallet, removed a stack of bills, then started to pull the curtain aside. "What's the other guy's name, do you know? I want to stick this on him. No point me leaving here empty-handed, eh?"

"Wait."

Hoon stopped.

Hoon turned.

"You really think you can help me?" Greig asked.

"Help you? I'm going to do more than help you, son." Hoon returned the money to the wallet. "I'm about to save your fucking life."

———

Hoon led the way to the circle of empty floor that served as the ring, cutting a trench through the crowd with shoves and swear words. Greig, his hands now properly strapped up thanks to Hoon's intervention, followed a couple of paces behind. A glance back at him confirmed Hoon's suspicions that the lad was absolutely shiteing himself.

"Don't worry about this jug of fucks," he said, raising his voice to be heard over the jeering and whooping and stamping of feet. "They don't matter. Just ignore them."

Ignoring them wasn't easy, of course. Now that the punters had clapped eyes on the second combatant, the betting was in full flow. A handful of harassed-looking bookies did their best to keep up with demand, while the muscle-bound bouncers worked to keep things from spiralling into chaos.

Hoon stopped, giving the lad a chance to catch up, then put an arm around his shoulder and fell into step beside him. "What's your name, anyway?"

"Eh? I thought... Didn't Frankie...?"

Hoon caught the doubt on his face and moved quickly to stamp it out. "No, I know it's Greig. I remember that. What's your surname? I forgot."

The younger man leaned in closer, straining to hear. "What?"

"Greig what?" Hoon all but bellowed into his ear.

Greig nodded. "Yeah."

"Jesus. No... I said Greig *what*?"

"And I said..." Greig rolled his eyes. "Oh. Right. Funny. Yeah. Very good. I haven't heard that one before. Greig Watt. *What*? Aye, that's a new one, right enough."

Hoon stared back at him, his brow furrowed into deep grooves. "What the fuck are you talking about? What's your surname?"

"Yes!"

"Yes fucking what?"

Greig stood a little taller than Hoon, but what he had in height he lacked in presence, and he gave a nervous swallow before replying. "Yes... sir?"

"Is this a fucking wind-up?" Hoon asked, but by then they'd reached the ringside, and he had no choice but to drop the subject.

Greig's opponent was even more intimidating up close than he had been from a distance, despite the fact he was wearing a tiny pair of cut-off denim shorts that showed half his arse. If anything, those somehow made him even more terrifying.

Hoon wasn't worried by the bastard personally—he'd dealt with his share of violent bams in his time—but Greig seemed like a nice enough lad. Too nice to be turned into a greasy smear on the floor of a pub cellar in front of a live audience, at any rate.

And that, Hoon reckoned, was precisely what this mad-looking fucker in the denim shorts would do to him. He was a little shorter than Greig, and there was no denying that Greig was physically in better shape. Probably mentally, too, given the way the other guy kept muttering below his breath and striking himself on the forehead. Of course, being a total headcase was rarely a disadvantage when it came to a street fight, so the fact the guy was clearly off his meds wasn't really working in Greig's favour. Greig did, however, have a distinct advantage when it came to reach.

Still, fat lot of good that would do him. Based on what Hoon had seen on the way down in the lift, this wasn't a boxing match. It was a full-on, no-holds-barred, gouging and grabbing, down in the dirt sort of scrap, and a few extra inches of reach wasn't overly useful when some bastard was chewing your nose off.

The other guy had a solid eyeballing game going on, too. He'd locked his sights on Greig as Hoon had led him through the crowd, and was still giving him both barrels now. Greig, for his part, occasionally returned the look, but then averted his gaze when the intensity of the other man's stare became too much.

This, Hoon thought, was not going to end well.

There was another lad standing beside Greig's opponent who Hoon was betting was an older brother. He had a similar height and build to the headcase in the cut-offs, but with a few more years of weathering to his face, and some flecks of grey in the stubble of his shaved head. They both had the same glassy-eyed stare, and the older sibling had complemented his with a long vertical scar. It ran from his forehead, down his nose, and through the lines of his lips, and while it was old, it had healed badly. It would do nothing for his love life, but down here it was just the sort of finishing touch that made people take you seriously.

Amanda, the bag of bones in the fancy dress, was standing on the elevator. It had been stopped halfway to the hatch that led up onto the street, affording her an elevated view of the whole cellar. Hoon caught her watching him, her freshly filled glass of champagne still clutched in the same hand at shoulder height. He nodded, acknowledging her, and she tilted her glass towards him as if toasting his luck.

"Shit. He does look like a mad bastard, doesn't he?" Greig muttered.

"Oh aye. Absolutely fucking dead behind the eyes," Hoon

confirmed, then he realised this probably wasn't the reassurance the lad had been looking for. "But, on the other hand, he also looks as thick as pigshit."

"What are you saying? You think we can outsmart him?"

Hoon puffed out his cheeks. "I mean, you're trying to kick his head in, no' challenging him to a game of *Trivial Pursuit*, so I'm not sure how, but... aye. Maybe. Fuck knows. We'll play it by ear and see what happens."

Greig met his opponent's eye again, held it for as long as he could, then buckled and turned back to Hoon. "I thought you were meant to be helping me out here!"

"I am helping you out!" Hoon retorted.

"In what way?"

"I'm going to chip in with advice once you get going."

"And how's that going to help?" Greig hissed. "I need a game plan before then. This guy looks fucking mental."

There was no disputing that. He was currently pacing back and forth like a wild animal in its cage, eyes locked on Greig. Occasionally, he'd slam the side of a clenched fist against his forehead, and each time he did his features became wilder and more savage.

"What were you going to do if I hadn't rocked up?" Hoon asked.

"I don't know. I was just going to sort of, I don't know, wing it."

Hoon tutted. "Good fucking job I got here when I did. How about you just try and no' die in the first minute while I figure out his fighting style, then I'll tell you which bit of him to hit and when?"

"But what about now? You must have some advice you can give me now?" Greig said, and despite all the muscles and the facial hair, Hoon felt like he was talking to a terrified wee boy.

"OK, fine. The best bit of advice I can give you right now?" He put a hand on the younger man's shoulder and pulled him in closer. "After this, you should get that shit off your face."

Greig frowned. "What? What do you mean? What shit?

"This fucking atrocity of a thing you've got going on," Hoon said, indicating his own lower jaw.

Greig touched his chin self-consciously. "What, my beard?"

"Beard?" Hoon snorted. "That's no' a fucking beard, son. That's a pubic wig that's wandered off course. That's a parody of a beard. In fact, no. It's no' even that. It's a fucking primary school play *loosely inspired* by a parody of a beard. That's how shite it is. Soon as we're done here, assuming you survive and have full use of your faculties, get rid of it."

"But... My fiancée loves it."

"Your fiancée? Fuck me, seriously?" Hoon gasped. "How've you got a fiancée? You look about eight. Should you no' still be pulling lassies' pigtails and running away at your age?"

"We're twenty-one," Greig protested.

"What, combined?"

"Both of us. Individually, I mean. We're both twenty-one."

Hoon pulled a 'well I never' sort of face, then shrugged. "Right. I see. And which is she, blind or stupid?"

"Neither!"

"Well, then I hate to fucking break it to you, son, but she's lying about liking that beard."

Before Greig could respond, a man in a shiny satin jacket stepped into the ring and started *clanging* an old-fashioned handbell for silence.

"Fuck, fuck, fuck," Greig whispered. He started to dance from foot to foot, but Hoon put a hand on his arm and held him in place.

"Ladies and gentlemen," the guy in the jacket bellowed above the din, which hadn't diminished in the slightest since the bell-ringing. Quite the opposite, in fact. His accent was all plums and silver spoons. Born into money. Privately educated,

Hoon assumed. Eton or somewhere. A classic rich-boy Oxbridge wanker if ever there was one, and Hoon despised him from the first syllable. "Our third bout of the evening is about to get underway!"

He paused then, for both dramatic effect and to let the drunken mob get the frenzy of cheering out of its system. Across the circle, the headcase in the denim shorts gave himself a flurry of smacks on the forehead, then threw a few wide-armed downward jabs like he was pummelling the shit out of a couple of dwarfs. Still staring down his opponent, he bounced on his toes and exhaled noisily through his nostrils, and looked for all the world like a bull getting ready to charge.

Greig, to his credit, stood his ground. Hoon kept holding his arm, just in case. Yes, it probably would've been in the lad's best interests to make a run for it, but Hoon didn't want him doing that. The truth was, he had seen something in Greig the moment he'd first set eyes on the lad.

Not potential, and certainly not a younger version of himself. Christ, no, nothing cheesy like that. He'd seen something far more valuable than either of those. The same thing he'd seen in the white supremacist back at the jail.

He'd seen an opportunity.

If he was going to get to know the score around here and find this Godfrey West bastard, then being a punter wasn't going to cut it. He needed a man on the inside. And, if that man could be him, then so much the fucking better.

"In the red corner," the announcer boomed, despite the fact that there were no corners of any description in the vicinity, red or otherwise. He dragged the words out like he'd no doubt heard them do in the *Rocky* films, which only made him sound even more of a knob than he already did. "All the way from Wexford in Southern Ireland."

"It's just Ireland, ya fucking ponce," Denim Shorts spat. It was the first time Hoon had heard him speak, and the thick Irish accent was impossible to miss.

This was potentially a problem. Some of these Irish lads— particularly those from the travelling communities—had been fighting since the day they were born. They could be savage, vindictive bastards in the ring, without a shred of compassion for their opponents or remorse for the damage they inflicted upon them.

The twat in the shiny jacket offered a smile by way of apology, then continued with his announcement.

"Weighing in at one-hundred-and-eighty-three pounds... Tony 'The Tiger' Mulllll-lllligan!"

The audience went wild, clapping, stamping, and roaring their approval. Hoon let out a snort that was lost amongst the din of it all.

"Tony the Tiger? Seriously? Is that no' trademarked?" he scoffed. "Who is it you're fighting after him? Snap, Crackle, and fucking Pop?"

Greig, however, wasn't listening. From the look of him, he was way beyond being able to listen. He was licking his dry lips and shifting his weight from foot to foot like he was desperate for the toilet. His hands were clenched into fists, but they were tucked in tight against his washboard stomach, like he was already anticipating having to protect himself from a kick, knee, or punch.

This was not the stance of a winner. It was not even the stance of someone likely to leave this room alive.

Hoon leaned in closer and hissed in the younger man's ear. "Keep moving. Don't let the bastard get a hold of you. You're not boxing, you're scrapping, but if you see an opening you jab and get the fuck out of his way before he can get you back. He'll tire himself out before you do."

Greig turned, stared wide-eyed at Hoon for a few seconds,

then jammed a finger in the ear on the opposite side of his head and leaned closer. "What?"

Hoon groaned. "Oh, for the love of—"

"Aaaaand in the blue corner..." the announcer boomed, drowning him out. "Weighing in at one-hundred-seventy-six pounds and hailing from Glasgow, Scotland..."

Even the way the prick pronounced 'Glasgow' so it rhymed with 'cow' made Hoon want to hurt him badly.

"Greig 'The Godkiller' Waaaaaattttt!"

More cheering erupted, though it didn't feel as enthusiastic as the previous outburst. Not by a long shot.

Hoon clicked his fingers. "*Watt*. Not *what*. Right. Aye. Makes sense now," he said.

Greig shot him a look that was part questioning, part bowel-shattering terror. "What did you say?"

"Nothing. Forget it," Hoon told him. He patted the younger man on a rounded shoulder and winked. "You go get him, *Godkiller*," he said, trying very hard to keep a straight face.

"It wasn't my idea. The name," Greig said, and for a moment—just a brief one—he looked more embarrassed than scared. "It was my fiancée. She came up with it."

He glanced over his shoulder at his opponent, then leaned in closer to Hoon and spoke urgently into his ear.

"Her number's in my phone. If anything happens... Anything bad... Can you tell her that, you know, like... that I love her, or whatever?"

"Last of the true fucking romantics, eh?" Hoon replied, then he nodded. "Aye. I'll tell her."

"And Benji, too."

Hoon frowned. "Who's Benji? That your dug?"

"He's my wee boy."

Hoon closed his eyes.

Fuck.

Fuck.

His eyes snapped open. "Your wee boy? You've got a *son?*"

"Aye."

"What do you mean you've got a son?"

"I mean... I've got a son. Benji."

"That's definitely a fucking dog's name," Hoon insisted. "Are you sure he's no' a dug?"

"No! He's my son. He's four months old."

"Fuck's sake," Hoon spat. He drew in a breath so deep and so sharp that some of the older occupants of the room may have started to feel light-headed due to a sudden lack of oxygen. His hand tightened on Greig's forearm again. "Listen. You should ditch this. Walk away. Away home to the missus and the wee man. No shame in bottling it."

"Aye, there is." Greig shook his head. "Anyway, I can't. I need the money."

"You don't have to pay us back. Me and Frankie. You're fucking absolved." Hoon made a hand gesture like a half-hearted priest blessing a member of his flock. "There. Debt cleared."

"It's not just you. I need rent, we need food, we need everything."

"There are easier ways to make money than this, son."

"Well, aye, but..." Greig's gaze flitted momentarily to Amanda, sipping her champagne on her raised viewing platform. He lowered his voice. "Once you're in, you're in. I can't back out now. There's no saying what they'll do."

Hoon glanced from the woman in the dress to the psycho in the denim shorts, then met Greig's eye and saw nothing there but desperation. The kid was so far out of his depth that the shore wasn't just a distant memory, it was a half-remembered legend only spoken of in whispers.

"Fuck. Alright, fine," Hoon said. He squeezed Greig's arm. "Go out there, try your best no' to get killed in the first thirty seconds, and leave the rest to me."

CHAPTER SEVENTEEN

THERE WERE VERY few advantages to being old. Everything ached, sleep was a haphazard affair, and the internal plumbing rarely operated in the ways it was designed to.

There was a perceived wisdom that came with getting older, of course, but Granny Porter had always felt like a bit of a fraud on that front. A few of the younger guys he encountered at the poker games or the lads he trained at the gym would occasionally ask for life advice, assuming his advanced years offered him some great insight that they could only aspire to.

Besides, 'Always walk closest to the kerb when escorting a lady,' and a step-by-step guide on how to poach an egg, however, he had very little to offer.

That was not to say, though, that being old didn't have *any* benefits. People tended to get out of your way, whether through courtesy or the fear that you might talk to them. That was why, in a room full to the gunnels with adrenaline-charged, testosterone-filled fight fans, he was able to help himself to the second best view in the house.

It was a walkway of sorts—a couple of wooden stairs, a three-foot-long bridge above a row of dented silver beer barrels, and then another two stairs at the other end. It wasn't high—certainly nothing like the view the woman up on the elevator had—but it put him above the head height of most other folks in the cellar, and gave him a relatively clear line of sight at the two combatants facing each other in the shifting circle of bodies.

He'd had a flutter, of course. You took your fun where you could get it at his age. Fifty on the Irish lad. He'd been given evens, so not a lot of profit to be had, but a fairly safe bet. The Irishman had the air of a killer shark about him, and his opponent, for all his height and muscles, was nothing but a bucket of chum.

"Alright, Granny? I got you a drink."

Granny beckoned for Dale to come join him on the platform. It creaked ominously when Dale put his weight on the first step, and he decided to go no higher. He passed Granny a small plastic tumbler with an inch of amber liquid at the bottom then raised his pint glass in salute, and slurped the lager's foamy head.

"Anything happened yet?" Dale asked, raising himself on his tiptoes rather than risking going any higher on the rickety steps.

"Just a lot of staring. You put a bet on?"

"Yeah. The Irish guy."

"Sensible boy," Granny remarked. He sipped his whisky, winced as it burned down his throat, then gestured to where Hoon had gone sidling up to the Irishman's coach. "How'd your friend get involved in all this? I thought he was here to watch, like us?"

"No idea," Dale admitted. "I suppose... I don't know. Maybe he knows the guy?"

"Maybe," Granny said. He shrugged. "Bit weird, though."

"Yeah," Dale said. He regarded Hoon in silence for a few seconds, then nodded. "Bit weird."

"Here. Pal. You know the rules for this? Like, are the old cock and bollocks off-limits, or are they fair game?"

Tony the Tiger's older brother turned and fixed Hoon with the briefest of looks, scowled, then directed his attention back to where both fighters were having their hand wraps and shorts checked for concealed weapons.

"Fuck off," the coach grunted.

As well as looking like his brother, he sounded like him, too. His voice was harsher, though, like he'd either recently recovered from throat cancer, or should be making an urgent appointment to get himself checked for it.

"Well, that's fucking charming," Hoon said. "I was just asking a question. No need to be an arsehole about it. I thought Irish folk were meant to be friendly? I mean, look at fucking Bono. He does all that charity work, and he doesn't ask a thing in return."

The coach's brow furrowed around the line of his scar, and this time when he turned he did so slowly and deliberately.

"Apart from all the constant fucking adulation and tax breaks, of course," Hoon continued. "Still, he seems nice. I bet he wouldn't have told me to fuck off. You should maybe make that your motto. 'Be more Bono.' He's an asset to your country, that man."

"Are ye deaf, or something? I just told you to—"

A bell rang, cutting him off. His head snapped to the front as the officials merged with the front row of the crowd, and the two fighters began to circle each other, each sizing the other up.

"And then there's them wee fellas," Hoon continued, leaning in closer to the other coach. He gave him a nudge with an elbow, drawing his attention. "The wee lads you've got kicking about over there. Wi' the funny wee hats and the pots of gold. They always seem happy as a pig in shite. Unless you try and nick their lucky charms, of course. I hear they can lose the fucking rag then, right enough."

The coach glowered at him. Hoon smiled, adopted a high-pitched and outrageously thick Irish accent, then announced: "They're always after me lucky charms!"

This earned him a hissed warning and a shoulder nudge from the Irishman.

That would do for now.

In the circle, Greig was bobbing and weaving with his fists raised in front of his face, while cautiously side-stepping his way around the empty space. If he wasn't shiteing his satin shorts, he was doing a good impression of it.

Tony the Tiger looked far more confident and relaxed. His fists were clenched, too, but they were kept low, like he wasn't even entertaining the possibility of taking a hit to the head. Or maybe he was actively inviting one. He'd certainly given himself enough of them in the run-up to the fight, and they'd only seemed to make him angrier.

Where Greig was retreating, the Irish lad was constantly on the advance. Greig bounced around on the balls of his feet, but Tony hadn't come here to dance. He was a plodder, conserving his energy, tirelessly stalking his opponent.

This was how humans had made it to the top of the food chain all those years ago. Other animals were faster and stronger, but humans were relentless. Humans kept coming. Humans did not, would not fucking stop until total dominance had been achieved.

That was what this was, Hoon thought. This, here, now. Despite his name, Tony the Tiger was the human being in this situation, and Greig was each and every species that had ever been hunted to extinction. He was the woolly mammoth. The giant armadillo. The fucking dodo.

He was, unless Hoon did something about it, a dead man walking.

"Which one are you supporting?" Hoon asked, leaning closer to the other coach again. "The young fella, or the big daft Mick?"

Tony's brother was roughly the same height as Hoon and just a handful of years younger. He carried himself like he was the hardiest bastard in the room, and when he fixed his gaze on the man beside him it was a level of contempt usually reserved for dogshit stains on a new carpet.

"What did you fucking say?"

"Fuck me, what happened to your face? If you don't mind me asking?" Hoon's gaze followed the line of the other man's scar. "Did you try and cut it off and swap it for another one? I mean, I wouldn't fucking blame you. If I looked like you, I'd be going demented."

A flurry of movement and a roar from the crowd stopped the conversation before it could escalate any further. Hoon turned, wincing at the thought of the horrors he might be about to witness, and was pleasantly surprised to see Greig skipping back to avoid a telegraphed right hook. The lad followed up with a quick left jab that made a satisfying *thwack* against his opponent's eye socket.

Maybe Hoon was worrying about nothing. Maybe this wouldn't be a total massacre, after all.

"Go on, son!" Hoon urged. Grinning like he couldn't believe he'd just landed a punch, Greig turned in the direction of the voice, and Hoon's confidence evaporated. "Don't look at me, look at him for fuck's sake!"

Tony seized on the distraction. He swung again with a big wild left, and this time Greig barely had time to avoid it. He certainly didn't have time to avoid the follow-up right hook to the ribcage, and in the time it took him to register the pain, Tony was past his defences, grabbing at him, tearing at him, the momentum of his charge sending them both flailing into the circle of onlookers.

The crowd jeered and shoved them back. Beer was thrown over them, soaking them both. Plastic glasses rained down as they staggered back towards the centre of the ring.

Another punch slammed into Greig's ribs, and pain burst as a bubble on his lips. He was caught in a headlock now, Tony's tattooed forearm locked across his throat. Greig slapped at the arm, pulled at it, tried to jam his fingers underneath and prise it away.

"Use your legs, for Christ's sake!" Hoon hollered. "Hoof the fucker!"

The advice was quickly taken. Unfortunately, it was taken by the wrong man. A foot was driven into the back of Greig's leg, and he collapsed onto his knees, all tears and hot snotters. Half-empty plastic pint glasses rained down on the circle as the audience voiced its dismay. For the most part, their man was winning, but did he have to win so quickly? Where was the drama? Where was the bloodshed?

"Gwan, Tone!" the man at Hoon's side cheered. Both fighters were more or less facing their coaches, the Irish lad standing tall above the kneeling and helpless Greig. "Break that black bastard's fucking neck!"

Hoon turned sharply, to be met by a yellow-toothed grin from Tony's big brother.

"Wassa matter? Ye got a problem?"

Hoon made a sudden lunge, but didn't hit the Irishman. Instead, he reached past him and snatched a shot glass from the grasp of the next man along. Then, he spun on a heel, and tossed the contents straight into Tony's eyes.

The effect was instantaneous. Agonising, too, by the looks of it. Hissing and blinded, the Tiger released his grip and staggered back, his palms pressed into his eye sockets.

"Ye dirty cheating bastard!" Tony's brother spat. He

grabbed for Hoon, then his eyes widened and his breath escaped him in one low, rumbling *huff* as Hoon's fist slammed into his solar plexus.

His arm was caught, jerked, twisted. He had nowhere to go but down.

By the time his face hit the floor, one of the bouncers was already upon them, demanding to know what the fuck was going on.

"It's no' my fault," Hoon protested, giving the fallen man's arm one more big wrench before releasing his grip. "Blame post-apocalyptic Daniel O'Fucking Donnell here. He started it."

The bouncer shot a questioning look to the raised elevator, and to the woman in red standing on it. She waved him away with her glass, let her gaze linger on Hoon for a few moments, then turned her focus back to the circle, where Tony was gradually regaining the power of sight.

"Get up, for fuck's sake," Hoon hissed, urging Greig back onto his feet. "Stop fannying about!"

There was movement from the floor beside him. He applied a foot to the fallen coach's neck and pinned him there.

"Not you," Hoon warned.

Greig, who was clutching at his throat like he was trying to strangle himself to death, managed a shaky nod, then struggled upright. He'd clearly caught a punch or something during their tussle, because his bottom lip was split, letting blood wash down over his chin and into his sparse, wiry beard.

He formed his hands into fists again, struggled through a few unsteady breaths, then bounced from foot to foot just beyond Tony's grabbing range.

"What are you fucking waiting for?" Hoon demanded. "Get stuck into him!"

Greig shook his head, but it wasn't clear if he was refusing the instruction or just trying to shake the cobwebs loose.

"He can't see anything," he croaked.

"Exactly! This is the best fucking chance you're going to get!"

Another shake of the head, and this time there was no mistaking the purpose of it. "That's not fair."

A bit of a cheer rose up at that. Over the racket, Hoon could just hear Granny Porter shouting, "Good for you, son!"

Hoon, however, was having none of it. "Fuck fair. Life's no' fair. Hit him now, or he'll do you in. And where will poor wee fucking Rover be then, eh?"

Greig blinked and shot a glance back over his shoulder. "Do you mean Benji?"

Hoon gave a dismissive wave of a hand. "Benji, Rover, it's all the fucking same. The point is—shite! Watch out!"

Tony the Tiger had shrugged off the blinding effects of the Scotch. His mood, unsurprisingly, did not seem to have been improved by the face full of whisky, and he practically ran at Greig, one hand grabbing for him, the other drawn back, ready to swing.

The punch was wide and wild. Greig bobbed back, weaved in, and delivered two solid jabs that sent the other man into a sideways stagger.

Hoon kept his mouth shut. There was no saying that Greig had learned his lesson after last time, and the last thing he needed was a distraction.

The Tiger recovered quickly, but his anger was getting the better of him. He fired a big wide-legged kick at Greig's midsection which was easily blocked. Greig moved in quickly for a follow-up, snapped off a couple of jabs, then ducked to avoid a looping right hook that *whummed* above his head.

Hoon spotted the trap. Greig, unfortunately, did not. As Greig bobbed back up, the elbow of the returning arm cracked him across the cheek. The impact was sharp. Solid. Greig staggered, his vision blurred by a flash of white.

"Kick right, kick right!" Hoon bellowed.

Greig swung blindly with his leg and felt the jolt of it connecting with Tony's thigh, just above the knee. It wasn't a particularly graceful move, but it was enough to make the Irish lad hiss in pain and dissuade him from following through with his attack.

Tony grimaced as his weight went down on the leg. He hobbled backwards, finally bringing his arms up to protect himself. He shot a look over to the edge of the circle, expecting to find his brother there offering advice. Instead, he found Hoon grinning at him and flashing a double thumbs-up like he was auditioning for a West End musical adaptation of *Happy Days*.

And then, with a roar, Greig's shoulder connected with him just below waist height. With his leg injured, Tony had nowhere to go but down, but he punched and gouged and grabbed all the way to the floor.

The sound the Tiger's head made when it hit the concrete immediately silenced half of the room, though the eruption of gleeful cheering from the other half more than made up for it.

Arms that had been attempting to wrap themselves around Greig's neck flopped limply onto the ground. A series of big, heaving convulsions from the Irishman sent Greig scrambling back off him, his face a mask of shock and horror.

"Shit. Shit. What's happening? What's happening?" he babbled. Eyes filled with tears flitted from the motionless Tony to Hoon and back again.

Another convulsion. An arching of the back. And then, with a sound like a long, drawn-out sigh of relief, Tony fell still.

"Wh-what's happening?" Greig muttered, then he cried out as strong arms caught him from behind and dragged him backwards. He tried to twist free, to swing a punch, then realised the men were pulling him into a celebratory hug, jumping up and down with their winning betting slips thrust to the sky.

By the time he wrenched himself away, Hoon was kneeling over the downed Irishman. He had two fingers on his neck, and his ear angled so he could listen at the lad's mouth while watching for the rise and fall of his chest.

"Get your fucking hands off him!" Tony's brother barked, marching out of the crowd. A glare from Hoon stopped him in his tracks.

"Don't even think about it, pal," he warned, then he straightened and pointed to the nearest bouncer. "You. Get a fucking ambulance." When the man made no move to comply, Hoon clapped his hands like he was trying to startle him into life. "Well, don't just stand there staring like a panda at a fucking porno, move!"

The reply, when it came, did not come from the security man. Instead, it came as from on high.

"I'm afraid that's not how it works," purred the skeleton in the red dress. "Everyone knows the risks. Everyone understands."

Hoon fixed her with a look that would've made most people turn and run in the opposite direction. Amanda didn't flinch, though. She held the stare, her champagne still held at shoulder height, the suggestion of a smile playing across her lips.

"He could fucking die," he told her, which drew a sob of anguish from Greig, who was pacing back and forth now, both hands clutching his head.

The crowd had fallen almost silent now. Fights were something they saw every night, but this? This was something different. This was something new.

"He knew the risks," Amanda said. "He knew what he was getting into."

"Oh, fuck off! He's a young lad!" Hoon cried, jumping to his feet. He stabbed a finger towards Tony's older brother. "With just this bag of boiled cocks to advise him. He is *not* fucking dying here. Not like this. Even if I have to go steal a fucking ambulance and bring it here myself."

Hoon became dimly aware of the men behind him. There

were four of them, all from the security team, and all with the same steroid-inflated physiques. Two of them had moved into position on either side of Greig, too, although from the look on the younger man's face, one strong gust of wind would be enough to knock him over at this point.

"Very well. If you feel so strongly about it, we'll take care of it," Amanda said, still nursing that glass, still smirking, still radiating a level of confidence Hoon had rarely seen in anyone but himself. "We won't let him die. You have my word. But you are *not,* under any circumstances, bringing an ambulance here."

"The day a big boney bag of right angles tells me what to do, is the day I fucking die, sweetheart," Hoon retorted. "I'll do what I fucking like."

It was the silence that told him he may have made a mistake. It had been quiet a moment before, when the crowd had been watching and listening to the exchange, but now they were into pin-drop territory. The only sounds in the place were Greig's fast, heavy breathing, and the creaking of shoe leather somewhere at Hoon's back.

He could take them, he thought. He'd have to move now, and move fast, but he reckoned he could catch them off-guard and cut all three of them down.

And then...

What? What happened then? How did he possibly help this kid lying broken on the floor?

And how did he do it without blowing his chance of finding Caroline?

"Sorry," he said, gritting his teeth. "That was out of line."

Up on her raised platform, Amanda held his gaze as she sipped her drink, then waved a hand. "Let's put that outburst down to first night nerves," she said. "And let's make sure it doesn't happen again, shall we? Hmm?"

Hoon conceded with a nod. "Fine. Aye."

"Good," Amanda said. "Now, as I say, we'll take care of Mr Mulligan here, and I think that you..." She pointed to Hoon and Greig with her glass. "Both of you, that is... should get out of here before I change my mind."

CHAPTER EIGHTEEN

GREIG'S FLAT was in the south-east of London. At least, so he said, but the length of time it took the taxi to get there—and the money it had cost—made Hoon doubt whether the flat was technically in London at all. He wasn't entirely convinced it was even in England, for that matter.

They had travelled out past Bexleyheath, Greig had explained—so far past it, in fact, that they were dangerously close to being in Dartford.

Were either of those places still London? Hoon had no idea. It didn't look much like London. It was leafier, and the oppressive tower blocks had given way to terraced houses and small gatherings of flats in groups of sixes and sevens. Once out of the taxi, it was one of these low-rise blocks that Greig had led Hoon towards.

They'd barely been given a chance for Greig to gather up his clothes before being escorted from the premises, and his face —including the travesty of a beard—was caked in dried blood, and lumpy with bumps and bruising.

He'd insisted he could get home on his own, but Hoon was having none of it.

"You're in bad shape, son," he'd said. "My conscience just won't let me," he'd said.

Those weren't the reasons, of course. Not really. If Hoon still had a chance of getting closer to this Godfrey West fucker and of finding Caroline, then Greig was currently his best shot.

Although, it had to be said that the lad had seemed relieved to have company. He'd asked a dozen questions—"Do you think he'll be alright? What's going to happen to him? Am I going to get in trouble?"—and insisted several times that it had been an accident, that he was sorry, and that he really hoped the poor guy was OK.

By the time they arrived, Hoon was grateful to no longer be trapped in the car with the chatterbox big bastard.

From the outside, the flat was... not a complete shit-tip. This was the kindest thing Hoon could think to say about it, though he was surprised he was able to be even that generous. Given what Greig had said about his money problems, and how desperate he obviously was for cash, Hoon had been bracing himself for something with a definite third-world feel to it. The fact that all the block's windows were present and accounted for was a pleasant surprise.

It went downhill quite quickly when Greig unlocked the building's front door. The thick, pungent aroma of weeks-old rubbish raced through the gap to greet them. The heavy door scraped on the stone floor as Greig shunted it inwards enough for them both to squeeze through into a narrow, dimly lit hallway with paint peeling from the walls.

"I'm fine from here," Greig said, but Hoon countered with a shake of his head.

"Are you fuck. I said I'd get you home, and I'm getting you home," he said, and he tried to usher the younger man on.

Greig shuffled a single step, but then turned and squared his shoulders towards the older man, blocking his path. "You're not... You're not going to do anything, are you? Because... I won't let you."

"Do anything?" Hoon asked. "Like what?"

"Like... I don't know. You're not going to hurt them?"

"Hurt them?"

"Because, if you try, I'll put you on your arse," Greig said, gritting his teeth like he was showing off his fangs. "I mean it, I'll fucking... I'll do you in, if I have to."

Hoon regarded him in silence for a few seconds, then snorted out a laugh and patted him on the shoulder. "Aye, good one, son," he said. With a gentle shove and a nod, he tried once again to make Greig walk on.

Greig, however, was going nowhere.

"Promise me," he demanded. "Promise me you're not going to do anything to hurt them."

Hoon tutted. "Fuck's sake, son. Where's this come from? I've done nothing but stick my neck out for you all night. I even paid for that fucking taxi! And by the way, wee word of advice for next time, you might have told me before I offered to do that just how fucking far away it was. I mean, Jesus Christ. They can send people into fucking space these days for less than that taxi cost."

"We could've got an Uber," Greig said.

Hoon's lips drew back into a sneer. "If I want to be driven around by a clueless bastard who just happens to have access to Google fucking Maps, I can steal a car and do that myself."

"You still haven't promised," Greig pointed out, getting back to the matter at hand. "Promise me. Swear you're not going to hurt them, or you're not coming in."

"Oh, for God's sake." Hoon rubbed his eyes, sighed, then held three fingers up like he was taking some sort of oath. "Fine. I swear. I fucking cross my heart and pinkie swear that I'm no' going to hurt your lassie or your baby. Alright? Happy?"

Greig didn't look entirely convinced, but he gritted his teeth and gave a single nod of his head.

"I mean, no' unless the wee man starts shit first," Hoon said. "Because, if he does, then I'm liable to kick off *big time*."

Greig stared back at him in mute horror. Hoon sighed again, and blew out his cheeks.

"That was a joke, son," he said. "I don't actually think your baby's going to pick a fucking fight with me."

"Oh. Right. Aye." He looked Hoon up and down, then began to hobble along the hallway. "Well then, I suppose you might as well come in."

———

The flat was a studio with a combined kitchen and living area, and a small bedroom and bathroom visible through the half-open doors in the hall. It was on the second floor, making it the uppermost apartment in the compact block.

It was sparsely decorated, and what little furniture was in the place had been cobbled together or improvised. A low-armed couch, its floral pattern faded and worn, took pride of place in the centre of the living room, turned so it faced towards a thirty-two-inch supermarket telly, and away from the dated, sagging kitchen area with its cluttered worktops and full sink.

The untidiness wasn't confined to the kitchen, either. Toys, clothes, and all the other bric-a-brac that came along with having a young child in the house, lay scattered across the floor, or draped over the back and sides of the couch, or piled up on top of a padded footstool that had been pushed against the wall beside the TV cabinet.

Most of the walls were covered in woodchip wallpaper. It had been painted so often over the years that a couple of scratches on the wall showed a rainbow of creams, magnolias, and eggshell shades below. Scrape all that paint away, and you'd probably buy yourself a couple of inches of space on every side of the room.

There was a Moses Basket-style crib on a stand in the corner. It was devoid of its occupant when Greig led Hoon inside.

Instead, the baby lay on a towel on the floor, wide awake and kicking his legs like a frog launching itself off its lily pad. His nappy was off, and he seemed to be thoroughly enjoying the feeling of fresh air on his undercarriage.

But then, Hoon thought, who could blame him for that?

A girl, even younger-looking than Greig, knelt over the baby, tickling his tummy and making *goo-goo* noises with an enthusiasm that was only slightly tempered by her obvious exhaustion. Her hair was on the redder side of blonde, tied back in a ponytail, and badly in need of a wash. She wore an over-sized *Guns 'n' Roses* t-shirt that reached to just above her bare knees.

She looked up at the sound of Greig entering, and her face rattled through a range of expressions in under a second. It started with relief and ended with horror, with brief intermissions at confusion and trepidation along the way.

"Who's that?" she demanded. Her accent was more or less identical to Greig's, and Hoon immediately wrote them up as childhood sweethearts.

Even as she spoke, she angled herself to block Hoon's view of the baby, and the look of horror that she had momentarily settled on now crystallised into something stern and threatening.

Maybe Greig wasn't the one who should've been out there fighting tonight.

"It's fine, Cassie. He's just... He's a guy," Greig mumbled. Clearly, he was getting the same *don't fuck with me* vibe from the young woman as Hoon was.

"I can see he's a guy, Greig. *What* guy? Why's he here?"

"He, eh... He works for Frankie," Greig said. He looked down at her on the floor, and there was something very deliberate in the way he widened his eyes. "You remember Frankie, Cass."

There was that look of horror again. "*Frankie* Frankie?" she asked, and her voice broke into a whisper at the mention of the name. Her gaze shifted to Hoon, but then darted back to Greig, like it didn't dare linger on the stranger. "Oh, God. Oh no."

"Whoa, whoa, back up, cool the fucking beans," Hoon said, raising both hands. "I told you, I don't work *for* Frankie, I work *with* Frankie, and even then, it's more..." The words tumbled into silence. He tutted and shook his head. "Actually, that's all bollocks. Frankie's dead."

Greig and Cassie both stared wide-eyed at Hoon.

"Dead?" Greig said.

"Aye. I mean, I assume so, anyway. He got on the wrong side of his uncle, and I'd be highly fucking doubtful if he came out the other side of that without all his bits and pieces in bits and pieces."

Greig appeared to have run out of questions, and just stared blankly while he processed this news.

Fortunately, his fiancée had enough for both of them. "When did that happen? Are you taking over, or something? Is that why you're here? You're collecting his debts?"

"A few months back," Hoon said, raising a thumb like he was ticking off the questions. He thought for a moment, then raised the rest of his fingers in one go. "And no to the rest. I'm not here to cause trouble, and I'm not after your money. As far as I know, nobody is."

"He's dead?" Greig asked again, apparently still playing catch-up. "What do you mean, he's dead?

"Fuck me, is he always this slow?" Hoon asked the woman on the floor. "Or did he just take one too many blows to the fucking head tonight? I mean he's dead, son. He's deceased.

No more. He's expired. He's an ex-scumbag. He rests in fucking peace." Hoon shrugged. "Well, hopefully no' too much peace."

He looked from Greig to Cassie and back again. Neither of them, it seemed, had got the *Monty Python* reference.

Kids.

"Did... did you win?" Cassie asked. "The fight, did you win?"

"Uh, yeah," Greig said, though he practically bowed his head in shame. "I did. Sort of."

"Sort of?"

"There was... an accident," Greig said. "The other guy, he... He sort of..."

"He's going to be fine," Hoon said. "He hit his head, but he's going to be fine. They're going to take care of him."

"You believe that?" Greig asked, and there was a note of hope to it. A wish that it might be true. "You think they're going to get him help?"

"I do," Hoon said. He had no idea if they would, of course—and he had his doubts—but the lad didn't need to carry that on his shoulders.

Greig smiled. "Yeah. Yeah, they'll get him help," he agreed. "He'll be fine."

"Of course he'll be fine. They're hardly going to leave him injured, are they?" Cassie said, practically laughing off Greig's concerns. She had more pressing concerns of her own, after all. "So... you got the money?" she asked. "They paid you?"

Greig's smile faded. He side-eyed Hoon for a second, then shook his head. "Not exactly. I mean, not yet, but I'm sure..."

"Jesus, Greig! Why not? You said you were going to get paid! Three hundred quid, that's what you said we'd get. We need that money!"

"Yeah, I know, babe, but—"

"Report them," Cassie instructed. "Report them to, I don't

know, the Boxing Commission, or something. Is that what they're called? Report them. They can't just keep your money."

Hoon groaned.

Boxing Commission.

She didn't know. Not really. She knew he was fighting, but she thought it was a legitimate bout with rules, and safety, and other quaint notions like that. She had no idea he'd been fighting for his life in a pub cellar.

"It's not that simple, babe."

"So, what? You're just going to let them walk all over you?" Cassie demanded. "Because I'm not. Give me their number, and I'll—"

"Hold your fucking horses," Hoon announced. He had his wallet in his hand and was counting out a bundle of notes.

Greig stared in confusion at the cash for a moment, then firmly shook his head. "No. We don't want another loan. We can't. Not after last time."

"It's no' a fucking loan," Hoon told him. He thrust the bundle of notes at the younger man.

Greig eyed the offered cash with suspicion. "Then... what is it?" he asked.

"The fuck does it look like? Three hundred quid. It's your payment."

"But... they didn't pay me."

"No, they paid me," Hoon said. "As your manager. I'm not going to take my cut this time, but from now on, I get ten percent."

"I don't need a manager," Greig said.

"Oh, right," Hoon said, taking the money back. "And here I thought you'd walked out of there empty fucking handed, then needed me to pay your taxi fare home. I didn't realise you had everything in hand."

"Greig," Cassie said, and Hoon knew that with just that one word, she'd won his argument for him.

Greig hesitated, but only for a second. He nodded, muttered, "Cheers," and then accepted the cash that Hoon pressed into his palm.

"You earned it. This was all you," Hoon said. "You did good."

"Uh, thanks." He smiled. Nodded. "And yeah. I suppose I did, didn't I?"

"Alright, let's no' get fucking ahead of ourselves, son. It was skin of your teeth stuff for a while there, let's no' kid ourselves. You're lucky it was a taxi you left in, and no' a fucking ambulance," Hoon told him. He turned to Cassie and started referring to the stunned Greig like he was no longer in the room.

"We need to get some ice on that face of his, by the way. Unless you want him giving the wee man there nightmares for the rest of his fucking life. You got any peas in the freezer?"

Cassie didn't have to think about the answer. "No," she said. "We don't like peas."

"And? No one likes peas, but it's just a fucking thing you have around."

"We've got fish fingers," Greig offered, which earned him withering looks from both of the other adults in the room. Even the baby appeared to do a double-take.

"I'm no' sure a box of fucking fish fingers is going to mould to the shape of your face in quite the same way, son, but fuck it, needs must. I'm game to give it a go if you are."

"Could you not swear?" Cassie said.

Hoon frowned, then blinked several times, like his brain was struggling to process this request. "Sorry, what?"

"Could you not swear, please?" Cassie said again. Despite the addition of the 'please' it sounded even less like a request and more of an instruction than it had the previous time. "We don't want Benji copying that sort of language."

"Ah well, you're in luck, then. He's, what, three months old?

He might as well be a bag of fucking Spam at this point. He can't copy fuck-all yet."

"He's four months. And he's taking it all in," Cassie insisted.

Greig quietly cleared his throat. "It's true. They're like sponges at this age," he added. "There was a thing on YouTube."

"Jesus. Well, far be it from me to argue with the fount of all fucking knowledge that is YouTube," Hoon said. He looked to the ceiling, shook his head, then tutted. "Fine. I'll stop fucking swearing right after this fucking sentence. Alright? Happy? Wee Bonzo there, or whatever the fu—" He gritted his teeth. "Or whatever he's called, is safe from my corrupting influence."

"Thank you," Cassie said. "And his name's Benji."

"Cheers, man," Greig added.

Hoon rolled his eyes. "Aye, whatever." He pointed to the couch. "Now, get yourself sat down, while I go find them fish fingers."

Before he could get to the freezer, a sudden rasping *buzz* from a handset on the wall rang out, startling Hoon to the point where he almost—but not quite—broke his promise not to swear.

He looked back at Greig and Cassie. They were both completely motionless, like time itself had frozen around them.

"Who's that going to be?" Hoon asked, indicating the now silent intercom.

"Someone at the front door. Downstairs," Greig said. He spoke in a hushed whisper, like he was worried whoever was out there might hear him. "It's an intercom buzzer thing."

"Aye, I understand the concept, son," Hoon said. "You've got no idea who it is?"

"We don't know anyone," Cassie said, her voice even quieter than her partner's. "No one who would be coming over at this time, anyway."

Hoon sidled to the window, where a pair of thin yellow

curtains hung from a rail improvised from a bamboo cane and a couple of screw-in hooks. He cautiously nudged the outside edge of one of the curtains aside, and pressed himself in close to the wall, trying to see down into the car park below.

A black Ford pick-up with a hardtop canopy covering the flatbed rear, stood idling in the centre of the block's shared parking area. Its headlights were picking out flecks of drizzle that had recently started to fall, its wipers *thunk-thunking* a steady rhythm.

"Who is it?" Greig asked. "Can you see?"

"I don't know," Hoon admitted. He beckoned the younger man over and they swapped places. "Any idea?"

Greig shook his head. "No. I don't know. Maybe—"

The buzzer went again, and this time it was Benji who took the brunt of the fright. His legs jerked, his face screwed up, and he let out a cry that threatened to wake the neighbours, and not necessarily just the ones in this block.

"Oh, shh, shh, you're alright, baby, you're alright," Cassie whispered, picking the child up and holding him to her chest.

Hoon marched towards the intercom, which drew a hissed, "What are you doing?" from Greig.

"They're not going to go away," Hoon said. "And they know we're in here, so might as well find out who it is."

He snatched up the handset before anyone could object, and spat, "Yes, what?" into the mouthpiece.

There was an echo down the line that, combined with the screaming baby, made the response hard to make out. He picked out his name, though—the fake one given to him by Miles at MI5—and what sounded very much like a question left hanging.

"Aye. That's me. Who's this I'm talking to?"

Again, the reply was garbled, but Hoon got the gist of it. "No, I'm not buzzing you in until you tell me who you are."

Another blast of feedback. Another few jumbled words. He

understood the meaning of the message, if not the actual content, and after a glance at the other three occupants of the room, he gave his final response.

"Wait there. I'll come to you," he said, then he replaced the handset with enough force to crack the flimsy plastic, and turned to Greig. "What's your phone number?" he asked, fishing his phone from his pocket.

It was the one that had been included in his official Stephen White Prison Pack, and he hadn't taken any time to figure out the workings of it. He tossed it to Greig, and told him to add himself to the contacts, then continued issuing instructions.

"When I go out, you keep the door locked unless I phone you, alright? Not text. Phone. If I say the words 'monkey tits' then do not under any circumstances open the door, alright?"

"Monkey tits?" asked Greig, looking up from Hoon's mobile.

"Aye. Monkey tits."

"Why monkey tits?"

"Because it's no' a phrase that's likely to come up in casual conversation, is it? Monkey tits. Nobody just says 'monkey tits.'"

"Can we stop saying it now, please?" Cassie objected, and she shot a meaningful look at the crying baby in her arms.

Hoon groaned. "Jesus. Fine. I'll say 'monkey breasts.' That better? If I phone, and you hear me say monkey breasts, you'll know I'm being forced to make the call. If that happens, keep the door locked, and call the polis."

Greig nodded and handed the phone back. "Gotcha," he said.

Cassie, however, was determined to drill down further. "But... they'll know that's why you're saying it," she pointed out. "Like you said yourself, nobody would say that for no reason, so they'll know it's some sort of code."

"So?" Hoon asked, returning the phone to his pocket.

"So, why not just say, 'It's a trap. Don't let me in'?" Cassie asked.

Hoon opened his mouth like he was going to offer some pithy and clever explanation, hung there saying nothing for a moment, then nodded. "Aye. Fine. I'll say that, then," he decided. "In the meantime, stay here, stay put, and keep the front door shut. Alright?"

There were nods all around. Hoon beckoned for Greig to follow him, then headed out into the hallway.

"Shut it and lock it at my back," he said, once they reached the door.

Barring a jump from one of the windows, it was the only way in and out of the flat. It seemed heavy enough, with a couple of locks and a sliding security chain. It wouldn't keep anyone out forever, but it would buy Greig and Cassie enough time to arm themselves, if it came to it.

"With a bit of luck, I'll be back in a few minutes. If not, I'll be in touch. Alright?"

"Uh, yeah. Yeah, OK," Greig said. He put a hand on Hoon's shoulder before the door could be opened. "Sorry. This is a bit embarrassing, but what was your name again? I know you told me before the fight, but I was a bit frazzled."

"It's Stephen," Hoon lied, and he felt a tiny pang of guilt about that. "Stephen White."

"Right. Yeah. That's it," Greig said. He stepped back, making room for Hoon to open the door. "Good luck, Stephen."

"Aye. Cheers," Hoon told him, then he pulled open the door, stepped out onto the upstairs landing.

There was a *clang* as the door was slammed closed behind him, followed by the rattling of its locks.

Hoon shivered in the sudden cold. The flat hadn't been particularly warm, but here on the top floor landing, the air had a real bite to it. He felt the skin on his arms sprout goosebumps and the fine hairs on the back of his neck standing on end.

The cold air wasn't static, either. It was moving. *Gusting.* Almost like someone had left the downstairs door wide open.

Shite.

He turned too late to avoid the black sack being pulled down over his head. He grabbed for it, blinded, but something solid crunched into his ribs, forcing him to bring his arms down to protect himself.

A drawstring was pulled tight. The bag got a grip around his throat. He twisted, drove an elbow back, but found nothing but empty space.

A lot of empty space.

His ankle rolled. He sensed a yawning void in front of him.

Someone hissed, "Catch him!" but he was already falling, head first, down the stairs.

Pain fractured across the top of his skull. Blood filled his mouth. The rest of him tumbled, end over end, then stopped, upside-down against what he guessed was a wall.

The last thing he heard was a man's voice, angry and exasperated.

"I *told* you we should've just asked him," it said.

And then, the darkness inside the hood became deeper and richer, and he was dragged down by the long, flowing tendrils of sleep.

CHAPTER NINETEEN

HOON WOKE up in a bed that was neither his own, nor familiar. It was ridiculously comfortable, though, and despite his brain screaming at him to get up, his body was determined to enjoy the soft mattress and silken sheets for as long as it possibly could.

This gave him a few moments to try to figure out where he was. The hood had been removed, and he didn't appear to be restrained to the bed in any way. There was a dull, lingering ache on the top of his head, just above his hairline, that became sharper and more insistent when he reached a hand up to tentatively explore the damage.

There was a lump there. Nothing too major, but big enough. If he'd had longer hair, it might've gone unnoticed, but on his head of short stubble it'd rise up like a mountain ridge.

Despite his body's continuing protests, he summoned the strength to slide himself up towards the head of the bed. Pain pressed down on his skull, and the dimly-lit room became a nauseating swirl of plush decor and tasteful furniture, before gradually settling back down again.

There was a TV fixed to one wall. A fifty-incher, maybe

more. Below it was a desk, on which sat a tray with tea-making facilities and some packets of biscuits he didn't recognise, but that looked like some right old artisanal gobwankery. They'd be olive and mascarpone oatcakes, or bramble and yoghurt short-bread, or some other such bollocks.

A single armchair was tucked away in the corner, and there were far too many cushions and pillows piled up beside him on the king-sized bed.

So, he was in a hotel, then. A posh one. This was better than being folded up in the back of the Ford pick-up, which was where he'd expected to wake up as he was slipping into uncon-sciousness. Although it meant that he'd been out of the game for far longer than he'd have liked.

There were two doors standing almost side by side across from the window. One had a switch mounted on the wall beside it. Bathroom. The other door had to be the way out, then. Unlikely the fuckers back at the flat would've gone to all this bother just to give him a nice night in a hotel, so the room was almost certainly being guarded.

The window it was, then.

The curtains were thick and heavy, and it took him almost half a minute to figure out where the break in them was. He threw them open and immediately recoiled at the morning sunshine streaming in through the glass.

"Jesus fuck!"

The dull ache in his head roared up to full volume. He screwed his eyes shut, grabbed a handful of curtain fabric, and used it to hold himself upright as he waited for the pain and the blindness to fade.

It occurred to him, as he was standing there with his eyes closed, that he was not wearing the clothes he had been wearing when he'd been grabbed. Or, for that matter, many clothes at all.

Socks? Yes. Underwear...? He ran a hand down to his hip. Yes. Everything else, though, had been stripped off him.

"This just gets better and fucking better."

He forced an eye open. It took a few seconds to adjust to the brightness, then the other opened, too. There were blue skies over London. A few planes trailed white plumes across the sky. In the middle distance, the Shard and the London Eye both stood proudly amongst the city's skyline. Beyond them, Greater London stretched off towards the horizon.

He quickly deduced two things from this view. Firstly, he was high up. Too high up to attempt to go clambering out of the window, even if it had been possible to open—which it wasn't.

Secondly, he had been unconscious for several hours at least. A blow to the head wouldn't have been enough to keep him under for that long without lasting brain damage.

He quickly ran through his personal info in his head— name, date of birth, home address—then rattled through most of the nine times table before concluding that his mental faculties were still for the most part intact.

If not the wallop to the skull, then...

He rotated his shoulders and hugged himself, patting down both upper arms. He soon found an aching spot on his left bicep where a needle had gone in. They'd drugged him.

The absolute fuckers!

He started for the door, anger uncoiling itself like a serpent in his stomach. They'd attacked him, abducted him, then pumped him full of God knew what to keep him unconscious. Any one of which would've been bang out of fucking order, quite frankly, but all three? No. No way he was letting them off with that. No-siree-fucking-Bob.

Sense prevailed just before he reached the door of his room. He had no idea who was out there. He had no clue what he was walking into. He needed to be prepared. More prepared than running out in just his pants and socks, at any rate.

He listened at the door, his ear pressed almost to the wood. There was a low murmur of voices, but he couldn't gauge the distance. It could be a couple of people talking very quietly right outside, or a regular volume conversation somewhere along the corridor.

For safety, he had to assume the former. Two guards, then, at least.

He turned his back to the door and took in the room, initially searching for a weapon, but quickly becoming side-tracked by the neatly folded bundle of clothes sitting on one of the shelves of the room's storage unit.

His pineapple shirt and trousers had been laundered, ironed, and left there for him. He glowered at them for a few moments, like they'd somehow betrayed him by collaborating with the enemy, but then he succumbed to their charms and quickly pulled them on.

This immediately made him feel better. More in control. He was no longer semi-naked. Things were headed in the right direction.

He couldn't find his shoes anywhere, which was annoying. Everything was easier with shoes. Everything he had in mind, at least. Still, the clothes were a bonus, so he wasn't complaining too much.

Finding a weapon was more difficult. There was nothing obviously sharp in the room, and while the TV looked heavy, it was a bit too cumbersome to effectively wield in a fight.

There was a notepad on the bedside table, but the pen had been removed. Shame. You could do a lot of damage with a biro if you put your mind to it.

Still, the printed logo at the top of the pad at least told him where he was. The McGinlay Hotel on Park Lane. He'd never heard of it, so the information wasn't particularly helpful, but he filed it away for later.

There was no phone in the room, and his pockets were

empty, so there was no saying where his mobile was. No means of contacting the outside world, then.

He sat on the end of the bed and considered his options. They'd taken care to remove everything stabby. There wasn't anything heavy and club-like, and breaking up the furniture to make one would inevitably bring the guards rushing in.

"Aye, well, you forced my fucking hand on this one," he muttered, then he got up, quietly filled the kettle from the bathroom tap, and set it on to boil.

While he waited for the water to heat up, he removed one of his socks, stuffed one of the room's teacups inside all the way to the toe, then gave it an experimental swish. The cup was small, chunky, and angular in all the right places. With enough of a swing, it would do some damage. Not much, but hopefully enough for him to turn the tables on whoever was waiting out there in the corridor.

The water reached boiling point, and the power clicked off. Hoon removed the lid, then picked up the kettle in his left hand, while holding onto his cup-in-a-sock weapon with his right. He hummed quietly to himself as he crossed to the exit, pushed down the handle with an elbow, and yanked the door open with a foot.

"Right, you fucks—" he began, then he stopped.

He had emerged not into a corridor as he'd been expecting, but into a living area that would've been large enough to accommodate the boat he'd been living on for the past few months, with room left over for a couple of couches and a good-sized coffee table.

It was a light, airy space, with furnishings that managed to look both antique and brand new at the same time, and a wall of floor-to-ceiling windows that offered a panoramic view of the city.

Most notable of all, on a raised platform by the window, a woman lay in a free-standing iron bathtub, only her head and one hand visible above the sea of foamy white bubbles. The hand clutched what appeared to be the same champagne glass she'd been holding the night before, and as Hoon clapped eyes on her, a lopsided smile played across her garish red lips.

"Good morning, Stephen," she drawled, and there was a twinkle of mischief in her eyes. "So nice of you to finally join me."

CHAPTER TWENTY

HOON, after concluding that there was no immediate threat—or not one that warranted a face full of scalding water and a mug to the side of the head, at any rate—placed both weapons on a glass-topped coffee table, and asked the question that had been on his mind since he'd first woken up.

"What the fuck is this?"

Amanda, the woman in the bathtub, continued to smirk. "What the fuck is what?"

"This. Everything. Why the fuck am I here? Why was I drugged? Why is there a bath standing on an expensive fucking carpet? What clump-eyed fudd thought that was a good idea?"

"I did, actually," Amanda said. "I like to lie here and enjoy the view." Her other arm slid out from below the bubbles and she tapped the curled rim of the tub. "Come. Sit. Join me."

"Nah, you're alright, hen," Hoon replied. "I'm no' in the mood for... well, any of this shite, really. So, are you going to tell me why I'm here?" He pointed to an enormous curved TV that sat on a glass unit in front of one of the couches. "Or am I going to see if the cable of that telly stretches as far as your bath there?"

Amanda laughed. It was a delicate and musical giggle, but it sounded wrong, like some of the notes were being played out of order. She took a deep breath, then slipped down under the surface of the water, leaving only the arm with the champagne glass sticking up above her like a periscope.

When she emerged again, she kicked herself higher than before, so her shoulders and the top of her flat, bony chest crested above the waves. Her hair was fizzing with foamy bubbles, and she ran a wet hand down her face, clearing the suds away.

"Sorry about..." She gestured with her champagne flute. "... everything. I had asked some of my assistants to go extend an invitation for you to come here to talk."

"Extend an invitation? Fuck me. Is that what you call it?" Hoon spat. "I'd have loved to have seen your fucking birthday parties when you were wee. Just a load of frightened five-year-olds waking up wondering where the fuck they were."

"I didn't expect them to be quite so forceful," Amanda told him. "The head injury was accidental. I'm told you fell down some steps. Still, I can't help but feel partly responsible."

"*Partly* fucking responsible? Well, that's very fucking big of you, thanks very much," Hoon retorted. "And what about the drugs you pumped into me? What fucking degree of responsibility are you taking for that?"

"That was actually my... employer's suggestion," Amanda admitted, hesitating a bit on the word choice. "It was late, and he thought we both needed our beauty sleep. He felt it best that we help you rest so we could tackle this fresh this morning."

"Tackle what?"

"Why, your future, of course. Yours and young Greig's."

A memory from the night before jolted him so hard he physically twitched. He'd just stepped out of the flat when the bag had been pulled over his head. Had the door been closed behind him? He couldn't remember. Had the bastards gone inside?

"What have you done to him?" Hoon demanded.

"Greig? Nothing. I give you my word," Amanda promised. "He and his family are fine. In fact, they're better than fine. I wasn't happy with how things were left yesterday, so I had one of my assistants post his payment through the door of his flat. Plus a little extra for the inconvenience. He earned it, after all." That smirk returned. "You both did. You put on quite the show, the two of you. You made quite the team."

"And that's why you knocked me out and brought me here, is it?" Hoon asked. "So you could fucking butter me up?"

"No. I brought you here so I could offer you an opportunity. Both of you, in fact."

"Seems a fucking extreme way to go about it," Hoon said. He folded his arms to signal he still wasn't happy, but then nodded for her to continue. "Go on then, let's hear it."

She took a sip of her champagne, then slid down until her shoulders were covered by the bubbles again. "I know who you are."

Hoon felt a fluttering in his chest, like his heart had skipped a couple of beats.

"Do you now?" he asked.

"I do. I know why you really came to the fight last night. And I know why you lied about your real identity."

Shit. *Shit.*

Don't look at the door. Don't look for an exit.

"I don't have the first fucking clue what you're on about, hen," Hoon insisted.

Amanda giggled her out of tune laugh again. "Yes. You do. Do you want to know what else I know?"

"Is it the lottery numbers?" Hoon asked. *Stall for time. Figure out the next step.* "Because if it is, I'm all ears."

"I know what you're looking for," Amanda continued. "And, well, I'd like to help."

Hoon's eyes narrowed. "Help?"

"If you'll let me."

"And what is it, exactly, that you think I want?"

"Well, it's obvious," Amanda said. "You might think you're hiding it, but I know exactly why you're here." She paused for a moment, letting him stew. "Glory."

Some of the tension that had been bunching up Hoon's muscles eased off. "Glory? You think that's what I'm after?"

"I do," Amanda confirmed. "I could see it right away, the moment I set eyes on you. I knew you weren't like the rest of them. See, most of the people that turn up to the fights, they don't belong in that world. Not really. They like to visit, yes. To take holidays in it. But they don't belong there. But you do, don't you, Stephen? You belong down here in the dark with us."

Hoon looked very deliberately around the plush room and out through the towering windows. "You've got a strange fucking concept of what darkness looks like."

"It comes in different shades, Stephen, as I think you're probably well aware," the woman in the bathtub replied. "I knew you weren't with Greig. But he was on his own, and I didn't fancy his chances, and when I saw you... Well, I saw the benefits of putting you both together. That's what I do. I see things. Connections. Possibilities. Opportunities. I'm told I have an eye for that sort of thing." She raised her glass in toast. "And, what do you know, it worked out rather nicely."

"No' for the lad who got his head smashed in," Hoon pointed out.

"Taken care of. As promised," Amanda assured him. "He's recovering as we speak. He's going to be just fine. We are only as good as our word, Stephen, are we not? And I gave you mine."

"Right, fine. Let's hear this fucking opportunity, then, so I can tell you to ram it up your arse and get going."

She giggled again. "You're refreshing, Stephen, you really are," she said. The laughter died in her throat. "But I'd be careful. What is it they say? 'It's all fun and games until somebody loses an eye.' I like you. Let's not do anything to change that. My employer wouldn't like that."

Amanda scooped up a little handful of the soapy bubbles, studied them like they were precious gems, then blew them off her fingers.

"We're down a fighter," she said. "He was supposed to be taking part in one of our... more prestigious events later this week. Bigger audience. Better quality, too. People more like us. People who inhabit the dark. But wealthy. Very wealthy. He's had to drop out, unfortunately."

"Bottle it, did he?" Hoon asked.

"No. He had whisky thrown in his eyes and his head smashed off a stone floor," Amanda said, and the look on her face said she was toying with him. "Perhaps you're familiar with the incident?"

"Might be ringing a bell."

"We had high hopes for young Anthony. He needed a rebrand, of course—I mean, Tony the Tiger? I don't know what they were thinking. But he had potential. He had scope. And now, thanks partly to you, he has a feeding tube and a catheter."

"I mean..." Hoon shrugged. "Oops, I suppose."

Amanda waved her Champagne glass like she was dismissing an apology Hoon hadn't given.

"It's fine. Don't worry."

"I wasn't."

"But it does leave us with a problem. His debut in the big leagues was planned for Friday. Last night meant to be plain sailing for him—an easy victory to give him some form for the betting at the weekend. And then you happened. You and your new protégé."

"Sounds like you've got a problem," Hoon replied.

"One of us does, certainly," Amanda said. "But, thankfully, we also have a solution. See, I thought Greig was nothing. Fodder. Collateral damage, call him what you will. But last night, when he refused to attack while his opponent was blinded?"

She drew in a breath and gave a full-body shudder that formed ripples across the surface of her bathwater.

"That changed things. You could feel it, couldn't you? In the crowd. Even people who'd bet against him had to respect that. They had to. And that's when we knew he had it. The thing more important than fighting ability, more important than strength, or speed, or stamina."

"And what would that be?" Hoon asked.

"Story!" Amanda beamed. "The noble warrior. Decent, through and through. A white knight come to conquer the darkness. A *hero*."

"A hero? Him?" Hoon asked, jabbing a thumb back over his shoulder as if Greig was standing right there behind him. "Are we talking about the same guy? Shite beard, almost got his head kicked in?"

"You mean snatching victory from the jaws of near-certain defeat?" Amanda said. "Yes. Exactly! Everyone loves an underdog, don't they? A noble underdog fighting to provide for his family? That's not just a fighter, that's a *draw*. People will come to see that. To see *him*."

"And what's in it for him?" Hoon asked. "Aside from getting leathered into a fucking coma, I mean."

"Money, obviously," Amanda said. "Five thousand appearance fee. Potentially a lot more, depending on how far he goes on the day."

"And what's in it for me?"

A slender bare leg emerged from the water and hooked over the edge of the bathtub. Amanda held his gaze as she swung her foot back and forth, letting foam drip from the tips of her toes.

"Anything you like," she purred.

Hoon's gaze lingered on the leg for just a few moments, then he shrugged. "Aye, well, I'll probably just take money too, ta," he said.

"You'll get a share of the spoils, of course," Amanda drawled. She swung the leg again like she was worried he hadn't noticed it. "But there could be other benefits, too."

"To be honest, sweetheart, you're no' my cup of tea," Hoon said. He pointed to her foot. "So I'd cut that shite out before you fucking embarrass yourself."

The coy smile that had been teasing up the corners of the woman's mouth fell away. For a moment, Hoon could've sworn he even saw her blush.

"I beg your pardon?"

"Listen, I'm sure there's plenty of guys who'd jump at the chance, but I prefer a woman who's no' just a fucking vertical line with a head at the top. No offence," Hoon told her. "So, how about we pretend this whole weird flirty thing hasn't happened, and get down to talking business like a couple of fucking grown-ups?"

CHAPTER TWENTY-ONE

IT DIDN'T TAKE LONG for them to reach an agreement. He'd persuade Greig to take part. In return, they'd both come away richer. If they happened to come away in one piece, then there was scope for future earnings, too. This could be the making of young Greig, Amanda had insisted. If things went well, and everyone played their part, this could very well set his family up for life.

There had been no more dangled legs or lascivious looks. Amanda had taken the hint, though she'd have had to possess skin like a fucking rhino not to. The talk had been strictly business after Hoon shot her down, and ten minutes later she raised her voice to summon a couple of big lads in dark suits from the adjoining room.

Hoon had no idea if these were the bastards who had snatched him the night before. Not that it really mattered, as he intended to treat them all with the same level of contempt, regardless of the individual roles they might have played.

They were given their orders to give Hoon back his belongings, then escort him downstairs and call him a taxi, and each silently confirmed their understanding with a nod.

There was no physical contact until the door to Amanda's hotel suite *clunked* closed behind them, then a hand slapped down onto Hoon's shoulder and forcibly turned him to face along the corridor to the right.

There was something ape-like about the hand. The fingers were thick, but also disproportionately long. Hoon studied it almost admiringly for a few seconds, then met the eyes of the owner.

"You like that, son?"

The guard, or henchman, or whatever the fuck his job title was, stared back at him, utterly impassive and devoid of all emotion, like a robot with skin.

"What?"

"Your hand," Hoon said. He gave a little tilt of his head towards it. "You like it? Because if you do, and you want to keep enjoying the benefits of ownership, I suggest you remove it from my shoulder ASA-fucking-P."

The bear in the suit did not seem in the least bit concerned about the threat, despite Hoon's boggle-eyed stare, and the vein that was throbbing on the side of his head.

"Just walk," the other suited ape instructed, and he sent Hoon stumbling forward a few paces with a well-placed shove to the back.

Red flashed before Hoon's eyes. He felt his stomach twist and his muscles drawing tight. The temptation to turn around and get stuck into these pricks was almost overwhelming, but he swallowed it down.

He was getting somewhere. He was getting closer to finding Caroline, he could feel it. He couldn't do anything to jeopardise that now.

"No bother, lads," he said, forcing a smile that was mostly clenched teeth. He looked back at them. "What's your names by the way?"

"Shut the fuck up," the first man barked. "And keep walking."

"No bother," Hoon said again. "You don't feel like sharing, that's fine. But I need to call you something, so how about...?" He stole another look at them both as they plodded along the corridor. "Bingo and Butterfuck?" He nodded, pleased with his decision. "Aye. Aye, that works for me."

The newly christened Bingo and Butterfuck swapped impatient looks, then another prod to Hoon's back made him pick up the pace.

"Shut the fuck up," the man now known as Bingo ordered for a second time.

Hoon held his hands up in surrender, then continued along the corridor. There had been no identifying marks on the door of Amanda's suite, but he'd noted the numbers of the rooms they'd since passed, so he'd be able to find it again if he had to.

The corridor was just as plush as the suite had been, and the number of 'Do Not Disturb' signs and empty breakfast trays left outside the doors suggested this floor was populated exclusively by lazy bastards.

Up ahead, just twenty or thirty feet away, a door opened and a young man came out, tucking his shirt into his jeans with the sort of swagger that suggested he'd recently got lucky. He hummed or sang below his breath, and as he danced around fixing his clothing, Hoon had a horrible moment of realisation.

He knew this wee fuck.

And, more importantly, this wee fuck knew him.

It was Humpty Dumpty, one of the rapey bastards he'd stripped naked and tied up in his van. They'd both seen his face, and given the situation, it was a face neither of them was likely to forget.

This was not good. This was a fucking nightmare, in fact.

"Everything alright, Mr West?" one of the goons escorting

him grunted, and Hoon immediately bowed his head just as the younger man turned.

Mr West? It couldn't be Godfrey West, Hoon knew—MI5 Miles wouldn't have let him go, if it had been—but a relative maybe?

"What? Oh. Yeah, yeah, great!" Humpty Dumpty replied. Hoon snatched a look at the bastard, who was now gesturing into the room he'd just left. "Could you... You know? Tidy this shit up?"

"We'll take care of it, Mr West," the other henchman drawled, and Hoon could hear the contempt in his tone, even if the shitesack along the corridor appeared as oblivious to it as he was of Hoon.

"Cheers, guys, you're lifesavers!" Humpty said, then he turned and went sauntering along the corridor, whistling happily as he fixed his collar and finished tucking himself in.

"Who's that prick?" Hoon asked once the younger man was out of sight and earshot around a corner at the far end of the hallway.

"None of your fucking business," was the response, and it was followed by another encouraging shove. "Just get going."

Hoon didn't need telling twice this time. The door to the room that Humpty had come strutting out of still stood open, and he wanted a look inside. He picked up the pace until he was practically jogging, then stopped just outside the room.

There was a narrow sort of passageway just inside the door, that opened up into a wider room of which Hoon could only see a fraction. The bottom of a double bed was just visible, its covers piled up in a heap on the floor beside it.

There were legs. Two of. Female. They stuck out over the end of the bed, feet pointing down, one bare, the other partially covered by a white ankle sock that had slipped down over the heel.

"The fuck is this?" Hoon asked, hanging a sharp right and

stepping into the room.

A hand grabbed for his shoulder, just like before. This time, he disposed of it, and the goon it belonged to hissed sharply as his thumb bent inward to touch his wrist.

Hoon was in the room before they could try to stop him again, standing over the bed, staring at the girl lying face down on it, surrounded by sex toys, ball gags, and the detritus of a bondage session that had gone too far.

Her hair was blonde with streaks of blue. She was so skinny that her mostly naked body looked emaciated—perhaps even more so than Amanda's, which was saying something. Her face was buried in a pillow like she was trying to inhale it. One of the many cushions from the bed was tucked under her middle, just a few inches down from her flat stomach, angling her so that her bare backside was being presented to all those standing behind her.

There were deep red welts across her buttocks and back, and bruising up her legs and along both arms. The sexual encounter had not been a tender and loving one. Quite the opposite.

This wasn't Caroline. This wasn't the woman he was looking for. But that didn't matter.

She wasn't Bamber's daughter.

But she was somebody's.

Had been somebody's. And now, she was—

"Jesus! What the fuck?!"

The woman twisted around like an electrical current had been fired up her jacksie. At the sight of the men, her eyes became two big saucers of horror, and she kicked out with her bare foot like she was trying to knock Hoon through the wall. He stepped back, getting clear. She snatched up one of the pillows and covered her breasts with it, then fired the foot in Hoon's direction again.

"What the fuck are you doing in here? You fucking

perverts! Jesus!"

"You're not dead," Hoon said.

"What the f...? Why would I be dead? Of course, I'm not fucking dead!"

And she was right. She definitely wasn't dead. Only the living could screech like that.

"Fuck off! Get out of here, you sick fucks!" she cried. "What are you doing here?!"

"Sorry. My fault. Total misunderstanding," Hoon admitted. "I thought you'd been raped and murdered. So, you know..." He gestured at her very much alive body with both hands. "Congratulations on not being."

"Raped and murdered? Fuck *off!*" Her head jerked as she searched the room. "Where's Charlie? Where did he go? Charlie?"

It was one of the goons who stepped in then. "Mr West had to leave. He's asked us to make sure you get safely off the premises."

She glared back, all defiance and disbelief. "Bullshit. Where is he? I want to see him."

"Yes, well, that won't be possible," the henchman insisted.

The woman on the bed raised her voice to a shout. "Charlie? Charlie, where are you? What the fuck is going on?! I swear, if this is—"

A hand caught her ankle, and she gave a yelp of pain as she was jerked off the bed. Her arse hit the floor with a *thump*, and the defiance gave way to fear as the brute in the suit snarled down at her.

"Cut the shit, you little slut," he hissed. "Wipe yourself clean, get your fucking clothes, and go. In the unlikely event that Mr West wants to contact you again—and I wouldn't hold my breath, if I was you—then he'll be in touch. Otherwise, you mention this to anyone, and you'll have me breathing down your neck. Do we understand each other?"

Despite her nakedness, aching arse, and obvious tactical disadvantage, the young woman spat out an impassioned, "Fuck you!"

The henchman who'd given her the warning—the one Hoon had christened Bingo—bent forward so suddenly that all her bravado disappeared. She yelped and shielded her face with her hands.

"Believe me, darling," he whispered. "That can be arranged."

Hoon pulled the man back. "Alright, alright, let her up then, Casanova. She can hardly fucking go anywhere with you hanging over her, can she?"

The goon spun like he was going to take a swing. He was bigger than Hoon. Both henchmen were. Violence was their language of choice, and while part of Hoon would've dearly loved to engage them both in conversation, now wasn't the time or the place.

"Sorry, Bingo, if it's a dick-swinging competition you're after, I'm not interested," he said. "Your boss told you to see me out, so are you going to do as you were fucking telt, or are you going to leave me to my own devices? Because this place is lovely. I'll happily wander the corridors for a while."

Both men, Bingo and Butterfuck, stood like they were squaring up to him. He didn't rise to it, but he didn't back down either, and when the woman on the floor pulled herself up on the edge of the bed, Bingo turned from Hoon and jabbed a finger in her face.

"Get dressed and get out," he barked, then Butterfuck used his bulk to steer Hoon back in the direction of the corridor.

"Sorry for the intrusion again," Hoon said, leaning to look past the men in suits. "I'd maybe reconsider my choice of men in future."

"Piss off, you creepy old bastard," the woman retorted, then she wrapped herself in the sheet from the bed, stormed off into the bathroom, and slammed the door.

Hoon tutted. "Kids today, eh?" he said. "No respect for their elders."

"Just shut the fuck up and get walking," Hoon was told, though this time there were no hands on his shoulders or shoves in his back.

"Aye, you say that now," Hoon replied. He looked deliberately to where Bingo was nursing his wrist, then fixed them both with a grin. "But I just know you're going to miss me when I'm gone."

———

"Go."

Godfrey's tone was as curt and abrupt as ever. She had learned, long ago, not to take it personally.

"We've had to make a change to the schedule," she said, cradling the phone to her ear as she sat on the edge of the bath, drying her legs. "One of the fighters got himself killed."

"Right. You took care of it?"

"Of course, Mr West" Amanda replied. "All squared away and dealt with."

"Which one was it?"

"The Irish one."

She could hear the disappointment down the line. "The Gypsy? Damn. I love watching our boy get stuck into those. He really goes to town. He can't stand them."

"I think he'll enjoy the replacement," Amanda said. "He might even get two for the price of one."

"Good. I'll look forward to it," Godfrey replied. "Was that all?"

"That's all," Amanda confirmed, and the line went dead before she'd even finished speaking.

CHAPTER TWENTY-TWO

THERE WAS a cafe across the street, perfectly placed to watch the front door of the McGinlay Hotel. He was able to claim one of the stools at the window, giving him an uninterrupted view of the building on the other side of the road.

That was the good news. The bad news was that the cafe was a *Starbucks*, so anything resembling real coffee was off the menu.

He sipped his disappointing Americano and tried hard to ignore the rainbow of ridiculous beverages being slurped up straws at the tables behind him.

He'd been given the chance to 'upgrade' his order to some sugar-soaked milky nonsense with a big swirl of cream on top, and while he'd been tempted to spell out his full thoughts on this offer to the fuck-fringed twenty-something who'd taken his life in his hands by making it, he'd been in a hurry to get to his seat, and so had declined with just a shake of his head and a muted, "Christ, no."

He sat there for an hour. Hour and a half, maybe. He counted sixteen people coming and going—wealthy looking men, mostly, in suits and long wool coats. The woman he'd seen splayed out in the room didn't emerge, though.

He gave it another twenty minutes, watching for her without moving. Nothing. Not a sign.

Hoon took out the phone that Miles had given him and opened up the contacts list. There were dozens of names in there, almost all of which were in there to help with his cover story. If someone was to get into the phone, a contact list with just one name in it was likely to arouse their suspicions.

He scrolled down until he found Donnie Watson—the name that Miles' number was listed under. His thumb hovered above it, but didn't yet move to make the call.

The would-be rapist he'd bundled into the van—Humpty Dumpty, Charlie West, call him what you liked—had to be related to this Godfrey West character Miles had told him about. It was too much of a coincidence, if not. Miles must've known about the connection. He *must* have. But he hadn't mentioned it. He'd kept Hoon in the dark.

Why? What was he hiding? If Hoon called him in on this now, what would he do? Could he be trusted?

If he couldn't, then what the hell had he done with Welshy and Gabriella?

"Fuck!" Hoon spat, and a man who had been sitting alongside him at the counter in the window quietly moved to the next stool over.

Hoon clicked the button on the side of the mobile and returned it to his pocket. He wasn't bringing the MI5 man in. Not yet. Not until he knew more.

He was lingering over the last few dregs of his below-par coffee when he saw a flash of blonde and blue in the doorway of the hotel across the road. The woman he had met in the bedroom was being led from the building by yet another man in yet another dark suit. This one looked a little older than Bingo and Butterfuck, but other than a few more lines and smattering of grey at his temples, there was very little to differentiate them.

The woman was swearing. Hoon couldn't hear her through the glass, but he didn't need to be a lipreader to recognise most of the words she was using. The emphatic way in which she was spitting them out made them easy enough to identify.

He abandoned the rest of his coffee, barged through the throngs waiting for their Fairy Sprinkle Frappucinos, or whatever the fuck they were having, and hurried outside in time to see the woman firing twin single-finger salutes up at the hotel.

"Fuck you!" she screeched to the building at large. In classic London style, none of the pedestrians passing on the street gave her so much as a glance.

The suit who had ejected her from the hotel had returned inside now, but Hoon didn't risk making his move quite yet. Instead, he followed on the opposite side of the road when she turned and hoiked her floor-length dress up to just above knee height, then went teetering away on her stilettos.

She walked for thirty yards or so, then raised a hand and shouted for a taxi. It swept straight past, earning itself a mouthful of abuse so vile it almost made Hoon wince.

Stealing a glance back at the hotel to make sure nobody was watching from the doorway, Hoon dodged the traffic, hurried across the road, and got the woman's attention with an, "Excuse me, doll."

She spun to face him like she was auditioning for a remake of *The Exorcist,* her lips drawn back over her teeth, her face contorted in fury. The fact that her running mascara had left her with long black lines down her cheeks only added to the overall effect, and the, "Jesus!" was out of Hoon before he could stop it.

"What do you—?" she started to ask, then her eyes became two slits of suspicion. "Wait a minute. You're that creepy bastard from the room."

Hoon tried his best not to take offence at that. "I wouldn't say I was a creepy bastard, exactly, I was—"

"What the fuck do you want, you pervert?"

Hoon blinked. "What? Hold on, how am I the fucking pervert here? I wasn't the one with all the ball gags and handcuffs, and my red raw arse sticking up in the air."

"Are you kink-shaming me?" the woman in the dress demanded. It was a nice dress, too. Not cheap. It seemed out of place on this foul-mouthed, blue-streaked train wreck. "Is that what you're doing? Are you fucking kink-shaming me?"

"What the fuck is...? What's kink shaming? I don't even know what that is," Hoon fired back.

She made a sound like an exasperated teenager who'd just been grounded for a month, then turned and started to storm off. Hoon picked up the pace until he was walking beside her, which immediately prompted her to stop again.

"I'll scream rape," she warned. "If you don't piss off, I will, I'll scream rape."

"Look, calm down, I just want to ask you a few questions," Hoon explained. He kept his voice light and friendly—impressively so, given what he was dealing with. "I'm hoping you can help me."

The woman looked him up and down, like she was properly taking him in for the first time. "You police?"

Hoon gestured down at himself, putting particular emphasis on his pineapple patterned shirt. "Do I look like the fucking police?"

She sighed, then ran a hand down her face, further smudging her already ruined makeup. "You've got thirty seconds. What do you want?"

"I'm looking for a girl," Hoon said, then he shook his head and tutted. "A young woman. Her name is Caroline Gascoine. Do you know her?"

"Never heard of her." The woman in the dress turned and

started to walk on, but then muttered something under her breath and turned back. "Who is she?"

Hoon hesitated before speaking. Telling her the truth was a risk. If she reported back to Humpty Dumpty, his cover would be blown.

But he had to know.

"She's the daughter of a friend," Hoon explained. "She's in trouble. She's missing. Has been for a while. I think your man in there might be connected. I think he might know something."

"Charlie?"

"If you say so, aye," Hoon confirmed. "How much do you know about him? No' in the Biblical sense, I mean, in general."

She looked past Hoon and up at the hotel, like she was seeing this, too, for the first time. "I mean... I don't know. Not a lot. Nothing, really. I just met him last night."

"Where?"

"Cocktail bar in the West End. Under. Seemingly, he goes there all the time."

"Under what?"

"That's what it's called. Under. It's in a basement. They're pricks about the dress code, but my mate really wanted to go, so..." She glowered down at her dress like she despised it.

"And what? He just came up and invited you back to his place?"

The woman scowled, suddenly back on the defensive. "Something like that, yeah. You got a fucking problem with that, granddad?"

Hoon glossed over the outburst. "Did he have anyone else with him? Guys? Girls? Anyone?"

"Well, I don't fucking know, do I?"

He caught her by the upper arms, and the intensity of his stare stopped her from pulling away. "Think," he instructed.

She swallowed. Shook her head. "No. No, I think he was on his own."

Hoon released her and stepped back. "You're sure?"

"Yeah. Yeah, he was sitting in a booth by himself. I remember. Thought it was a bit weird," she continued. "But, you know, it's London. Everyone's fucking weird. He came up to me, he bought me a few drinks, and then we went through to a little private room. We chatted, then we went back to his hotel."

"And he didn't say anything?" Hoon asked. "Anything that might help me?"

"What, about abducting women? No, funnily enough, that didn't come up in the conversation."

She looked off along the street like she was searching for a way out of all this. Just as it looked like she was going to walk off, though, she turned back to him.

"There was one thing," she said. "That was, you know, like... weird."

"What?" Hoon asked.

"When we went in—I mean, I was pretty drunk, so I'm not sure it..." She shut her eyes for a moment, touched her head like she was nursing a pain, then continued. "When we went up in the lift, he went to a room and opened it with his keycard. Just, like, tapped it to the pad. So, I thought, that must be his room, but when he opened it there were people in there. On the bed. Like... doing it. A guy with a couple of girls."

"Girls?"

"Well, about my age, I think," she said. "Twenty, twenty-one. Pretty."

Hoon, more than anything, wished he had Caroline's picture with him, but it was tucked in the notebook back at his hotel room. Just as well, too. Had Amanda or her goons found that on him when they'd stripped him, there was no saying he'd have ever woken up.

"Can you describe them?"

"I just fucking did," the woman told him. "That's all I saw. Twenties. Hot. Good tits."

Hoon abandoned that line of questioning and focused on another. "So the room, it wasn't his?"

"No. I mean... I don't know. I suppose not. But his key opened it. And, like, the people in there didn't seem to mind us being there."

"What do you mean?" Hoon asked.

"They didn't stop. When they saw us. The guy just sort of gave us a thumbs-up, and then Charlie turned around."

"They knew each other?"

"God, I don't know. It was weird, though."

"What about the women? How did they seem?"

"I don't... I don't remember. I'm not sure they even noticed us. I think they might have been drunk, too."

"Could they have been drugged?" Hoon asked.

"Drugged?" Her voice was a sharp gasp. "I mean... Jesus. I don't know. How would I know? I don't... They were just... They were just sort of lying there, so I don't... I don't know!"

The thought of it appeared to horrify her, and she danced on the spot like she was getting ready to run. Like she'd rather make a break for it than dwell any further on what she might have seen.

What she could've stopped.

"And then what?" Hoon pressed, steering her back into calmer waters. "You left there and went to his room?"

"What? Oh. Yeah. Yeah, we left there, then we... Wait. No." She tilted her head, like she was trying to shake the memory loose. "No, it happened again. I mean, sort of. I think. We went to the next room and he opened it, but I didn't go in this time. He just sort of poked his head inside for a few seconds, said something I couldn't really hear, and came back out."

"You think there was someone else in that room, too?"

"I don't know," the woman admitted. "Like I said, I was drunk. It's all a bit vague. But that's weird, isn't it? That's fucking weird. The key opening different doors like that. I asked him if he worked there, but he just sort of laughed."

"Aye," Hoon agreed. "Aye, that's weird."

"You think they're OK? The girls I saw? You think they're going to be OK?"

Hoon looked back at the hotel, and up to the penthouse floor. "Don't you worry," he told her. "I'll make fucking sure of it."

CHAPTER TWENTY-THREE

IT TOOK him the best part of an hour to get back to the mooring, and even though he hadn't been away from it for long, he felt oddly comforted by the sight of the boat bobbing gently on the murky brown surface of the water.

He had half expected it to have been dragged away, set on fire, or otherwise sunk. Quite who would have done these things, he wasn't sure, but it was a relief to find it where he'd left it, and apparently none the worse for wear.

As was customary, he checked the windows of the tower blocks overlooking the towpath for any signs that he was being watched, then hopped aboard the boat and made his way down the narrow steps that led below deck.

It was bright outside, but the size of the windows meant the inside of the boat never reached above 'gloomy' without switching the lights on. Now, with the sun almost directly over-head, almost the whole interior was cast in shadow.

Not wishing to draw any unwanted attention to the yacht, Hoon left the lights off as he went through to the galley kitchen and opened the door of a wall-mounted cabinet. Bookish had used it for storing drinking glasses. Technically, Hoon used it for the same thing, he just hadn't got around to washing any of the used glasses and returning them to the cupboard yet.

He prodded the thin square of veneered plyboard at the bottom right corner so it sprang free from the groove that held it in place. Peeling it aside, he reached in and found the hunk of metal and wood he had taped to the wall behind it.

The gun was a fucking abomination—a garish, jewel-encrusted Desert Eagle that Welshy had brought back as a souvenir from some mission or other during his private-sector days. The Colombian flag was emblazoned across the grip in shiny wee gemstones, and all the various metal parts were coloured gold. It was, without question, the most hideous gun that Hoon had ever seen.

No wonder Welshy had kept it. He'd have done the same.

The bullets were in a small cardboard box tucked right at the back of the cutlery drawer. It would've been a decent hiding place had there actually been any cutlery left in there, but as it was the box slid forward in the empty drawer as soon as he pulled it open.

He had just released the magazine so he could slide in the fifty cal shells when the voice spoke behind him.

"What are you doing?"

He turned with the unloaded gun raised, ready to pistol-whip whoever the fuck had snuck up behind him. Miles the MI5 man quickly held his hands up to indicate his complete surrender.

"Whoa, whoa. It's just me," he said. "Relax."

"What the fuck are you doing here?" Hoon demanded.

"I was going to ask you the same thing," Miles replied. "This wasn't the plan."

"Aye, well, plans change," Hoon said. He sat the gun down on the kitchen worktop, picked up the magazine, and opened the box of shells.

"Why? What happened?" Miles asked.

"I think I might have found her," Hoon said. He picked up a couple of bullets and began sliding them into the mag. The movements were fluid and seamless, muscle memory taking over. "I might have found Caroline."

"What do you mean you might have found her?" Miles asked.

"I mean I might have..." Hoon tutted. "You can put your fucking hands down now."

Miles caught sight of his raised arms and gave a little jump, like they'd caught him by surprise. He lowered them, fiddled with his fingers as if he didn't now know what to do with them, and then stuffed his hands in the pockets of his trousers.

"Where is she?"

"A hotel. The McGinlay. You know it?"

Miles nodded. "Yeah. It's owned by a company we think could be connected to the Loop."

"Aye, no shit it's connected," Hoon said. He finished loading the magazine and slotted it into the base of the Desert Eagle's grip. "I think they might be holding her there."

"Might be? You mean you don't know?"

"I've got a pretty fucking good idea," Hoon said. His lips drew back into something like a snarl. "They know. Someone there, they know where she is."

"How can you be sure?"

"I'm no' fucking sure, pal. I'm no' sure about anything right now. But I'm going to fucking well find out."

Miles shook his head. He raised his hands again, but this time appealing for calm rather than offering his surrender. "No. No, this isn't the plan. This isn't what we discussed."

"And what the fuck did we discuss, exactly?" Hoon demanded. "Remind me, because there's a few fucking gaps I wouldn't mind you filling in. Charlie fucking West for one. That name ring any bells?"

Hoon wouldn't have heard the groan Miles gave had he not been listening for it.

"Aye, I fucking thought it might," he spat.

"Look, I get that you're unhappy with how I handled some things—" the MI5 man began, but Hoon stopped him there.

"Unhappy? I'm no' unhappy, son. Well, I am, aye—unhappy's my default fucking state—but now? With you? About this? I'm no' unhappy, I am *fuming*. I am the physical fucking manifestation of rage itself, in fact. You let that prick go. You knew who he was, and you let him fucking walk away."

"He's nobody," Miles insisted. "He's Godfrey West's nephew, yes, but he's nothing. He's minor league. They keep him in the dark. He doesn't know anything."

"We could've fucking used him," Hoon hissed. "He was a fucking bargaining chip."

"A bargaining chip? Ha! You think the Eel gives a shit about the welfare of his idiot nephew? You think the Loop would... what? Hand your mate's daughter back so you'd let him go? Do a swap?"

"Worth a fucking try," Hoon spat back.

"No. No, it really isn't," Miles insisted. "If they thought for one second that he'd been compromised, they'd kill him. Then they'd kill you, then anyone else they thought you'd been in contact with. If they thought Caroline was more trouble than she was worth, they'd kill her, too. If they haven't already—and, let me tell you, that's a big if."

Hoon said nothing, just barged past the other man and headed for the bedroom. Miles followed, still trying to reason with him.

"What are you going to do, exactly? Storm in there and shoot the place up?"

"If that's what it fucking takes," Hoon replied. He fished around in the piles of dirty clothes on the floor and pulled out a crumpled red-and-black checked shirt. It was less conspicuous than the one he was currently wearing, but only just.

"How far do you think you're going to get?" Miles asked. "Ten feet? Fifty? How is that possibly going to help anyone?"

"It'll help my current fucking mood," Hoon insisted. He tore open his pineapple shirt, sending buttons pinging around the room. "There are girls there. Women. Being made to do Christ knows what. Caroline could be in there."

"And if she isn't?"

Hoon pulled off the shirt, revealing his naked torso, and all the scars from a lifetime of violence that he wore like medals.

"If she isn't, then I'll get any others I find there out, and I'll burn the fucking place to the ground."

"And then you'll never find her," Miles said. "Then, she's gone. She's lost to you. Forever. Is that what you want? I know it isn't."

Hoon closed the gap between them. His hand caught Miles by the throat and slammed him up against the wall. "And what the fuck am I supposed to do, eh? Just leave them in there? Just turn a blind eye?"

"We're not... turning a blind eye," Miles wheezed. His face was turning a brooding shade of purple, but he wasn't fighting back. "We're just...ak...*Jesus*. We're just waiting for the right time."

Hoon searched the other man's face. "You knew," he realised. "About what's going on there. About the women. You fucking knew."

Miles tried to shake his head, but only managed a few tiny movements. "No! Not... We didn't..." He coughed. Or tried to. "I can't... breathe. Can't breathe."

Hoon did not appear to care. He held his grip, even when Miles started to slap pitifully at his arm, and only released the MI5 man when his eyes were starting to roll back into his head.

Miles collapsed onto his knees, coughing and gagging, tears rolling down his cheeks and dripping onto the bedroom floor.

"We didn't know," he spluttered, and his voice was a shaky croak. "We *suspected*, yes. But nothing was confirmed. It still isn't. We still don't know what's going on in there."

Hoon pulled on the checked shirt, clicked closed the pop studs, then picked up the gun. "Aye, well, high fucking time we found out."

Miles heaved himself to his feet, one hand gingerly rubbing at his throat. "You're killing her," he said. "If you do this, and if she's not already dead, you're killing her. And probably dozens more like her."

Hoon tucked the gun into his belt at the back of his trousers, but didn't yet make for the door.

"You go in there guns blazing, you won't get past reception. They'll kill you. Then the police will come, and what do you think they're going to do then, Bob? You think they're going to risk things escalating like that? You think they're going to risk those women being found? Or all the other shit they've got going on in there? You think they're going to leave loose ends like that?"

"I won't give them the fucking chance," Hoon said.

Miles ejected a raw sounding laugh. "What are you, the Terminator now? You bulletproof all of a sudden?" He sat on the end of the bed, cleared his throat a few times like he was trying to dislodge a blockage, then shrugged. "Look, I can't stop you. If you want to go, there's nothing I can physically do about it. But I'm asking you to think for a minute. To really think this through."

"I'm done thinking things through," Hoon retorted.

"Seriously? You're actually saying that out loud, are you? Jesus. Listen to yourself!" Miles said, jumping to his feet. "These people are not amateurs. They know what they're doing. They plan. They *think things through*. Now, we've got a chance here—a real chance—to take down a key player. We can hurt them. Will it help you find Caroline? Honestly? I don't know. But it's the best chance you've got."

Hoon said nothing, just ground his teeth together and breathed deeply through his nose.

"You can charge in there. You can throw your weight around. But you'll be handing them the win," Miles continued. "If Caroline is there, if there are other women being held, then we'll get them out, Bob. We will. But it's a marathon, not a sprint. We rush it, we fail. We fail, they die. Or they get moved somewhere we'll never find them. Is that what you want?"

"Of course it's not what I fucking want," Hoon hissed.

He drew the gun from the back of his trousers, and Miles flinched like he was about to be fired upon. Hoon saw the reaction and sneered.

"Get a fucking grip, man. I'm no' going to shoot you," he said, then he set the weapon down on the bedside table with a *clunk*.

He didn't let go of it, though. Not yet. He stood there, fingers wrapped around the gem-encrusted grip, a frown troubling his brow. He turned slowly and raised his head until he was eye to eye with the man from MI5.

"How the fuck did you know where to find me?" he asked.

Most of Miles' face didn't move, but Hoon saw it flashing behind his eyes. The panic. The moment of horrible realisation that he'd been caught out.

"I just... You didn't come back to the hotel, so..."

Hoon raised the gun again, and this time he did point it at Miles. "Cut the shite," he spat. "How the fuck did you know I was here?"

Miles cowered, his hands raised in front of his face like they might repel a hail of bullets. "Jesus! Stop, alright? Calm down!

Just... just put the gun down, Bob. Please, just put the gun down!"

The hammer of the Desert Eagle drew back. The safety *clicked* as it was disengaged. "How... the *fuck*," Hoon repeated, more slowly this time for added emphasis. "Did you know... where I was?"

"Alright, alright! Your phone! The phone I gave you! I tracked that!"

Hoon took a step closer, forcing Miles to retreat until he was backed up against the wall. "You put a fucking tracking device in the phone?"

"What? No! I mean, sort of but not really. It's built in. It's standard. They've all got them! They just share GPS location data. Yours is set to share it with me!"

Hoon kept the weapon trained for a few more agonising seconds, then tutted. "Oh, right." He lowered the gun. "Fucking technology."

"I should've told you," Miles admitted between sighs of relief. "I should've said."

"Here, hold on a fucking minute," Hoon began. "So, you knew that I'd been fucking taken prisoner? Where was the rescue mission, eh? For all you pricks knew, I was having my fucking fingernails torn out in there."

"Taken prisoner? Shit. I didn't know you'd been taken," Miles explained. "I could see you went to the hotel, yes, but I didn't know it was against your will. Who took you?"

"Couple of arseholes," Hoon said. "Knocked me out, then drugged me up. Took me to see some fucking bag of bones in a bath."

Miles' lips moved silently as he ran over that last sentence, before coming to the conclusion that he had no idea what the other man was on about.

"A bag of bones in a bath?"

"Aye, no' literally. Jesus. A woman. Amanda something."

"Amanda what?"

"I don't know!" Hoon ejected. "Fucking...Holden."

Miles raised an eyebrow. "Amanda Holden?" he said. "Off *Britain's Got Talent*? Les Dennis's ex-wife? That Amanda Holden?"

"Well, clearly it wasn't actually Amanda fucking Holden," Hoon fired back, the lines of his face tightening in anger. "I don't know her surname was the point I was making. Amanda. That's all I know. Amanda. Skinny bastard, flirty as fuck, seems to be in charge. You're the one with all the fucking intel, you tell me who she is."

"We'll look into it," Miles promised.

"Meaning you don't have a clue who she is. Well, that's reassuring that is. The full combined might of the British Security Service and you can't ID one brassy tart in a fucking bathtub."

"What did she want?" Miles asked, quickly moving the conversation on.

"A damn good seeing to, I think, but I knocked that on the fucking head before she got carried away with herself. No way I'm sleeping with the fucking enemy. Especially no' one that looks like a pile of sticks with a sheet over it."

Miles frowned. "What?"

"Doesn't matter," Hoon said. "She wants Greig to fight in some big event they've got coming up. Big money thing. High fliers."

"Oh. Right. OK," Miles said. His frown deepened. "And, sorry, who's Greig?"

"Greig," Hoon said, as if that explained everything. "Have I no' told you about Greig?"

"No. I mean, I haven't seen you since yesterday, so..."

"Fuck's sake," Hoon snapped, and his tone suggested that the lack of communication was all somehow the other man's fault. "Right, go get a beer from the fridge and take a seat at the table."

"I can't drink, I'm driving," Miles pointed out.

"Aye, well, just as well I didn't tell you to get one for yourself. I meant for me," Hoon said. "You and I have got a lot of fucking catching up to do."

CHAPTER TWENTY-FOUR

THE DOOR finally opened after the third knock. It made it as far as the security chain allowed, then a face appeared at the gap. Clean-shaven, he looked even younger than he had the night before, even if the bruising had made the contours of his face a little less symmetrical.

"Jesus Christ, I've changed my mind, can you put the beard back on?" Hoon asked. "You look like a fucking potato."

The one eye of Greig's that Hoon could see swivelled as it checked out the landing behind him. "How'd you get up?"

"Door wasn't shut properly downstairs," Hoon replied. "Fucking security issue that, if you ask me. I'd put in a complaint."

"Are you alright?" Greig asked.

"I'm hunky-fucking-dory," Hoon assured him.

"You've got a big lump on your head," the younger man pointed out.

"That? That's nothing."

"Does it hurt?" Greig asked, transfixed by the monstrous lump.

"Only when I talk about it, so let's move on," Hoon said.

"Anyway, you don't exactly look a picture of fucking health yourself."

"What, this?" Greig self-consciously touched his swollen top lip. "Perks of the job."

"Aye, suppose so." Hoon indicated the door between them. "Now, are you going to keep me standing out here all fucking day, or are you going to let me in?"

"Oh. Yeah. Sorry. Hang on."

The door was closed. Hoon listened to the scraping of the chain, then the door opened again and Greig stood aside and motioned for him to enter.

"Benji's sleeping," the younger man said, closing the door at Hoon's back.

"Tired himself out playing fetch did he?" Hoon asked, sauntering along the short hallway towards the living room.

"Benji's not a—"

"I know he's no' a dug, I was joking," Hoon said. "Still a stupid fucking name, though."

He entered the living room to find Cassie sitting forward on the couch, a plate balanced on her knees while she attacked the food on it with her knife and fork. A second plate sat on the empty seat beside her, and Greig quickly swooped in to claim it.

"Whoa, whoa, whoa. What the fuck's this?" Hoon demanded, pointing to Greig's plate.

Greig looked down at the food. "It's a fry-up. We didn't have any breakfast, so I made us this."

"I can see it's a fucking fry up. I meant that. Is that a square sausage?" Hoon asked, pointing to something on the plate that was currently sort of triangular, but which may well have had four sides in the not-too-distant past.

"Uh, yeah," Greig confirmed.

"Where the fuck did you get that?"

Cassie swallowed the mouthful of food she'd been chewing on. "My mum sent it down."

"Jesus, you've got tattie scones, too!" Hoon all but shrieked. "Did she send them down, too?"

"Yeah," Cassie confirmed. "And can you please stop swearing?"

Hoon looked around the room. "I thought he was sleeping?"

"He is."

"Then I wouldn't get my knickers in a twist, sweetheart. He's no' going to take it in through fucking osmosis."

"I'm asking you to stop," Cassie said. "Or you can leave. It's your choice."

Hoon started three different responses—"The..." "I..." "How the..."—then sighed, threw his arms up into the air, and sulkily conceded. "Fine. I won't pollute the adorable wee brain of your chubby dog-named wean with all my terrible bad words. Happy?"

"Not really," Cassie said. She stuffed a bit of bacon into her mouth and went back to chewing. "What do you want?"

"A bit of square sausage if it's going."

"It isn't," Cassie said.

Hoon tutted, then pointed to Greig's plate. "You shouldn't be eating that, anyway. You're in training."

"Training?"

"I got you a new gig. Better paid. Higher profile. There's five grand in it *at least*. Maybe more."

"Five grand?" Cassie spluttered. "For one boxing match?" She gave Greig a dunt with her knee. "See? Told you things would pick up!"

Greig shot Hoon an imploring look, and forced a smile. "Yeah. You did say that," he agreed, then he set his plate on the arm of the chair and got up. "That reminds me, eh... Mr White. He fished in the back pocket of his jeans and pulled out a folded envelope. "The money came through for last night. They posted it just after you left."

"Greig," Cassie muttered through a mouthful of grub.

"We can't keep it," Greig told her. "We agreed."

He turned back to Hoon and held out the envelope.

"What's this?" Hoon asked.

"It's the money you gave us last night. You didn't have to do that."

"That's your money," Hoon insisted.

"No. It isn't, though, is it? It's yours. They posted ours."

Hoon shook his head. "Look, son, it's no' my fault if there was some sort of admin error. You got paid twice. Don't knock it."

Greig kept the envelope held out between them. "I can't... I don't want to owe anything. Not again."

"Then you're in fucking luck."

"Language!" Cassie scolded.

"Jesus. Then you're in luck, because you don't. It's not a loan, it's not a trick, it's all yours. Alright?"

Greig looked from Hoon to the envelope and back again. It was only when Cassie cleared her throat that he finally returned it to his pocket and took his seat again.

"Right. Well, you know, thanks," he said, picking up his plate.

"No, son, thank *you*," Hoon replied. He held up what was left of the square sausage, grinned, and took a big bite. His eyes closed as he chewed, and he put a hand on his chest like he was experiencing something beautiful and pure. "Aw, yes. Yes, that's the stuff," he mumbled, his voice distant and dream-like.

With great reluctance, he finally swallowed the mush of mashed-up sausage meat, let out a long, satisfied, "Aaaah," then opened his eyes and held out a hand. "Now, give me that plate and go get your gear on," he instructed. "You've got training to do."

Greig resisted for all of five seconds, then passed the plate across. Hoon had already picked up what was left of the tattie scone when Cassie threw a spanner in the works.

"He can't go out training. I've got work in twenty minutes."

"Shit, yeah, she does," said Greig. "I've got to look after Benji."

Hoon shrugged. "That's fine. We'll take him with us."

"Eh, no. You won't," Cassie insisted. "You're not taking my baby to that smelly lock-up."

"Perish the thought," Hoon said. He shoved half a tattie scone in his mouth and chewed noisily while he looked from one of Benji's parents to the other. "But what smelly lock-up are we talking about?"

———

"Cassie's going to go mental," Greig said, sliding the key into the rusted metal handle fixed to the centre of a graffitied garage door.

"What she doesn't know won't hurt her," Hoon insisted. He had one hand on the handle of a battered old pram, and was rolling it slowly back and forth in the hope of keeping the sleeping occupant from waking up. "Anyway, good for the wee man to get a bit of fresh air."

With a bit of difficulty, Greig shunted the key around in the lock, then shot a glance back at the busy road just a few feet from where Hoon was standing.

"I'm not sure that's the description I'd have used," he said, but the thunderous roar of a passing truck drowned him out. The racket of it made Benji stir, and Hoon added to the forward and back movement with a wee sideways shoogle that settled the baby straight back off.

It was short-lived, however, as the *screeching* of the garage door being lifted jerked the lad wide awake. The wee petted lip came on at once, and when he saw the unfamiliar face peering down at him, Benji clenched his fists, opened his mouth, and howled.

"Shit, sorry, was that me?" Greig asked.

"Now you mention it, that two-hundred-decibel, high-pitched scream you just caused might've had something to do with it."

"Here, I'll get him," Greig said, sidling up to the pram. He leaned down and put a hand on the blanket tucked across the baby's chest, but the crying continued unabated.

"You're just making him worse," Hoon said.

"How am I making him worse?" Greig asked.

"Well, look at him. He's still bawling his eyes out, isn't he?"

"That's not worse though, is it?" Greig countered. "He was already bawling his eyes out."

Hoon tutted. "Right, fine. Well, if you're going to be pedantic about it, you're no' making him any better then, and oh for fuck's sake, what in the name of God is this?"

He had raised his head and was now peering into the dark confines of a cluttered garage. A heavy punchbag hung from the ceiling, about a mile of silver tape the only thing preventing its contents from spilling out onto the floor. A barbell with weights on the end stood propped against a stack of filthy car tyres in the corner, and as Hoon watched, a somewhat startled looking rat shot out from inside the lock-up, ran in a panicky circle on the pavement, then fucked off down the street as fast as its legs would carry it.

"It's my gym," Greig said, he kept his hand on Benji's chest, and the weight of it slowly settled the wee man down. "It's where I train."

"Jesus Christ, son. What are you training for in there, an outbreak of fucking cholera?"

Greig's head tick-tocked between Hoon and the garage. "What do you mean?"

"I mean it's an absolute shit tip, son. We can't bring a baby in there. I mean, Christ, even I don't want to go in there and, generally speaking, I have zero fucking concern for my own wellbeing whatsoever."

He kept his feet planted but leaned a little closer, trying to get a better view of the inside of the garage, while still keeping his distance.

"It's alright," Greig insisted. "It's a good space. And it's cheap."

"Cheap?!" Hoon virtually shrieked. "You mean you pay for this?"

"Thirty quid."

"I hope that's a fucking lifetime subscription!" Hoon said.

"A week," Greig clarified. "Thirty quid a week."

"Christ, someone well and truly saw you coming," Hoon told him. He shook his head and motioned for the younger man to close the door. "No, bollocks to that, shut that over. We're not training here."

"Well, where, then?" Greig asked. "I don't know anywhere else."

"Aye, well," Hoon said. "It's lucky for you that I do."

CHAPTER TWENTY-FIVE

HOON'S GAZE drifted around the gym that was spread out before him, flirted briefly with the heavy bags and speed balls, then settled on the full-size boxing ring that took up the majority of the available floor space.

None of the equipment looked new, and the ring could've done with a clean and its ropes tightened, but he wasn't bothered about any of that.

"Aye, this'll do," he remarked. "This'll do nicely."

Beside him, Granny Porter twirled a set of keys around on an arthritic finger, then hooked them onto a clip on his belt. "Well, we got a club starting at seven, but it's all yours until then." He shot Hoon a meaningful sideways glance. "And I should say that all donations are gratefully accepted."

Hoon patted the old man on the shoulder like he was greeting an old friend. "Oh aye," he said. "I bet they fucking are."

With a smile and a wink, he descended the set of metal steps that ran from the door down to floor level. The gym had been put together in a windowless basement, and the only light came from the half-dozen old-style filament bulbs that were screwed into fittings fixed high up on the walls. There were thirty or more such fittings, but less than half of them were working, so the place was lit more like an old jazz bar than a sports facility.

Dale had arranged it after Hoon had got in touch. He'd tried to invite himself along, but had been given short shrift. This wasn't a fucking social gathering, Hoon had told him. This was serious stuff.

The place smelled of damp and hard graft. The odour of sweat hung in the air, like the walls themselves were perspiring.

This was a real gym, Hoon thought. A *proper* gym. It wasn't one of those glitzy, overly lit spaceships full of gadgets, gizmos, and self-obsessed wankers mentally undressing themselves in the big wall mirrors.

Nor, mind you, was it a shitty wee garage with a rodent infestation and a lingering sense of despair. No, it was somewhere slap bang in the middle—right in the Goldilocks zone between those two extremes—and it was exactly the sort of place that he'd been hoping for.

"Can you give me a hand with this?" Greig asked from the top of the stairs. He indicated the pram that he'd successfully squeezed through the narrow door, but was now struggling to get much further with. "Just grab the front."

He had directed the request at Hoon, but Hoon was too busy admiring the space to even notice.

"Allow me," Granny Porter said. He bent with some difficulty and caught the bottom of the pram with both hands. Then, despite Greig's protestations that, actually, it was fine and he could probably manage, the old man helped guide the pram and its sleeping occupant down to join Hoon at the bottom of the steps.

"Eh, cheers," Greig said. "I was worried the bumping might wake him up."

"Aye, very good, Supernanny," Hoon said. He indicated the

boxing ring. "Away get the kit on and get in there. Gloves and head gear. Let's see what you've got."

"Who am I fighting?" Greig asked.

"Who do you think?" Hoon asked, puffing up his chest.

Greig looked around, then shrugged. "I don't know. Who?"

"Fuck's sake. Me, obviously."

Greig's gaze tracked up and down, studying the man standing before him. As it did, a smirk tugged upwards at the corners of his mouth. "You? Are you not a bit...?"

"A bit what?"

"You know, like, old?"

"You watch your fucking lip, son."

Greig laughed. "I mean, no offence, like. I don't want you having a heart attack on me or something."

"Don't you worry about me, pal," Hoon told him. "Just you concern yourself with doing what you're fucking told. Get the kit on. Get in the ring. And brace yourself for a fucking hiding."

Granny Porter sidled his way between the men, pointed into the pram, and lowered his voice to a whisper. "You want me to keep my eye on the little fella?" he asked. "Case he starts making a fuss?"

Greig looked a little uncomfortable about this suggestion. He made a few non-committal mumbling sounds while he tried to think of an excuse as to why it probably wasn't a good idea. Or an excuse that wouldn't cause massive offence and get them chucked out, at least.

"I don't know. Probably best if I just get him if he wakes up. He's a bit... finicky," Greig finally said.

Granny smiled. "I have four children, thirteen grandchildren, and five great-grandchildren," he said. "And I've had three wives and two divorces. I am well used to finicky. I've been dealing with finicky all my damn life."

"There you go, nothing to worry about. Granny's got him. The wee man's going to be fine," Hoon said. He gave Greig an encouraging shove that propelled him the first few paces towards the ring. "Now come on, get your arse in that ring and let's see what you've fucking got."

Greig shrugged, and went swaggering towards a big net bag full of gloves, pads, and headguards. "OK, well, you asked for it, old man," he said. "But don't say I didn't warn you!"

———

Hoon padded around the ring, his gloved hands raised in front of his chest, his sights set on the younger man bobbing and weaving in front of him.

"You know where you're going wrong?" Hoon asked.

"Shut up," Greig mumbled through his mouth guard.

"You keep letting me punch you in the face," Hoon continued, goading him. "I mean, I don't know where you learned to box, but that's the exact fucking opposite of what you're meant to be doing."

Greig lunged with a right jab. He was fast, Hoon would give him that much, but he was holding back. Hoon sidestepped the punch and gave the boy a tap on the back of the headguard as he went staggering past, off-balance.

"I mean, what the fuck was that meant to be?"

"I'm just going easy on you," Greig said, then he turned, feinted with a left, and let fly with another right that *whummed* through the space that had, until that very moment, been occupied by Hoon.

A couple of fast, light uppercuts caught him on the ribcage. Not enough to do damage, but enough to get his attention.

"I really hope that's true, son, because otherwise, this is just fucking embarrassing," Hoon continued to taunt. "It's a good thing your son's no' awake to see this, or he'd be cringing himself inside out."

The mention of Benji made Greig look over at the pram,

which earned him a shove and a couple of swift punches to the lower back. Again, there was no force behind them—just enough for the glove leather to sting the skin—but there could have been, and that was the point.

"Eyes on me. Don't let me out of your fucking sight."

Greig advanced again, and this time threw a jab with his left that was easily deflected by Hoon's gloves.

"Did you no' tell me you went pro?" Hoon asked, and the note of disbelief in his voice was unmissable.

"No. I said I *nearly* went pro," Greig corrected.

"How nearly are we talking?" Hoon teased. "Did you buy the *Rocky* boxset on DVD?"

Greig stopped and let his arms fall to his side. "This is stupid. What are we even doing?" he sighed.

"You were in the middle of getting your arse handed to you," Hoon said. He made a beckoning motion with his gloves. "Come on. Hands up. Let's go."

Greig raised his guard for all of two seconds, then lowered it again and shook his head. "This is pointless. How is this helping?"

Hoon tutted and put his fists on his hips. "What do you mean? You've got a bare-knuckle fight coming up tomorrow, and to the casual fucking observer, you don't have the first clue how to handle yourself."

"I can handle myself fine," Greig insisted.

"No' from what I've seen," Hoon countered.

"You're not wearing a headguard. I've just got bag gloves on. I can't very well hit you, can I? I'll knock you out."

Hoon let out a cackle that echoed around the gym. "You've got my full fucking permission to try," he said, then his head snapped back when a punch caught him on the chin from out of nowhere, and he stumbled back with a, "Fuck!"

"See?" Greig said. His hands were back by his sides. Hoon

hadn't even seen them move. "It's not fair. You've not got protection"

Hoon dabbed his bottom lip on his bare forearm, and it came away bloodied.

"Sorry," Greig said with a wince. "Do you want me to see if there's some ice?"

"Do I fuck. I want you to do that again," Hoon instructed. He shook out his arms then brought them up to guard his head. "Hit me."

"I don't want to hit you," Greig protested.

Hoon flew at him, and this time the punch that connected with the right side of Greig's stomach had some weight behind it.

"Tough shit. Hit me," he urged. He banged his gloves together, then swung with a big telegraphed right that Greig leaned back to avoid. "Don't just dodge, fucking hit—"

His body reacted to the headshot before he even had a chance to register it happening, his arms grabbing for the ropes to catch himself before he could go tumbling through them.

The ringing in his ears happened a second or two later. The pain, a moment after that.

"Right. Fuck. Aye, that's more like it," Hoon said. "That's what I want to see."

"Are you OK?" Greig fretted. "I tried to pull the punch."

Hoon blinked, and gave his head a shake, clearing away the fuzz that was rushing in to fill it. "What, that wasn't full power?"

"No!" Greig replied, and he looked horrified by the very idea. "I can't just punch you at full power when you don't have a headguard on!"

Hoon almost scolded him for that. He almost told him he could take it.

Almost.

"Aye, well, fair enough. That's no' a bad hook you've got

there," he said, then he launched himself off the ropes, drove his shoulder into the younger man's midsection, and slammed him backwards onto the mat.

A knee pinned an arm, a foot trapped a leg. Hoon's blood-smeared forearm pressed down on Greig's throat like an iron bar, cutting off his air so there was nothing he could do but croak, "Stop! Stop! *Stop!*"

Hoon kept his arm there for a few more agonising seconds, then relented. He put a gloved hand on Greig's head and used it as support to get himself back up onto his feet, while the lad lay there coughing and wheezing on the mat.

"But you're no' going to be in a boxing match, son," Hoon reminded him. "A solid right hook's all well and fucking good, but it goes out the window when some bastard's got his thumbs buried up to the knuckles in your eye sockets, and his teeth clamped round your tadger."

Greig spent a moment trying to visualise this, but gave up when Hoon clarified by adding, "No' necessarily at the same time."

Before Greig could offer any sort of response, a sharp cry rang out from the pram and echoed around the gym. Granny, who had been sitting next to the pram watching events in the ring, leaned over to *coochie-coochie-coo*, then drew back in horror and waved a hand in front of his face.

"I draw the line at nappy changing," he announced. "Those days are over."

"Right, yeah. Yeah, I'll get him," Greig said.

Hoon offered a hand, which was regarded with suspicion for a moment, then accepted. Greig was hauled up to his feet, then given a pat on the back as he headed for the ropes.

"Nice couple of punches there, though, son," Hoon told him. "You're maybe no' the useless bastard I thought you were. No' quite, anyway."

Greig moved skittishly out onto the apron, then down to the

ground, like he was worried Hoon might jump on him at any moment.

"Cheers," he said, when he was safely out of lunging range, then he pulled off his gloves, fished the changing bag out from below the pram, and tended to his crying child.

———

Ten minutes later, Benji had been inexpertly changed, and was now nestled in his father's arms, gulping his way through a bottle of milk.

Like Greig, Granny Porter sat on one of the folding chairs that got set out when spectators came along to the occasional exhibition nights they held at the gym. Hoon sat inside the ring, his legs sticking out below the bottom rope, his arms resting on the middle one.

"That wasn't as bad as I thought," Hoon said. He moved his jaw around, and something went *click*. "You weren't, I mean. The punches to the face were quite a bit fucking worse than I was expecting."

"Sorry!" Greig said. He leaned back so the front legs of the folding chair were off the floor. "You did tell me to hit you, though!"

"Uh, I wouldn't do that, son," Granny said, putting a hand on Greig's knee and pushing down until all four of the chair's legs were back in contact with the ground. "Half these things collapse right out from under you if you lean back like that."

Greig warily eyed the metal and plastic chair beneath him. "Oh. Right. Cheers."

"One of the many things we need to spend some money on," Granny said. He looked between the two men. "So, I been wondering since last night, how is it you two know each other, exactly?"

Greig started to reply, but Hoon interjected. "We're Scottish. We all know each other up there," he said. "There's only about six of us."

Granny chuckled, obviously not believing a word of that, but choosing not to pursue it any further. Hoon could feel Greig looking at him, but he avoided the younger man's gaze.

"And when did you start boxing?" Granny asked.

Greig blinked. "Me? Eh, when I was thirteen. My mum got me into it. She thought it would be a good idea if I joined the local club."

"You have a coach there?" Granny asked.

"Eh, yeah. Just volunteers, though. Not anyone, you know, like proper."

"Aha. That explains it," Granny said.

"Explains what?" Hoon and Greig both asked at the same time.

Granny pointed to the bottle of milk that Greig was holding. "You're left-handed."

"Uh, yeah. So?"

"You stand like you're right-handed," Granny told him. "You lead with your left."

Greig looked down at his hands like he hadn't really given them much thought before. "I just did what they told me," he said. "Like everyone else was doing."

"I'm sure you did. And some left-handed fighters do make that choice. Orthodox stance. Some of them do that. But most? Most left-handed fighters, they're southpaws."

"Yeah. Yeah, I'm a southpaw," Greig said.

"No, you're left-handed," Granny corrected. "But you don't stand like a southpaw. You stand like you're right-handed."

"Oh. Right," Greig said. He mulled this over in silence, then frowned. "So, what does that mean?"

"It means you jab with your strong hand and follow through with your weaker one. And, it means your coach wasn't worth shit," Granny concluded.

"Ha. Yeah, no. No, probably not. But it wasn't really about getting good. Not to start with," Greig explained. "We were in a bit of a rough area, and it was meant to keep me out of trouble."

Granny nodded, like this was a story he was all too familiar with. "And did it?"

"Sort of. Yeah. For a while, anyway," Greig said, then he turned his attention back to the baby in his arms.

Granny wasn't letting him off the hook that easily, though. "And what brought you down this way?"

"Just, eh..." Greig shrugged. "Dunno. Fresh start. I heard there were, you know, like... opportunities, and that. For fighters."

"Always opportunities," Granny conceded. "Just not always ones you'd be wise to take."

"What do you know about this underground stuff?" Hoon asked. "You ever come across it before?"

"Rumours and hearsay," Granny said. "Never saw it for myself until last night. Wasn't quite how I'd heard it painted."

"What had you heard?"

Granny considered his answer carefully. He was a man who considered most things carefully, Hoon thought. "Way I heard it, it was some kind of high society bullshit. Full of the who's who, not the hoi polloi."

"The what?" asked Greig.

"For the toffs, no' the peasants," Hoon translated, and Granny pointed to him like he'd just won himself a prize.

"Lot of rich, powerful men watching the little guys hurting each other for a handful of pennies," Granny continued. He sucked air in through his teeth. "But then, I guess that's always been the way of it."

"They're paying me five grand," Greig said.

"May as well be pennies for these people," Granny countered. "I saw some life-changing injuries last night. I mean, don't get me wrong, it was thrilling. Hell, it was the most fun

I've had in a long time, but five grand won't do anyone much good if they can't use their hands. Can't walk. Can't talk."

"That's not going to happen," Greig insisted, though he pulled the child in his arms in a little closer.

"You show promise. You're still young. You could go pro," Granny continued. "But at boxing. Real boxing, not this... whatever it is."

"I can't," Greig said. "I can't wait that long. We need money now."

Granny nodded. "Yes, well, I hear that, alright," he said. He leaned back in his chair, then quickly thought better of it and sat forward again. He appraised Greig with a long, slow look. "And that's why you fight? For money?"

"I mean... yeah."

Granny raised an eyebrow. "That's it?"

Greig wriggled uncomfortably. "Yeah. I mean, I suppose, like, not just for that"

"For what, then?"

The boy was blushing now, wishing he'd kept his mouth shut. "I suppose, sort of, like, for him," he said. "For Benji. To give him a better, like, life, or whatever. Better than I had."

"And?" Granny pressed.

It took several seconds for the reply to come. "And, I mean, I want to, you know, like, make him proud, sort of thing."

"Uh-huh," Granny said. He slapped his hands on his thighs, gave a groan of effort as he got to his feet, then pointed to Hoon. "You. Down here. Take the baby."

Hoon and Greig both offered the same response at the same time. "You what?"

Granny turned his attention back to the younger man. "You, hand the kid over, and go get your ass in the ring."

A look of horror registered on Greig's face. "You want me to fight you?"

"Shit, no, son. I'm eighty-four years old. There are only two things I'm fighting these days—dementia..." He stuck out a thumb and forefinger like he was counting with them. "...and dementia."

Greig looked up at him, concerned. "Um, you said 'dementia' twice."

Granny chuckled, and turned to Hoon. "Nice kid, but not the sharpest knife in the drawer, is he?"

"Aye, you can fucking say that again," Hoon agreed.

"What do you mean? He did say it twice," Greig pointed out.

Granny smiled, but made no further comment on the matter. Instead, he pointed to the baby again. "Pass him over, and get in the ring. I'm too old to fight you, but I'm not too old to give you some pointers."

"Can you no' just stick the bairn back in his pram?" Hoon suggested, peering at Benji like he was an unexploded IED of unknown origin. "That's probably best for all concerned."

"I've not finished feeding him, though," Greig said. "And he's going to need winding before I put him down."

Granny bent over and prised the child from Greig's arms. Benji's mouth searched hungrily for the teat of the bottle, then his bottom lip turned outwards and the waterworks started.

"It's not rocket science," Granny said, raising his voice to be heard over the racket. He held the crying infant out for Hoon to take. "You'll figure it out."

"Jesus fuck," Hoon muttered, but he slid under the bottom rope, and awkwardly took hold of the child.

The handover appeared to cause Benji some confusion—enough so that his screeching died down into some petted-lip grizzling. Hoon held the boy at arm's length, and they both regarded each other in silence for a few seconds, like they were sizing one another up.

And then, with a kick of his legs and a screwing up of his face, Benji erupted into tears again.

"Christ. OK. Right. Shut up," Hoon instructed. "Enough with the whinging, you gurning-faced wee bastard."

This stern talking to didn't have the effect on the child that Hoon hoped it would. Benji, unsurprisingly, continued to sob.

With a tut, Hoon manoeuvred the boy into the crook of his arm, then pointed to the bottle Greig was still clutching. "Right, give me that fucking thing," he instructed. He took the bottle and brought it closer to the baby's mouth. "And we'll see if that makes him shut the fuck..."

Silence fell, save for the faint *slurp* of the baby taking his milk. Hoon rocked his weight from one foot to the other, and gave a nod that bordered on the self-satisfied.

"Piece of piss," he said. "Now, go get in the ring and do what Granny tells you. Because, frankly, you need all the fucking help you can get."

CHAPTER TWENTY-SIX

"WHERE THE FUCK HAVE YOU BEEN?"

Hoon stopped just inside his hotel room, and let the door close behind him before replying.

"Who are you, my wife?" he asked, hanging his jacket on a peg on the wall.

Miles was standing in the middle of the room, and from his position it was clear that he'd been pacing back and forth, presumably for quite some time.

"Speaking of which, why are you always here? Have you no' got a fucking family to go home to?" Hoon asked, sauntering further into the room. "I mean, I doubt they'll be missing you, but they might be idly wondering where you are."

"You turned off the tracking," Miles snapped, ignoring the question.

He was angry. Positively fuming, in fact. Hoon had never seen him like this. Truth be told, he liked him better this way. It felt more honest.

"Obviously, aye," Hoon said.

"I didn't know where you were!"

"Well, aye. That was the entire fucking point," Hoon

explained. "If I wanted you to know where I was, I wouldn't have turned it off, would I? You need to think these things through."

He raised a hand to give the MI5 man a patronising pat on the cheek, but Miles caught his hand and held it. For a moment —just a moment—there was real fire blazing behind his eyes.

"You need to start taking this fucking seriously," Miles spat back.

"Aw, were you worried I'd got hurt?" Hoon asked.

"I was worried you'd screwed this whole thing up! I was worried you'd been killed! You and this lad you're using."

"Here, I wouldn't say I'm fucking *using* him..."

"No? What would you say, then?" Miles demanded. "How would you describe it, Bob?"

Hoon hesitated. "I'm helping him. He wants to do it. He knows what he's getting into."

"What?!" Miles threw back his head and laughed at that. "No, he doesn't. He has no concept of what he's getting into."

"He knows he's there to fight," Hoon said.

"And do you remember why you're there? Do you remember the point of all this? Or are you just enjoying being a part of the show?"

"Of course, I fucking remember," Hoon retorted, and the vein on his temple pulsed. "I'm there to find Caroline and bring her home."

"No! No, you're not!" Miles cried. "It's bigger than that. It's much bigger! You're there to get access to Godfrey West. To the Eel. You're there to infiltrate his part of the network and bring it down. And yes, that's how you find Caroline. Maybe. Hopefully. But he's the target. He's the priority."

"No' for me," Hoon said. He stared into the MI5 man's eyes, like he was trying to implant that last statement deep in his brain, then turned and headed for the fridge containing the minibar.

Miles breathed out, rubbed his temples, and then tried a different approach.

"Where is he now? Your fighter?"

"Sent him home in a taxi. Told him I'd be in touch tomorrow when I knew what was happening."

"Right. Right, I see. And have you eaten? I was going to get room service."

"What, delivered to my room? That's taking fucking liberties, is it no'?" Hoon asked, squatting by the fridge.

"I am paying for it," Miles reminded him. "I mean, we are. The agency. We're paying for everything."

"Aye, well, speaking of which, I'm going to need more cash," Hoon said. "I'm running low."

"How the...? You had two grand yesterday."

"Aye, and now I don't," Hoon said. He opened the fridge and couldn't contain his irritation at the sight of the empty slots. "Fuck's sake. They haven't filled this up since yesterday. How the fuck's that allowed?"

Miles picked up the receiver of the room's phone. "I'll call room service. What do you want?"

"Just get me the most expensive thing on the menu," Hoon said. He closed the fridge door and stood up. "I mean, like you say, you pricks are paying. Might as well make the most of it while I can."

———

It was after eight when the food arrived. Hoon lay propped up on the bed, polishing off a thoroughly enjoyable T-Bone steak with all the trimmings, while Miles sat at the desk, picking away at an apology for a chicken dish.

"We looked into the woman you mentioned. Amanda," Miles said. "Couldn't find anything."

Hoon dunked a bit of lightly seared fat into a little pot of peppercorn sauce and swirled it around. "What, nothing?"

"No. Name not pinging up anywhere. You sure she's in charge?"

"She certainly seemed to think so," Hoon said.

"We'll keep looking." Miles sliced off a thin piece of chicken breast and pronged a couple of carrot chunks onto the fork alongside it. "We dug around into your young friend a bit, too."

"Greig?"

"Do you know he's been banned from boxing?"

Hoon stopped swirling the fat around and shoved it in his mouth. He took a moment to savour the taste, then motioned with his fork for Miles to continue.

"Performance-enhancing drugs at some European contest. Ten-year ban. Think they were making an example."

"Oh. Right." Hoon chewed thoughtfully for a minute. "Wonder if he can get his hands on some more? He might fucking need them tomorrow."

"I've been thinking about tomorrow," Miles said. He put down his knife and fork and swivelled the chair around to face the bed. "They haven't told you anything? You don't know where it is?"

"Not a ghoster," Hoon told him. "They said they'd pick us up."

"But they didn't give you a time?"

Hoon shoved a pinkie right to the back of his mouth and unhooked a bit of meat from a rear molar. "Nope. Not yet. Said they'd give us a bit of warning, though, and that they'd get the pick-up address at the same time."

"Right. OK. Well, you'll need to turn the tracking on the phone back on, obviously."

"You don't fucking say," Hoon replied.

Miles started to turn back to his dinner, then abandoned it. "I was also thinking about who's going to be there."

"What, at the fight?"

"Yes. In an ideal world, West himself will be there. If he is, you have to tread lightly. Don't antagonise him, whatever you do."

"Antagonise him? When the fuck do I ever antagonise anyone?" Hoon asked.

Miles raised both eyebrows, but passed no further comment on the matter. "My worry is the nephew. Charles."

Hoon paused with a plump, sauce-covered mushroom halfway to his mouth. "That wee cocksplash? I thought you said he wasn't worth stressing about?"

"He isn't. Not really," Miles said. "But... he could be there. Tomorrow. He could be at the fight. And he knows you. He's seen your face."

There was a *clink* as Hoon returned his fork to his plate. He stared at the darkened TV on the wall across from the bed, and his reflection stared back.

"Fuck."

"Yeah."

"He could fucking blow everything."

"He could," Miles agreed. "He really could. If he's there, you'll just have to try to stay out of his way."

Hoon winced. "Risky. I'm going to be right there in the fucking middle of it all. If he's there, he's bound to see me. Fuck!"

"Yeah. It's a problem," Miles said.

Hoon chewed his bottom lip for a moment, then spat it out. "Aye, well, you know what they call a problem in Japan? A fucking solution," he announced.

"I don't think that's how the saying goes," Miles said, but Hoon was up off the bed now, and completely ignoring him.

"No' to put too fine a point on it, but if that wee prick's there, the whole thing's fucked," Hoon declared. "So, the answer is simple." He made a weighing motion with his hand. "Problem, solution, like they say in Japan."

"Again, I don't think they do say that..."

"That cash I mentioned earlier," Hoon said.

"What about it?"

"You might want to get your arse to an ATM," Hoon told him. "Because I'm going to need you to get me it pronto."

CHAPTER TWENTY-SEVEN

HOON HAD SPENT a good couple of minutes perusing the menu when he'd first arrived at Under, the cocktail bar where the blue-haired S&M queen had first hooked up with Charlie West. She'd told Hoon that he came here 'all the time,' and he was counting on the bastard being here tonight.

The drinks ranged from old-school classics like *Sex on the Beach* and *Singapore Sling* to the bar's own recipes like *Moonlight Dalliance, Electric Nylon*, and—Hoon's personal favourite—*Cheeky Wee Fuck.*

While the name of that last one appealed, the contents very much did not. Any mix of alcohol that included a peppermint flavoured gin liqueur could, quite frankly, fuck right off.

He settled on a vodka martini, but stopped short of asking for it shaken and not stirred, since only arseholes did that.

The *mixologist*, as he insisted on fucking calling himself, was in his mid-thirties, with a twirly moustache and a hairstyle that appeared half-finished—long on one side, shaved almost down to bone on the other.

He was dressed like he'd stepped right out of a saloon in the late eighteen hundreds, with a thick pair of braces holding up his trousers, and a matching pocket square sticking up from the pocket of his collarless white shirt.

While Hoon waited for the posing bastard to whip the drink together, he checked himself out in the big mirror behind the bar. The website for Under had made it clear that there was a strict dress code, but nobody appeared to be enforcing it. At least, not where the men were concerned.

Most of them had fallen well short of the tuxedo and bow tie combo that Hoon had plumped for, settling instead for shirts, suit jackets, and ties where they could be arsed. They hung mostly in groups, barking out laughter and swapping tales of how much money they'd made that day, or how many cars they had parked in their fucking driveways.

Bankers. Why was this whole city full of bankers?

A few of them had wandered off to chance their arms with the dozen or so women dotted around the place, some in pairs, others flying solo. The women were kitted out in dresses of various styles and colours, some long and elegantly figure-hugging, others short, sparkly, and more or less arse-revealing.

The women smiled graciously at every scrap of attention thrown their way. Surprising, given how fucking pig-ugly some of the guys cracking onto them were. Either they were soulless money-grabbers looking to latch onto the first rich bastard who came their way, or they were unbelievably fucking desperate.

Or, Hoon thought, maybe they weren't here through their own free will.

Whatever, behind the smiles and fluttering eyelashes not one of them was genuinely having a good time.

Hoon's drink was placed in front of him, and he bit down on his tongue to stop himself shouting, "Eighteen fucking quid?!" when the bill was presented. He paid it in cash, told the barman to use the two quid change to, "Go buy yourself the rest of that fucking haircut," then headed to an empty booth in the corner that would give him the best possible view of the rest of the bar.

He removed the olive from his drink, flicked it onto the floor, then took a sip. It had been several years since he'd had a vodka martini, and he immediately remembered why. They were shite. Quite what James Bond saw in them, he'd never know.

Before he'd even set his glass down, a woman appeared at the booth. She was young—far too young to genuinely be interested in a grizzled old bastard like himself—and he got the sense that she was nervous when she opened the conversation.

"Hi. Would you like to buy me a drink?"

"No' particularly, sweetheart," he told her. "Have you seen the fucking prices in this place? They're through the roof. Besides, I've only just sat down."

"Um, oh. OK."

She looked back over her shoulder at nobody in particular. When she turned to face him again, he was holding out a twenty. "Tell you what, you go get yourself something. Save my old legs."

The money was quickly plucked from his grasp. He watched her as she *clopped* over to the bar and placed her order, the tight hem of her shimmering thigh-length dress forcing her legs to rub together.

She wasn't used to walking in heels, that much was obvious. They were big bastards of things, too—five or six inchers—and from behind she looked like a wee girl playing dress-up with her mummy's clothes.

Hoon scanned the rest of the room while he waited for her to come back. There was some Grade A arseholery going on more or less everywhere he looked, and while there were plenty of Charlie West types in the place, there was no sign of the actual Charlie West himself.

Still, the night was young. There was time for him to put in an appearance yet.

He heard the approaching footsteps, and turned to find the

young woman teetering back to his table. "Thanks," she said, sliding into the booth directly across from him. Her frizzed-up 80s style hairdo all but blocked his view of the door. "I'm Brandi, by the way. You're new here, aren't you?" She gave a little shake of her head. "I mean, I haven't seen you here before."

She stuck her straw between her pouting red lips and sucked. The level of the pink-tinged liquid in her glass dropped half an inch before she removed the straw from her mouth and used it to poke around in her ice.

The tip of her tongue flicked across her teeth and skimmed her glossy lips. Presumably, this was meant to be a sultry and suggestive gesture, but the mechanical, well-rehearsed way in which she did it had the opposite effect to the one intended.

"No, first time. Heard a lot about the place, thought I'd check it out," Hoon said. He made a gesture with his left hand. "Can you shift your arse that way a bit?"

"What? Oh. Sorry." Brandi's arse shifted, as requested. "You waiting for someone?"

"Something like that, aye," Hoon said. He stole another look around the bar, checked out a couple of new arrivals, then leaned closer to the girl across the table and lowered his voice. "I'm looking for Charlie."

"Oh. Right. OK," Brandi said. Her eyes darted left and right. She leaned in, mirroring Hoon's body language. "I know someone who can probably hook you up."

"Aye?"

"Yeah. How much do you want?"

Hoon frowned. "How much do I...?" The penny dropped. He tutted. "No' Charlie as in cocaine," he told her. "Charlie as in Charlie. A guy. Called Charlie. Comes here a lot."

"Oh. Shit. Yeah. Sorry. Forget I said anything!" Brandi implored. "Um, Charlie? You a friend of his?"

"Oh aye. We go way back," Hoon told her. "You know him?"

There was something about the way her eyes turned down, and how she adjusted herself on the chair that made Hoon's skin crawl.

She knew him, alright. More than that, he'd hurt her. It was written right there on her face and in the angle of her shoulders.

He didn't wait for her to confirm anything. "He going to be in tonight, do you know?"

"Um, I'm not sure," she said. "What day is it?"

"Thursday."

She almost flinched. "Oh. Then, yeah. Yeah, he's usually in on Thursdays."

"You don't sound overly pleased about that prospect," Hoon said. "What's the story there?"

Brandi brought the straw to her lips again. This time, a couple of inches of liquid disappeared in one gulp. "No story. He's just..." Whatever the end of that sentence was, she didn't get to it. Instead, she turned and looked back in the direction of the door. "He won't come in that way."

Hoon leaned out of the booth a little, allowing himself a better view of the entrance. "Only way in and out, isn't it?"

Brandi shook her head. "No. He uses a different entrance. There's a room they have, through the back. It's..." She pulled up the strap of her dress, like she was securing it in place. "...a private room."

"Where?" Hoon asked.

"I can't... I'm not supposed to say."

"Don't say, then," Hoon told her. "Just look."

Her eyes went back to her drink. She hunched over it, like she was trying to squeeze herself down the straw and into the glass.

"I'm not going to let him hurt you, Brandi. You're not going to get into trouble," Hoon promised. "Just point me in the right direction, then get up and go talk to someone else. I'll give it a minute. No one will ever know you said anything."

She raised her gaze to meet his. It didn't shift from there, not at first. Not for a while. Then, it flicked to a door set in between two bookcases in a roped-off area just to the left of the bar. It remained there until Hoon muttered a, "Thank you," then she got up without a word, picked up her drink, and toddled off to meet some of the boorish new arrivals.

Hoon gave it five minutes. Just long enough for him to force down the vodka martini and then quietly make some uncomplimentary remarks about it.

That done, he got up, sauntered nonchalantly towards the bar while he made sure the barman was occupied elsewhere, then diverted and made for the door between the bookcases.

The rope was easy enough to unhook. He was just replacing it behind him when he heard the first shout of, "Sir?" from somewhere behind him that told him he'd been spotted.

"Toilets this way, aye?" he called back over his shoulder, then he pushed the door open and stepped into a low-lit lounge with a horseshoe-shaped red-leather couch, and a glass coffee table that fit neatly into the curve.

A man was bent over a table, snorting white powder through a short plastic straw. Two women sat next to him, one on either side, neither one apparently keen to get too close.

Hoon heard the clattering of footsteps behind him. "Sir, sir, you can't be in here."

With a snort, the man at the table threw himself upright, and Hoon recognised the bastard at once. Judging by the way Charlie's mouth fell open and how the colour drained from his cheeks, he recognised Hoon, too.

"Well, well, if it's no' Humpty fucking Dumpty himself," Hoon said.

"Oh, fuck! What the fuck?" Charlie coughed, and a cloud of cocaine misted the air in front of him.

A hand caught Hoon by the shoulder. Pulled him back. Turned him in a half-circle. Hoon caught sight of the metal drinks tray arcing towards him just in time to bring up an arm and deflect the worst of the blow.

Wrenching the tray from the barman's hands, he *thwanged* it down hard onto the half-finished haircut, denting the metal and sending the stunned mixologist staggering backwards, just as the two women began to scream.

He heard a door swinging open and he spun on the spot, hurling the circular tray at the fleeing Charlie like it was Captain America's shield. It wobbled through the air, thudded limply against the wall, then spun on the floor like a giant coin.

"Fuck's sake," Hoon hissed, shooting daggers at the useless bastard of a thing.

The barman grabbed for him again. It was far less enthusiastic this time, and the elbow Hoon delivered to the centre of his face robbed him of what little motivation he had left.

Bounding over the couch, Hoon charged through the door, collided with the metal rail of a spiral staircase, then hurried up it in hot pursuit.

He emerged into a drab, largely featureless space that reminded him of a doctor's waiting room. The door was open, and through it he could hear the sound of fleeing footsteps.

"Come here, you wee prick!" he bellowed, launching himself out of the room and into a plush hotel foyer, where guests and staff alike had stopped what they were doing and were staring in confusion at the two men racing towards the revolving front door.

Charlie had an age advantage, but even with the speed-boost afforded to him by his sheer, wide-eyed terror, he wasn't particularly fast. By the time the bastard reached the exit, Hoon had started to close the gap, and the lazy rotation of the revolving door only slowed him down further.

As he shuffled around, Charlie risked a glance back through

the glass, and yelped in fright when he saw Hoon hurtling towards the hotel's other exit. This one was manually operated, and not of the revolving variety, and by the time Charlie went stumbling out onto the street, Hoon was almost upon him.

"Wait, no, don't, don't!" Charlie screeched, a final burst of speed propelling him through a knot of late-night pedestrians.

Hoon launched himself after him, hand grabbing for the trailing tail of Charlie's untucked shirt. As he reached for him, he felt the first little niggle of concern. It spoke to him, a little nagging voice, asking him what the fuck he thought he was playing at.

In truth, this had all happened much more quickly than he'd been expecting, and while his plan had been to corner Charlie West, he hadn't really thought things through much beyond that.

Oh sure, he'd been workshopping a few ideas. The one he had been leaning towards involved kicking so many shades of shite out of Godfrey West's nephew that he couldn't possibly attend the fight the next day. And, if it came to it that he could never walk again, or needed a straw to be able to eat, then so much the fucking better.

Much of this plan relied on some degree of privacy, though. A dark corner. A quiet room. That sort of thing.

What was he going to do if he caught him now? What was the next step after that?

He couldn't exactly pummel the fucker in front of all these witnesses, right at the side of a busy street, could he? Someone would see him—*everyone* would see him, in fact.

This was still London, so it was unlikely that anyone would actually intervene, but they'd stand there filming him, streaming him, uploading him. His face would be everywhere. His cover would be blown.

Shite.

This wasn't good. That was an understatement, in fact.

This was quickly shaping up to be a disaster of the highest fucking—

A horn blared. Brakes wailed, and tyres screeched.

The impact was so hard and so sudden, that Hoon could swear he felt it from several feet away.

Someone who did actually feel it was Charlie West, although the shock of the collision was likely quite quickly replaced by the freeing sensation of flight.

Hoon slid to a stop and watched as Humpty Dumpty had a big fall. Charlie flipped in mid-air, all arms and legs and howling.

There was the sound of bone hitting glass.

Then of flesh hitting tarmac.

Then of the front tyre of a twelve-tonne London bus meeting a flailing skin-sack full of organs.

That last one would really stick in the mind of all those who heard it.

And then, there was silence. Just for a moment—a perfect, absolute stillness that blanketed the area like the first snow of Christmas.

It was shattered, soon after, by the screaming.

But by then, Hoon was no longer around to hear any of it.

CHAPTER TWENTY-EIGHT

MILES WAS STILL in the room when Hoon returned. He shot up out of the armchair like it was spring-loaded, and intercepted Hoon before he could get the door shut.

"Well?" he asked.

"Well, what?"

Miles tutted. "What do you mean, *well what*? Did you see him?"

"Aye," Hoon confirmed. "I saw a surprising fucking amount of him, in fact."

"What's that supposed to mean?" Miles asked.

Hoon unfastened his bow tie, whipped it from inside his collar, then disposed of it on the floor. "It means we don't have to worry about Charlie popping up tomorrow and blowing my cover."

"You sure?" Miles asked. "You sure he won't be there?"

"No' unless they're carrying him in a bucket," Hoon said.

Miles' face took on a sepia sort of shade. "What? Jesus. What are you saying? You didn't... You didn't kill him, did you?"

"No! Fuck's sake. No, of course, I didn't fucking kill him, what do you take me for?" Hoon spat. He shook off the tux. "I mean, did he die? Yes. Very fucking much so. But was it my fault? No. Well, I mean, maybe partly. But did I kill him? No, I did not." He sniffed, shrugged, then dropped his jacket on the floor beside the tie. "Although, I suppose it depends on your definition."

Miles clutched at his head like he was afraid it might topple backwards off his shoulders. "Shit. Shit, shit, shit, shit! Shiiiiit!"

"Alright, keep your fucking hair on," Hoon said. "It's fine. Job done. We wanted him out of the picture, and now he is."

"You weren't supposed to fucking *murder* him!"

The icy coolness of Hoon's reply was in stark contrast to the MI5 man's shrill whine.

"I didn't murder him. I didn't even want to kill him. I mean, no, I did want to, aye, but I wasn't really planning on it," he said. "But this is a fucking war. I didn't start it, but that's where we are. And every war has its fucking casualties. Believe me, I know that better than most. So, I hope you'll find it in your heart to forgive me if I don't shed any tears for that rapey wee prick."

Miles sat on the edge of the bed, and looked surprised by this, like his legs had made the decision all on their own. He ran a hand through his hair, shut his eyes, then took a series of deep breaths that seemed to calm the worst of his panic.

"What actually happened?" he asked.

"He basically exploded."

Miles opened his eyes. "Exploded?"

"Aye, no' with a bomb. Under a bus," Hoon clarified. "Like, imagine the full weight of a double-decker rolling over a—"

"Right. Right, yes, I get the picture," Miles said.

"Never mind the picture, it was the fucking noise that got me," Hoon continued. "Well, that and the smell..."

"Stop!" Miles raised a hand to shut down the description before it could get any more vivid. "And were you seen?"

Hoon thought back to the bar, the girl, the mixologist, all the people in the hotel foyer, and the hundreds of pedestrians and drivers on the street outside.

"No," he said. "No, don't think so."

"OK. Well, that's something," Miles said. He closed his eyes and snatched another few steadying breaths, then stood up. "Right. Well, no point crying over spilled milk."

"Some of him did look a bit milky, right enough," Hoon said. "Or, like, I don't know. Cottage cheese."

"Fuck. OK, enough," Miles said, wincing at the thought of it. He checked his watch, which triggered a stretch and a yawn. "You should get some sleep. Tomorrow's going to be a big day."

"Aye," Hoon conceded. "Aye, it'll be that, alright."

"You're, eh, you're going to be fine. It's going to be fine," Miles told him. "I've got your back."

"Oh right, well that's filled me with fucking confidence, that has," Hoon told him. "If things get out of hand, I'll just wait for you to come rushing in with your fucking spreadsheets and PowerPoint presentations."

"I don't... When have I ever mentioned spreadsheets or PowerPoint presentations?" Miles asked.

"You don't fucking have to, it's written all over your face," Hoon told him. "Now, off you fuck so I can have my room to myself." He pointed to the TV. "Do they have porn on this, do you know?"

Miles side-eyed the screen. "Uh..."

"No' that I'm particularly into that sort of thing, I just like the idea of Her Majesty's Secret Service picking up the bill."

Miles arranged his features into something like a smile. A weary one, but a smile all the same. He patted Hoon on the shoulder. "Knock yourself out."

Hoon followed him when he turned and headed for the door. "Aye, that's the general idea, right enough," he confirmed, then he ejected a, "Here, listen. Before you go..." just as Miles reached for the handle.

"What's up?"

It was Hoon's turn to take a breath. He shoved his hands deep into his pockets and shifted his weight from foot to foot, not quite looking the MI5 man in the eye. "Gabriella and Welshy. They're alright?"

"They are."

Hoon did meet his eye then, just long enough to glower. "You fucking swear?"

"I swear. They're both fine."

"Right. Aye. Good," Hoon said. "So, eh, if anything happens. To me. Tomorrow, or whatever."

"Nothing's going to happen."

"Aye, but if it does, will you tell them something? Will you tell them something from me?"

Miles nodded. "Of course."

"Will you tell them I'm sorry? For, you know, for dragging them into this shite. Will you tell them..." He sighed. "Fuck. I don't know. Maybe just think of something clever and say I said it, eh?"

Miles looked upwards, like he was racking his brains. "I'm sure I can come up with something," he said. "Goodnight, Bob."

"Aye. Fuck off," Hoon instructed. He tilted his head back in the direction of the telly. "Some of us have got shagging to watch."

He stepped back to give Miles room to leave, then watched as the door swung shut again. He stayed there as he took his mobile—Stephen White's mobile—from his pocket, and ran a thumb across the screen to wake it.

He didn't have the number stored in this phone, but that didn't matter. He knew it off by heart. He'd sat there in the dark staring at it often enough. Building up the courage to call. Going over and over what he'd say if someone answered. What he'd tell them. How he'd explain.

He opened the dialler app and punched in the number. His

thumb hovered over the icon that would make the call, start the ball rolling, force him to face what he'd been putting off for so long.

"No," he said, tapping the delete key and erasing the number.

Not like this. Not from this phone. He couldn't link it to them. Any connection might put them at risk, and he couldn't do that to them. He wouldn't. Not after everything they'd been through.

Hoon opened up the settings, reactivated the tracking function, then threw the phone down on the bed. That done, he wriggled his feet back into his shoes without undoing the laces, unhooked his rain jacket from the hanger behind the door, and after a quick check in both directions to make sure Miles wasn't hanging around, he headed out into the corridor.

———

He had wandered for a while until he'd found a phone box. It was a red one, near Parliament Square, and to his amazement, it still accepted payment in coins. He'd slid them into the slot, punched in the number on the sticky plastic buttons, then listened to the *burring* down the line.

The interior of the box had been decorated with the business cards of some of the area's more enterprising—and if the descriptions of the services on offer were anything to go by, open-minded—escorts. The cards blocked most of the little windows, affording him a level of privacy from the late evening revellers strolling past outside.

The phone continued to ring. He whispered, "Come on, come on," and his breath fogged on the few undecorated squares of glass.

And then, there was a click from the other end. The coins

he had loaded into the phone dropped all the way inside, and a voice on the other end said, "Hello?"

It wasn't the voice he'd been hoping for. But it came as no surprise.

"Eh, Lizzie?"

He heard her gasp. Swallow. Struggle to get her reply out. "Robert?"

"Aye. Aye, it's me," Hoon said.

"Has something happened? Have you... Have you found her? Have you found..."

She couldn't say her daughter's name. It got stuck somewhere in her chest.

"No. Not yet," Hoon said. "But, well, I want you to know that I'm still here. I'm still working on it. I haven't stopped."

There was no reply, just the rustling of a mouthpiece being covered, and the muffled sounds of a mother in mourning.

He wanted to tell her he had a lead. He had a chance. That, for the first time in weeks, he actually believed that he might find her. That he might yet bring her home.

But how could he do that to her? To either of them? How could he give them that hope when he had nothing to truly base it on.

"I'm never going to give up, Lizzie. I promised you that much," Hoon said. "Whatever happens, I won't stop. Can you tell Bamber that for me? Can you make sure he—"

There was another click, louder this time, and the line went dead. Hoon's fingers tightened on the handset until the knuckles went white. He swung it back, raised it above his head like he was going to smash it to pieces on the walls of the phone box.

But then, the fight went out of him, and he settled for slamming it back in its cradle.

"Nicely fucking done, Bob," he muttered. "Nicely fucking done."

CHAPTER TWENTY-NINE

GODFREY WEST WAS LYING on his back with his legs in the air when the news came through. He had just had a delightful piss, and was enjoying the way the warmth of it seeped into the absorbent layers of his bulky underwear, when his phone rang.

"Shit."

He didn't reach for the mobile right away. Let them fucking wait. Let him lie here and make the most of this for a while. His time was never his own these days. He never got to savour the little things.

The phone continued to ring. He didn't have voicemail set up, because he had neither the time nor the inclination to listen to messages from the assortment of mundane bastards he was forced to interact with. The downside to this was that, unless he cancelled the call, the phone would ring, and ring, and ring until the person on the other end gave up.

And they were not, it seemed, giving up quickly.

He rolled over on the plastic mat he had set out on the floor, crinkling as his weight shifted, and reached for the trousers he'd left folded on the chair. His full nappy squelched, and he let out a little childish giggle of delight at how it sounded, and the way it felt between his legs.

His mood darkened considerably when he saw the name on his screen. Eddie. One of his more... *specialised* employees. A call from him this late at night was rarely a sign of anything good.

"Yes, what?" he spoke into the phone. "What's happened?"

He listened to the voice on the other end, then slowly lay down on his changing mat. They weren't easy to find in his size. He'd had to have it shipped in from the States, where his particular tastes were more widely catered to.

The waterproof plastic was cold against his back, and he let out a little gasp as it pressed against his bare skin.

"What do you mean?" he asked. "*Dead?*"

He gazed up at the ceiling while he listened to the response. A spinning mobile of zoo animals crept around in circles, while a lullaby chimed softly from some in-built speaker. His eyes followed the movements, round, and around, and around.

"Well, then find whoever is responsible," he spat into the phone. "It's not rocket science, Eddie. This is what I pay you for, is it not? Find out who killed him, and then deal with it. And someone tell his mother. Let her know it's in hand. Send her, I don't know, send her flowers or something."

He gave Eddie just enough time to confirm he understood these instructions, then he spoke emphatically into the mobile.

"Now, unless the building I'm in is on fire, I don't want to be disturbed again tonight. It's a big day tomorrow, and I'm trying to unwind," Godfrey said. "Is that clear? Good. It had better be."

He thumbed the button to hang up, then tossed the phone so it flew several feet across the nursery. It bounced on the carpet, then rolled the rest of the way until it came to a stop among the pile of cuddly toys in the corner.

Charlie was dead. His only nephew was dead. Chased into

the street and run down. Messy, by the sounds of things. Painful, one had to assume.

"Oh well," he said, then he slipped one hand down the front of his nappy, reached for his bottle of room temperature breast milk with the other, and snuggled down for a feed.

CHAPTER THIRTY

THE CALL CAME THROUGH JUST after ten. A man whose voice he didn't recognise told him a car was being sent, asked for the address, and then instructed him to be out front in twenty minutes.

Hoon, who had fallen asleep shortly before eight, and had still been there when the phone rang, leaped out of bed the moment the call ended, informed the phone that it was an, "Absolute fucking bawbag," and then tried to get dressed, call Miles, and have a slash all at the same time.

Miles double-checked that the phone tracking was working, confirmed that he could see Hoon's location, and then rattled off a list of instructions that were mostly focused on Hoon not doing anything stupid.

Hoon said he'd do his best, but made no promises, then he ended the call and went on the hunt for the rest of his clothes.

Once dressed, he fished in the carrier bag of shopping he'd picked up on the walk back from the phone box the night before, and slaked his thirst with a lukewarm can of *Fanta*.

Next out of the bag came a padded envelope. That had

been the real reason he'd stopped in at the shop. The two cans of *Fanta* and three bags of *Frazzles* had just been a bonus.

It took a bit of effort to cram the sequin-covered notebook into the envelope, but a wee outburst of swearing seemed to hasten its journey on. He peeled off the covering of the sticky strip and sealed the envelope shut.

He wrote Bamber's name and address on the front, then scribbled a note to Miles on the branded hotel pad. It was short and to the point, and said simply: 'Post me.'

All that done, he checked the time. Twelve minutes since the call had come in. Eight minutes to go. No point in hanging around.

He left the room, took the stairs down to the ground floor, then exited onto the street. The rest of London had been awake for hours now and had settled into all its usual rhythms. Hoon had a quick scan of the traffic, but while there were plenty of taxis and Ubers around, none of them were waiting outside the hotel.

He waited for a gap, then darted across the road and took up position under the awning of a shop on the other side, half-hidden by shadow, with a clear view of the hotel he'd just left.

There, he took his phone out, called up Greig's number from his contacts, and listened as the connection was attempted.

Greig sounded groggy when he answered. Not so much like he had just woken up, more like he hadn't been to sleep in the first place. "Hello?"

"Morning, sunshine," Hoon said. "You sound like a bag of shite."

"Yeah. Rough night. Benji didn't sleep much," Greig replied. "Did you get a call? Because some guy phoned me to say—"

"They're picking you up?"

Greig yawned before replying. "Yeah. In, like, five minutes."

"Same here," Hoon confirmed. He watched a black BMW SUV slowing as it passed the hotel, then tracked it as it picked up speed again. "Hold on," he said, taking the phone from his ear.

He opened the camera app, snapped off a picture of the vehicle, then sent it to Miles' phone. The SUV indicated left at a junction a little further along the street, potentially preparing to do another lap.

"Sorry, back," Hoon said, returning the phone to his ear.

"Right. So, eh, I guess I'll just see you there then, I suppose."

"Aye. See you there," Hoon replied. "Wherever the fuck 'there' is."

"Oh, wait!" Greig said. "What if it's, like, busy? How will I find you?"

"What do you mean?" Hoon asked. "Just look for the guy with my face. Chances are that'll be me."

"Uh, yeah. Ha. OK. Right. Well... yeah. See you soon, then," Greig said.

"Aye," Hoon said, and this time it was his turn to call out. "Oh, but Greig."

"Yeah?"

"Maybe don't bring the fucking baby this time, eh?"

He ended the call, took a moment to delete the message to Miles and the photo of the BMW from his phone, then spotted the vehicle approaching again for a second pass of the hotel's front door.

Spying a gap in the traffic, Hoon darted across the street just in time for the SUV to roll to a stop. The driver didn't give him so much as a glance of acknowledgement. Instead, the rear passenger-side door opened, and a familiar figure squeezed himself out.

It was one of the men who'd escorted him from Amanda's room back at the McGinlay. Hoon grinned like he was greeting an old friend. "Which one were you again?" he asked. "Bingo or Butterfuck?"

"Just get in the car," the goon instructed.

"You look like a Butterfuck," Hoon told him, then he climbed into the back of the Beamer and found Bingo sitting directly behind the driver. "Great, the gang's all here."

He was given a shove to help him inside, then the man he'd christened Butterfuck squashed in beside him. It wasn't that the rear of the car was small—it was pretty roomy, actually—but between them, the two goons were taking up around seventy percent of the available seating space.

"Do you maybe want to do me a favour and breathe in, lads?" Hoon suggested. "I'm feeling like a fart trapped between two arse cheeks here."

Neither of the men complied. If anything, their bulk seemed to press more firmly against him.

Up front, the driver checked his wing mirror, indicated, then pulled out into traffic, forcing a taxi behind them to slam on its brakes and sound its horn.

"I'd say I'd better put my fucking seatbelt on, but the weight of you two bastards should keep me safely pinned in place," Hoon remarked.

He turned to the man on his left, and was confronted by a black cloth bag with a drawstring opening. He held a hand up like he was declining the offer of a cup of tea.

"That won't be necessary," he said.

"Yes. It will," said Butterfuck. "I can put it on, or you can. Up to you."

"Oh, you do it, then," Hoon said. He stuck out his chin and winked. "I bet you're a fucking dab hand at putting bags over guys' heads. I want to see how the pros do it."

"Suit yourself," the goon grunted, then the bag came down, the tie pulled tight, and Hoon was plunged into a hazy not-quite-darkness.

"Aye, thought as much. That was fucking textbook," Hoon said.

He turned his head and craned his neck several times in every available direction. He wasn't trying to see—he'd realised immediately that this was pointless—but he *was* trying to get on the tits of the men sitting on either side of him, and judging by their tuts and sighs it was working well.

When he got bored of that, he wriggled himself upright, placed his hands on his knees, then sat there humming. He knew there was little point in him trying to figure out the route the car was taking, given that he didn't know his way around London even with his eyes open.

He tried though, all the same. He made a mental note of a big left turn, but when it was followed up by a couple of rights in quick succession, and then a long, gradual left, he concluded that he was already hopelessly lost, and completely wasting his time.

Better to go back to his original plan of pissing off the two men beside him.

"Right, then," he announced, slapping his hands on their knees to get their attention. "I Spy, with my little eye, something beginning with B..."

———

The drive took an hour, give or take. Or, to put it another way, seventeen games of *I Spy,* all of which only Hoon participated in, and all ending in him saying the word, "Bag!" like it was a surprise.

It was, he thought, a miracle he made it to the venue alive.

The SUV had descended a ramp near the end of the journey. The echo of the engine had changed, and Hoon knew they were inside somewhere now. That didn't really help him figure out where they'd taken him, although technically he supposed it did narrow things down a bit.

The car eventually stopped. He was ordered to stay where he was, and Bingo got out. He'd heard a brief discussion, but it had been too far away for him to make it out over the sound of the running engine.

Bingo had returned to the car a couple of minutes later, and Hoon had been ordered to keep the hood on while getting out.

He had, against his better judgement, complied, and had emerged into what felt like a multi-storey car park. There were several engines running, and the sound reverberated off walls. A cold wind swirled around him, though, which told him he was neither inside nor outside, but somewhere in between.

That didn't leave many options—train station or car park, mostly, and only one of those felt likely.

A hand fell onto his shoulder and manhandled him in a direction of its choosing. As he was steered along by it, he couldn't shake the feeling that he was being led to face the hangman's noose.

Soon, a door creaked open, and he was guided inside a building. There had been light seeping through the fabric of the bag until then—not enough to see by, but enough to give an impression of a world beyond the hood. Now, though, the light was gone, and there was nothing to see but the dark.

They stopped him with a tug on the shoulder and a muttered, "Wait."

He heard a button being pressed. The clank and hum of an elevator. It grew steadily louder until the doors opened ahead of him with a jolly little *ping,* and he was marched forward three paces.

By this point, he was almost completely disorientated, and despite his best efforts, he couldn't work out if the lift took him up or down. He was sure they didn't turn him around though, and when the elevator stopped and gave another cheerful *ping,* he was led straight ahead through what he assumed must be a second set of doors.

Another few corridors followed—brighter again, so the inside of the hood developed some texture—and then a door was opened ahead of him, and the voice at his back said, "In."

"Mr White?"

That was Greig's voice, and the relief in it was unmistakable.

The hand was removed from Hoon's shoulder, and he tore off the hood right before the door behind him clicked closed.

He made a grab for the handle, only to find that the door had already been locked from the outside.

"Well, that's a fucking health and safety hazard if I ever saw one," he muttered.

He ran a hand down the inside of the door, but found no way of opening it from that side. Not without the liberal application of a shoulder or the heel of a boot, anyway.

"I'm glad you're here, Mr White," Greig gushed. "I was starting to get really worried."

Hoon turned to the lad and, sure enough, that worry was written all over his face. He was dressed in jeans and a hoodie, and had twisted an empty can of *Red Bull* into a sort of tornado shape which now *cu-clunked* as he fiddled anxiously with it.

They were in what looked to be a dressing room in an old theatre, albeit one that hadn't put on any shows in a very long time. There were no personal touches here, just some beige decor, a couple of worn swivel chairs, and a long dressing table with a mirror mounted to the wall behind it. A crack ran from the top of the mirror almost all the way to the bottom, jagged and forked like a bolt of lightning.

"They put a bag on your head, too?" Greig asked, glancing at the hood Hoon still held in one hand.

"No, I just brought my own from home," Hoon said, then he

sighed when Greig failed to recognise the sarcasm. "Aye, son, they put a bag on my head, too."

"Guess they don't want us to know where we are."

"So it would seem," Hoon said. "Daft bastards obviously don't know about..." He patted his pockets, his face falling. "Where the fuck's my phone?"

"I think they took them," Greig said. "They took mine, anyway. Said I'd get it back at the end."

Hoon's brow furrowed and his nostrils flared. "What, they fucking *confiscated* them? Bastards!"

"They seem pretty serious about security," Greig said. He squeezed the can again. *Cu-clunk.* "I mean, I know *technically* it's not legal, the whole fighting thing, but it feels a bit, you know... much. I get quite travel sick on long journeys, and it got quite hot in that hood. I was sure I was going to spew."

Cu-clunk.

Cu-clunk.

"Did it seem a bit much to you?"

"OK, first of all, I'm going to break your fucking fingers if you don't put that can down," Hoon told him.

He waited until Greig had sheepishly placed the empty can down on the dressing table before continuing.

"Right, good. Now, secondly, I'm not best pleased about how my morning's been shaping up, either, but you don't hear me fucking whinging about it. We know why we're here. We know what we've come to do."

"To fight."

"Aye. Like I just said, we know why we're here, you don't need to sign it out for the fucking deaf, son." He pointed to the *Everlast* kit bag that was currently taking up one of the room's two available seats. "That your gear?"

Greig picked up the bag and cradled it to his chest, almost exactly like Hoon had seen him do with his infant son. "Yeah.

Yeah, all my stuff's in here. Should I get changed, do you think?"

"Aye, may as well."

Greig hesitated. "What if there's, like, a meeting, or something?"

"A meeting?"

"Or, I don't know, a press conference sort of thing."

Hoon snorted, like Greig had just made a joke. When the lad didn't join in, though, Hoon realised he was being serious.

"I don't think you need worry too much about a press conference," Hoon told him. "But, in the unlikely event that they do decide to hold a fucking photoshoot, I'm sure they'd prefer you in your fighting gear than dressed like a wee ned. Either way, I'd say you're safe to get changed."

Greig nodded. "OK. Thanks, Mr White," he said. "I couldn't do this without you."

His tone was nothing but sincere, and Hoon felt a pang of guilt as he returned the lad's smile. "Aye, well. Likewise, son," he said. He turned away and caught his warped reflection in the damaged mirror. The crack split him in two right down the middle. "Likewise."

CHAPTER THIRTY-ONE

IT WAS NOT A THEATRE. That much was obvious when they were eventually collected from their dressing room by yet more men in suits, and led through a network of corridors and stairways to the vast, hangar-like windowless room that stretched out before them now.

It wasn't an arena, exactly. It wasn't quite *that* big. But nor was it far off. It had to be an exhibition centre of some sort, Hoon thought, and he wished he'd paid more attention to the city he'd been living in for the past few months. Maybe then, he'd have been able to work out where they were.

Greig wasn't being much help either, and was instead just staring in mute disbelief at all the activity going on around them.

On Hoon's instruction, he had changed into his shorts, boots, and a vest-style top that left little of his impressive physique to the imagination, while hiding some of the bruises around his abdomen and ribs. A half-decent opponent would hone in on those right away, so it was best to keep them out of sight for as long as possible. No point painting a target on the poor fucker's injuries.

Hoon had then strapped up Greig's hands. This time he'd bound his feet, too, if only to remind the lad that this wasn't a boxing competition, and that when it came to causing harm to his opponents, kicking was one of the many options available to him. And, in fact, a preferred one.

"There's a lot of people here," Greig muttered.

He was not wrong. The hall had been split into sections, with ten-foot-tall freestanding barriers dividing it up into five or six areas of various sizes. From where they stood, they could only see the two closest sections. Two cages, domed at the top, had been assembled in each space, elevated to make them easier to see from the rows of chairs around them.

Nobody was seated yet, but there had to be seventy or eighty people milling around the cages, and presumably plenty more still in the sections of the hall beyond the walls.

They were all kitted out like they were headed for an afternoon at Ascot. The men sported top hats and tails, the women—of which there were notably far fewer—wore more colourful dresses with elaborate headwear that lent the place something of a carnival atmosphere.

None of these were the most remarkable detail of their outfits, though.

"Are they... Are they wearing masks?" Greig asked.

"Either that or there's a rogue plastic surgeon on the fucking loose," Hoon replied.

While the outfits varied—the women's, anyway—the masks were all uniform. They were all made of the same semi-transparent plastic, and while the design of the mask itself was plain and uninteresting, the curves warped and magnified the features of the wearer into something grotesque and barely recognisable as human.

"Fucking posh folk," Hoon muttered, and there was some real bile behind it. "They love all this shite."

"What shite?" Greig asked.

"Fancy dress stuff. Masquerade bollocks. They'll all be shagging each other before this thing's over, just you fucking wait. It'll be a fucking carpet of twisting limbs and heaving bodies."

Greig turned and cast his eye across the milling crowds again. Right now, they were mostly just shaking hands, but there was a definite buzz about the place that threatened the possibility of more to come.

"Jesus. You think?"

"Oh aye. Trust me. It'll be wall to wall bumming in here before the afternoon's out, I know what these bastards are like."

"I mean, that's not technically on the schedule, but who knows where the day will take us?"

Hoon and Greig both turned to find Amanda standing behind them, her apparently compulsory glass of champagne held in its usual position. She was wearing a satin silver dress, with matching hat and heels. Unlike most of the others in attendance, she wasn't wearing a mask, and so the smirk on her face was plain to see.

"What have you come as?" Hoon asked her. "A roll of fucking *Bacofoil*?"

"Ha! There's that wit of yours," she said. The smile held, but not without a few cracks. She glanced down at her outfit, then gave her champagne flute a dismissive little wave. "It wasn't my first choice, I'll give you."

"What happened, did someone come and wrap you in it after you finished a fucking marathon?" Hoon continued.

The smile lost a little more of its shine. "Haha. Well, it certainly feels like I've run a marathon, given the work that's gone into this."

Hoon scoffed at the comment. "My arse," he remarked. "What, up all night building the walls and setting out the folding chairs, were you?"

Amanda took a sip of her champagne, and it felt like she

was stalling for time, trying to figure out her next move, or her next line.

Clearly, she'd had enough of Hoon, and turned her attention to the younger man beside him, instead. "We really appreciate you stepping in at such short notice," she said.

"Eh, yeah. No bother. Thanks for, like, inviting me."

"You really impressed the other night. We all loved your..." She waved the glass, searching for the word. "Virtuousness."

Greig raised both eyebrows and rocked back on his heels. "Cool. Thanks."

"I'd play into that today," she advised. "Everyone loves a hero."

"Who's the fucking coach here?" Hoon demanded, stepping between them.

"Ha! Yes, you're right, of course. Far be it from me to intrude. Just some friendly advice, that's all. I know what this sort of audience enjoys."

"Caviar and fucking croquet, I'm guessing," Hoon said.

"Some of them, yes. It's a real mix of old money and new. There are actors, business leaders, lawyers, politicians, royalty..."

Greig whistled. "Seriously? Royalty?"

"It's Andrew, isn't it?" Hoon guessed, and his nostrils flared like they were picking up a bad smell. "I bet it is. I bet it's fucking Andrew."

"I don't get to know names," Amanda said.

"I thought you were the boss?"

There was a bitter note to her laughter. She brought her champagne quickly to her lips, almost like she was trying to stop herself saying something she might regret. "No. Definitely not," she said, once she'd finished drinking. "Not by a long shot."

"How does it all work?" Greig asked. He indicated the hall with a nod. "Like, what's actually going to happen?"

Amanda looked to Hoon for his permission, then beamed when he granted it with a grunt and a roll of his eyes.

"Good question," she said. "Basically, we'll be starting soon with eight fights. Two at a time, opponents randomly drawn. We've got a real mix of styles and experience levels, though you're the new kid on the block, so to speak."

She laughed like this was a joke, and Greig felt compelled to chuckle along with her. Hoon didn't crack so much as a smile.

"And is it, like, a knock-out thing?"

"Well, I believe that's the general idea, yes..."

Hoon tutted. "He means is it like a tournament? The four winners are paired off in the semis, then the winner of them two fight in the final? That the plan?"

Amanda mulled her answer over for a while before coming out with it. "We tend to play it by ear after those first bouts," she explained. "Perhaps a winner isn't in shape to continue. Maybe another competitor wants to spice things up a bit by taking on two other fighters at once. After those first fights, think of it like jazz. It's a bit wild, and fun, and freestyle."

"That's no' jazz you're describing, that's BMXing," Hoon told her. "So, it's a big fucking free for all, basically?"

"I mean, I wouldn't say that, exactly, no. But the audience is... open to possibilities."

Hoon gave Greig a nudge with an elbow. "See? What did I tell you? They'll be knobbing each other like bloody rabbits."

Greig had zoned out of the conversation and was instead staring at the man who had just entered through the same door he and Hoon had used.

At least, he thought it was a man.

"What the fuck is that?" he whispered.

He was the shape of a man, just not the size, or any of the traditional colours. His skin was chalk-white, like he'd been carved out of a block of ivory. At first, Greig thought he was bald, but then realised that the short-cropped hair on his head and the fuzz of his goatee beard were as devoid of pigmentation as the rest of him.

He had a hand cupped over his eyes like he was shielding them from the light. When he became acclimatised enough to remove the hand, the eyes were a pinkish-red that crept across the other occupants of the hall, sizing them all up.

"Jesus Christ," Hoon remarked. "He's a big 'un."

"I'm thinking about... what? Seven-foot?" Greig mumbled.

"Can't be a kick in the arse off it," Hoon agreed.

"Big, too," Greig added. "Bulky, I mean. He looks strong."

"He calls himself 'The Wraith,'" Amanda explained.

"What, was Mr Spooky Ghostface already taken?" Hoon asked.

"Ha. Maybe. You should ask him. Might be a bit of a language barrier, though. He's Lithuanian."

"I thought they were all tiny?" Greig said.

Hoon shook his head. "You're thinking of Lilliput."

Greig turned to him. "Is that near Poland?"

"Forget it," Hoon said, with a resigned sort of sigh.

"He's pretty terrifying," Greig remarked. A thought struck him and he turned to Amanda, his eyes alive with worry. "I don't have to fight him, do I?"

"You don't have to do anything you don't want to," Amanda said. "But there might be an opportunity."

"An opportunity to do what?" Hoon asked. "Get pummelled into a stringy paste?" He shook his head. "No way he's fighting that fucking thing. Not a chance."

"I'm sure he can make his own decisions," Amanda said. She looked pleased with the comment, like it was some startlingly original comeback. Her smile didn't last, though. It fell away at the sight of the man trailing in the wake of the albino giant, then was hastily dragged back into action again when the man spotted her and started to walk her way.

"Ammie," he purred, holding both hands out like he was

coming in for a hug, but never actually following through with one.

His voice had a South African twang to it, though it was muffled by the mask he wore. The mask was made of the same semi-clear plastic as those the rest of the punters were wearing, but the design was different.

This one had an elongated mouth and chin that made Hoon think of the Joker from Batman, or the grinning mask from the Comedy/Tragedy theatre pairing. It contorted his features so they appeared even more bulbous and grotesquely exaggerated than everyone else's. Only his eyes, visible through two holes in the plastic, were unaffected, yet somehow Hoon found them even more monstrous and harder to look at than the rest of the face.

"Mr West! Good morning!" Amanda said, and her enthusiasm was as gushing as it was bullshit.

So, this was him, then. The Eel. In the fucking flesh.

Hoon noted the shift in Amanda's body language—the lowering of the champagne glass, the slight stooping of the head and curving of the shoulders, like she was showing deference to some apex predator, in the hope of having her life spared.

She was afraid of him. That much was obvious.

"Almost afternoon in fact, Ammie," the man in the mask replied, and despite his smiling eyes, there was a suggestion of reproach in his voice. "We should be underway soon, should we not?"

"It's almost ready to start," Amanda assured him.

"I hope so." He pointedly tapped a watch that Hoon suspected cost as much as a house, then tucked his hands behind his back and gave Hoon and Greig a curt but efficient once up and down. "And who do we have here?"

"Stephen. Stephen White," Hoon said, stepping forward before Greig could put his fucking foot in anything. "This here's the Godkiller." He thrust a hand out for the other man to shake. West regarded it with disinterest, then turned to Greig.

"The Godkiller?" He smiled, and the lines of the mask twisted it into a mockery of a grin. "Why do they call you that?"

Greig, who had been gazing slack-jawed at the still-wandering albino, turned when he realised he was being spoken to. "Eh, well, I mean, they don't, really. My fiancée came up with it. Thought it sounded good."

"It does! I like it a lot," West crowed. "It's... what would I say? Dynamic. I'm looking forward to seeing how you—"

"Here, what's that noise?" Hoon asked.

West stopped talking and became very still. "I'm sorry?"

"Noise? I don't hear a noise," Amanda quickly said. "Probably just the crowd."

Hoon shook his head. "No. It's like... a rustling noise. Like a crinkling."

Amanda stared at him, stuttering like a malfunctioning robot. "I don't... There isn't... I think you're imagining it," she said, and something in her eyes told him not to push the matter any further.

"Aye, maybe," he conceded.

"Yes. Well, I'd best get on. Very best of luck. I'll be watching with interest," West said. Then, with another meaningful look and a tap of his watch, he went striding off after the Wraith.

"There was definitely a fucking crinkling," Hoon said, once West was safely out of earshot. He turned to Greig. "Did you hear a crinkling?"

"I heard something," the younger man confirmed.

Hoon fixed Amanda with a deadly serious looking. "Answer me honestly. Look me in the eye. Yes or no, was that man wearing a big fucking nappy?"

Greig slapped the heel of his hand against his head. "Yes! That's what it sounded like! Knew I recognised it."

"I don't think that's any of our business," Amanda said.

"No, you're right. You're right," Hoon conceded. "I mean, each to their own, we've all got our crosses to bear." He managed to hold off for a full three seconds before continuing his enquiries. "But, like, is it a health issue, or a weird fetish thing? Because that's the sort of shite you fucking toffs are all into, isn't it?"

"I'm hardly a toff," Amanda replied. Still, she raised the glass again and once more held her head aloft like she was the lady of the manor, master of all she surveyed. "And, like I said, that's none of your business."

A gong chimed somewhere over near the centre of the hall, and the volume of the chatter rose in anticipation.

"Saved by the bell, eh?" Hoon teased.

Amanda ejected a final joyless, "Ha," then gestured with her glass towards where the crowd was thronging excitedly around the towering red-eyed giant. "If you're ready, gentlemen," she drawled. "We're about to begin."

CHAPTER THIRTY-TWO

FIVE MINUTES INTO THIS THING, Hoon knew how animals in the zoo felt.

He'd motioned for Greig to walk ahead of him, and they'd both followed Amanda to where much of the action seemed to be happening. Many of the masked toffs were taking seats around the cages, and Hoon could see them pointing and hear them passing judgement as he and Greig, on Amanda's instruction, stood together on a blue circle on the floor.

Hoon looked around at all the masked faces. Considering the plastic was mostly see-through, they were surprisingly effective at hiding the identity of their wearers. Hoon reckoned his own father could be sat there in the audience, and he'd be none the wiser.

It'd be a hell of a turn-up, mind you, considering the old bastard had been dead for over a decade.

"I had a dream a bit like this once," Greig whispered.

"I don't suppose it ended with you being ritualistically buggered, did it?" Hoon asked.

"What? No!"

"Thank fuck for that," Hoon said.

He waved sarcastically to some of the spectators, thinking it might shame them into looking elsewhere. This lot had that born-and-bred overconfidence of the upper classes, though, and they continued to regard him like he was some sort of lab experiment gone horribly wrong.

Hoon noticed that most of them were holding drinks, and all of them—with the exception of a few women—clutched tablet devices a little larger than a mobile phone. A couple of them looked Greig up and down, then tapped a button on their screen.

"What's that?" Hoon asked, catching Amanda's attention. "What are they doing?"

"Hm? Oh. They're betting."

"On me?" Greig asked.

"Or against you. That's between them and the house. There'll be a lot of money changing hands."

"Aye, there'd fucking better be," Hoon said, holding out his palm and prodding it with a finger.

Amanda smiled. "You'll get your payment, as agreed. Hopefully more. Everything will be settled up at the end of the day." She tapped Greig on a shoulder with the rim of her glass. "You're on."

Greig blinked. "What? When? I didn't hear anyone say anything."

Amanda put a finger to the back of her ear and pushed it out, indicating that he should listen. Even before she'd finished the gesture, a voice rang out from an overhead PA system.

Unlike back in the pub cellar, there was no forced fanfare to the announcement this time. The MC wasn't trying to get the audience all fired up, and Hoon got the distinct impression that a whoop or a cheer would both be unwelcome here.

Instead, the voice was low and measured. Boring, even.

"Ladies and gentlemen, it gives us enormous pleasure to

welcome you to this, the latest in our ongoing series of combat-centric events held here in the capital."

"Combat-centric events?" Hoon scoffed.

"I think he means fights," Greig whispered.

"Do you think?" Hoon asked, but Greig completely failed to pick up on the sarcasm.

"Many of you have been in attendance at past events, and will be familiar with how things work," the voice continued. "Those of you who are new, welcome, and I'm sure you'll have little problem in following along."

A brief explanation was given—eight fighters, four initial match-ups. Essentially what Amanda had already told them. Hoon only half-listened, though, and instead diverted most of his attention to the big Rastafarian-looking geezer who had practically danced onto the red spot on the opposite side of the cage.

He wasn't particularly big—Greig had the advantage when it came to height and muscle—but he had an air of confidence about him that Greig didn't share. Greig's eyes were darting around like those of a mouse anticipating the snap of hungry jaws, but his opponent appeared to be completely relaxed.

More than that, in fact, he looked like he was having fun. Or expecting to be soon, at any rate.

"You think that might be the guy I'm fighting?" Greig whispered, following Hoon's gaze.

"I think there's a pretty solid fucking chance, aye."

"He doesn't look too tough," Greig remarked. "Cool dreads, though."

"Aye, well, thankfully it's no' a Best Hairstyle contest," Hoon said.

There was a smattering of polite applause, and Hoon pointed upwards towards the now-silent speakers. "Did you take all that in?"

"Eh, most of it, I think."

"Thank fuck for that, because I wasn't listening," Hoon told him.

The voice returned with the same calming tone as before. "On the red spot, joining us from Kingston Jamaica, please give a very warm welcome to Judge 'One Drop' Lambsbread."

There was some more polite applause, completely devoid of any energy or enthusiasm. Nevertheless, the Rastafarian thrust his bandaged hands in the air like he was soaking up the adulation of an adoring crowd. Then, he danced into the cage, slowing only to eyeball Greig as he passed. It was quite an effective display of eyeballing, too, with one eye wide and staring, and the other fixed in a narrow squint, so he looked like a fucking nutter.

"He seems friendly," Greig muttered.

"And on our blue spot, a relative newcomer to the sport, here fresh off the back of an impressive victory in one of our lower leagues. From Glasgow, Scotland, please show your admiration for Gregory 'The Godkiller' Watt."

"Gregory?" Greig said, turning to Hoon. "I'm not Gregory, I'm just—"

"That's the least of your fucking problems," Hoon told him. He took one of the lad's arms and held it aloft, like he was already claiming victory. When he spoke, it was through a fixed smile and gritted teeth. "Remember what Granny said. Lead with your right, follow with the big left. But don't get fancy. If you can hoof him in the bollocks straight off the starting blocks, do that. You're not here to put on a show for these fucks, you're here to win, so do it quick. Don't fight well, fight smart. Or, even better, fight dirty."

"That woman said I should play up the noble thing..." Greig reminded him, which came very close to earning him a clip around the ear.

"Doesn't fucking matter what she said. She's one of them. Do what I say, not what she tells you."

"Right. Right, sorry. Any other advice?" Greig asked.

"Aye." Hoon lowered his arm, turned him towards the cage door, and slapped him on the shoulder. "Try and no' die."

"Die? Why would I...? I'm not going to die!"

"Watch out!"

Greig turned just in time to see a foot flying at him. He staggered sideways, and the cage shook as the kick slammed into the bars.

"Fuck's sake, is there no' a bell?" Hoon demanded.

Amanda appeared at his side, armed as ever with her Champagne. "No. All that was explained in the rules at the start," she said, and she was clearly fighting back a smirk. "Maybe if you'd been paying attention..."

"Fucking watch this prick!" Hoon barked, ignoring the stick-thin woman behind him. He scowled and pointed when Greig looked over in their direction. "Him! Watch him! No' fucking me!"

He realised his voice was carrying clearly around the hall. The audience members were sitting in silence, with only the occasional cough or clearing of the throat to indicate their presence.

Inside the cage, Greig had brought his hands up to protect his head, and was rotating slowly in the centre of the ring while Judge 'One Drop' Lambsbread—a name, Hoon thought, that somehow managed to be even more ridiculous than the sum of its parts—jigged around the outside.

"This is fine, this is good," Hoon encouraged.

The Jamaican was going to tire himself out if he kept this up. Greig was conserving energy. Biding his time, waiting for the right moment to—

One Drop danced aside as Greig went lumbering in with a big swinging punch. The strike missed its target, and Greig barely turned in time to stop his face clattering into the bars.

Instead, he managed to twist at the last moment, and his back took the brunt of the impact.

"What the fuck was that meant to be?" Hoon demanded, but Greig was already on the move again, staggering clear of a kick that *whummed* through the spot where he'd been standing.

One Drop's leg came right through the bars of the cage, and Hoon actually left the ground in his excitement. "There! Get stuck into the fucker!" he cried, but Greig kept his distance, giving his opponent time to free himself from the cage's grip.

The crowd made some positive noises at that. There was some more applause. Hoon saw a few of them tapping at their screens.

"See? The nice guy thing is having an impact," Amanda said.

Hoon grunted. "Aye, they'll all be betting against him, if they've any fucking sense."

The fight continued. It was quite a sedate affair, with both combatants sizing each other up, occasionally throwing a punch or a kick that didn't quite land.

"Fuck's sake. Glad I'm no' paying to see this," Hoon muttered. He threw a thumb back over his shoulder. "This gaggle of flumps don't exactly seem to be loving it, either."

"They're actually quite engaged. They'd usually all be shagging by now."

Hoon shot her a sideways look. She raised her glass and winked.

"Kidding," she said. "But they're enjoying it. They just don't show it like the rest of us."

"You talk as if you're no' one of them," Hoon said. He winced as a wild punch caught Greig on the shoulder, but it didn't appear to do any damage.

"Oh, I'm not," Amanda said.

"Aye, you keep telling yourself that, sweetheart," Hoon said, then he cupped his hands around his mouth and shouted, "Don't forget the bollocks!"

He waited to see if Greig would immediately land a solid kick to the goolies, but both fighters just continued to bob and weave around each other in silence.

"I'm really not," Amanda insisted, refusing to let the matter go.

"OK, you're not fucking royalty, or whatever, but you're part of the show," Hoon reasoned. "You're part of this whole fucking deal."

"So are you," Amanda reminded him.

Hoon opened his mouth to offer an argument, but couldn't find one compelling enough to counter her point.

"We've all got our own reasons for being here, Stephen," she continued. "Some of us are here for the thrill of it. Some for the money. Others because we have no choice but to be here. Because we are... compelled."

"Oh aye? And what one are you?" Hoon asked.

She smiled back at him. "And who says we have to be only one?"

There was a murmuring of appreciation from the audience, and they both looked up at the cage to find One Drop moving his head like he was shaking off the after-effects of a solid hit.

"Good lad!" Hoon said, and Greig flashed him a smile. "Keep that up."

He lowered his voice and spoke out of the side of his mouth to Amanda.

"Did you see what he did there? I don't have a fucking clue."

"No, but it obviously impressed the crowd, so that's good," Amanda said.

Hoon glanced back over his shoulder at the sea of expressionless masks. "Oh aye," he muttered. "Sent them into a right fucking frenzy."

He faced front again, and they watched another half-minute of ring pacing before another flurry of punches came to nothing for either fighter.

"Is there no' another fight going on?" Hoon asked. "Or some paint drying somewhere? Be more interesting than this."

"I'm fine here," Amanda told him. She wet her lips with her Champagne. "How's your head, by the way? I still feel bad about what happened, and how they brought you to see me at the hotel."

"It's fine. But, aye, a fucking phone call would've been easier," Hoon told her, his gaze trained on Greig.

That punch or kick, or whatever he'd landed, had given him a confidence boost. While he still didn't have the same swagger as his opponent, at least he didn't look like he was thinking of running away.

"Speaking of the hotel," he ventured. "Seemed a bit... grubby."

Amanda frowned. "Was it? They have an excellent cleaning team, so I don't know why that would be the case."

Hoon shook his head. "No, like... There was a lot of grubby stuff going on."

"Oh! You mean sex?" she asked. "Nothing grubby about sex between two consenting adults, Mr White." She smirked and watched his reaction closely as she added, "Or more."

"Aye, key word 'consenting,'" he said.

"What do you mean?" Amanda asked, and the levity dropped right out of her voice. "What are you implying?"

Hoon turned to look at her. "Nothing. I'm just saying, aye, I'm all in favour of that sort of thing. Fire away, stick whatever you want wherever you like. As long as everyone's happy to be involved."

There was a long pause before she answered. Even when she did, there was an awkwardness to it. "Sex is like this," she said, gesturing around them. "Some do it for the thrills. Some for the money."

"And some because they've got no choice?" Hoon said, firing her earlier response back at her.

"I never said that," Amanda replied.

"Oh, bravo!"

The voice from behind them was the sort of nasal, braying, upper-class affront to the ears that would usually be like a red rag to a bull for Hoon. The fact that one of the posho pricks had reached the relative fever pitch of opening his mouth, though, made him quickly turn his attention back to the ring.

From the way One Drop was stumbling, Greig had landed a big left hand. He followed with a right hook to the stomach that drew a grunt and a gasp from the Jamaican.

"I should go check out the other fight," Amanda said.

"Just as it's getting interesting?" Hoon asked.

Amanda leaned in and pressed her cheek against his, and the smell of her perfume hung around her like a shroud. Her parting sentence was a low whisper in his ear. "Be careful, Stephen. Be very careful."

———

"Did you see me?" Greig asked. He was bouncing on his chair like an excitable child, adrenaline still pumping through his veins. "Did you see when I ducked that kick and caught his leg?"

"Aye, I saw it," Hoon said. He dabbed at a cut above Greig's right eye, and tutted when the lad flinched at the sting of the TCP. "Which word's the fucking problem, son? The 'hold' or the 'still'?"

"Sorry," Greig said.

He gripped the sides of the folding chair, closed his eyes, and sat bolt upright.

It lasted all of three seconds.

"And that punch at the end!" he crowed, leaning back on the seat just before Hoon could apply the cotton swab. "The left. The hook, I mean, not the uppercut, though that felt good. Did it look good?"

"It looked better than your fucking face is going to look if you don't let me fix you up," Hoon told him.

"Granny was right, flipping the stance made it way easier. Can't believe nobody's picked up on that before. I should thank him. Do you think I should thank him? I should probably thank him."

"Jesus Christ! I think you should fucking shut up for two minutes! That's what I think," Hoon snapped. "How come you're the one getting kicked in the face, and I'm the one with the fucking headache?"

"Sorry! Sorry, I know!" Greig grinned. "I just... that's five grand I've made. Five grand! From one fight!" He raised a bloodied hand and gestured to the dressing room door. "And they said I can make more! I'm supposed to have a wander about. Get involved. See what takes my fancy."

"Or you could call it quits now," Hoon suggested. "Take the money and run."

"What? No way! You saw me against that guy! I won!"

Hoon took a sticking plaster from a box in the first aid kit, lined it up with the cut on Greig's head, then pressed it in place.

"You got lucky. He was all mouth and no fucking trousers, that one."

Greig's body language became defensive. It was a shame, Hoon thought, that it hadn't done the same right before the kick that had led to the lad's head injury.

"Well, the crowd seemed to like it," Greig said. He shifted on the seat. "I mean... I think. Amanda said they enjoyed it."

"Aye, well, I wouldn't trust her as far as I could fucking throw her," Hoon said.

"You could probably throw her pretty far," Greig pointed out. "She doesn't look very heavy."

"Here's what we're going to do, son," Hoon told him. "You're going to stay here, sit on your arse, and wait for me to come back. And stop fucking frowning like that, you'll pull that plaster off."

Greig's eyes crept upwards like he was trying to look at his own forehead, then the lines that had been furrowing it into ridges faded. "Where are you going?"

"I'm going to go scope out the competition," Hoon replied. "I'll go for a wander and see what's what. That way, you don't do anything stupid."

"So, what, I'm just meant to sit here?"

"Exactly. Right in that fucking spot," Hoon told him. "You don't move unless I come and get you, alright?"

"What if there's a fire?" Greig asked.

Hoon opened the dressing room door, then stopped. "Why would there be a fire?"

"I don't know. I'm just thinking out loud."

"I reckon the word 'thinking' is bigging yourself up a bit much there, son," Hoon told him. "But, aye. In the highly unlikely event of fire, flood, earthquake, swarm of killer bees, or any other fucking disaster-movie style misadventure, you have my full permission to get up off your arse and leave. Alright?"

Greig replied with a nod and a thumbs-up.

"Alright," Hoon said, then he stepped out into the corridor, promised he'd be back soon, and shut the door behind him.

CHAPTER THIRTY-THREE

THE SAME LACKLUSTRE atmosphere permeated the place when Hoon returned to the main hall, where two more fights were currently in progress.

One of the fights looked interesting. Two Middle-Eastern men were firing kicks at each other at almost exactly the same time. Both were blocking, but it was only a matter of time before one of them broke through the other's defences and did some real damage.

They were fast. Strong, too. Had Greig been drawn against either of them for his opening match, he'd probably be missing a head by now.

It had been a mistake to bring him here. Yes, it had worked out OK so far, but he had no chance against either of these two men, and based on what Hoon had managed to catch of the fight that had taken place at the same time as Greig's, the winner of that one was way above his league, too.

He had made himself five grand. He had escaped with a few cuts and bruises, and he hadn't accidentally caused anyone to suffer any life-changing injuries. Stop now, and the day was a roaring success.

Don't, and it could all go to shit very quickly.

The problem was whether he could convince Greig to bow out now. Or, for that matter, if the bastards running the show would even let him. Amanda had said they weren't going to make him do anything he didn't want to do, but she'd also insisted she wasn't in charge. If that was true, then it probably wasn't up to her what happened to the fighters.

"Enjoying the show?"

Hoon turned away from the fight, and every part of him went into a state of high alert at the sight of the man in the grinning plastic mask.

Godfrey West—the Eel—pointed at him, paused for a moment, then said, "Stephen, wasn't it?"

"Aye, that's me," Hoon confirmed.

There was a faint, but unmistakeable crinkling sound as West walked over to join him, but Hoon chose not to pass comment. Instead, he accepted the flute of Champagne he was offered and *chinked* it against the other man's glass.

"Those who are about to die, we salute you," West said, before chuckling like he'd just said something funny.

"Aye, very good," Hoon said, then he knocked back the bubbly in one gulp. "How do you drink with the masks on, by the way?"

"Very carefully," West replied. He placed the rim of the glass to a small slot in the mouth of the mask, then gently tipped it back. "It's an inconvenience, but people do seem to enjoy the anonymity. It's very liberating, pretending to be someone else for a while. Wouldn't you agree, Mr White?"

Hoon shrugged. "I wouldn't know."

"Wouldn't you?" Godfrey asked. He regarded him for a while with his head tilted to one side, then let out another little laugh. "You should try it sometime. You might find you enjoy it."

"I don't think it's really my scene," Hoon said, indicating

West's mask. "You all look like Cher fell asleep with her head on a radiator. No offence."

"None taken," West assured him. "We don't do it for how it looks, we do it for how it feels."

"Uncomfortable and largely humiliating?" Hoon guessed.

West didn't laugh. Not this time. "Freeing, Mr White. So very freeing. It's ironic, don't you think? Wearing a mask—pretending to be someone we aren't—may provide us with one of our only opportunities to actually be ourselves."

There was some applause from the fight fans that came within spitting distance of sounding enthusiastic, and Hoon turned back to the cage to see one of the men standing victoriously over the fallen body of the other.

"Actually..." West began. "Here's a thing. I'm throwing a small celebration after this. Not for everyone, just a select few."

"What, a party?"

"More of a gathering," West told him. "An intimate sort of thing. Masks are optional, though most people like to wear them." His mouth, Hoon thought, pulled itself into a distorted smile. "Some of the people who're going to be there have expressed that they'd like to meet you."

"Meet me?" Hoon asked. "The fuck do you they want to meet me for?"

"You're a breath of fresh air, Stephen," West replied. "We've all heard you. You say things as you see them. You don't hold back. Many of us would like to get to know you—the real you—a little better."

Hoon nodded slowly. 'The real you.' What did this fucker suspect? What did he know?

"Where is it?" he asked.

"Ahaha. Don't worry about that," West said. "The driver who picked you up will take you. He knows the way. Don't worry about getting dressed up, either. You'll be perfect as you are."

Hoon looked down at his tracksuit bottoms and t-shirt combo. "No' exactly a party outfit," he said.

The Eel leaned in closer. "That rather depends on the party, doesn't it?" His breathing echoed behind the mask. "By the way, did I mention there'll be women? So many women." He winked, and Hoon had to swallow back the urge to grab his throat and squeeze.

"No," he said. "You hadn't mentioned."

With the fight over, the spectators had started to get up from their seats. They swept past Hoon and Godfrey like a fast-flowing stream, headed for some other part of the hall.

"I'd best go mingle," West said. "But you'll come? I'd adore it if you came. I'd love to have you."

Hoon resisted the obvious response to that, and confirmed his acceptance with a nod. "Sure, aye. Never pass up a party, that's what I always say."

"Wonderful. *Wonderful!*" He looked around until he spotted the woman in the tinfoil dress, then beckoned her over. "Amanda will add your name to the list, and take care of the details." He waited for her to join them. "Won't you, Ammie? You'll make sure Stephen makes it to the gathering after we're done here?"

Amanda failed to hide her surprise. "Yes! Of course!" she said, practically bowing to the man in the mask. "I'll take care of everything."

"Wonderful!" Godfrey sang. He traced a thumb down her cheek, cupped her face in a hand, then marched off, following the rest of the audience towards the other end of the hall.

"He invited you to the gathering?" Amanda asked, the moment West was out of earshot. "You?"

"Aye. What's so fucking shocking about that?"

"Nothing. No, nothing," Amanda said. "It's just... I'm surprised, that's all."

"Why?"

"Because he doesn't know you," Amanda replied. "He's just met you."

She gestured with her glass for them to start walking, and they fell into step together, following behind the rest of the crowd.

"I've got a trustworthy face," Hoon said, which earned a snigger from the woman beside him.

"You really don't," she said.

Her gaze flitted across some of the audience members ahead of them. A few of them, men and women alike, were looking back over their shoulders, apparently transfixed by the foul-mouthed Scottish thug trudging along behind.

"Ah. I think maybe that's it," she remarked.

"What?"

"I think some of our guests want to fuck you."

Hoon almost choked on his own tongue. "Sorry?"

"Or be fucked by you. You never know until the lights go down."

Hoon tutted. "Oh. Right, aye. Winding me up again. Funny."

Amanda shook her head. She wasn't laughing. "No. I'm being serious this time. This place is for fighting. This is the foreplay." She wrapped an arm across herself, like she was suddenly feeling the cold. "The gatherings? Those are for everything else."

"Oh. Shite," Hoon said. They walked on in silence for a few seconds, then he side-eyed her. "You going to be there?"

Amanda smiled, but it was paper-thin. "Always."

Hoon was prevented from asking any more by a Kamikaze-like screech from the other side of one of the freestanding walls. He hurried around it to look, and saw One Drop, the Jamaican who Greig had fought earlier, throwing himself at the giant albino, fists flailing.

"Here we go," Amanda muttered. She took a big swig of her

Champagne and hugged herself even tighter. "This is why they're all really here. To see this."

One Drop rained blows on the Wraith, snapping out jabs, and landing a few powerful hooks to the giant's midsection. Which, to be fair, was almost as high as he could reach.

This fight, like the others, was taking place in a cage. This cage was larger than the rest, though, with loops of barbed wire wrapped around the bars.

"The fuck is this?" Hoon muttered, but Amanda offered nothing in response.

There were no seats set out around this ring. It was standing room only, and the members of the crowd seemed more than happy to be on their feet. They closed ranks around the cage, forming a circle around the outside, fingers flying across the screens of their tablets.

There was a big red digital clock on a stand just outside the cage, Hoon noticed, its digits counting down. One-twenty-one. One-twenty. One-nineteen.

One Drop landed another couple of blows, then jumped back, his fists rising like he was getting ready to go again. There was something different about the way he was moving, though. An air of confusion hovered around him.

"He knows those should've hurt him," Hoon remarked. "Big fella or not, those punches should've put him down."

"Ha. Of course, you've never seen him in action, have you?" Amanda asked. "It's impressive, if you like that sort of thing."

"What sort of thing?" Hoon asked.

Up in the cage, One Drop lunged with a kick. It was the same move he'd tried on Greig, and the outcome was even more disastrous. The giant's hand caught him by the ankle, his long fingers looping all the way around it.

There was a jerk, a pop, and a scream. Hoon could only watch as One Drop was swung around and launched against the side of the cage.

Blood sprayed from where he hit, and for the first time since this had started, Hoon heard some actual cheering. It came from the front row of onlookers, some of whom had been hit by the flying droplets.

One Drop slid down the bars, crying out in pain as the metal barbs tore through his flesh and skin.

"That sort of thing," Amanda said. She turned away, unable to hide her disgust. "If you'll excuse me, Stephen, I have some things to attend to."

"Eh, aye. Aye. No bother," Hoon said.

Try as he might, he couldn't tear his eyes from events going on inside the cage. The Jamaican was upright again, albeit not under his own steam. The big albino had hoisted him up by the throat, and was holding him so just the tips of his toes were touching the floor.

A crunching left hook exploded against the Rastafarian's ribcage. It would almost certainly have elicited a cry of pain, had it not been for the long white fingers constricting his throat.

One Drop tried to protect himself, but his movements were slow. Groggy. Unfocused. He took a swing at thin air, like he was trying to land a punch on a ghost.

BAM! Another uppercut from the giant was followed by another spontaneous cheer from some members of the crowd. This was what they were after. This was why they were here.

Without so much as a grunt of effort, the Wraith hoisted the Jamaican high into the air so his feet were dangling half a metre from the mat. With the other hand, he caught the lad's injured leg, pulled in opposite directions like he was trying to tear him in half, then swung him down quickly while bringing up one of his legs.

One Drop's back formed a letter C across the albino's knee, and Hoon would've sworn that, even from that distance, he heard something break. The giant released his grip then, and the crowd fell silent as the Jamaican slid to the floor, eyes rolling, whole body convulsing like he was suffering a seizure.

On the stand outside the cage, the clock stopped with sixty-seven seconds to go.

The audience went comparatively wild. There was a lot of enthusiastic clapping, some whistling, and even a slightly self-conscious *whoop*.

The timer may have stopped, but the Wraith hadn't. He stamped twice on the fallen man's chest, and Hoon definitely heard a crack that time.

"Jesus fuck," he whispered.

The cage door was opened, and the albino backed off when two men entered with a stretcher. Hoon watched them loading the Jamaican onto it, and then became distracted when he spotted Godfrey West standing on the other side of the cage, talking into a phone.

It was impossible to tell what was being said, and the mask meant lip-reading was out of the question. From the way he moved, though, it seemed that West wasn't pleased about something.

"Ladies and gentlemen, the Wraith thanks you for your support. And, as always, we wish his opponent a swift recovery," the announcer said, and Hoon realised that he was standing beside the countdown clock, just another posho-prick in a plastic mask.

There was laughter at the MC's comment. It made Hoon think of horses, and generations of inbreeding.

"As ever, we welcome anyone who wishes to accept the Wraith's challenge to step on up," the announcer continued. "Ten thousand pounds to anyone who can survive just three minutes in the ring. Ten thousand pounds for three minutes of your time. Who could possibly refuse such an offer?"

Hoon made his way through the crowd, trying to get close enough to West to hear what was being said. The audience was really starting to find its voice now, though, and short of getting within spitting distance of the bastard, listening in was going to be impossible.

West checked his watch, said something into the phone, then rubbed the forehead of his mask like he was trying to fend off a headache, and this somehow might help.

Then, he shoved the mobile into his pocket, wheeled around on his heels, and went marching towards one of the side doors of the hall, apparently unnoticed by anyone else.

Hoon set off after him, head down, hands in his pockets, trying to make himself as close to invisible as he could get. All eyes were still on the big albino, and he was almost at the door when he was forced to stop dead in his tracks.

"Wonderful news, ladies and gentlemen, we have a challenger," the announcer said, almost managing to convey the slightest suggestion of excitement for once. "Trying their luck against the Wraith next will be our newcomer, Gregory 'The Godkiller'—"

"What?" Hoon hissed, turning back to the cage. Sure enough, there, right outside it, stood a grinning and dangerously overconfident Greig.

Hoon looked to the door that Godfrey West had gone through. The bastard might be alone in there. Now could be his chance.

He heard the creaking of the cage door being opened, and the murmurs of a crowd excited at the thought of what it was about to see.

"Sit on your arse, I told him. Stay where you are, I told him," Hoon muttered, then he turned back the way he'd come, and raced on down to ringside.

CHAPTER THIRTY-FOUR

GREIG WAS daft enough to look genuinely pleased when he spotted Hoon charging towards him. He raised a hand to wave, like he was trying to get his self-appointed coach's attention. Hoon, however, already had the lad in his sights, and all but pushed his way through the crowd to get to him.

"The fuck do you think you're doing?" he demanded.

Greig motioned to the ring. "This."

"Did I no' tell you to wait in that fucking dressing room?" Hoon asked. "Do I not distinctly remember fucking saying that?"

"Well, I mean, yeah, but... I wasn't sure you were coming back. You were away for ages."

"Bollocks! I've been gone about five fucking minutes," Hoon told him. "I've pissed for longer than that."

"No, but—"

"Just shut your fucking mouth," Hoon warned. He turned to the announcer and waved a hand. "He's no' doing it."

The announcer leaned down from the elevated ringside so his face was level with Hoon's. He was wearing the standard-issue plastic mask, devoid of all expression. There was a microphone clutched in one hand, but he kept it far from his mouth while he replied.

"His name's on the list now."

"Well, fucking take it off the list," Hoon instructed. "He's not doing it."

"It's three minutes!" Greig protested. "It's ten grand for three minutes! I can last three minutes!"

"Against that? You couldn't last three fucking seconds," Hoon said. He pointed up at the announcer. "Score his name off. He's not fucking doing it."

"I can do this, Mr White. I can keep moving," said Greig. He puffed up his chest, and Hoon anticipated the next words before they were even out of his mouth. "And who knows? Maybe I could even beat him."

"You couldn't beat him if he was made of fucking pancake batter," Hoon told him. "You get in the ring with that thing, and you won't be leaving here in a fucking ambulance, you'll be leaving in a number of plastic bags."

"His name's down. He's committed to fight," the announcer said.

Hoon spun and caught the irritating wee prick by his bow tie. "Take his name off. Now. I won't fucking ask you again."

As he hissed out the warning, Hoon became aware of shapes closing in around him. Henchmen types, including his old pals Bingo and Butterfuck, were positioning themselves in a semi-circle at his back.

"I can't do that," the announcer said. Hoon's threat didn't seem to have had any effect, judging by the way his voice maintained its usual calm monotone. "His name's down. He has to fight. That's the rules." Hoon saw the other man's eyes smiling. "Unless you want to step in, of course?"

Hoon released his grip and the announcer straightened

again. The goons were still surrounding him, saying nothing, but only too ready to jump in if needed.

Up in the cage, the big albino was staring down at them, his features slack and devoid of all emotion, like nobody had thought to switch him on.

"What, I can stand in for him?" Hoon asked.

"You can."

"And he won't have to fight?"

"No. He'll be off the hook."

Hoon shrugged. "Right, fine. Fuck it. I'll do that, then."

"Wait, what?" Greig yelped. "No! You can't fight him. You're too old."

"Fuck off! I'm no' old, son, I'm experienced," Hoon told him.

Greig caught him by the arm. "No. You can't. I'll do it. I want to fight him."

Hoon pulled his arm free. "Aye, and there's your fucking problem, son. You want to fight him. I don't."

"Then let me do it!"

"I wasn't fucking finished. I don't want to fight him, so I'm no' going to," Hoon explained. "I'm going to go in there and I'm going to avoid the big fucking plank of wood." He looked to the announcer for confirmation. "Three minutes, right?"

"Three minutes."

A range of emotion registered on Greig's face, starting with confusion, then giving way to betrayal. "Are you... Are you just after the money?" he asked. "Is that it?"

"Jesus Christ, Greig. If I wanted a crack at the money I'd have put my name down after yours, so he'd at least have tired himself out a bit when he pulled your fucking arms off," Hoon said. He sighed, looked around at the crowd, then stepped in closer to the boy. "I want to bring you home in one fucking piece, alright? You're engaged. You've got a baby. I'm no' having you eating through a fucking straw like that last poor bastard."

"What poor bastard?" Greig asked.

Hoon buried his face in his hands. "Fuck's sake. You mean you didn't even see what happened to the last guy? You just put your fucking name down willy-nilly without checking to see if he'd recently paralysed someone?"

"Paralysed?" Greig said, and finally, not before time, there was a hint of worry on his face.

"Aye. Bent him fucking head to heels," Hoon said. "So, away you go back to the dressing room, and leave this to me."

Greig swallowed. Shook his head. "No. No, I can't, Mr White. It's me who put my name down. I can't just let you go in there and—"

He didn't see the punch coming. Then again, he wasn't expecting it. It was a big right hook that put him to the floor and left him there long enough for Hoon to make his way up the steps.

By the time Greig came round, Hoon was already in the cage, and the door was being locked behind him.

Throughout all this, the audience had remained almost supernaturally silent, like every single member was holding their breath, waiting to see how things were going to play out.

Now that Hoon was in the cage, they were starting to become a bit more vocal. This wasn't just a fight now, this was theatre. This was art.

This was *glorious*!

"Dramatic scenes here today, ladies and gentlemen," the announcer said, his voice now booming through the PA system. "Standing in for the Godkiller is..." He brought an ear closer to the cage, listening for a response.

"Can we just get fucking on with it?" Hoon spat.

The albino hadn't moved a muscle since he'd entered the ring. He stood with his arms limply at his sides, and zero expression on his face. He wasn't making an effort to be intimidating, but then again, he didn't have to. His very existence was unnerving enough.

"You need a name," the announcer insisted.

"Start that countdown clock and then give me three minutes to think of one," Hoon said.

"The White Knight."

Hoon looked down to see Amanda at ringside. She tilted her glass first towards him, then at Greig.

"It would seem appropriate," she said, smirking. "Stepping in to save the day."

The announcer wasted no time debating it. "Ladies and gentlemen, the next bout is scheduled to last for three minutes," he said. "Our reigning champion, the Wraith, will be facing his second challenger of the day, the White Knight. Place your bets now. Place all bets now. Will our champion emerge victorious again, or will our challenger be the first-ever to survive for a full three minutes in the cage?"

Hoon's head snapped to the right at that. "First-ever?" he said. "What do you mean, the first-ever?"

A bell rang.

A countdown started.

And the whole cage shook as a giant with eyes like red-hot coals came thundering across the ring.

———

He was fast. Much faster than he had any right to be, given his size. Hoon avoided a big lunging grab from the bastard, but it was a clumsy retreat that threw him off-balance, and he was barely able to avoid a follow-up punch that would've reduced his head to atoms.

"Right, whoa, whoa, easy there, big guy," he said, pacing backwards, keeping his distance. "I don't suppose we can just talk about this, can we?"

"Watch your back!"

That was Greig calling from the front row. Hoon stopped retreating just in time to avoid ripping himself open on the barbed wire, and quickly side-stepped out of the albino's considerable damage radius.

"So, eh, do you come here often?" Hoon asked.

He wasn't quite sure why he was talking. It wasn't like the giant was going to engage him in conversation. But maybe he could get on the Lithuanian's impressively firm tits enough to make him lose the rag. If he was angry, he might get careless.

And if he got careless, Hoon might survive for another—he checked the clock—two-minutes-and-forty-eight seconds.

Jesus. Twelve seconds? Was that all that had passed?

The Wraith dived for him, arms outstretched like he was planning a wrestling hold that Hoon had no intentions whatsoever of being caught by. There was nowhere to go but down, though, and Hoon grunted as he threw himself into a less than stellar forward roll that sent a shockwave of pain through his shoulder.

Maybe Greig was right. Maybe he *was* too old for this shite.

"Go for his goolies, Mr White!" Greig suggested.

"Shut the fuck up!" Hoon barked, not convinced he could even get his leg that high. "This is all your fucking fault."

"Sorry, Mr White."

"I said shut the fuck—"

A fist like a speeding train caught him a glancing blow to the chin. He was able to roll with the punch, but it still filled his mouth with blood and his head with stars, and for a moment, he wasn't quite sure of where he was.

He heard the sound of thunder behind him. Felt the ground shake.

Something hit him like a wrecking ball, launching him sideways, setting his ribcage on fire. He started to fall, but he couldn't. He wouldn't. If he fell in here with this ghostly white monster of a thing, he was a dead man. No two ways about it.

He managed to keep staggering towards the bars, and gritted his teeth in anticipation of the barbed wire. A hand caught him by the wrist and jerked him to a stop, though, saving him from a whole host of painful lacerations.

A moment later, though, he was moving again, this time headed straight towards the giant ivory statue in the centre of the ring.

The Wraith's forearm was like an iron bar across his throat. Everything below that point on Hoon's body continued forwards and upwards, while his head swung backwards and down until he was horizontal in the air.

There was no way of avoiding a fall this time, he realised, not unless someone switched off the room's gravity in the next two seconds. He went as limp as he possibly could, in the hope of a fast recovery.

A hammer-blow hit him on the chest in mid-air, driving him harder and faster into the mat. The impact echoed around the vast room, accompanied by the *oohs* of the masked spectators.

Most of Hoon decided it was best to stay there on the floor, but a tiny voice at the back of his mind overruled the rest of him, and he rolled quickly onto his front before an ogre-like stamping foot had a chance to turn the whole of his upper torso into a two-dimensional image.

He saw the giant's leg lock, and went for his knee, driving a shoulder against it, trying to slow the Lithuanian down.

A hand grabbed him by the head, fingers squeezing like they were powered by pistons. Hoon was hoisted up, up, up until he was level with the expressionless face of the other man, then he was returned to the floor with another ear-splitting *bang*.

"It's OK, you've got this, Mr White!" Greig cheered.

Hoon didn't have the time, the energy, the wherewithal, or

even the breath to respond to that. Which was a shame, because he would've very much liked to.

How in the fuck have I got this? he'd have asked. *In what fucking world has this been got?*

But he didn't. Instead, he spat quite a concerning amount of blood onto the ring floor, and tried not to pass out.

"Don't fight well, Mr White, fight smart!" Greig suggested.

Hoon really fucking hated that kid sometimes.

He had a point, though. Down there on his knees, the Wraith's crotch was almost within striking distance. He just needed the bastard a step closer. One step, that was.

It would be the David and Goliath story all over again, except rather than felling the giant with a stone and sling, he'd do it with a God Almighty punch to the bollocks.

"Come on then, Casper," he whispered, beckoning the big man closer. "Bring it on."

He listened for the scuffing of feet. Waited until the Wraith had closed the gap. Then, with a roar, he launched an uppercut that he told himself would've been very effective, had it not been caught by an enormous white hand.

"Fuck," Hoon wheezed. He was suddenly up on his feet again, spinning around, his movements no longer his to control.

The bars came rushing up to meet him. The barbed wire, too. He managed to stick out a foot and kick himself back towards the middle of the ring with only a couple of minor scrapes to his ankle.

Hands like mechanical pincers clamped down on his shoulders. He dropped and rolled again before they could collapse him into the mat, or rip his arms right out of their sockets.

He heard Greig say, "One minute left, Mr White!" and the audience murmuring in anticipation, then the big spooky red-eyed fucker was on him again, plucking him up off the mat like he weighed nothing.

As he was being lifted, Hoon brought up a knee that connected hard with the giant's stomach. The Wraith's face didn't show any reaction, but Hoon's upward momentum faltered, and he was able to wrench himself free of the Lithuanian's grip.

"Thirty seconds! You've got this, Mr White!"

The albino shot a look to the announcer, and Hoon could've sworn he saw worry zipping between them. The giant lunged again, but this time Hoon was ready for him. He skipped back out of reach, pushing down the pain that was threatening to consume the right side of his ribcage.

Something was grinding in there. Something hard and sharp was digging into something soft and wet.

He couldn't think about that now. He had to keep moving. Keep dodging. Keep out of this fucker's reach for just a little while longer. Just a few more seconds. Just a—

A jagged metal point caught his arm when he stumbled too close to the bars. It dug in deep, forcing him to backtrack a pace and unhook it from his flesh.

The Wraith seized on his mistake. Of course he did. His fist connected hard with Hoon's stomach, and Hoon doubled over, all the fight leaving him along with the last of the air in his lungs.

He tried to grab for the bars, for some sort of anchor point, but missed completely. The world turned upside down. He felt a hand gripping him by an ankle, and another around the back of the neck.

The image of the Jamaican being snapped in two came, unbidden, into his head. He saw the shape he had formed across the giant's knee. Heard the cracking of his spine.

There was nothing he could do to stop this. Nothing he could do but shut his eyes, brace himself, and wait for the inevitable.

"That's time."

Amanda's voice rose up from the sidelines, and as suddenly as it had started, his movement stopped.

"Three minutes. That's time," she said again. "He did it."

"He did it! He actually did it!" agreed another voice in the crowd.

"Put him down!" Greig demanded. "He did it. Let him go!"

"He's right." That was the announcer's voice, though there was a note of bitterness to it now. "Put him down."

Hoon was suddenly moving freely again. He grabbed at thin air like it could hold him up, then he hit the canvas and lay there, staring up into the eyes of a monster. Hurt, injured, but somehow still alive.

"Ladies and gentlemen, I'm sure you're all equally as excited as I am," the announcer droned. "That our challenger has successfully survived three whole minutes in the ring with the Wraith. What a feat. What an achievement. Please show your admiration for the White Knight."

Hoon didn't hear the applause. The ringing in his ears and the rushing of blood inside his head conspired to drown it all out.

It was only when he dragged himself to his feet that he realised everyone was clapping with much more enthusiasm than he'd seen them demonstrate so far. He acknowledged their applause with a raised middle finger, then limped towards the door of the cage just as the announcer swung it open.

"Anything you'd like to say, White Knight?" the man with the microphone asked.

"Aye. Can someone call me a fucking ambulance?" Hoon said. The crowd whooped and cheered like he'd just made some clever and insightful comment when, in fact, he genuinely did just want some urgent medical attention.

Greig appeared beside him and hooked himself under one of Hoon's arms like a human crutch. "I've got you, Mr White.

I've got you," he said. "And wow, I'm glad that was you in there and not me. That guy's brutal."

Hoon risked a look back at the towering albino. He was back to his 'powered down' mode, arms drooping at his sides, his face a blank canvas.

"Meh, he's no' that tough," Hoon said, then he quickly fucked off out of the ring in case the big bastard had heard him.

CHAPTER THIRTY-FIVE

"DOES IT HURT?" Greig asked. Under other circumstances, Hoon might've found the sincerity on the young man's face vaguely amusing. Here and now, though, with bruising spreading across him like a rash, and his ribcage in the process of trying to relocate itself to somewhere else in his body, he wasn't really in a laughing mood.

"Yes," he confirmed.

"It looks sore," Greig said. "Is there anything I can do?"

"No' unless you can fucking wind time back and no' put your name down on that list," Hoon said.

Greig winced. "Yeah. Sorry about that. I think you were right. That was probably a mistake."

Hoon removed the ice pack from the side of his face so he could more effectively glower at the younger man. "*Probably?*"

"OK, definitely. It was definitely a mistake. I shouldn't have done that. I just... I saw pound signs."

Hoon grunted. "Aye. Well." He kicked the bag at his feet. Amanda had brought it in a few minutes earlier. She'd offered to hold onto it until after the party, but he'd given her short shrift. "Take it," he said.

Greig looked down at the bag. "What?"

"Take it. You can have it."

"No. No, I can't do that, Mr White," he said. "You're the one who got the shit kicked out of you."

"I wouldn't go that fucking far," Hoon retorted.

"OK, well, you're the one who did the fighting," Greig said. "So, I can't take it. Anyway, they've given me my five grand. That's still amazing."

"Just take the fucking money, son. Alright?" Hoon insisted. "I don't want it."

"I can't. It wouldn't be fair."

Hoon ran a hand down his face and noted a few places where it had changed in shape. "Will you just take the fucking cash, son?" he sighed. "I wasn't in this for the money. I had my own reasons for coming."

"What reasons?" Greig asked.

"Does it matter? I'm just—"

There was a knock at the door. Amanda didn't wait to be invited before opening it. A couple of black-suited henchman-types lingered like a bad smell behind her.

"Cars are ready," she said. "Greig, they'll take you home. Stephen, they'll take you to get cleaned up and ready for the gathering."

"What gathering?" Greig asked. He looked from Amanda to Hoon and back again. "What, like a party? Can I come?"

"No you fucking cannot," Hoon told him. "Grown-ups only. You've got a family to get home to." He looked over to Amanda. "Can you give us a minute?"

"Just one," she said. "We need to get the drivers back for the guests."

Hoon confirmed with a wave that he understood, then heaved himself up off the chair as the door was closed.

"Right, here's what's going to happen," Hoon said, standing face to face with Greig. "You're going to take this money—both bags—and you're going to get out of London. You're going to go somewhere else. Somewhere away from all this shite."

"But... that lady, Amanda, she said I could fight again if I wanted. Next time."

Hoon caught him by the shoulders. He wanted to give the daft bugger a shake, but couldn't face the pain. "Aye, I bet she did. Because she knows that, sooner or later, the house always fucking wins. They paid you five grand today. How much do you think they made from all them rich bastards? A fuckwad more than that, that's for sure. They'll keep paying you as long as you keep fighting, but one day—maybe next time—something'll happen so that you can't fight. So that you can't walk. So that you can't wipe your arse without some poor bastard having to give you a hand. Is that what you want, son? You want someone else wiping your arse?"

Greig shook his head. "I don't," he said. "I don't want someone else wiping my arse."

"Good answer," Hoon said. "So, take the cash. Round up the family. Get tae fuck. Start again somewhere. Build something nice for that bairn. Alright?"

Greig chewed his lip for a while before answering. "Where should we go?"

"Jesus Christ, son, I'm no' going to draw you a fucking map. Pick somewhere. It's a big world."

"What about America?" Greig asked, and he had that sincere look on his face again that Hoon found simultaneously endearing and infuriating.

"Aye. Maybe. I don't fucking know," Hoon told him. "But, maybe start by setting your sights a bit lower. Like Elgin or Perth, or somewhere."

"Dundee?" Greig suggested.

Hoon scowled back at him. "No' that fucking low," he said. "Things aren't that desperate."

The door opened again. Amanda appeared in the gap. "We

really have to go, I'm afraid," she said. "We have quite a strict schedule."

"Fine. We're just coming," Hoon said. He bent, picked up both bags of money, and handed them to Greig. "Go on, son. Go make a life, eh?"

Greig swallowed. He ran an arm across his eyes, then put an arm around Hoon and hugged him. It hurt tremendously, but Hoon was big enough and ugly enough to take it.

"Thanks, Mr White. Thanks for everything."

"Aye, on you go, fuck off," Hoon said, but he patted the younger man on the back, and let the hug linger just a little while longer.

Amanda cleared her throat. Greig stepped back.

"Right then," the lad announced, switching the handles of the bags around so he was carrying one in each hand. "I guess it's time we were off."

———

Hoon peered into the back of the BMW SUV, and was unable to hide his disappointment when he saw the goon he'd named Butterfuck slouching at the far end of the rear bench seat. The bulky big bastard's weight had been uncomfortable enough on the ride in. Now, with his body a mess of bruising, and something grinding in his ribcage every time he took more than a sip of air, even the thought of it was unbearable.

"Fuck off. Can I no' go in the front?" he asked.

"No," Bingo told him. He pointed to the middle seat in the back. "Get in."

"No chance. I'm no' being the cock between you two sweaty bawbags again," Hoon insisted. "I'll just sit up front. You can stick your bag back over my head, and I'll just have a nice wee doss until we get to wherever the fuck it is we're going. You fat bastards don't crush me, I don't get on your nerves. Everyone's a fucking winner."

Bingo shook his head and started to refuse again, but it was the driver who had the last word. "Just put him up front if it means he'll stay quiet."

"You're a fucking saint, you are," Hoon said, jabbing a finger in the driver's direction. "I mean it. I thought you had a bit of a seedy paedo vibe with you no' saying anything on the way here, but fair's fair. I take it back."

"Just shut the fuck up and get in," Bingo ordered, pulling open the front passenger-side door. He held up a black holdall that Hoon hadn't noticed he was carrying. "I'll put this in the boot."

"What's that?" Hoon asked.

"Your winnings," Bingo said. "Your little pal said he'd taken it by mistake. Personally, I'd have kept it."

"That daft wee bastard," Hoon muttered. He didn't have the energy to worry too much about it right now, though, so just sighed and clambered into the car. Reaching for his seatbelt brought a burst of agony up his side and he shut his eyes while he waited for it to pass.

The slamming of the boot shook the car. The passenger-side rear door opened and closed a moment later as Bingo climbed in.

Butterfuck thrust the black cloth hood through from the back and instructed Hoon to put it on.

"Gladly, pal," Hoon said, slipping it over his head and pulling the cord to tighten it around his neck. "Like I say, just give me a dunt to wake me up when we get there. And apologies in advance if I snore. But, you know, I recently had my head kicked in by a spooky giant, so we all need to make a few fucking allowances."

"Can he see anything?" Bingo asked.

Hoon heard the *whoosh* of air, and the snap of a fist stopping an inch from his face. Even if he had seen it coming, he doubted he'd have had the energy to react.

"Doesn't look like it," the driver said, then the engine started, and Hoon let his head drop back onto the padded headrest, and gave the impression that he was shutting down for sleep.

Instead, he silently catalogued his injuries. All things considered, he'd escaped the wrath of the Wraith quite lightly, he thought. Yes, his nose was bunged with corks of dried blood, the lumps and bruises on his torso were like a topographical map of the world, and one of his ribs was moving in a way neither God nor nature had ever intended.

But, on the bright side, he wasn't paralysed from the eyebrows down, and he could still remember his name. Or most of it, anyway. So, all things considered, it definitely could have been worse.

Should he be going to the hospital? Almost certainly. Was he going to? Was he fuck. He was en route to the dragon's lair. The inner sanctum. The belly of the beast.

Godfrey West had promised women. *So many women.*

And there was one, in particular, that he was interested in.

This could be his best chance of finding her. This, today, could be when he finally saved Caroline.

For a moment, his thoughts drifted back to Greig. He felt bad about just sending him packing like that. He'd already been mixed up in all this, yes, but Hoon had dragged him deeper into it.

Amanda had been right. Some people belonged in the darkness, and some didn't. Greig, most definitely, did not.

Still, Hoon consoled himself with the fact that the lad had done well out of the day. Just walking away in one piece would've been achievement enough, but he'd walked away richer, even without the money the silly bastard had given back.

He had a nest egg now. A chance to build something for his family.

Hoon just prayed he took his advice and got the fuck out of London. There was nothing here but trouble and pain. A fresh start would be just what the doctor ordered.

The car went over a bump, and Hoon realised his eyes had been closing. He inhaled, trying to keep himself awake, but the air in the bag was warm and stale, and tainted by his own sweat. There was nothing refreshing in that breath, and his eyelids grew heavier as the Beamer rumbled along its route.

A phone rang behind him, so piercing and shrill that his tiredness instantly lifted. He listened to the grunt of acknowledgement from Bingo, then the long, frantic babble of a response. Even from that distance, and through the fabric of the hood, the voice on the other end of the line sounded even more urgent than the ring tone had.

The words themselves were far off and scratchy, like a telephone conversation sound effect from an old cartoon. Hoon couldn't make any of it out, and Bingo had chosen that moment to become virtually monosyllabic.

"Yeah," he said.

More babbling.

"Right."

Another garbled response.

"No. Happy to. Believe me."

There was a *bleep* as the call was terminated. Hoon cocked his head and listened, trying to tune into the low murmuring from the men in the back as they discussed the call.

"Everything alright, lads?" he asked, and then he gasped as the cord of the hood went tight around his throat, powerful hands pulling him back against his seat.

His fingers clawed at the cord, but it was pulled too tight for them to find purchase. Change of plan, then.

He threw a wild punch at the driver and grabbed for the

steering wheel. The car swerved violently, throwing him sideways so his head walloped the glass of the side window, and the wheel slipped beyond his reach.

The other goon in the back caught his right arm and pinned it down, stopping him throwing a second punch, or attempting another grab. He pushed back with his legs, driving himself harder into the seat, giving himself just enough room to bring up a foot. He fired it wildly, hunting for the driver, but finding only dashboard and windscreen.

There was a rushing in his ears. A roaring, like the sands of time running out. The darkness inside the hood was replaced by a brilliant bright light that swam and danced before his eyes.

His left hand searched for the door handle, but his fingers were thick and clumsy, and not obeying his commands.

His lungs were tight. Shrivelled. Pain burned across his throat, and panic surged up his spine like a jolt of electricity as he realised that there was nothing—not a damn thing—that he could do to stop this.

He thought of a life lived poorly.

He thought of a scared young woman, lost and all alone.

He thought of death. And, God help him, part of him ached for the release of it.

And then, all his thoughts themselves fractured into fragments, and the roaring rush of sand swept them down

down

down

into the dark.

CHAPTER THIRTY-SIX

COLD.

Raw, brutal cold. Cutting right through him, freezing his insides, dragging him back from whatever empty void he'd escaped to.

Icy water ran in twisting rivulets down his face, and as he instinctively gulped in a breath, he inhaled enough of it to trigger a violent fit of coughing.

The sound was harsh and brittle, like broken glass scraping on a rough brick wall. Pain seared a line across his throat and pounded on his skull like a big bass drum. His eyes felt too big for their sockets. His damaged ribs gave him a moment or two to adjust, then the agony of them detonated like a bomb that drew a cry from his bloodied lips.

He was in a bad way. No two fucking ways about it.

But he was alive. Somehow, for better or worse, he was alive.

He was on a chair. Tied, he thought, though he didn't yet have the energy to test that theory.

There were spots of blood on the floor between his bare feet, their edges spiked like the outside of a virus particle. He watched them for a while, the water that came dripping from his nose and chin diluting them, breaking them apart.

There was something about the floor. Something familiar. Something nagging at him. Grey. Rubbery. Worn and scuffed beneath the blood and water stains.

And that was when it clicked. That was when he knew where he was.

He raised his head and hissed as the beam of a freestanding spotlight burned into his retinas. He screwed his eyes shut, but not before he saw the three horizontal ropes, and confirmed where he was.

A boxing ring. And not just any boxing ring, either.

Granny's gym.

"Finally! I was starting to think you were never going to wake up."

Godfrey West's voice was light and cheerful, and seemed to float around the ring like a butterfly. Hoon brought his head up more cautiously this time so he wasn't staring directly into the light, and found the bastard standing at the top of the staircase that led down to the gym floor.

He came down them like a gameshow host at the start of each episode, sidling down with a sideways skip, and a smile like some benevolent angel descending from the heavens.

"What... what the fuck is this?" Hoon asked.

Adrenaline had started to work its magic, and while his head still felt like it was in the process of being jackhammered, the fog was lifting.

He became aware of his arms. They had been pulled straight down and tied to the back legs of the chair he was sitting on, while his ankles had been bound to the legs at the front. He tried to drag his hands free, but the restraints across his wrists dug painfully into his flesh.

Godfrey reached the steps at the corner of the ring and darted up them. There was a definite crinkling sound as he climbed between the top and middle ropes, but Hoon felt this probably wasn't the best time to pass comment.

"What the fuck is this?" Godfrey mimicked, his South African accent temporarily becoming a mangled attempt at a Scottish one. "That's a very good question. But that's not how this is going to work." He put his hands on Hoon's knees and squatted in front of him. He had removed the mask, yet something about his face looked even more twisted and warped. "I'm going to ask the questions, and you're going to answer them."

"I have my fucking doubts about that," Hoon said. It wasn't one of his more memorable retorts, but it was the best he could come up with in his current condition.

Godfrey gave a shiver. There was something creepily sexual about it. "I got a shudder there. Very macho. I do love the tough guy talk before these things." He adopted a deep, booming voice. "*You won't break me! I'm a big, strong man!*" He laughed, then ran one of his hands up and down Hoon's thigh, before giving it a friendly pat. "But we do. Break them, I mean. In the end. Just like we will with you."

"Good luck, you nappy-wearing bellend," Hoon said, finding some of his usual rhythm again. "Better fucking men than you have tried."

Some of the smug superiority that had been plastered all over Godfrey's face ebbed away. "What? 'Nappy-wearing?' I don't know what..."

"Oh, fuck off. Seriously?" Hoon spat. "You honestly think it's a fucking secret? You crinkling about like a fucking *Pampers* advert with your arse twice the size it should be?"

"Shut up."

"I'd say it's nothing to be ashamed of, pal," Hoon continued. "That we've all got our fucking health problems, but you're no' doing it for that, are you? You're one of them pervy weirdo bastards who gets off on it. So, aye, it's absolutely something to be fucking ashamed of. I'm ashamed on your fucking behalf, in fact. I'm ashamed by association."

The strike to Hoon's face was neither a slap nor a punch, but some half-arsed middle ground that glanced off his cheek.

"Shut up!" Godfrey hissed.

"Everyone fucking knows, pal. They're just too embarrassed to say anything."

Godfrey sprung to his feet. He stabbed a finger past Hoon to one corner of the ring. "You. Do you have any idea what he's talking about?"

"Uh, no, sir," came the grunted response.

"What about you?" Godfrey demanded, pointing to the other corner out of sight at Hoon's back.

"He's just... He's making shit up, sir. He's lying." That one was Butterfuck, Hoon thought, meaning the first man was probably Bingo. "Don't listen to him."

Godfrey nodded, pleased with the responses. He ran a hand down the front of his waistcoat and seemed to find his composure again.

"Ah, but I want to listen to him," he said. "I either want to hear him answering my questions, or I want to hear him begging me to stop."

He clicked his fingers and pointed to a spot in the ring in front of Hoon. Butterfuck appeared suddenly on Hoon's right, and Hoon tensed like he was getting ready for a beating.

A chair was unfolded and set down where Godfrey had indicated, then Butterfuck vanished back into the shadows again.

Godfrey pulled his trousers up an inch or two and lowered himself onto the chair. The spotlight stood behind him, so his features were cast into silhouette, like a whistleblower on TV who couldn't risk being identified.

"You're probably wondering why this is happening," Godfrey began. "How it all went so wrong in such a short space of time. One minute, you're heading to the most exclusive party in the whole of London—and, by extension, the whole of the UK—the next, you're here. Tied to a chair and bleeding."

Hoon didn't give him the satisfaction of a response. He knew exactly why he was here. Of course he did.

Godfrey sat back and crossed one leg over the other. The chair *creaked* its objections, but he ignored them.

"The thing about Charles was that he was a useless little bastard," Godfrey announced. "Had he not been family... Well, let's just say that his career trajectory would've been very different. *Very* different. But... you do what you do for family, don't you, Stephen? You know what I mean. You've got a niece, don't you?"

The drumbeat that had been filling Hoon's chest fell silent. Godfrey smirked and gave himself a tap on the forehead. "Wait, no. Stephen White doesn't have a niece. But Robert Hoon does. Doesn't he?"

Shit.

Shit. Fuck. Shit.

"Who?"

Godfrey waved a hand. "Oh, please, no. God, no. Don't embarrass yourself. We're way past denials. We know everything, Bob. See, turns out you were on our radar for a while, but it was only when we ran the footage of you throwing my nephew under a bus that we put two and two together." He placed his hands on his knee and smiled. "You must've suspected there'd be cameras in the hotel you chased him through, yes? On the street itself? We have access to all of that. Not to mention all those people sharing it online. Even ghouls can be useful."

He turned to where Bingo was standing and gave him a nod. Hoon heard a rustling of fabric behind him.

"And from there? Well, from there it was easy, really," Godfrey continued, bringing his attention back to Hoon. "Algorithms. Face ID. That sort of thing. Tracking you everywhere. Not just the cocktail bar. Your hotel. That phone box where you called your friend. The shop. How was the *Fanta,* by the way? Rather too sweet for my tastes."

The rustling noises behind Hoon became the sound of something heavy being dragged across the ring. Godfrey uncrossed his legs and sat up straight, then indicated the gym with a twirl of a finger. "And here, of course. It led us here. And I thought, what better place for a demonstration? What better place to show you just how serious we are?"

Hoon didn't want to look. There was almost nothing in the world he wanted less. But he couldn't not. He owed him that much.

Granny was alive, but not by much and not, Hoon knew, for long. His face was barely recognisable, a mush of flesh and bone. One eye had swollen shut. The other stared blankly ahead, only the occasional bubble of spit and blood bursting on his lips to indicate he was still in the land of the living.

At the sight of him, Hoon's muscles ignited. He wrenched on the restraints holding him to the metal legs of the chair, heaving and twisting, and hissing through gritted teeth. "You fucks! You fucking *fucking* fucks—"

An arm wrapped around his throat from behind. It pulled, squeezed, stretching his neck and cutting off his air. He continued to fight for as long as he could, then relented as darkness came creeping in from the corners of the gym, and lights sparkled before his eyes.

Down on the mat, something in Granny's chest gave a rattle. Another bubble formed and grew, and Granny Porter's final breath ended with a *pop*.

"I think that was a pretty effective demonstration, don't you?" said the Eel.

Hoon studied the lifeless old man, scrutinising the raw

burger meat of his face like he was committing it to memory. Then, slowly—ever so slowly—he turned to Godfrey West.

"I want you to know, that I'm going to fucking kill you for that," he said. There was no bravado to it. No boasting. It was just a statement, straight to the point and matter-of-fact. "It might not be today... Though, actually, what time is it?"

"Nine-thirty," Godfrey said, humouring him.

Hoon raised his eyebrows. "Oh, then it might be today. Thought it was later than that."

Godfrey laughed and wagged a finger. "You're funny." He looked to his henchmen like he was sharing some exciting news. "He's funny."

His gaze returned to Hoon, then he clapped his hands on his thighs and stood up, scraping the legs of his chair on the mat.

"I hope you maintain that sense of humour throughout everything that's going to happen next. I really do. Sadly, I won't be around to see it, but I'm leaving you in very capable hands. You will talk, Robert. You will. You'll tell them everything you know."

"What, about the Loop you mean?" Hoon took a moment to savour the look of surprise on the other man's face, then shrugged. "I wouldn't know anything about it."

Godfrey recovered quickly from his shock, and started doing up the buttons of his jacket. "Yes, well, I suppose we'll find out. Sooner or later. And I actually sort of hope it's later. Is that cruel of me?"

"Your wee fucking bum chums can torture me all they like, you *DryNites* paedo fuck," Hoon told him. "You won't get anything."

"No? Hm." Godfrey finished fastening his jacket, adjusted his tie, then shrugged. "That's OK, because they're not going to be torturing you," he said.

He closed the gap between them in a couple of big strides,

put a hand on Hoon's head, and jerked it sharply to the right until he was looking back over his shoulder.

Another chair was there, the occupant bound to it in the same way he was, only slumped forward, unconscious.

Greig.

Godfrey's voice was a whisper in Hoon's ear. "They're going to be torturing him."

CHAPTER THIRTY-SEVEN

HOON HAD SHOUTED and threatened as Godfrey had gone crinkling away out of the ring and up the stairs. He had bounced violently in his chair, trying to smash it against the floor. He had spat warnings and rage at the two suited henchmen as they closed in on Greig, their glee written all over their faces.

Granny had warned him about the chairs—they were flimsy things, he'd said, and half of them collapsed when you leaned onto the back legs—and yet, try as he might, he couldn't damage the one he was in, and the way his legs were tied meant he didn't have the reach to push himself backwards.

He was stuck. Trapped. And all he could do was watch.

Watch, and know that this was his doing. Know that, without his interference, Greig would probably be sitting in his cosy little flat right now. He'd be holding his baby, or eating his dinner, or arguing with his missus. Something else, anyway.

Something that wasn't here. Something that wasn't this.

"Don't you fucking touch him," Hoon hissed. "Don't you fucking touch him. He's just a kid."

"That's a bit condescending, isn't it?" Butterfuck said, his bloated face heaving itself into a smirk.

"Didn't hear you saying that when you had him in there fighting," Bingo agreed. "Can't have it both ways."

Greig didn't have long enough hair for the goon to grab, so Butterfuck caught him by the nose and pushed his head back. It lolled back for a second, then flopped forwards again.

"Wakey wakey," the henchman sang. "Rise and shine. No point doing this if you're not awake to appreciate it."

"Here, give us a go," Bingo said. He bent down and slapped Greig across the cheek a few times, each harder than the one before. The *crack* of the last slap sent Hoon into another frenzy of thrashing and swearing, his muscles burning, sweat and blood and foamy spit falling like rain onto the canvas as he tried to shake himself free.

"Leave him alone. You want me to talk? Fine, I'll fucking talk. Just let the kid go."

"Nah, doesn't work like that," Butterfuck told him. "See, we've been given orders. We're going to keep cutting bits off him until we're absolutely sure you've told us everything. If we think there's more to tell, we'll get his girlfriend in here. The *wittle* baby. We'll go through them all until we're absolutely sure you've spilled your guts."

"But it's not just because we've been given orders," Bingo continued. "Is it?"

"Oh, no," Butterfuck confirmed. "No, it's not just that. Fact is, we *like* this shit."

"This is our favourite bit," Bingo said, and his excitement was clear from the way he was jiggling his legs. "All the other shit... Driving people around, making sure that no one escapes, we could take or leave that. But this? Fucking someone up? And getting *paid* for it? That's dream come true stuff."

For once, Hoon was lost for words. What could he say to

that? Clearly, he couldn't appeal to their better nature, and he was in no position to intimidate the bastards.

He tried to throw himself backwards and tip the chair, but barely managed to raise the front legs half an inch off the boxing ring floor before gravity pulled it back down again.

Meanwhile, Butterfuck caught Greig's shoulders and shook him violently. Greig groaned in his sleep, but otherwise didn't register what was happening.

Both henchmen stepped back and crossed their arms. "So, we know he's not dead," said Butterfuck. "That's something."

"Maybe cold water again?" Bingo suggested. He jabbed a thumb in Hoon's direction. "Worked on him."

Butterfuck looked down at the floor on Hoon's left. Hoon followed his gaze and saw a bucket with a dribble of water left at the bottom.

"It's empty. I tipped it all," Butterfuck said.

"Well, we can fill it up," Bingo suggested.

Butterfuck tutted, bent down suddenly, and shouted, "Lalalalala!" in Greig's face.

Nothing.

"Christ. Maybe he's brain-damaged or something," the henchman mused.

"Just get the water," Bingo insisted.

"How come I have to get the fucking water? It's your idea," Butterfuck countered.

Bingo sighed. He marched up to the metal bucket, and it clanked as he grabbed it by the handle. "Fine. I'll go get the water. But shout if he wakes up. And don't fucking start without me."

He clambered out of the ring, then went stomping off towards the doors at the back of the gym. Hoon watched him as far as he was able to, then listened for the sound of one of the doors squeaking open and closed.

"He won't be long," Butterfuck said, and he almost sounded apologetic. "Then we can crack on."

Hoon coughed, snorted up a wad of something thick and bloody, and spat it onto the floor. "Aye. Better wait for the boss, right enough," he said.

Butterfuck gave a little laugh. "Ha. He's not the boss."

"Oh. No. I get that. You're just, what, partners?" Hoon said.

"Something like that," Butterfuck said. He put a hand on Greig's head and moved it around like he was operating a lever. Greig, to the fuckwit's visible disappointment, didn't react.

"Like Cagney and Lacey, but with bigger tits," Hoon continued. "Or Batman and Robin. He's Batman, you're Robin."

"He's not fucking Batman. I'm Batman," Butterfuck retorted.

Hoon sucked in air and winced. "Shite. Touched a nerve there. Sorry."

"Just shut up."

"I didn't want to hurt your feelings or anything," Hoon told him. "It's just, you know, from where I'm sitting, there's only one fucking Batman in your wee pairing, and it's no' you."

"Oh yeah? Then how come he's the one off filling up the bucket?"

"Because it was his fucking idea," Hoon countered. "He's the brains of the outfit, but he's also no' afraid to get his hands dirty. That sounds like Batman to me, which means you're just the Boy Wonder tagging along. Or maybe the butler, in fact. Just bringing him cucumber sandwiches and getting the stains out of his Bat-fucking-Y-fronts."

Butterfuck's face darkened for a moment, then a lightbulb switched on. "Ah. I see what you're doing," he said. "You're trying to turn us against each other. You think you can get us arguing, buy yourself some time to try to escape. Is that it?"

Hoon shook his head. "Naw, the thought hadn't crossed my

mind. I mean, it's obvious that you two are close. Very close. In fact, maybe you're no' Batman and Robin at all. Maybe you're Superman and Lois Lane." He grinned, a bit toothy, shit-eater of a thing. "Is that what you get up to when you're no' on the clock? Does he fire it up you faster than a speeding bullet?"

"Shut the fuck up," the goon said again, but there was anger behind it now. A narrowing of the eyes, a hissing of the words.

"I was just thinking, is he really more powerful than a loco-motive?" Hoon continued. "That must play havoc on the old bahookie. Look! Up my arse! Is it a bird? Is it a plane? Naw, it's Supercock, the Tadger of Steel!"

The blow struck him dead in the centre of the face. He saw it coming—he'd been hoping for it, in fact. He snapped his head back, used that and the punch's momentum to launch the chair onto its hind legs, and rode the impact all the way to the floor.

———

Bingo whistled quietly while he waited for the bucket to fill. The sink was a large, deep ceramic thing, scuffed and scratched through decades of use. He'd last seen one like it back in primary school, and he traced a hand across the porcelain, letting his mind wander back to those far off days.

They had, he quickly concluded, been shit, and he didn't waste any more time dwelling on them.

There was a little freezer filled with cool packs and bags of ice just to the right of the sink. No doubt these were designed to help with bruising. And that, he thought, as he removed one of the bags and tore it open, was precisely what this one would be used for. Just in the opposite way in which it was intended.

He had decided that he was going to be the one to throw the water this time. It had looked like fun, and it was only fair that they both got a turn. He could almost picture how the young lad's face would look when the water hit—the shock of the cold bringing him round, then the slower dawning expression of horror when he started to realise just how deep in the shit he was.

Yes, this was better than driving and guarding. This was what had first attracted him to the job. This was what it was all about.

The bucket was almost full now. He turned off the tap, and the pipes rattled and clanked as if celebrating a job well done. He continued to whistle as he poured in the ice, then grunted with the effort of lifting the now substantially heavier bucket back out of the sink.

The door behind him opened. "Yeah, I'm coming. I'm coming," he said.

He turned. The man in the doorway was not the one he was expecting to see. Nor was it one he *wanted* to see.

The handle slipped from his grip, and the bucket *thunked* against the floor, spilling icy water up over the edge.

Hoon entered without a word. He smiled. And then, once inside, he quietly closed the door.

CHAPTER THIRTY-EIGHT

GREIG ROUSED SLOWLY and of his own free will. One eye opened first, like a scouting party checking for danger. When it saw Hoon standing there, all bloodied and bruised, it quickly shut again, then returned a moment later with reinforcements.

"What... What's happening?"

Hoon beamed down at him, and greeted him with a double thumbs-up. "You're no' deid! Well done, son."

"What? Why would...? Why would I be dead?" Greig muttered, then he realised his hands were tied, and panic flushed through him like a dodgy curry. "What the fuck? What are you doing?"

"Calm down, for Christ's sake," Hoon instructed. "I just left you tied there so you didn't faceplant onto the fucking mat. Here."

He knelt down beside the lad, unfastened the restraints that pinned his arms to the chair, then stood back up again.

"You can do your feet yourself."

Greig didn't waste any time, and immediately started working loose the knots of the ropes around his ankles. As he did, his gaze went to the broken chair in the middle of the ring, and then over to the corners, where two large men in bloodied shirts had been gagged and tied to the padded posts.

"What the hell is all this?" he asked. "What's going on, Mr White?"

"It's Hoon."

Greig kicked free of the ropes and stood up. He swayed on the spot for a moment, blinking and waving his hands at his sides like he was trying to stay upright on a surfboard.

"What do you mean?" he asked.

"It's no' Mr White. It's Mr Hoon. In fact, it's Bob to you. No point standing on fucking formality now."

Greig's mouth moved, like he was talking but his sound had been muted. Eventually, though, he managed to get a word out. It wasn't really worth the wait.

"What?"

"Jesus. My name is Bob Hoon, son. No' Stephen White," Hoon explained. "I've been undercover."

Greig stared at him. The look was either one of fear or of awe, but Hoon couldn't tell which.

"You're a policeman?"

Hoon's lips curled up in disgust. "Am I fuck. I'm more... freelance."

"Like a private detective?"

"Something like that, aye. But no." He thought for a moment. "Have you ever seen the TV series *The Equalizer*?"

Greig nodded. "With Queen Latifah, yeah."

"Who?"

"*The Equalizer*. Queen Latifah." Greig stared at him for a moment, then gasped. "Are you like Queen Latifah?"

Hoon scowled. "Who the fuck's...? No! I'm like Edward Woodward."

Greig shook his head. "I don't know who that is."

"Forget it," Hoon muttered. He pointed to the two men tied

up in the corners. "These two pots of shite were going to kill us. You'll be pleased to hear I put the kybosh on that."

"Kill us?" Greig muttered, then he jumped back in fright when he turned and saw the lifeless form of Granny Porter on the mat behind him. "Jesus Christ! Jesus Christ, what the fuck? What the fuck did you do?!"

"Deep breaths. Come on. That wasn't me, that was this pair of Granny-bashing fucks."

"They murdered him? Jesus! We need to call the police!"

"You're right," Hoon agreed. "We do need to do that. And I'm going to leave you in charge of that bit."

Greig stared back at him, wide-eyed and terrified. "I don't... I haven't got my phone."

"Allow me," Hoon said. He crossed to one of the corners and rummaged in the pockets of Butterfuck's suit jacket until he found his mobile.

He tapped the button on the side, held the phone at arm's length so he could read the stupidly small text on the screen, then he pulled down Butterfuck's gag and turned the mobile towards him.

"They'll fucking kill you if you try to—" the henchman began, but by then the screen had unlocked and the gag had been pulled back in place.

"Yeah, yeah. I've heard it all before, pal," Hoon said. "And you're no' the first one to tie me to a chair, either, by the way. You pricks need to get together and workshop some new fucking strategies."

He wheeled around on his heels, marched to the opposite side of the ring, then climbed out between the ropes.

"Well?" he called, glowering up at Greig. "Don't just fucking stand there. Get your arse down here."

"Oh. Sorry," Greig mumbled. With a few final glances at Granny and the two men tied up in the corner, he clambered out of the ring and joined Hoon at floor level.

Hoon had his eyes closed and was whispering to himself, his thumb poised over the on-screen keypad of the phone.

"It's just... It's nine-nine-nine."

Hoon tutted. "Fuck's sake. Shut up. I nearly had it there."

"What, the police? It's nine-nine-nine," Greig said, then doubt seemed to strike him. "Isn't it?"

"Will you shut your mouth for a minute?" Hoon sniped. He looked down at the phone, paused, then tapped out a series of digits he'd pulled from his memory. "Aye, I'm phoning the police," he confirmed, putting the mobile to his ear. "But no' the fuckwits round here." He listened to the ringing tone and tilted his head like he was conceding a point. "I mean, still a fuckwit, aye, but a different one."

———

Several hundred miles north, Detective Chief Inspector Jack Logan pounced gratefully on his ringing phone. He had, until that moment, been enduring a horror film with not only the lowest production quality he'd ever seen, but also a plot that made absolutely no sense whatsoever, and acting performances that made him want to claw his eyes out.

"Will I pause it?" asked the woman beside him, though her Irish accent and the half-a-pound of popcorn in her mouth meant it took him a moment to work out what she'd said.

"No!" he said, a touch too passionately. He picked up the phone and heaved himself up off the couch. "Just you keep watching. I'll catch up."

He checked the phone's screen as he headed out of the living room and into the kitchen, the sound of a chainsaw and overacted screaming blaring out at his back.

Whoever was calling him was doing it from a mobile he didn't recognise. Possibly a wrong number, but with a bit of luck, he could keep them talking through the whole third act of the movie, then appear disappointed when he walked back in to find the credits rolling.

"DCI Logan," he said.

He immediately regretted answering when he heard the voice on the other end of the line.

"Jack. Long time no fucking see."

"Bob? I was starting to think you were dead."

"Only on the fucking inside," Hoon replied.

"No change there, then."

"Aye, very good. No time for a fucking chinwag, though, got a couple of guys to kick the living shite out of."

"Fair enough," Logan said, deciding he'd rather not know any more.

"I'm going to stick someone on in a minute. Name's Greig. Good guy."

"Is this his phone?" Logan asked.

"Naw, this is Butterfuck's phone."

"Who the hell is...?" Logan began, then he shook his head, and just said, "OK."

"I want you to hook Greig up with your old pal Deirdrie at the Met. Like, now, I mean. Like, in the next five fucking minutes."

"What? It's after ten. How am I supposed to do that?" Logan asked, then he moved the phone an inch from his head to protect his eardrum from the outburst that followed.

"Jesus fuck! I can't think of fucking everything here, Jack! You're a big fucking boy, I'm sure you'll figure something out. She needs to get him and his family somewhere safe. And it's got to be her. She can't fucking delegate this to one of her wee tit-headed minions. Tell her I said that. Use those exact fucking words. It's got to be her. Got that?"

"Aye," Logan confirmed.

"Aye, but have you? Have you really? This is fucking important, Jack. No' like your fucking day-to-day shite up there. I don't care what you're doing right now, drop it. This is priority fucking one. OK?"

"OK, Bob. Fine."

"Right. Good. See that it fucking is. I'm putting you on to him. Hang on."

There was a rustling sound, like the phone was being handed over, but it was Hoon's voice that spoke again a moment later.

"By the way, there's a guy down here wears fucking nappies."

Logan waited for more information, but it wasn't forthcoming. "What do you mean?"

"Aye, like, just for fucking kicks. He's no' got bladder issues or anything," Hoon clarified. "Fucking weird that, eh?"

"Aye," Logan confirmed. "Aye, that's weird."

"Thought you'd appreciate that one," Hoon said. "Right. Say hi to everyone for me. In fact, no, don't, because they're all dicks."

There was more rustling. The next voice that spoke was younger, and significantly less foul-mouthed. "Um, hello?"

"Hello, son," Logan said. "I'm guessing you must be Greig...?"

———

Greig took up residence in what had been Granny's office. He was left in there talking to DCI Logan, with strict instructions not to come out until Hoon came back to fetch him, even if he heard screaming.

Especially if he heard screaming.

Hoon returned to the ring with a notepad and pen he'd found on Granny's cluttered desk. There was a note on it about, 'Aubrey's school play' along with a date and a time just a few weeks from now.

Hoon flipped to the next page, slid the pad under the bottom rope so it came to a stop in front of Bingo, then climbed up onto the ring apron and started to untie one of the henchman's hands.

As soon as one hand was free, Bingo grabbed for the dressing gown cords that were wrapped around his middle, tying him to the post. Hoon put a stop to this by reaching over the top rope, hooking his fingers into the bloodied nostrils of Bingo's broken nose, and pulling. Hard.

Once he was sure his message had been received, he climbed into the ring, walked to the centre, and addressed both his captives.

"Right, pin back your fucking lugs, lads. Here's what's going to happen," he began. "The three of us are going to play a game." He pointed to himself. "I'm going to ask a question." He pointed to Bingo. "You're not going to say a word. You're just going to write down the answer. Then..." He shifted the finger in Butterfuck's direction. "You're going to tell me the answer out loud, and we'll check it against what he wrote. If the answers match, *ding ding!* You win that turn! Everything's hunky-fucking-dory, big smiles all round."

He lowered his pointing finger and looked at each man in turn. They both stared back at him, neither of them making a sound.

"If the answers don't match, then *I* win that round. And I get to do whatever the fuck I want to whichever one of you I happen to dislike most at that particular moment in time. And, I'll be honest, I'm not a big fucking fan of either one of you, so it could go either way. Then, whatever happens, whoever wins the round, we go again. Next fucking question. Boom. And around and around we go."

He grinned and gave a wave of his hand, like he was dismissing concerns they hadn't yet voiced.

"I know, I know, it sounds complicated, but you'll soon get

the fucking hang of it. It'll be fine. We'll fucking freestyle it, and see where we go, alright? Alright. Question one." He turned to Bingo, snivelling behind the bloodied rag that was pulled tight over his mouth. "Where the fuck's this wee gathering I keep hearing about?"

CHAPTER THIRTY-NINE

IT HAD BEEN cold sitting outside the gym, waiting for the others to come out. He had turned the engine on to warm himself up, but had quickly shut it down again when Mr West had emerged. West didn't like them sitting with the engines on. It was harmful to the environment, he said. Not to mention financially wasteful.

Luckily, the boss had gone over to the other SUV and climbed in the back. It had pulled away shortly after, but such was the power of Godfrey West that it took the driver a full five minutes before he dared start his engine again.

He was warmer now, the heated air blowing in through the vents bringing the temperature up to a relatively toasty twenty degrees. He drummed his fingers on the steering wheel, listening to the voice coming from his radio.

"In English, we say, 'goodnight,'" explained the man on the audiobook. He had a calm, soothing voice, like he was delivering the lesson to someone standing on a window ledge on the thirtieth floor of a high-rise. "In French, we say, 'bonne nuit.' *Bonne nuit. Bonne* - meaning good. *Nuit* - meaning night. Bonne nuit. *Bonne. Nuit.* Say that with me."

"Bonne," began the driver, but his door was pulled open before he could get out the second part.

Hands grabbed at him. Fingers tangled in his hair. For a moment, he thought that the steering wheel was rushing towards him, then dismissed that as impossible, and realised it was his head that was moving towards—

His nose exploded on the top of the wheel. Over the sound of his squealing, he heard the passenger door opening, and felt his seat belt retracting across his chest.

And then, he was falling, tumbling out of the car and onto the ground. The SUV was quite tall as vehicles went, and he had always enjoyed a high sitting position.

That was why, when he landed, he heard his wrist snapping beneath him.

And why, just a moment later, he felt it, too.

"Fuuuuuck!" he wailed. He scrabbled inside his jacket with the hand whose palm wasn't currently folded in against his wrist, and managed to wrestle his handgun from its holster.

It was taken from him immediately. This time, he didn't even hear the bone in his arm breaking.

He saw it, plain as day.

While the man on the ground screamed, Hoon took a moment to appraise the weapon. SIG Sauer P365 SAS with a bullseye sight to help with a smooth draw, and reduce the risk of snagging. 9mm rounds, ten in the mag, and one locked and loaded in the chamber.

"Don't fucking mind if I do," he said, tucking the gun into the back of his trousers. Then, he drew back a foot, took aim at the head of the man lying squealing on the tarmac, and—at least for the moment—kindly put him out of his misery.

He pointed through the open doors of the car to where Greig stood with the phone still pressed to his ear. "You still got that fuckwit on the line?"

Greig nodded. "He's asking what you're doing."

"Tell him he doesn't want to fucking know," Hoon said.

"He says you don't want to know," Greig relayed. He listened, nodded again, then looked back at Hoon. "He says you're probably right."

"Tell him no' to worry, nobody's actually dead," Hoon said. He glanced back at the gym and shrugged. "I mean, I'd imagine they might be fucking wishing they were, but that's their fault, not mine."

Greig did his middle man thing again, then passed on Logan's reply. "He says he's going to pretend he didn't hear any of that."

Hoon bent, grabbed the arms of the unconscious driver, and began dragging him back in the direction of the gym. "Right, I'm going to stick this prick in there with the rest of them," he said. "How long until Deirdrie gets here?"

Greig started asking the question, but Logan had evidently heard it and answered before he could finish.

"He says ten minutes."

Hoon opened the door to the gym, heaved the driver inside, then shoved him down the metal staircase. The clanking and thudding of him rolling down the steps was only silenced when Hoon closed the door.

"Right. Listen," he said, approaching Greig. "You're going to be alright. Deirdrie's sound. I mean, as sound as anyone in the fucking polis can be."

"I heard that," a tinny voice announced from the mobile.

"He says he heard that."

"I know he heard it, he was fucking meant to," Hoon said. "But listen to me, son. You tell her everything you know, alright. You tell her everything that's happened."

Greig glanced sideways at the car, then over at the door to the gym. "I'm not actually sure what happened."

Hoon tutted. "Just fucking tell her what you do know, alright? And then, she's going to get you, your missus, and the wee man to safety. She's going to look after you. It's all going to be fine. Do you still have the money they paid you?"

Greig looked down at his empty hand, like he expected to find himself holding the bag.

"The money!" he cried. "No. It must still be in the car. I never made it home. They got a phone call while we were driving." He frowned and touched the back of his head as he pieced everything together for the first time. "They hit me with something, I think."

"Well, good job you were fanny enough to give me mine back. Grab the holdall from the boot," Hoon instructed. When Greig didn't move, Hoon sighed, marched past him, and felt under the back rim of the boot until he found the switch to open it.

It rose slowly, with a faint electronic whine. Hoon saw the bag right away, but as he reached for it, a long plastic box caught his attention. It was pushed up against the back seats, ran the full width of the boot, and was fastened with a couple of metal latches.

Curiosity got the better of him, and he flicked both fasteners open, allowing the lid to be lifted. The low whistle that escaped through his teeth drew Greig over to the back of the car to see what he'd found.

"Are those...? Are those guns?" the lad asked.

"Aye," Hoon confirmed. "Aye, those are guns."

"They're big."

"They are big," Hoon agreed.

Greig pulled the phone from his ear and pointed to it. "He says he doesn't want to know anything about this, either."

Hoon pulled the lid down on the weapons, then grabbed the handle of the holdall. When he lifted it off the floor of the boot, he discovered that the phone that had been taken from him on the way to the fight venue was pinned underneath it.

"Bonus," he said, retrieving the mobile.

He tapped the screen, but it remained dark. He pressed and held down the button on the side until the *Apple* logo appeared, and then shoved the device in his pocket.

"Here," he said, dumping the bag at the lad's feet. "You're down five grand, but it's better than nothing."

"But this is your money. I can't take it, Mr White. I mean... Mr... Bob."

"Mr Bob? Seriously?" Hoon replied. He sighed. "Just fucking drop the nice guy shite and take it, alright? I told you, I don't need it. I don't want it. Maybe best if you don't let Deirdrie see it, if you can help it, though."

Greig looked sideways at the phone that was still held to his ear, then back to Hoon. "Your friend says she's less than five minutes away."

"He's no' my friend," Hoon said, raising his voice so he could be sure that Logan heard.

"He's asking if he can get that in writing," Greig relayed.

Hoon looked both ways along the street. The gym was tucked down a quiet side road, and though there was still over an hour until midnight, only a handful of vehicles had passed since they'd first emerged from inside the building. The kid should be safe enough on his own until the cavalry arrived.

"Right, I need to get going. I can't be here when she arrives. But, like I said, it's going to be OK, son. You and your family are going to be fine. The woman who's coming, Deirdrie, she'll make sure of it."

"What about you?" Greig asked.

"Me? Oh, don't worry about me. I'm going to be having a great time," Hoon replied, and an unsettling sort of half-smile crept across his face. "I'm going to crash a fucking party."

————

Hoon hadn't been able to figure out how to get his phone to connect to the SUV's sound system. Although, to be fair, he hadn't actually bothered to try.

He'd sped away from Greig and the gym, and watched the lad waving as he grew smaller and smaller in the rearview mirror. Hoon had done all he could for him for now. Maybe later, if they all survived the night, he could get Miles to help with the family's relocation. If the might of MI5 could get Gabriella and Welshy to safety, they could do the same for Greig.

"Aye. Aye, it'll all be fine," he said, as if speaking the words out loud would somehow make them true.

Once he'd made it a few streets away, he'd programmed the address of the McGinlay Hotel into the car's satnav, waited for it to plot a route, and then set off following the red line on the map.

He hadn't done a lot of driving in London. It had always seemed like far too much hassle. The road network itself was a jumblefuck wrapped up in a shambles, like someone had tossed a handful of cooked spaghetti in the air, pointed to where it landed, and said, "Let's just build it like that."

And it was best not to even get him started on the fucking traffic.

Still, the streets were quiet enough at that time of night that he was able to tear his eyes from the road long enough to call Miles and put him on speakerphone.

Miles' voice, when he answered, was tinny and hard to hear over the rumble of the BMW's tyres.

"Hello?" he asked, cagey and giving nothing away.

"Aye, it's me. All clear. Nobody's with me."

"Jesus Christ. What happened to you?" Miles asked, and though the road noise made it hard to be sure, Hoon thought there was genuine relief there. "Your phone's been off all day."

"Aye, they swiped it from me as soon as they picked me up."

"Shit. Right. OK," Miles exhaled the tension that had been building up all day. "And? How did it go?"

"Bit of a mixed bag," Hoon said.

"What do you mean? What happened?"

Hoon almost missed the turning marked on the map, wrenched the wheel, and narrowly avoided ploughing through a pizza delivery guy on a moped on the other side of the road.

"Oh, you know," he said. "Kidnapping, murder, torture, a giant albino with a head like a fucking concrete block. The usual."

There was a change to the sound on the other end of the line, and Hoon imagined Miles leaping to his feet. "What? What are you talking about?"

"He knows. Your man, Godfrey. He knows who I am."

"Oh God," Miles whispered. "Oh, God. How?"

"Been tracking me since I went after his nephew yesterday. Then, I don't know, got into the fucking CCTV network and worked backwards from there."

He glanced at the screen, swore below his breath, then swung across the road, mounted the pavement, and roared onto the indicated side street just in the nick of time.

"He left me tied up with a couple of his boys. Told them to get me to spill my guts, then left for a big fucking party he's throwing."

"Jesus Christ. What happened?"

"Well, let's just say I'm currently driving their fucking car, and we'll leave the rest to your imagination," Hoon said. "The party's at the McGinlay. Big secret masked ball, full of a fucking Who's Who of these Loop bastards."

"God. Right. OK. What's the plan?" Miles asked.

"Is that no' you're fucking department? Can you no' just swing in with a hundred armed bastards and a couple of heli-copters?"

"It doesn't work like that," Miles said, after a moment's

pause. "I'd have to go through the channels to get it approved. Making a move like this on home soil would mean involving the Defence Secretary, and there's no saying he's not already compromised. Plus—"

"Fuck's sake. Alright, alright. I get it, you're a useless bastard."

"I can meet you there, though," Miles said.

"What are you going to do?" Hoon spat. "Reorganise their fucking filing cabinets?" He thought of the handgun pressed uncomfortably against his lower back, and the case full of weaponry in the boot. "It's fine. I've got a plan."

"It's not the same as your last plan, is it?" Miles asked. "You're not just going to storm in there and shoot the place up?"

"I'm no' that fucking stupid, give me some credit," Hoon said.

He raced to beat a changing traffic light, then hung a hard left, tyres screeching.

"I mean, it's a variation on that plan, aye," he admitted. "But I've refined it. I've given it a wee twist."

"God. And what's the twist?"

"I'm going to cause a big distraction first," Hoon said. He glanced down at the phone propped up in a dookit on the dashboard. "And that's where you're going to come in."

CHAPTER FORTY

TWENTY MINUTES LATER, the SUV sat in the shadow of a tree on Park Lane, close enough to the McGinlay Hotel that Hoon could see people coming and going, but far enough away that the evening's suspiciously burly doormen hadn't yet clocked him.

He checked the time. After eleven. Godfrey may well have been expecting his guys back by now. For all Hoon knew, he was now well aware of what had happened back at the gym, and was already on the move.

The front of the hotel's twenty-plus floors were lit up in electric blue. The light was projected from two spotlights at ground level, each one slowly ticking from side to side, so the shadows on the front of the building shifted and moved like they were alive.

"Come on, come on, where the fuck are you?" Hoon muttered, peering along the length of Park Lane. "Where are you pricks when I need you?"

They had been the bane of his life in the police—the one thing that detectives on high profile murder cases despised perhaps even more than the killers themselves. They arrived on crime scenes like an invasive fucking species, poking their noses into places they didn't belong, getting under the feet, and generally making arseholes of themselves in the name of press freedoms.

Usually, all it took was a whiff of scandal and they'd come weaselling out of the woodwork. A pretty young female victim would usually attract a good few of them. A suggestion of police corruption would have them descending like a fucking plague.

But here was a terrorist organisation holding a gathering of the créme de la créme of British high society, and the fuckers were nowhere to be seen. Not even *The Sun*, and those bastards would usually be jizzing themselves into dry, dusty husks over something like this.

Of course, there was no saying their owner or editor wasn't on the fucking guest list, which might explain their failure to...

A white van passed the SUV, close enough and fast enough to shake it. Hoon watched as it pulled in at the side of the road, its arse-end angled out like it had been abandoned in a hurry.

Two men jumped out, one carrying a microphone, one hurriedly swinging a camera up onto his shoulder. Beyond them, from the opposite direction, a battered old Ford Focus screeched to a stop, and a slovenly looking man, unshaven and untucked, heaved himself out.

All three men hurried towards the front door of the hotel, forcing the two brutes on guard duty to intercept.

Another two cars passed Hoon and braked hard outside the McGinlay. He watched the occupants—a man from one, two women from the other—come oozing out, cameras, notebooks, and microphones at the ready.

"Now you're fucking talking," Hoon muttered.

Miles had done it. A few phone calls, a couple of 'hot tips' shared online, and the bastards came running, just like Hoon had hoped they would.

So much for their covert wee gathering.

He watched as another couple of goons stepped out through the front door. One of them took out his phone and started talking urgently into it.

That was Hoon's cue.

He got out of the car, went around to the back, and threw open the boot. The clasps of the gun case opened easily, and he stared down at the contents, considering his next move.

The weapons were big. Serious. Conspicuous. There was no way he was sneaking in with any of those slung over his shoulder. No way he was going unnoticed.

"Fuck it," he said, closing the case. "Maybe next time."

There was a black bomber jacket in the boot. He grabbed that, pulled it on, and zipped it up. The jacket was a little on the large side, but not ridiculously so, and it was far better than walking down the street in his torn, blood-stained t-shirt.

He shut the boot, locked the car, then checked the SIG Sauer in the back of his belt. It was a compact gun, easily concealed beneath the jacket. Far more so than Welshy's gold-plated Desert Eagle, although he knew which one he'd rather have with him right now.

Another couple of vehicles had rolled up outside the hotel, and the doormen were in real danger of losing control. The vultures were circling, and any moment now, they'd swoop. They'd break through the defences and get inside. He knew it, they knew it, and while the goons might not want to admit it, they damn well knew it, too.

They wouldn't be trying to stop the journos getting inside, just delaying them long enough for the contingency plan to complete. An operation like this was bound to have a contingency.

Hoon took a left down a side street well before the hotel, then immediately hung a right that Google Maps had assured him would lead him around to the back of the McGinlay. Sure enough, he very quickly found himself outside the hotel's private and gated car park. The whole place was chock-a-block with near-identical looking black cars and several SUVs just like the one he'd recently abandoned.

There were a few larger vehicles tucked away at the far end of the car park—a couple of small hotel-branded vans, plus a bigger truck with a roll-up back door and a logo on the side that was written in French.

He drew back into the shadows as some of the cars' headlights ignited and their engines woke up. He peered through one of the gaps in the tall metal fence and watched as the back door of the hotel was opened from inside, and a sea of men and women in masks came stumbling out in a panic.

There was a buzz from along the fence and the gates rattled as they rolled aside. Hoon sidled in quickly and ducked out of sight behind an industrial-sized wheelie bin before any of the headlights could come sweeping in his direction.

He crouched there in the dark, watching the rats flee the sinking ship. Yet more of the suited henchmen pushed through them, spitting orders, the urgency of the situation shifting the balance of power in their favour. It didn't matter who the people in the masks were now—film stars, politicians, members of the fucking nobility—it was irrelevant. All that mattered now was getting them off the premises before a long lens got a snap of them.

"Aye, toddle on, you bastards," he whispered. "Your time'll fucking come."

It took less than three minutes for all fifty or so masked guests to get to their cars, where their drivers were already primed and ready to go. Unfortunately, being a shower of self-important pricks, they all tried to be the first to leave, and the entire car park quickly descended into gridlocked chaos.

The henchmen, who had looked pleased at the progress of the evacuation, now saw success slipping through their fingers. They hurried between the trapped cars, barking commands and doing their best to play at being traffic cops, and in doing so left the hotel's rear entrance completely clear.

"Bonus," Hoon said, barely able to believe his luck.

Keeping to the shadows at the side of the building, he hurried up to the back door, stole a quick glance through it to make sure nobody was standing there waiting to twat him, then carried on inside.

The entrance led to the kitchen area, where half a dozen white-clad staff members were fixated on their cooking and cleaning, while making a very clear point of not looking up. The whole circus must've come through that way a moment before, but from the way they were pretending to be oblivious to Hoon's presence, they evidently knew better than to get involved.

It wasn't that he was in disguise, exactly, but the jacket he'd taken from the car was clearly familiar enough to the kitchen staff that they assumed he was just another henchman.

There were a couple of doors leading off from the kitchen. One led to a restaurant where a handful of diners were snuggling together at tables, far enough from the drama not to have picked up on any of it.

The other door, which he chose, took him out into a corridor which, after a couple of turns, almost spat him out into the hotel's foyer.

He stumbled to a stop when he saw the suited goons scurrying across the wide-open space, varying expressions of anger, outrage, and confusion written on their faces.

The gaggle of media bastards out front had grown substantially since he'd last seen it. As he watched, one of them pointed to the left along the front of the building and shouted something, and a splinter group broke off and vanished out of sight. Presumably, the gridlock had ended, and the first of the cars had started to flee the scene.

Some of the guards gave chase, and a few of those in the foyer rushed to take their place.

Hoon watched them go, his gaze following them across the entranceway until he became aware of a flash of red over by the elevators.

There was a small group of people waiting for the lift. Godfrey West stood at the centre, flanked by three of his thugs.

The red that had caught his eye belonged to the dress of the woman standing a step behind him. She had changed out of the silver outfit, and into something shorter and more revealing.

Amanda was looking back over her shoulder, and had spotted Hoon before he'd seen her. Her eyes were wide, and her mouth had dropped open into a little circle of surprise.

Hoon froze, waiting to see what she would do. Bracing himself for what would happen next. If it came down to a straight firefight, he might be able to nail West, but that didn't help him. If he was going to find Caroline, he needed the bastard alive.

The doors to the elevator opened, and the Eel was all but bundled inside by his bodyguards.

Amanda turned away from Hoon. She stood there for a moment, coming to a decision.

Then, without a word, she stepped inside and the doors slid closed behind her.

Hoon watched the numbers above the door creeping up.

And up.

And up.

Through the teens, past the low twenties, and on towards the penthouse floor.

"Of course. Might've fucking known," he muttered, then he jogged back along the corridor until he found the staircase, and set off up them as fast as his legs would carry him.

CHAPTER FORTY-ONE

THERE WERE twenty-eight floors to the hotel, with seventeen steps between each one. Hoon tried to do the maths, if only to take his mind off the pain that was rampaging unchecked through his entire body, but gave up somewhere around, "Far too fucking many."

He had dragged himself up to just below the twenty-fourth floor when he heard a door up above screeching open, and two sets of feet come running down towards him. Hurrying up the last few steps, he eased open the door on the landing and sidled quietly into the corridor on the other side.

Slipping his hand behind him, he wrapped his fingers around the grip of the SIG Sauer, and watched through the mottled glass of the door as two of the bodyguards he'd seen escorting Godfrey into the lift came racing past.

He waited until the clattering of their descent had faded, whispered a thanks to the Universe for this uncharacteristic stroke of luck, then snuck back out onto the staircase and continued his climb.

By the time he finally reached the top, he was struggling to breathe past the pain in his ribs, and felt like all the blood in his thighs had turned to acid. Still, the staircase felt safer than the lift. You had a chance to see what waited for you, and some hope of retreating, if necessary.

In a lift, though, you were going in blind, and if you found yourself face to face with some gun-toting hardman, it was unlikely they'd give you the chance to press the button for another floor before opening fire.

There was no window to the door on the penthouse floor, though, which meant he had no way of seeing if the coast was clear without opening the door itself.

Crouching, he reached for the handle, only to discover that there wasn't one. The door had been set up like a fire exit, and could only be opened from the other side. Hoon glared at the spot where a handle should have been, like he might be able to intimidate the door into suddenly sprouting one.

Unsurprisingly, it did not.

"Fuck," he hissed.

From what he could see, the door opened outwards, so a well-placed kick or shoulder was going to do precisely fuck all. He could shoot it, but that was unlikely to achieve anything except to blow his element of surprise and bring several dozen armed bastards rushing his way.

He was considering his options when the door was opened, almost knocking him off his feet. He yanked the gun from his belt and raised it, his body taking the wheel before his brain had a chance to process what was happening.

Amanda stopped dead in the doorway, going slightly cross-eyed as she focused on the barrel of the gun that was currently aimed at her forehead.

She held her hands up, and Hoon saw that she was holding a small piece of plastic roughly the size of a credit card. Amanda slowly lowered herself down until she was practically kneeling, jammed the piece of plastic against the door frame, then stepped out onto the landing and let the door close behind her.

Or *almost* close. The rectangle of plastic stopped the mechanism from catching. She gave Hoon a single nod and then, ignoring the gun, she swept right past him like he wasn't even there, and started off down the stairs.

She moved silently, and Hoon realised that she had taken off her shoes.

"Thanks," he whispered after her.

She stopped a few steps down, but didn't look back. "I'm not doing it for you."

And with that, she continued downwards and vanished out of sight.

Hoon inched the door open, revealing the same corridor he'd been escorted along just the morning before after waking up in Amanda's suite. Now, it was empty. Deserted. Silent, like the grave.

The piece of plastic jamming the door had the hotel's logo on it. A keycard. He picked it up and stuck it in his back pocket, then set off at a creep along the corridor, eyes open, ears pinned back and listening for trouble.

The door of the first room he came to was held open by a housekeeping trolley. He squeezed past it, gun raised, and found an unmade bed with a couple of empty vodka bottles on the bedside table.

The door to the next room was resting against the frame. He cautiously pushed it open, and found a similar picture to the one before. A messy bed, a few empty bottles. A smattering of white powder on the desk was a sign that a very private party had recently come to an abrupt end.

The doors to the next few rooms were locked, but Amanda's keycard soon put paid to that. The first two were in better condition than the others he'd seen, with neatly made beds and a full complement of teas and coffees in a metal box on the desk.

The third room went to the opposite extreme. Hoon smelled it as soon as he opened the door. The sheet had been partly pulled off the bed, so it hung, twisted like a rope, from one corner. Blood and piss pooled on a waterproof topper that had been stretched across the mattress, and an assortment of female sex toys, each one large enough to choke a horse, regardless of which end you inserted it, lay scattered around.

Hoon tried not to think of Caroline as he left the room and closed the door behind him.

The next few along were open. He didn't bother looking in. Instead, he stopped at the door to Amanda's suite, tapped the key against the lock, then slipped inside with the gun leading the way.

He saw the flash of white too late. The gun hand twisted across his body, trying to get off a shot, but fingers like iron bars clamped down on it, preventing him from squeezing the trigger, and a fist like a wrecking ball slammed into his broken ribs, reigniting the inferno in his chest.

Another blow came out of nowhere. The gun flew from his grip and went rolling across the expensive carpet. Through a haze of pain, he saw it slide to a stop against the side of a chaise longue, but before he could make a dive for it a third punch hit him, and this one sent him spinning all the way to the floor.

Ribs grinding, Hoon struggled into a kneeling position, one hand on the carpet beside him like a sprinter getting ready to run, the other wiping a smear of blood from his lips.

He looked up. And there, gazing impassively down, was a big spooky giant with chalk-white skin and eyes of ruby red.

"Oh, Jesus," Hoon groaned. "No' again."

CHAPTER FORTY-TWO

"ARE YOU EVER FUCKING DRESSED?" Hoon asked, indicating the giant's tiny shorts and naked upper body.

He used a side table to heave himself to his feet, wheezing and holding up a hand to indicate he wasn't ready. The Wraith, having apparently nothing whatsoever to fear from his opponent, gave him the time and space he needed.

Big mistake!

Snatching up a vase that was sitting on the table, Hoon made a wild lunge and smashed it against the side of the albino's head. The pottery shattered, forcing him to shut his eyes and turn away to protect himself from the flying shards.

A half-second later, when he looked back, the Lithuanian still didn't appear to have registered the attack.

"Ah, fuck," Hoon had time to mutter, then a punch like a horse's kick nearly took his head off. He wasn't aware that he was stumbling backwards until he hit the hotel room door.

His vision cleared just in time to see the giant striding towards him, fist already swinging. Flames of pain licked up Hoon's side as he ducked clear. The albino's fist powered a hole cleanly through the door, and Hoon took the chance to attack with a couple of elbow strikes that he was almost certain, hurt him more than they did the Lithuanian.

He sprang towards the chaise longue, reaching for the gun, but a hand caught him by a foot and he fell, face-first, onto the carpet. He felt a sudden sensation of pressure. Something in his knee *popped*, and then he was moving, spinning, arcing away from the floor, and the gun.

The grip on his leg was released, and he experienced a terrifying yet oddly peaceful second or so of free flight before he landed on a coffee table. It was a heavy, sturdy bastard of a thing, and pointedly refused to break his fall by collapsing. Instead, it stopped him dead, and he lay half on it, half on the floor. His brain screamed at him to get up, but his body decided it needed a moment to get its shit together.

His knee went *pop* for a second time as it slipped back into place. It hurt. A lot. But, he welcomed it, all the same. At least he'd be able to stand now. Assuming he could figure out which way was up.

The high-pitched ringing that filled his ears drowned out the sound of the footsteps behind him. It was only when he saw the giant's shadow that he realised the next attack was incoming.

His eyes fell on the handle of a small drawer sticking out from the side of the coffee table. He grabbed it, yanked the drawer free, then swung it in a wide *whumming* semi-circle up and around behind him.

Almost every part of his body objected to this movement, but he gritted his teeth and pushed the pain down, reinvesting it to be collected with interest at a later time.

He'd been aiming for the Lithuanian's head, but his position on the floor and the other man's height both contributed to him being quite some way off the target. The corner of the drawer cracked the giant on the hip, and while he didn't seem best pleased about it, it did very little to slow him down.

"Look, can we maybe just talk about this?" Hoon wheezed. "Have a wee fucking sit down and a blether?"

The Wraith swung a fist down like a sledgehammer. Hoon rolled clear, and this time the coffee table did collapse under the weight of the punch's impact.

"I'm taking it that's a no, then?" Hoon groaned.

Hoon grabbed a lamp and threw it, only for the cable to pull tight well short of the target.

"Fuck's sake," he complained, as the lamp *thunked* to the floor.

He needed a weapon. The gun was across the room, with the big spooky bastard between him and it, so that was currently not a possibility. Even at full health, he doubted he had the speed and acrobatic ability to get past the albino. Now, with somewhere in the region of two to three broken bones, a recently dislocated knee, and what he suspected was quite a lot of internal bleeding, he had no chance.

So, what did he have? He looked around. *Not a fucking lot* was the answer. Nothing within reach would make a particularly formidable weapon. Not without time to adapt it, anyway. Aye, he could upend a table and break one of the legs off, but he couldn't see the Lithuanian agreeing to give him the time-out that he'd need to get the job done.

The bath Amanda had been lying in when he'd first entered this room was over on the left. It was now empty, though, robbing him of the possibility of drowning this scary fucker. On the other hand, it also removed the much more realistic possibility of that very same thing being done to him.

Wait. The bath! Relative to where he was standing, it was almost exactly where it was when he'd first seen it. This was where he'd come in.

Turning, he saw the bedroom door just a few paces behind him. He lumbered for it, threw himself into the room, then slammed the door closed. He was just grabbing for a chair to jam under the handle when the whole thing flew inwards as if compelled by the wrath of God.

The albino ducked into the room, his features as blank and impassive as ever, his red eyes sparkling like gemstones in the dark.

Hoon backed off. There was no way out of the room except through the giant. The bastard knew it, too, and wasn't advancing. He was just standing there waiting, like he had all the time in the world.

A weapon. A weapon. Hoon needed a fucking weapon. But all there was close to hand were the bedclothes, an outrageous number of cushions and pillows, and the same kettle he'd filled earlier with a view to throwing the boiling contents into the face of his kidnappers.

He wondered briefly if he had time to fill that and set it to boil now, then told himself not to be so fucking stupid.

There had to be something, though. Something he could use. Something heavy and solid enough to make a dent in this one-man circus of horrors.

The TV! That would do it. Darting to it, he caught the telly by the frame and pulled. Clearly, whoever had installed the fucking thing had done a bang-up job, though, and it held firm until the burning in his side forced him to abandon the idea.

Fuck it, then, the kettle it was. He caught it by the handle, spun, and smashed it hard enough against the side of the albino's skull to dent the metal. The giant felt that one. He staggered a single step, and for a moment—just a moment—his previously expressionless face registered shock.

Hoon swung with the kettle again, but the giant deflected it, wrenched it from his grip, then hurled it across the bedroom.

Seizing the distraction, Hoon made a dash for the door. He made it all of three strides back into the suite's living area—back towards the gun—when a foot hit him in the lower back, and staying upright was suddenly no longer an option.

His head and one shoulder hit a wingback armchair that was either made of concrete or bolted to the fucking floor. It stopped him dead in his tracks and he slumped down until he was inhaling the carpet.

The pain he had tried to defer until a later date decided that payment was now overdue. He swore, although he couldn't be sure if it was out loud or inside his head, and managed to get both hands below himself so he could at least entertain the possibility of getting back up.

Not now, though. Not quite yet. He needed a few seconds first. A chance to get his breath back. Then he'd be able to take the bastard.

Just a little rest. That was all he needed. Just a moment's shut-eye, then this ghostly fucker was getting it.

His eyes closed all on their own.

In the darkness, he thought of a bed, all blood and piss.

He thought of a young woman. Naked. Afraid. And so very far from home.

He thought of her parents, waiting for her. Counting on him.

On your fucking feet, soldier.

His arms shook as he pushed himself up. The chair, which he'd been cursing a moment before, now proved to be a blessing as he used it to heave his bleeding, wheezing carcass the rest of the way upright.

He leaned against it, spat a dribble of blood down his chin, then exhaled painfully and made a half-hearted beckoning motion.

"Come on then, you rat-eyed vampire doughball," he growled. "Is that the best you've fucking got?"

A left hook almost unwound his head like it was a screw-on cap. A follow-up punch to the stomach emptied all the air from his lungs along with a thin thread of blood that coiled on the carpet beneath him.

"Shite," he croaked.

That was disappointing. That last-minute rally thing usually worked in the movies.

The Wraith was unstoppable. He didn't just look like he was carved out of ivory, his punches felt like it, too. He was apparently impervious to pain, an indestructible solid block.

No. He wasn't all solid. Nobody was. And there were at least two soft, dangly bits within arm's reach.

Gnashing his teeth against the pain, Hoon delivered a respectably powerful uppercut to the giant's groin. The impact sent a jolt of agony through his wrist, up his arm, and into his shoulder, and he actually winced at the thought of what it would be like to be on the receiving end.

The albino, however, didn't appear in the least bit fazed.

"Fuck's sake, seriously?" Hoon groaned, flexing his fingers and shaking his hand so it flapped limply on his aching wrist.

"You're wasting your time there, I'm afraid."

The Wraith took a step back and stood like a military man at ease, his hands tucked behind his back. From beneath a swelling eyelid, Hoon saw Godfrey West entering through the hotel room door. The bastard was smiling at him. *Smiling.*

"He's castrated," West explained. He came closer, stopped beside his albino giant, and ran a hand down his bare front, the fingers crawling likes the legs of a spider and stopping just above the waistband of his shorts. "Barbaric, I know, but he had it done himself as a teenager, long before I... acquired him. Obviously, as you've discovered, it brings with it certain advantages."

Hoon launched himself towards West, but a big open-hand slap from the Lithuanian spun him a whole ninety degrees to the right.

He spent a confused handful of seconds wondering where the fuck the other men had gone, then found them again when he turned to his left.

"I appreciate your spirit, Bob. I mean, it's really impressive what you've done." Godfrey started to count on his fingers. "You've cut my party short, you've..." He struggled to think of a second thing, then rallied and gestured to some debris on the floor. "You broke that vase! And then, yes, you got yourself caught. But still. You should be really pleased with everything you've achieved. Seriously." He grinned and gave him a double thumbs up. "Great job!"

"Maybe this was all part of the fucking plan," Hoon said, the words slurring through his bloated lips. "Maybe I was drawing you out."

"Huh! That had not occurred to me," West replied, though he didn't appear all that concerned by the possibility. "Fair enough. And what do you plan to do now that I'm here, then?"

"For starters, I'm going to bleed all over your nice fucking carpet," Hoon told him.

"We get a lot of blood on these carpets," West said, and there was a twinkle in his eye when he said it, like he delighted in that fact. "We factor it into the cost of the services we provide."

"Caroline Gascoine," Hoon said. "Where is she?"

Godfrey raised an eyebrow. "Sorry, who?"

"You took her. The fucking... caravan of cunts that you're part of. The Loop. It took her."

"Oh! I see! Is that what all this is about?" Godfrey asked. He laughed, and the *trill* of it bounced around inside Hoon's head. "I'm afraid I don't have a clue. We go through a lot of girls. I don't generally sit down with them and find out their names. Who they were before isn't important."

"Was she here?" Hoon asked. "You had women here. Was she one of them?"

"I wish I could help, Bob. I really do," Godfrey said. "But, well, even if I went and asked the girls one by one, chances are even she wouldn't remember her own name now." He put a hand to the back of his mouth, glanced from side to side, then spoke in a conspiratorial whisper. "They do a *lot* of drugs. The hard stuff, too. It's really quite sad." He ratcheted up his smile, then shrugged. "Still, whatever gets them through, I suppose."

Hoon tried again, and he almost got close enough to grab the bastard by the lapel of his suit before another slap caught him.

This time, he was more prepared for it. He caught hold of the albino's hand, brought his head down, then sunk his teeth into the fleshy ball at the base of his thumb.

Don't fight well, fight smart.

Or, even better, fight dirty.

He tore free a chunk of meat, and the white skin of the giant's palm suddenly pooled with red.

The Wraith grabbed him by the head and pulled him backwards until he felt like his spine might be about to snap.

The big man's bollocks might have been a no-go, but they weren't the only soft and fleshy parts of the male body. Not by a fucking long shot.

He tucked the thumb of his right hand in and straightened the other fingers until they formed a point like a spear. He feinted with a left jab, then powered through with a strike straight to the big man's throat.

That one did damage. The Wraith took a couple of lurching steps back and grabbed for his throat with his injured hand. Blood cascaded down his front, forming rivulets of red on the tightly stretched white skin.

"So, you've got a bit of fucking colour in you somewhere," Hoon said, spitting out the other man's flesh.

He moved in to finish the big bastard off, then buckled when West delivered a quick one-two to his broken ribs.

The floor was suddenly jelly under his feet. It wobbled and undulated beneath him, making it impossible to stay standing.

He was sure that the ground was a long way away, yet he hit

it almost instantly. His reunion with the carpet was painful, but short-lived. He felt hands gripping his head, saw a glimpse of a ghostly white finger, and then he was being hoisted up onto his knees, his head twisting until he heard the creaking of the bones in his neck.

He tried to shove the giant away, but there was no strength left in his arms, and it was all he could do to dig his fingernails into the other man's wrists until they left crescent moon shaped imprints on his skin.

West's voice sounded far off, like it was coming to him through a snowstorm.

"I want you to know, that he takes absolutely no pleasure in this," West said. Hoon saw his face emerge from the shadows, his grin so wide it looked like he was back to wearing the feature-distorting plastic mask. "But let me assure you, that I do."

Spikes of electricity surged down Hoon's spine as his neck was twisted just a little further, just a little more.

"He's not going to kill you, Bob. He's going to paralyse you. Then, when he does, you'll be mine to do with as I see fit. We have access to some truly excellent doctors, and they will keep you alive for a very long time." He came closer, until Hoon could feel the warmth of his breath on his face. "I assure you, you will wish otherwise. If you were still able to speak, you would beg them for the release of—"

There was the sound of thunder. Heat and wet hit Hoon in the face, and the pressure on his neck suddenly stopped. He fell backwards onto the floor, kicking clear, watching as the Wraith prodded gingerly at a hole in the centre of his chest.

Blood poured from the wound—a straight line down his front that rattled as it formed a puddle on the carpet between his feet.

And then, like some great felled oak, he began to topple. His shadow grew larger around Hoon, and it was only some frantic last-second scrambling that got Hoon clear of the crash zone.

The shock rang in the air with the echo of the gunshot. A second shot went off, and West ducked for cover, his hands wrapped around his head like they could somehow make him bulletproof.

Hoon looked for the gun that had landed by the chaise longue, but in its place he saw a pair of black and white trainers, and the bottom of some neatly pressed pinstriped trousers.

"Oh, thank fuck," he coughed.

"You alright, Bob?" Miles asked. He had the gun raised, training it on the wingback armchair that Godfrey was currently using for cover.

"Oh, just tickety-fucking-boo," Hoon said. "And, just for the record, I was just about to take him there. I was just waiting for the right moment." He shifted himself up onto his elbows and looked over to the open door. "That the Cavalry here, is it? About fucking time."

"Just me," Miles said.

Hoon hacked up a wad of blood and spat it onto the floor. "Oh, aye. *Proper channels*. How long until they get their finger out and get here?"

Miles shook his head. "They're not coming."

Hoon frowned. "What?"

"It's just us," Miles explained. The gun was trembling in his hands, and Hoon realised that the MI5 man's whole body was vibrating, like it was fighting off hypothermia.

"What the fuck do you mean?"

Hoon manhandled all his many injured parts into something that passed for a standing position. The whole hotel seemed to be swinging back and forth like a pendulum, though, so there was no saying how long that position would last.

Godfrey West raised his head above the armchair, then ducked again as the gun went off. One of the big windows looking out across London crystalised, and wind whistled in through the newly formed hole.

"Jesus! What the fuck are you doing?!" Hoon demanded. He tried to take the gun, but Miles pulled back out of reach.

"Don't!" the MI5 man barked, shooting Hoon a sideways look. The torment in his eyes stopped Hoon dead in his tracks. There was anger there, but other things, too. Hate. Grief. Fear. Sorrow. "I don't want to hurt you. I just want him."

"Aye, well, we've fucking got him," Hoon pointed out.

Miles shook his head. "Dead. I want him dead. I'm going to kill him." He gritted his teeth and sucked in air, like he was fighting to hold himself together. "Like he killed *them*."

"Killed them? Killed who? What are you...?"

Hoon felt his gaze being pulled down to floor level. The trainers had been a present from his wife—one important enough that he'd worn them ever since.

There had been a booster seat in the car, yet Miles had never mentioned a child.

Have you no' got a fucking family to go home to? That's what Hoon had asked.

He hadn't received a reply.

Not until now.

"Aw, fuck," he groaned, then the gun fired again, and one of the wings on the back of the chair became a whirlwind of fabric and stuffing.

CHAPTER FORTY-THREE

"WAIT, WAIT, WAIT!" Hoon hollered, throwing his hands up like he was surrendering on West's behalf. "We need him alive! We need him to tell us where Caroline is."

"Oh, grow up, Bob!" Miles spat back. The hand holding the gun was swaying now like the weight of the weapon was taking its toll. He clutched his wrist with the other hand and tried to hold it steady. "She's already dead. You know it, I know it, and he definitely knows it!"

"No! No, she isn't! What good would she be to us dead?" West called from behind the armchair. "I can help you. I can help you to find her if you just—"

The SIG Sauer kicked, and a painting on the wall behind the chair sustained a life-altering injury.

"He's lying!" Miles hissed. "He's trying to talk his way out of this. That's what he does. But he won't. Not this time."

"What did he do?" Hoon asked, sidling closer, his arms still raised. "Tell me what happened."

Miles' mouth became thin, his lips pursing together. His eyes seemed to shimmer, as tears formed, then rolled down his cheeks.

"I was investigating him. I was digging too deep," he said. "He had some of his men try to warn me off. Try to scare me away, but I wouldn't listen. I kept digging."

His bottom jaw trembled like it was going to shake itself free of the rest of his face. He ran an arm across his eyes, wiping his tears on his shirt sleeve.

"So, he killed them. Both of them. He killed my wife." His voice became a dry scraping sound at the back of his throat. "My son."

"I didn't. I didn't, I swear," West said. He raised his head just long enough to fire Hoon an imploring look. "I don't know what he's talking about. You've got to help me!"

"*Stop lying!*" Miles barked. He fired again, and another shot went wide of its target, shattering a lampshade across the other side of the room.

"We've got him. We can bring him to fucking justice here," Hoon said. "You said you wanted to bring down the Loop. This is how you fucking do it. We start with him. Alive."

Miles' face contorted into an anguished grin. He laughed, but it was a sound devoid of all happiness or joy.

"You still don't get it, do you? You can't bring down the Loop. It's everywhere. It's everyone," Miles told him. "How can you hope to get justice when they own everyone in power?" He shook his head and sniffed. "This was never about stopping the Loop. You can't. No one can. This was about getting me and him in a room together so I could kill him for what he did."

"No. No, was it fuck," Hoon snapped. "It was about finding Caroline. That's what you said."

There was an apology in the glance Miles gave him. It was apparently the only one he was going to get. "I lied. I just needed your help. I knew I couldn't do it without you."

Something cold and clammy crept up Hoon's spine. "Wait... are you even MI5?" he asked.

"Yes. Yes, I am. That bit was true," Miles assured him.

"Oh, thank fuck," Hoon breathed.

"I'm just..."

The icy fingers of terror returned. "You're just fucking *what*?"

"I'm on compassionate leave. I have been ever since they... Ever since *he* killed them. I called in some favours. With the police. That's how I got you to come on board"

"No. No, no, no," Hoon shook his head, refusing to believe it. "Welshy. You told me you'd got him somewhere safe."

"He is. They both are," Miles insisted. "I promise you that much. They're at my cousin's."

Hoon almost hit the roof. "Your *cousin's*?! What are they doing, having a fucking sleepover?" He practically hurdled the fallen albino, and closed the gap between him and Miles before the gun could be turned on him. "You fucking promised me! You said you had a team moving them!"

Miles tried to pull away, but Hoon grabbed the gun, wrenched it from him, and then shoved him in the chest with his free hand, sending him stumbling backwards across the room.

"You fucking stay down there. I'll talk to you in a minute," he barked, tucking the gun into the back of his trousers. "First, I'm going to go twist bits off our mutual friend over there until he tells me everything I want to know."

Godfrey, who had been spying on this exchange from behind the chair, suddenly launched himself to his feet.

"Look, we can talk this over," he insisted. "We can come to an agreement. I can get you anything you want. Money? Power? Whatever you need, I can make it happen."

"What I want is to know where Caroline Gascoine is," Hoon said, advancing slowly. "Then, you're going to tell me the names of everyone who was involved in taking her. All your wee secret fucking handshake pals. I already know who grabbed her, and he's at the bottom of the fucking Thames. I want to know everyone who so much as looked at her from that point on, and I want to know where to find them."

"I can't... I don't know," West insisted, backing away.

Hoon shrugged, and tried not to let on quite how painful the action was. "Fine. Just give me all the names you've got, and I'll go ask them myself if they saw her."

"I can't give you that information!" Godfrey said. "I mean... even if I had it, I couldn't. They'd kill me."

Miles piped up before Hoon could respond. "I'm going to kill you!"

"There we go, see? The Loop's the least of your fucking problems," Hoon said. "So, how about you tell me where she is, and we'll start from there? If you don't know, tell me who will. Then, I'll help you. I'll protect you. But I need to know about her. I need to know where—"

"Boss?"

Hoon turned to find a henchman standing in the doorway, hand already reaching into his suit jacket and grabbing for a gun.

Spinning, Hoon drew the SIG Sauer and fired off two shots into the goon's chest that launched him back across the corridor. He hit the wall and slid down it, leaving a trail of blood on the expensive wallpaper.

"He's running!" Miles cried, and Hoon turned back to see Godfrey sprinting at full-tilt towards the broken window.

"You'll never take me!" he bellowed. "Long live the Loop!"

There was a *thunk* as he hit the glass and rebounded off it, blood spurting down his face.

"Argh! Shit!"

He launched himself sideways and staggered, half-blinded, towards another of the suite's many doors.

Hoon raised the gun and took aim at the bastard's back.

"Stop right fucking there!" he warned, but West covered his head with his hands again and darted into the side room.

"Fuck!" Hoon spat, hobbling after him. The door wasn't locked, but it was blocked from the other side. He aimed low and fired a shot that drew a cry of pain from inside.

The door fell open, and Hoon stepped through into what looked like a giant version of a baby's nursery. He spent a few dumbstruck moments taking in the huge soft toys, bed-sized cot, and giant plastic changing mat, then turned his attention to the man currently lying on the floor amongst it all, blood pumping from a hole in his shin.

"This is just fucking weird, pal," Hoon remarked. "I mean... I wish I had something more insightful to say, or some sort of clever quip to deploy, but I'll be honest..." He sucked air in through his teeth and shook his head. "I'm at a bit of a fucking loss here, so I'm just going to pretend that I'm no' seeing any of this shite, and get back to what we were discussing."

He pressed a foot on Godfrey's injured leg and pinned it to the bunny rabbit patterned carpet. "Caroline Gascoine. Where is she?"

"Please... please! I don't know their names, I swear. I don't know who they are. I don't know anything about them. I just know they get moved around."

"To where?"

"Everywhere! All over the world!" West sobbed. His eyes widened in desperation, and he reached a hand up like he was begging for help. "But, hey, listen. You're right. You're right! I can help you. I can. We can find her together, but you have to let me go. If they think I've been compromised, they'll kill me, and you'll never find her. But... Yes. Now I think about it, maybe I do know who you're talking about! I think I do know her! In fact, I'm sure of it."

Hoon ground his foot on the gunshot wound, and stared through his one good eye at the snivelling wee fuckrag on the floor.

"What's her name?" he asked.

Godfrey's clutched at his leg, his chest twitching as his breaths came in tiny short bursts. "What?"

"Her name. I just fucking said it a second ago. If you know who I'm talking about—if you know where she is—what's her fucking name?"

"I... I... It's..."

Hoon saw it on his face. In his eyes. He was lying. This was a final desperate play, in the hope of earning himself a reprieve from what was to come. He didn't know who Caroline was. He had no idea. To him, she was just one in a hundred nameless women whose lives had been ruined by the Loop. One in a thousand. More, even.

This man couldn't help him find Caroline.

But that didn't mean he served no purpose.

"The women who were here. Where are they?" Hoon demanded.

"They're gone. They're gone. I don't know where."

Hoon pressed the foot down harder, drawing a scream. "Think."

"I don't know! Abroad, probably! I don't know!"

"How are they transporting them?" Hoon asked, but the answer came to him before he'd even finished the question.

The truck. The truck with the French logo. It had to be.

"Miles!" Hoon shouted back over his shoulder, then he jumped when he saw the MI5 man standing just a few feet behind him, watching on.

"Jesus!" Hoon scowled.

He handed Miles the gun. Miles stared down at it in his hand, like it was some sort of trick.

"I'm fucking trusting you here," Hoon told him. "I need to go. I think this half-chewed jebend can be useful. I think he can help bring these Loop fucks down, but I get it. I understand why you want to put a bullet between his fucking eyes. So, I'm making it your call. I'm leaving it in your hands. Alright?"

Miles was still staring down at the gun, and Hoon didn't have time to wait for an answer.

"Good fucking chat," Hoon said, then he patted Miles on the shoulder, and half-ran, half-hobbled out through the main living area and into the hallway.

It took him just a second or so to retrieve the dead hench-man's gun from his holster. He heaved his aching frame in the direction of the stairs, then thought, 'Fuck that for a game of soldiers,' and headed for the lift, instead.

CHAPTER FORTY-FOUR

HE GOT out of the lift one stop before the ground floor and took the stairs the rest of the way. By the sounds of things, the hotel foyer was still in chaos. There were a multitude of raised voices, some scuffling, and the occasional cry of shock or pain.

In the distance, sirens wailed. A few months ago, that would've been a welcome sound. But knowing what he did now —knowing how integrated into the system the Loop was—the sirens were a countdown. Whatever he was going to do, he had to do it fast.

His appearance had changed since the last time he'd passed through the kitchen, and all those chefs and KPs who had so pointedly ignored him before now watched, wide-eyed, as he limped through the steam and the heat, the gun held up to make anyone who might be considering challenging him to fucking well think again.

He made it outside, and the sudden cold snatched his breath away.

He saw a cloud of exhaust fumes and heard the rumbling of a diesel engine. The French truck trundled out of the car park, hanging a left.

"No, no, no," he ejected. He brought the gun up, tried to get a bead on the driver as the van completed its turn, but the angle was all wrong. "Fuck!"

He broke into the closest thing to a run he could manage, given the current state of his body. Nothing was moving properly, though. Nothing was working together. He watched the van vanish out of sight in the direction of Park Lane, and all hope went with it.

There were no other vehicles in the car park. No way for him to give chase. No chance of him catching it now.

From around the corner, he heard the blaring of a horn.

"Get the fuck out of the way!" a man's voice called. "Move your fucking vans!"

Yes! God, yes!

He continued to lumber out through the gate and saw a black-suited goon standing beside the open driver's door of the truck, shouting at two camera crews whose vehicles had blocked the exit onto the road.

God bless the fine men and women of the fucking press!

Hoon hobble-ran up to the truck, called, "Haw, fanny-baws!" to the driver, then floored him with a pistol grip to the forehead when he turned to look. Quickly tucking the gun into his belt out of sight, Hoon pointed to the camera operators.

"You lot. You want the story that'll make your fucking careers? This way."

Without waiting to see if they were going to follow, he turned and limped to the back of the truck.

The locking mechanism took a bit of working out, then a bit more shunting around until, with a *squeak*, one of the doors swung outwards a few inches, before Hoon helped it the rest of the way.

"Oh," he said, staggering back. "Oh, fuck."

"What the hell...?" asked a voice at his back. "Colin, are you shooting this? Can we go live? We need to go live."

Hoon pulled himself up into the truck, and the women sitting hunched at the far end lowered their heads and looked away, terrified he might single them out.

All but one.

"It's OK," Amanda said. She looked around at the others, and Hoon saw that they were all fastened together, her included. "It's OK, he's not one of them. He's not going to hurt us. Are you?"

Hoon shook his head. Words escaped him, so he cleared his throat a few times, like he was trying to kickstart his voice box. "Uh, no. No. You're OK. You're all OK. I'm here to help."

There were eighteen of them, including Amanda. Not that he counted them. Not yet. Not then.

They were young. Mostly. On the outside, anyway. But he could tell from the few eyes that flitted to look at him that they were old on the inside, where it counted. Older than most. Older than anyone had any right to be.

"You're OK," he told them again.

They were in various states of undress, with Amanda at one end of the spectrum, and a completely naked blonde girl shivering uncontrollably at the other.

Hoon removed his jacket and draped it over her. She didn't look at him. She didn't dare. But she pulled the garment tighter around herself, trying to trap some heat inside.

"You getting this?" he asked, turning to the journalists. Two cameras were rolling. A man with a microphone was standing in open-mouthed shock, staring into the back of the truck.

"Uh, yeah. Yeah, we're getting it," he said, pulling himself together.

Hoon turned back to Amanda. He wasn't sure what he wanted to say to her, exactly, but he knew he had to say something. Demand answers. Offer an apology. Tell her he understood. Whatever she'd had to do to survive, whatever deals she'd had to make with the devil, he understood.

But then...

But then...

It was his stomach that reacted first. It fluttered like it was lifting up into his chest, and for a moment he thought he might be having a heart attack.

Then, his brain registered what he'd seen.

Who he'd seen.

She was sitting over on the left, a black dress pulled down to her waist, revealing an intricately detailed one-piece undergarment designed solely with titillation in mind.

Her head was lowered, but he could see the side of her face.

She had her mother's cheekbones. Her father's eyes.

The world seemed to grind into slow motion. The floor became treacle, gluing him to the spot so it took all his strength to make a move. To take a step.

She shrunk back as his shadow fell across her. He knelt so that he was no longer some terrifying towering presence. She was scratching the back of one hand, and had been for a while, judging by the redness of her skin. He wanted to reach out and hold her. Pull her in close. Protect her. Promise her that everything was going to be OK now, and that nobody was going to hurt her.

But nobody was going to touch this girl without her permission again. Not him, not anyone. He would make fucking sure of that.

His voice shook when he said the word. The word he'd been waiting to say ever since that night Bamber had turned up at his house in Inverness.

"Caroline?"

She didn't look up. She didn't react, other than to stop scratching for a second or so, before resuming with even more determination than before.

"Caroline, my name's Bob. Bob Hoon," he said. "I'm a friend of your dad's. From his army days. He asked me to come and get you. He asked me to take you home, sweetheart."

She stopped scratching and wrung her hands together. Her eyes flicked to his, and for a moment he saw the girl he'd once known, long, long ago. She was buried deep, but she was still in there. Still fighting. Still holding on.

"H-home?" she whispered.

"Aye. I'm going to get you home," Hoon told her. He looked around at the other women, then stopped on Amanda. She held his gaze for as long as she could bear it, then hung her head just like the others. "All of you."

"You're... You're hurt."

Caroline was studying his face, taking in the blood, bruising, and general misshapenness of it.

"What, this?" Hoon asked. He smiled. It did hurt, but right now, he couldn't care less. "You should see all the other guys..."

———

It didn't take long for the rest of the press to get wind of what was going on around the side of the building, and by the time Hoon had untied the women, there was a semi-circle of journalists, camera operators, and other assorted nosy bastards monitoring his every move.

This, for the second time in the past few months, suited him down to the ground. Scrutiny helped keep people honest, even if only for a while. And, with the police sirens splitting the night air and flashing lights licking across the walls of the hotel, he was grateful for all the scrutiny the press could provide.

There was no sign of the suit-wearing goons now, most of them having wisely fucked off when they realised that the game was up.

The driver Hoon had pistol-whipped to the ground had attempted to run for it, only to find himself in the path of a police car. The vehicle had been slowing down at the time, but the impact had still launched the fleeing man several feet into the air, then deposited him unceremoniously back on the ground, where he remained until paramedics arrived.

Hoon, meanwhile, had been bracing himself for a battle with any jumped-up uniformed fuckwits who tried to separate him from Caroline and the rest of the women, and he had been surprised when the first officer on scene was the last one he'd expected to see.

"Mr Hoon. Why am I not in the least bit shocked to find you at the centre of all this?" asked Chief Superintendent Bagshaw. She was in her full uniform, though it looked like she'd thrown it on in a hurry.

"Deirdrie?" Hoon said. He contemplated jumping down from the back of the truck, then concluded that it'd probably hurt. He climbed down carefully, instead. "The fuck are you doing here? You're meant to be looking after Greig."

"Yes, I got that call, thank you," she said. "I had a very interesting chat with Jack, in fact, and I got the impression that tonight was going to turn out to be worth getting dressed for." She looked past him to where the women sat huddled together. "I see you have not disappointed."

"Greig," Hoon stressed. "Where is he?"

"He's safe. Him and his family. I've seen to it," she assured him.

"People you trust?"

"Yes. There are still a few of them. He's in good hands. I promise."

"He'd fucking better be," Hoon told her. "Or on your head be it."

Bagshaw looked entirely unimpressed by the remark. "The big scary hardman act might work with some people, Mr Hoon, but it doesn't hold water with me. So, best not to waste our time with it, eh?"

She turned to the constables emerging from the cars behind her and began demonstrating why she was the one in charge. Ambulances were called. Blankets were sourced. Cordons were set up, and backup was summoned. Uniforms were soon swarming through the hotel, securing the area.

Before they could get the back door locked down, a man with a broken nose and a hole in his shin stumbled out of it, each step drawing a whimper of pain.

Miles shuffled beside him, gripping his arm, holding it like he was never going to let the bastard go. By the looks of it, he had disposed of the gun. Probably best, for the avoidance of temptation.

"Is that...?" Chief Superintendent Bagshaw began.

"Aye," Hoon confirmed. "That's your MI5 man. And that shrew-faced sack of snake shit he's got with him is the fucker responsible for all this. Miles can explain better than I can. I reckon you two are going to have a lot to fucking talk about."

A couple of Uniforms moved to intercept Miles and his prisoner, but Deirdrie waved for them to be let through. Miles gave Hoon a slightly embarrassed nod, then indicated West with a sideways glance.

"I decided against killing him."

"Aye, well, you needn't have bothered. I've found Caroline, so go for your fucking life."

Chief Superintendent Bagshaw stepped in quickly. "No. No, don't do that. Definitely don't do that."

Miles shook his head. "No. No, I'm not going to. He's got information. He has names. Addresses. Bank account details, maybe. He's more use to us alive."

West spat a wad of blood onto the ground at Hoon's feet. "They'll kill you for this. You must know that? They'll hunt you down, and they'll flay the skin from your—"

"Wait, wait, hang on. I want to write this down," Hoon said. He turned to Bagshaw. "You got a notebook I can borrow?"

It was Miles who answered. "Here," he said, offering out a garish sequinned monstrosity of a thing. "Brought it from the hotel."

"Even fucking better," Hoon said. He opened the book to a random page, unclipped the pen from the spine, then held it poised over the page. "Sorry, you were saying?"

Godfrey regarded the notebook with some confusion. He resumed his rant, but it had lost most of its venom now, and just sounded a bit silly.

"They'll, uh, they'll flay the skin from your bones. They'll kill everyone you love. They'll, you know... It'll be a fucking horrible thing, is what I'm saying. Wherever you go. You won't get away from them. They'll hunt you to the ends of the Earth, if they have to. You'll never be safe. You'll always be looking over your shoulder. You and everyone you care about."

"Good. That's great. Just what I needed," Hoon said. He marked a full stop with a prod of the pen, then closed the book. "People saw that, you think?" he asked, glancing at Deirdrie and Miles.

"Cameras got it, yes. Few officers watching," Miles said. "Why?"

"Oh, no reason," Hoon said. "Now, can we get this nappy wearing weirdo fuck out of my sight, please? Otherwise, I'm likely to kill him myself."

"You'll never be safe. None of you will," West seethed. "You're all targets now. You're all marked, and—"

The toe of Hoon's shoe struck the hole in Godfrey's shin, and he went down screaming. Chief Superintendent Bagshaw pointed to a constable and a sergeant, and instructed them to keep West under observation in the back of a car until the paramedics had arrived and dealt with everyone else.

When he had been dragged away, she turned back to Hoon. "You're going to need medical attention, too."

"Eventually, aye," Hoon conceded. "But the girls first. And I'm staying with them until they've been seen."

Bagshaw followed his gaze. Female officers were wrapping blankets around the shoulders of the women. A few hot drinks were being sourced and pressed into hands that hadn't known kindness in weeks, months, or even years.

"I found her," Hoon said.

"Your friend's daughter? She's here?"

"She is," Hoon said. He smiled up at Caroline, who sat shivering under a blanket, gazing in mute disbelief at everything going on in and out of the truck.

She was a long way from home, and she had a long road ahead of her.

But she wouldn't have to walk it alone.

CHAPTER FORTY-FIVE

HOON DIDN'T MAKE the call. He couldn't.

He couldn't even be in the room when they arrived to collect her. It wasn't his place. He'd done his part, and now it was over to them.

Instead, he stood in a darkened side room, watching through the glass as Caroline Gascoine was finally reunited with her parents. There was sobbing. There were hugs. There were whispered promises, and grateful thanks, none of which he heard, as he'd insisted the microphones in the room all be turned off before Bamber and Lizzie had arrived to collect their daughter.

But he wanted to see. He wanted to know that she had been handed into their care. That she was back where she belonged.

That wasn't too much to ask, he reckoned.

There was a subtle clearing of a throat beside him. Hoon saw a flash of white, and looked down to find a box of tissues being offered to him. He took one without a word, and Chief Superintendent Bagshaw returned the box to the table.

"You've done a good thing there," she said.

Hoon shrugged, then grimaced at the pain. It had been

almost sixteen hours since his last sustained injury, and despite a strict regime of painkillers, each and every one of them hurt more now than they had the day before.

Still, things generally got worse before they got better, he knew. It was all just part of the healing process.

"I feel like there's a 'but' coming," he said.

"Well, you did cause really quite a lot of property damage, hospitalised a number of people, and killed a man."

"That was basically a fucking accident," Hoon protested.

Bagshaw frowned. "You shot him in the chest."

"Oh. Him," Hoon said.

"What do you mean, 'him'? Were there others?"

"No comment," Hoon said.

He looked ahead through the glass, and realised that Bamber was looking back at him. He was in his wheelchair, arms around his daughter and his wife, big hands stroking their hair and wiping their tears.

For a moment, Hoon would've sworn his old army pal could see him through the mirror. Or, if not see him, then sense him watching on.

"She's going to be OK," Hoon announced. "They're all going to be fine."

He turned away, allowing the family their privacy.

"And what about you?" Bagshaw asked. "Assuming I don't arrest you right now, of course."

"That'd be far too much fucking hassle, and you know it," Hoon said. "Did you pass on my messages to Greig and Gabriella?"

"All done," she confirmed. "They know what to do."

"Every week?"

"Every week. Thursday mornings. They'll make the call."

"Good," Hoon said. He didn't ask the question that was on his mind. He didn't have to.

"They're all fine," the Chief Superintendent assured him.

"They're all safe. And the calls will make sure of that. As long as the message gets passed on to those who need to hear it."

"Oh, don't worry, it'll get passed on," Hoon told her. "I'm going to make fucking sure of it."

———

They came that night. Three of them, all armed, but not nearly as fucking dangerous as they liked to think.

And nowhere near as dangerous as him.

He and the one he assumed was the leader sat down in the bowels of Bookish's boat, face to face across the little dining table. The groans and whimpers of the other two were only just audible over the lapping of the waves and the creaking of the old wooden hull.

"Thanks for coming," Hoon told the skinhead twenty-something currently bleeding on the chair across from him. "And sorry about the fingers. It's fucking amazing what they can do with prosthetics these days, though, so I wouldn't worry too much."

The goon stared in horror at the red-stained pillowcase that was currently wrapped around what was left of his right hand. His whole body was trembling like it was in the process of shutting down.

"I want you to pass a message on for me, alright?" Hoon continued. "I want you to go crawling away, back to the gaggle of fucks you work for, and give them a message on my behalf. Will you do that for me?"

When the other man didn't reply, Hoon slammed a fist down on the table to get his attention.

"Are you fucking listening, son? Or should I throw you overboard and see if one of your wee pals has got a better attention span?"

The skinhead nodded frantically. "N-no. I'm listening. I'm listening."

"Good. Here's the message," Hoon said. "I want you to tell them that I have a list. A list of names. Actors. Politicians. Members of fucking royalty. Everyone who frequented that fucking hotel last night. Everyone who was at that party."

He tapped a finger on the sequined notebook on the table beside him, then pinned it there. "I've got them all. Your man, Godfrey, spilled his fucking guts when he was being arrested. I'm sure you saw the wee chat on camera, if you watched the news."

He leaned closer, grinning from ear to ear. "Here's the good news. I'm not going to tell a fucking soul. This list? It stays our secret. *Unless* something happens to any of my friends or associates. They're going to phone in, once a week, and confirm they're still in one piece. The day they don't—the day any of them fails to call the number they've been given, for any fucking reason whatsoever—then all this goes public. Every fucking name and home address goes to the press and online. Your wee Pandora's Box will be opened, and there'll be no shutting it again. Ever."

He eyeballed the snivelling bastard across the table until he was sure his point had been made, then he sat back.

"You got all that?"

"I... I got it."

"You sure you don't want me to write it down?"

"N-no. I've got it. I'll remember."

"See that you fucking do, son," Hoon said. He held up two fingers. "Because you've got plenty fucking more where these came from."

He tossed the detached digits onto the table between them, then made a shooing motion.

"Now, pick up your shit, and get the fuck off my boat," he instructed.

The skinhead didn't hang around to be told a second time. He collected his fingers, jumped up from the chair, then went stumbling up the steps and out onto the upper deck.

Hoon listened to him shouting at the others, then heard the distant *thunking* of car doors closing, and the roar of an engine.

"All clear?"

Miles poked his head out of the bedroom, but looked ready to pull it back in the moment that anything kicked off.

"You're fine," Hoon told him. "They've gone."

Miles opened the door the rest of the way and emerged from the room. "Message received and understood?"

"Aye. Hopefully, it'll do the job," Hoon said. "And they'll all be safe."

Miles slid into the chair that had recently been vacated and tried not to think too much about the blood spots on the table.

"I passed on your other message. To Gabriella."

"At your cousin's, you mean?"

"He's part of the Security Service, too," Miles said. "It was just until we got somewhere more long term. Do you want to know what she said, or not?"

Hoon thought about this for a few moments, then shook his head. "No. I don't think I do."

"Well, tough. She says you've got nothing to be sorry for," Miles told him. "And that at least the hot water's more reliable at the new place, if that means anything to you?"

Hoon made a sound that was not dissimilar to laughter. "Aye. Aye, it does. Thanks."

"No problem. I can get you their details when they're settled into the new place."

"Probably best not to," Hoon said. "Don't want to push our luck."

"No," Miles agreed. "No, I suppose not."

"What's your plan now?" Hoon asked. "With your man Godfrey, and the Loop, and all that shite?"

"We're working on it," Miles said. "It's early days, but we've kept him alive for this long. We might get something useful from him yet. But he's more scared of them than he is of us, so I don't know."

Hoon nodded. "Aye. Well, good luck," he said. "And, for the record, I get why you wanted to kill him. I'm no' fucking impressed that you used me like that, but... I get it. Course, had I not found Caroline, I might be feeling very fucking different about the matter, but as it stands? I get it. No harm done."

"Uh, yeah. Thanks," Miles said. "You were right, of course. I couldn't just shoot him in cold blood."

"Personally, I'd have done it in a fucking heartbeat," Hoon replied. "Shoe on the other foot, I'd have painted the fucking walls with him. But evidently, you're a better man than I am."

"Obviously," Miles agreed. He glanced over at the steps, then back to Hoon. "What about you? What are you going to do now?"

"No' sure," Hoon admitted.

"Your message to the Loop. I heard it," Miles told him. "You said they had to leave your friends alone. Nothing about you."

Hoon shrugged. "Ah, fuck it. Let them come. Keeps life interesting."

Miles winced. "I don't think you understand who you're dealing with, Bob."

"Maybe," Hoon said. He sat back and interlocked his fingers behind his head. "Or maybe *they* don't. Either way, should be a lively fucking time ahead."

"Well, it's certainly been one so far," Miles said. He got to his feet, offered a hand across the table, and looked positively giddy when Hoon actually shook it. "You know where I am if you need me."

"If I ever need some typing done, I'll know who to call," Hoon said.

Miles chuckled. "Yes. Good. But I mean it. Anything I can do."

Hoon thought about all the many faceless enemies lurking out there. Watching him. Waiting. Biding their time.

He thought about the black SUV at the bottom of the Thames. About the hard-shelled case hidden beneath his bed, and about the arsenal of weaponry secured inside it.

"Thanks for the offer, pal," Hoon said.

He winked. It hurt.

Christ, it hurt.

"But something tells me I'm going to be just fine…"

Printed in Great Britain
by Amazon

78454365R00230